A complete list of books by James Patterson is at the end of this book. For previews of upcoming books and more information about James Patterson, please visit JamesPatterson.com, or find him on Facebook or at your app store.

Miracle at Augusta

JAMES PATTERSON
and PETER DE JONGE

LITTLE, BROWN AND COMPANY

LARGE PRINT EDITION

Copyright © 2015 by James Patterson

All rights reserved. In accordance with the U.S. Copyright Act of 1976, the scanning, uploading, and electronic sharing of any part of this book without the permission of the publisher constitute unlawful piracy and theft of the author's intellectual property. If you would like to use material from the book (other than for review purposes), prior written permission must be obtained by contacting the publisher at permissions@hbgusa.com. Thank you for your support of the author's rights.

Little, Brown and Company
Hachette Book Group
1290 Avenue of the Americas, New York, NY 10104
littlebrown.com

First Edition: April 2015

Little, Brown and Company is a division of Hachette Book Group, Inc. The Little, Brown name and logo are trademarks of Hachette Book Group, Inc.

The publisher is not responsible for websites (or their content) that are not owned by the publisher.

The Hachette Speakers Bureau provides a wide range of authors for speaking events. To find out more, go to hachettespeakersbureau.com or call (866) 376-6591.

Illustrations by Joel Holland

ISBN 978-0-316-41097-7 (HC) / 978-0-316-33928-5 (LP) / 978-0-316-34382-4 (international)
LCCN 2014959627

10 9 8 7 6 5 4 3 2 1

RRD-C

Printed in the United States of America

*To Sue, second-best player in
our house
—JP*

*For my brother William
—PdJ*

Miracle at Augusta

1

"ON THE FIRST TEE...from Winnetka, Illinois...the 1996 winner of the U.S. Senior Open...Travis McKinley."

I've never set foot on Augusta National before, let alone teed it up, so for thirty seconds, I just stand there shivering and let the polite applause of the patrons wash over me. Okay, "wash over me" is a bit of a stretch. How about "trickle over me"? Could you live with that? While the clapping subsides, I close my eyes and picture the shot I need to hit.

Because my grandfather gave me a book

on the Masters one Christmas, I happen to know that Augusta was originally a nursery owned by a Belgian horticulturist named Prosper Berckmans. That's why all the holes are named after trees. The first, Tea Olive, is a 445-yard par 4, which doglegs right and calls for a high fade to the right side of the fairway some 290 yards away. When the image of the shot is locked in my mind, I step up and launch my drive into the December gloom, aiming twenty feet right of the big wire net that keeps balls from flying into the parking lot of the CVS next door.

I'm happy to report that my tee shot comes off pretty much as planned, leaving me 165 yards to an uphill green, so I swap the driver for my 7-iron and aim for the right rear corner of it. When the ball lands softly and trickles—like that applause—toward the pin, tucked up front, just beyond the trap, I give myself the eight-footer for birdie and move on to the par-five 2nd, aka Pink Dogwood.

My body may be fifteen miles outside of Chicago, freezing its nearly fifty-two-year-old ass off at the Big Oaks Driving Range on Route 38, but in my mind it's in Georgia in April, and those color-corrected dogwoods and azaleas have old Prosper turning over in his grave.

The start of my third year on the Senior Tour is a month away. As some of you may recall, my rookie year went rather well— unkind sportswriters leaned heavily on the word *miraculous*—culminating in my win at Pebble, which the starter was gracious enough to mention. My sophomore season, however, was lackluster at best, so I'm doing everything I can to prepare for '98, particularly since the shelf life out here is so brief, what with me growing more decrepit by the day and fresh young blood bubbling up from below. If you think it's hard fighting for scraps left by Hale Irwin, Gil Morgan, and Hank Peters, and believe me it is, imagine what it will be like next year when Tom Watson, Lanny Wadkins, and Tom Kite flash their birth certificates and step up to the senior buffet.

I don't even want to think about that. I just know that this year is huge, and since the end of October, I've been at Big Oaks every afternoon, fifth stall from the left, chewing up these nasty rubber mats and whatever cartilage is left in my right elbow.

To relieve the tedium, I've been playing virtual rounds at Augusta, hole by hole, Flowering Crab Apple to Carolina Cherry, seeing if I can find the correct half of the fairway and then land it on the correct quadrant of the green. Along the way, I try to keep my scuffed range rock from rolling back into Rae's Creek or finding the pine straw or nestling up behind the Eisenhower tree. It keeps me sharper than mindlessly banging balls.

For the front side, the nine they never put on the air, I make do with the pictures and descriptions in my old Christmas present, but for the back nine, I have thirty years of TV viewing to draw on. When I get to 12, Golden Bell, that nasty par 3 at the end of Amen Corner, I even know which tree Byron Nelson used to look at to decipher the swirling winds. Instead, I gaze roofward and see if there are any plastic bags whipping around in the currents. My favorite holes are 13 and 15, Azalea and Firethorn, the two short par 5s that have been the scene of so much drama. In the last couple of weeks, I've even been working on a high draw to keep it on those slippery greens, which, in my mind at least, are never less than 13.2 on the Stimpmeter.

Today, at 15, I catch it solid off the tee, and since I get even more roll off the Big Oaks cement than I would from the hard, sloping fairways at Augusta, I've only got 215 left, a perfect yardage for my new pet draw. As I prepare to launch the ball into the azure sky, there's a bang behind my left shoulder. It sounds like a shotgun blast but is in fact a shank from Esther Lee, the housewife in the stall to my left.

"Sorry about that," says Esther, raising a hand in a pink glove.

"No problem," I reply. But the reverie is broken, and suddenly it's a lot harder to pretend I'm in Georgia and not a drafty warehouse in suburban Chicago. After a couple more swings, I pack it in for the day and deposit my bag in the closet behind the front desk, where the manager has been nice enough to let me keep it, seeing as I'm here five days a week.

Then I drive the nine miles to Winnetka and get in line with all the other trophy housewives and husbands and wait for Noah to be released from his kindergarten classroom at Belltown Grammar. Elizabeth and Simon were already well grown when Noah made a surprise appearance nearly six years ago, and as I watch the little gink shuffle out of the back, his backpack hanging off one shoulder and his baseball cap turned backwards, I appreciate how lucky Sarah and I are.

"Hey, Noah, how was your day?"

"Not bad. How about you? How was Augusta?"

"Shot thirty-two on the front."

"Give yourself a lot of eight-footers?"

"You know what I say, Noah?"

"Charity begins at home."

"Exactly."

Our house is less than five minutes from the school, and seeing Sarah's Cherokee in the driveway makes us both uneasy.

"Mom's home early."

"Yeah."

When we get out of the car, Sarah is standing in the doorway. "I have some sad news to share," she tells us. "Pop died."

2

AT 2 P.M. THE FOLLOWING Saturday, some two hundred of my grandfather's friends convene in the parking lot of the Creekview Country Club and follow him up the frozen first fairway. By now, Pop has been reduced to the ashes that fill the Tupperware container head pro Matt Higgins holds in the crook of his left arm. When Higgins reaches the first green, he pulls off one glove, pries open the lid, and sprinkles a bit of Edwin Joseph McKinley over the portion of the green where the hole is generally cut.

As the gray soot rains down on the winter green, Higgins utters the signature words with which my grandfather started a thousand rounds: "No gimmes. No mulligans. No bullshit. Let's play golf," and the ragtag army, some of whom have been forced by age and infirmity to ride golf carts with home health aides, hurl it back in unison like a battle cry: "No gimmes! No mulligans! No bullshit! Let's play golf!" Then Higgins hands Pop off like a football, and another volunteer takes the lead.

It's an impressive turnout, particularly considering it's fourteen degrees. Included in the boisterous band of mourners is my best friend and former caddy, Earl Fielder, who came up last night from North Carolina. No doubt my grandfather would be touched to see so many dear friends. Pop, who hated slow play, would also appreciate the brisk pace. In forty minutes, the procession covers thirteen holes, and with five left, the next two generations of McKinleys take over.

Simon, a freshman at Northwestern, leads us up the par-five 14th. He carries his grandfather over the longest hole on the course, then turns him over to his proud younger brother, and now the chilled brigade, many of whom have been fortifying themselves with frequent nips from their pocket flasks, fall in line behind a five-year-old. After Noah guides them to the 15th green, they take particular delight in the unlikely spectacle of a kindergartner leading them through another chorus of "No gimmes! No mulligans! No bullshit! Let's play golf!"

But it's the McKinley ladies, Elizabeth and Sarah, who get to me the most on this freezing afternoon. Elizabeth, because she is surely the most devastatingly beautiful radiology resident in North America, and Sarah...because she's Sarah. Sarah walks off 17, she hands off Pop with a kiss, and it's up to me to carry him home.

Affection for my grandfather is inscribed on every face in this unholy procession, many of whom are by now overfortified, but for me the affection and appreciation are overwhelming. Without my grandfather, I have no idea where, or even who, I'd be. I wouldn't be a golfer. When I was eight, he put a cut-down 7-iron in my hand, and for the last forty-three years or so he's been my only coach. And when Leo Burnett tossed me to the curb a couple of Christmases ago, he was the only one who didn't think my grandiose scheme of qualifying for the Senior Tour was insane. I've been so dependent on his guidance, on and off the course, for so long, I'm more than a little worried how I'll do without it.

I carry Pop the final third of a mile and sprinkle what's left on 18, banging the bottom of the container like a bongo to make sure every last particle of the beloved man has been set free.

"No gimmes! No mulligans! No bull-shit!" I shout. "Let's have a drink!"

"I think he means an indoor drink," says an old friend, turning over an empty flask, and we file into the clubhouse for one last round or three on Edwin Joseph McKinley.

3

AFTER EARL HAS RUN a gauntlet of McKinley hugs and kisses and accepted pats on the back and best wishes from a dozen of my grandfather's starstruck old cronies, I walk my friend from the clubhouse into the freezing Midwestern night. At the end of the flagstone path, a cab is waiting to take him to the airport, and as we approach the car, I realize, and not for the first time, that I also owe a great debt to Earl, without whom I never could have succeeded in my rookie year, and although I feel the urge to finally thank him in clear and explicit

English, I fall short, in the finest male tradition.

"Thanks again for making the trip" is about the best I can manage. "As you can see, it meant a lot to all of us."

"It meant a lot to me too, Travis. When you kick off, I'll come to yours, too."

"Promise?"

"Yup."

"Thanks."

"See you in a couple of weeks, then. You ready?"

"I better be. I've been working my ass off."

"Good. Because I don't want to embarrass you out there."

When we've exchanged as much of this as we can stomach, Earl gets into the car, and I walk to the back of the lot and get into mine. After letting the heat run for five minutes, I pull up in front, where Sarah, Elizabeth, Simon, and Noah pile in.

Creekview Country Club is an older

course and, like a lot of older courses, is in the center of a neighborhood that has deteriorated over the decades. On the way back to the highway we pass a series of strip malls, lined with liquor stores, pawnshops, and mini-marts that seem particularly threadbare on such a raw night.

In the last year and a half, I've done pretty well, almost embarrassingly so, and my one indulgence has been this Mercedes sedan. Although I've had it six months, I often still feel uncomfortable behind the wheel, an impostor, but the one time I never regret the purchase is on a night like this, when it's stuffed with McKinleys and I feel that, at least for the duration of the trip, the tanklike vehicle is protecting them all, not just from the wind and cold but from all life's other harsh realities as well.

Plus, as Noah often points out, it's kind of swank.

Up ahead, at the light, a broken-down old van sits on the side of the road. As I wait for the light to turn, a middle-aged woman climbs out of the driver's seat to gauge the extent of her problem, and when she walks in front of her car, we make eye contact. I know I should pull over, but the lateness of the hour and the sketchiness of the neighborhood lobby against it, and before I can offer a convincing counter-argument, the light turns green and the impregnable Benz rolls on.

Two stoplights later, my conscience gets the better of me, or maybe I just feel the heat of Elizabeth's gaze on the back of my neck. "I'm going to circle back," I say, more to myself than anyone else. "See if I can help her."

It's a four-lane road and half a mile before I can make a U-turn. By the time I get back to the woman and her van, I'm relieved to see that a second just as beat-up car has pulled over and parked behind it, and an older man, African-American with a gray beard, is wrestling a spare tire onto the right rear wheel. I roll down the window and the cold air rushes in.

"Need any help?"

"That's okay," says the man, taking in the well-dressed family from below.

"Sure?"

"It's just a flat tire, sport. We got it covered."

4

IF THERE'S A BETTER place to spend mid-January than Hawaii, let me know. Till then I'll have to make do with Waialae Country Club on the island of Oahu, where Earl and I are getting our last reps in before tomorrow's start of the Azawa Open and warming our bones in the tropical sun. It feels so good to be warm, and out of that stall at Big Oaks, I'm hardly bothered by the fact that fifty people are lined up on the range behind Earl, and two are watching me, one of whom is my new caddy, Johnny Abate. Earl's fans, who have taken to calling themselves Earl's Platoon, aren't content to stand and gape. Every time he pures another 4-iron, they ooh and ahh and shower him with love.

"This is your year, Earl!"

"Hell yeah, buddy."

"You're the man, EF!"

And my personal favorite—"Earl Fielder is EFing good."

"I guess they don't get out much," I mumble under my breath to the object of all this adulation.

"What makes you say that, Travis?"

To clarify, I should probably point out that Earl has enjoyed a dramatic change in fortune since caddying for me in my rookie season in '96. For starters, he is now a member of the Senior Tour himself. He earned his playing privileges by finishing second in the '97 Senior Q-School, then backed it up with one of the most consistent rookie seasons ever, ending the year with twenty-three straight top tens. But what changed everything and transformed him into a bona fide celebrity is that Reebok commercial, which juxtaposes Earl on tour with old footage and photos of him from the late sixties in Vietnam. No one is happier for Earl than me, but do I find the clamor for autographs and photographs at restaurants and airports just a wee bit annoying?

Of course not. I'm a bigger person than that.

"Work on anything in the off-season?" I ask.

"Just tried to tighten everything up a notch. Keep the arms and body more attached, have it all move in one piece."

"Jesus, Earl. You already got the most buttoned-up swing out here. To get it any tighter you'd need a monkey wrench." But as Earl stripes a couple more, I realize he may actually have succeeded. Watching Earl, his broad forehead beaded with sweat, is like watching an Old World Italian ma-son build a wall. There's no wasted motion. Every move and gesture is pared to the nub.

"You're striping it better than ever, Earl, and that's saying something. You're going to get that win this year, maybe two."

"I wouldn't bet on it," says Earl. "I'm too much of a grinder. I may not stink it up, but I rarely go real low, either. Don't roll it well enough. But I'd trade all those seconds and thirds for one win. And not just for the exemption. I want something to be remembered for, and once you get your name engraved on silver, it's hard to get it off. How about you, Trav? You work on anything up there on the tundra?"

"See for yourself."

I pull my 5-wood, aim my club face and feet slightly right of my target, and as I swing, I focus on keeping my hips turning and really letting my arms go, ripping down, through, and up. The ball takes off with the usual trajectory but, a hundred yards out, shoots up like a rocket when the afterburners hit. It bends slightly to the left before landing softly 215 yards away.

"Son of a bitch," says Earl. "I need to see you do that again."

I dislodge another Titleist from the pyramid-shaped pile, nudge it into place beside the long, shallow divot, and turn on the ball one more time.

"Well, I'll be damned. The high fucking draw. The suavest shot in golf. I just have one question."

"What's that?"

"Why? There isn't one hole out here where you'll need it."

"It's for Augusta."

"Augusta?"

"How else am I going to keep the ball on those reachable par fives, thirteen and fifteen in particular? Those are birdie holes, Earl. You're not birdieing those, you're losing half a stroke to the field."

"I know that, Travis. You're not the only one with a TV."

"You get reception down there?"

"How the hell are you going to get an invitation — steal it from Tiger's mailbox?"

"Haven't thought that far ahead. You know it's a mistake to get ahead of yourself in this game. I just have a feeling I'm going to need it."

5

THE DISPARITY IN STATUS between Earl and me is reflected in our Friday tee times. Earl goes off in the early afternoon with Chi Chi Rodriguez and Raymond Floyd, and I slip out at 7:03 a.m. with senior rookies Trent Smith and Elliot Brody. I hadn't heard of them either, until I looked them up in the media guide. Smith joined the navy out of high school. Back on dry land, he sold insurance, ran a nightclub, and repaired pin-setting machines at a bowling alley, then spent fifteen years in Grand Prairie, Texas, in the auto repair business.

He got into the field by Monday qualifying. Brody, who earned his spot through this year's Q-School, was a teaching pro outside Tacoma for thirty years.

It couldn't be a more congenial group. One look at each other and we knew we were all just slightly different versions of the same person—three guys who hadn't seriously considered making a living at competitive golf till it was almost too late, and now we're determined to make the most of our chance. What little chatter there is, is collegial and supportive, each of us giving the others the chance to do their best.

The setting isn't half bad, either. With no one in front of us, I feel like I washed ashore in paradise and just happened to find my sticks here waiting for me. The only sounds are waves, rustling palms, and birds. If anyone had gotten up at dawn and wandered over, they would have seen some quality golf. Among the three of us, we carded one bogey and fourteen birdies. All those sessions at Big Oaks must have paid off, or maybe it's the novel thrill of hitting off organic material, because six of those birdies are mine. For the next four hours, my 66 makes me the year's top player on the Senior Tour, and when the last player walks off 18, I'm tied for second with Gil Morgan, one shot behind the leader, Hale Irwin.

6

FRIDAY, I WENT OFF in the first group of the day. On Saturday, thanks to that 66, I go off in the final one. Instead of playing under the radar with two fellow journeymen, I'm trading shots with the two best fifty-somethings on the planet—Hale Irwin and Gil Morgan. Last year, Irwin won nine tournaments and more money than any golfer in the world, including an elegant young cat named Tiger Woods. Morgan won six times and earned more than Tiger, too. The last time I felt this out of my league was the summer afternoon in college when I got it into my head to play pickup basketball at a playground on the South Side of Chicago.

Everyone knows about Irwin, the former all–Big Eight cornerback with three U.S. Open titles, but it's the late-blooming Morgan who is the revelation. For one thing, he possesses a perfect swing. Literally. When he was a kid, his father, a small-town mortician, took him to see Harvey Penick, the legendary Austin pro who taught Ben Crenshaw and Tom Kite. Penick took one look at Morgan's move and sent him home. Said there was nothing he could do for him.

Irwin's swing is not nearly as lovely and he's much shorter off the tee, but he possesses a level of competitiveness and confidence that is borderline psychotic. As impressed as I am that Morgan hits it twenty yards past Irwin all day, I'm even more impressed by the fact that Irwin could truly not care less.

I don't want to belabor the point, but here's one last illustration of the chasm in golfing prowess between me and them. Last year Irwin led the tour with an average score of 68.93, and my average was a shade under 71. In other words, if we had a regular game at Creekview Country Club on Sunday mornings, he would have to give me a stroke a side. But at Waialae on Saturday afternoon, I didn't need any strokes from anyone. When our round is in the books, I've carded my second straight 66 to Irwin's 69 and Morgan's 70.

Those aren't typos. That's just golf.

7

FOR THE FIRST TIME since that U.S. Senior Open I keep bringing up, the name McKinley looks down from the top of the leaderboard. And it's in excellent company. Sharing my lead at six under are two of the best players and biggest personalities on the tour—Lee Trevino and Hank "Stump" Peters. As the patron saint of golfing long shots, Trevino has forever occupied a special place in my personal pantheon, and the thought of going off with him in the final group on Sunday is thrilling. But seeing that Hank Peters will be playing with us makes my stomach hurt.

You know how some competitors always bring out your worst? Peters has been providing that invaluable service for me since he beat me on the eighteenth hole of a college match when we were juniors, him at Georgia Tech, me at Northwestern. At the time, Northwestern was the kind of school a powerhouse like Georgia put on the schedule to pad their record, and that was one of the reasons I wanted to beat him so badly. Another was that Peters, an all-state quarterback in high school, exuded exactly the kind of big-guy swagger that has always stirred my darkest competitive instincts, probably because at 6'2" and 137 pounds, I exuded something quite different.

In our first encounter, back in college, I was two up with three to play, yet Peters never for a second thought he would lose, and of course he turned out to be right.

After he knocked in his winning putt, which thirty-two years later I still recall as an uphill twelve-footer that broke two inches to the left, he shook my hand and said, "You got a nice little game, son. Stick with it."

"Thanks, Hank."

I guess there's something about being condescending, patronizing, *and* better that leaves an indelible impression. Then again, I've always had a talent for nursing slights. I collect them like a wine snob collects Bordeaux. I never know when I might need to dust one off. Not that this one has been paying dividends. Since I got out here, I've been paired with Peters three times and gotten drubbed every time. Maybe it's because I try too hard. More likely, it's because Peters, who won eleven times on the regular tour, is better and always will be.

On Sunday afternoon, Trevino comes out sporting four shades of brown—beige cashmere sweater, light brown shirt, dark brown slacks, and darker brown shoes, and just watching him work his way through the crowd with his distinctive slightly bow-legged gait makes me smile. Peters arrives wearing a camouflage hunting cap and sweatshirt, with several pinches of chewing tobacco stuffed between his teeth and lower gum, but for some reason I find his version of populist charm less endearing. My expression must give me away, because Johnny A promptly walks over and puts his hand on my shoulder.

"Now, listen," he says, "we're not going to let this cracker take us out of our game."

8

EASIER SAID THAN DONE, when this particular cracker has been living in my head rent-free for three decades. Trevino plants his tee, doffs his cap, and busts his iconic open-stanced move. His flat, abrupt chop—somewhere between martial arts and grunt labor—produces the same low, hard fade it has a million times before and ends up smack in the middle of the fairway.

"I hit that sunnabitch quail high," he says to his adoring gallery. "But I guess there aren't a lot of quail on Oahu."

After ejecting a brown stream of tobacco

juice into a Styrofoam cup, Peters knocks it ten yards past Trevino, who at fifty-eight has lost some distance. Appropriately enough, I'm up last, and as I go through my routine, I can sense how anxious the gallery is for me to get it over with so they can hustle down the fairway and watch Trevino and Peters hit again.

Nevertheless, I catch it solid and roll it past them both. Having hit the longest drive, I'm last to hit again, and this time the gallery doesn't even pretend to wait. Halfway through my backswing, the scenery shifts like the furniture between acts of a play. I yank an easy wedge ten yards left, and when I fail to get up and down, I walk off the first green with a bogey.

"Only the first hole," says Johnny A. "Plenty of golf to be played."

True enough. And on the par-three 2nd, I hit my 6-iron to fourteen feet. Knock it in, I'm back to where I started and it's all good. Unfortunately, I'm so eager to undo my opening bogey, I charge my birdie putt five feet past and miss the comeback for another bogey, and on three, I'm so pissed about one and two, I bogey that as well.

Bogey. Bogey. Bogey. Not exactly the start I had in mind, and while I'm barfing on my FootJoys, Peters and Trevino are keeping theirs nice and clean, carding two birdies each. The round is barely fifteen minutes old, and I'm five strokes behind and well on my way to another traumatic defeat at the hands of my outdoorsy, tobacco-juice-spittin' nemesis.

At this point, I should summon my inner Lombardi and dig deep, but God knows what I'd dredge up. Instead, I relax and watch Trevino. For all I know, I'll never get a chance to tee it up with Super Mex again, and if I can't enjoy it, maybe I can learn a thing or two.

The first thing that stands out is the way Trevino parcels his concentration. Yesterday, Irwin and Morgan never peeked from behind their game faces. From the handshakes at the first till they signed the scorecards in the trailer, they never stopped grinding. Trevino has a different MO. For the thirty seconds it takes to plan and execute his shot, he and Herman are as focused as assassins, but once the ball stops rolling, they go right back to shooting the breeze, picking up the conversational thread—dogs, Vegas, barbecue—wherever they left it, as if trying to win a golf tournament is a minor distraction from an otherwise carefree afternoon.

And if the conversation lags, or we're waiting for a green to clear, as happens on 5, Trevino walks to the edge of the nearest hazard and fishes out balls with his 7-iron. He reminds me of my cheap buddies back home, except that Trevino tosses his plunder to the kids in his gallery.

I'm so captivated by the rare opportunity to observe Trevino in his natural habitat, I barely notice my own birdies on 7 and 8, and when I'm looking over my eagle putt on 10, the prospect of sinking it is such a nonevent, I roll it dead center from forty-five feet. Now I'm back in the hunt—two behind Peters and one behind Trevino—and the thought of evicting Peters from my brain is so tantalizing, I immediately start pressing again.

On the next seven holes, I give myself legitimate birdie looks on five and never scare the hole. Surprisingly, Peters and Trevino can't make anything either. Over the same stretch, Peters misses three putts shorter than mine—I guess legends and assholes aren't immune to pressure either—and we head to 18 exactly as we stepped off 10, with Peters one up on Trevino and two up on me.

9

THE PAR-5 FINISHING HOLE is a gauntlet of palm trees, mined by bunkers, which I avoid and Peters and Trevino don't. That means they have to lay up, and I have a chance to reach in two.

Johnny A paces off the distance to the nearest sprinkler head and checks his yardage book. "Two fifteen to the center," he says, "two twenty-nine to the flag."

As soon as that first number falls out of his mouth, I smile involuntarily, because it's a number close to my heart, the perfect distance for my new high draw that got me through the winter. Of course, as Earl was unkind enough to point out on the range, the high draw offers no tangible advantage, and since this isn't figure skating and there are no points awarded for degree of difficulty or artistic expression, there is no sensible reason to pull it out now. Except one. If I go with the high draw, I just might be able to foster the illusion that rather than coming down the stretch with Peters and Trevino on Sunday afternoon at Waialae, I'm back at Big Oaks on a Tuesday morning with Esther Lee. And maybe, with a little luck, I can sustain the illusion long enough not to choke my brains out. Plus, as even Earl concedes, it's the suavest shot in golf.

When Johnny A hands me my 5-wood and says, "Nice soft cut, center of the green," I don't bother to contradict him. Instead, I do what I did all winter...in reverse. Instead of savoring the reality of this Hawaiian paradise, I transport myself eight thousand miles away to a drafty, underheated warehouse in the midst of a brutal Chicago winter. The breeze rustling the palms? That's traffic whooshing by on Route 38. The waves breaking on the shore? Trucks rattling over the potholes.

I do such a thorough job of conjuring those chilly practice sessions, my biggest fear is that Esther will shank another one in the middle of my backswing. It's a feat of reverse double psychology that might not impress mental guru Bob Rotella, but when my ball drops softly on the green and settles fifteen feet from the hole, it impresses the shit out of Johnny A.

"I thought we said high cut. But let's not split hairs."

It also makes an impression on Trevino. "Golf shot, Travis," he says, and I swear I'm not making that up.

"Thanks, Lee," I respond, and I would have been more than happy to carry on back and forth like this for another ten minutes, but seeing as he and Peters have their second and third shots to contend with and I've got some work left on the green myself, I reluctantly cut our conversation short and follow Johnny A to the green.

10

When we get there, I discover I'm even closer than I thought, which is always nice. It's more like thirteen feet from the hole, and considerably closer than Peters's twenty-one feet and Trevino's eighteen. And they're lying three.

If you watch televised golf—and if you're reading this, that's more than likely—you've heard that pros never root against their competitors. You believe that, I have a warehouse conveniently located on Route 38 you might be interested in. When Peters attempts his birdie, I'm pulling so hard for it to miss, I may have given myself a hernia. If so, it's worth a little outpatient surgery, because his putt stops three feet short. Trevino misses too, although I swear, I wasn't bad-vibing my pal Lee…at least not as much.

Once they tap in, I've got those thirteen feet, a McKinley dozen, to force a play-off with Peters. Thirteen feet is no gimme. It's about three gimmes. But it's manageable, the kind of putt even I can stand over with a certain level of optimism, if not confidence, and Johnny and I are taking our sweet time / stalling, if only to get my heart rate down. Although our extended deliberations must be boring the crap out of Trevino and Herman, I know Peters is watching. For the first time in thirty-two years, I may have his full attention.

There is another reason Johnny A and I are taking our sweet time / stalling, and it has nothing to do with the enormous consequences or the fact that there is enough mental baggage between Peters and me to fill an airport carousel. The putt is dead straight. As long and hard as Johnny and I stare at it, we can't see any break, and the last thing a pro golfer wants to see when he squats behind a putt is nothing. *Nothing* is spooky. *Nothing* messes with your head.

Canvass a hundred guys out here, ninety-nine will agree. On a crucial putt of this length, they'd rather see two inches either way than nothing at all. A dead-straight putt is like looking at a mirror with too much light. It reveals way more about you and your stroke than any pro wants to share with himself, let alone his rivals. Then again, a lot of the people in that survey would say I'm barely a pro at all, which may help explain why I pour it dead center.

11

It would be an exaggeration to say that when Peters climbs out of the cart at 11 for the start of our play-off, he's a broken man. That's asking too much. But he's clearly dispirited by the recent turn of events, just as I'm buoyed by them. For the first time in our unhistoric rivalry, which may be a rivalry only to me, I'm the one feeling jaunty.

You can see it in my step as I hop from my own cart, and my uncharacteristic bonhomie as I chat with Marcus Azawa, chairman and CEO of Azawa Enterprises, the sponsor of the tournament. Judging from my social ease with him and his vice president of marketing, you might conclude I'm employable. And when I pump Peters's hand for the second time that afternoon and wish him, with utter lack of sincerity, good luck, there's a few extra pounds of pressure in my grip. I'm feeling so ebullient, I'm half tempted to ask Peters if he can spare a pinch of Skoal.

Eleven is a shortish par 4 with water left, and based on the numbers we draw from the chairman's palm, Peters has the tee. That's another break for me, because it gives him that much less time to recover from his disappointing finish. He closes his eyes and inhales deeply through his nose, trying to delete the memory of those missed short putts, but unless your last name is Woods or Irwin, that rarely works. As soon as Peters hits it, he knows it's wet, and when it dives into the hazard, the Azawa Open is mine to win or lose.

Now I'm the one taking New Age

breaths. Before Peters's ball has reached the bottom of that man-made lake, Johnny A has pulled the 3-wood from my hand and replaced it with a 4-iron. Somehow I keep it dry, and Johnny and I head up the right side of the fairway while Peters trudges up the left. He takes his drop and hits it about thirty feet left of the hole, and I hit my 6-iron about the same distance to the right.

On the green, the lengths are so close, it takes a rules official and a tape measure to determine that I'm far. Since we're on the same line, that's a break for Peters, but I still like my chances. If I can lag it close and tap in for par, Peters will have to sink his thirty-footer to tie.

Unlike 18, this putt has all kinds of break, at least four feet of break from left to right, but Johnny A and I are far more concerned with the pace, since the last thing we want to do is run it eight feet past or leave it five feet short. On lag putts, my grandfather taught me to feel the distance, not just see it, and as I walk back and forth between my ball and the hole, I process the contours of the green and the route my ball will travel, through my feet.

"Weight. Weight. Weight," whispers Johnny A when he finally hands me the ball, and as I place it in front of my marker, I repeat the message to myself like a mantra. My first practice stroke feels a hair tentative, the second a tad strong, and when I put the putter behind the ball for real, all I'm trying to do is split the difference.

The contact is solid, and the weight feels right. And even though we didn't grind over the line anywhere near as much as the speed, I got that right, too. Six feet from the hole, as the ball slows, takes the breaks, and swerves inexorably toward the hole, I know it's in.

12

WHEN THE BALL CATCHES the high side of the hole, my putter is already in the air. It glints in the sun like a saber as the ball drops from sight, and it's still pointing heavenward when the ball catches the back edge and comes flying out the low side twice as fast as it went in. (See *physics: gravity; centrifugal force; the combination thereof.*) When it stops rolling, I'm ten feet from the hole.

I appreciate that only Jack Nicklaus has earned the right to lift his putter when the ball is four feet from the hole, but I've never hit a better lag in my life. Ever. My only mistake was being too close on the line. Ten inches left or right, I'd have a kick-in par, but because I missed by a fraction, I've got ten feet.

Even worse, I've given Peters hope. Now he doesn't *have* to make. Despite his dunking his tee ball, two putts will likely extend the play-off, and one could end it. Since I've given him such a good read, he steps up and lets it roll while the line is still fresh in his mind. By this point, I'm too exhausted and traumatized to risk another hernia. I just turn away and glance at Johnny A... until the crowd explodes.

I've got to give Johnny credit. He doesn't bat an eye. "You already hit one good putt," he says. "We need one more."

He's right as usual, old Johnny, and it's shorter than the one I just made on 18. But that feels like a year ago, and I'm not the same golfer as the one who sank that putt. I wouldn't recognize that guy if I were sitting next to him. I tell myself not to hit the putt until I'm ready, but that could take a week and I doubt the networks would go for that. When I can't put it off any longer, I step up to the ball and give it a roll. It's not even close. Peters, that son of a bitch, is going to be living in my head for the rest of my life.

But wait. It's not over. First I have to watch two beautiful beige-skinned Hawaiian girls in grass skirts prance onto the green, kiss Peters on each jowl, and anoint him with red leis. As I'm enjoying this lovely native ceremony, Dave Marr, the on-course reporter, comes up from behind me, lays a consoling hand on my shoulder, and asks me to tell the viewers "how I feel."

"Like puking," I say. "And please take your hand off my shoulder."

13

FOUR HOURS AFTER PETERS hoists his crystal pineapple, Earl and I are lifting filthy shot glasses at the horseshoe bar of the Ding Dong Lounge, a gritty dive on the border of Honolulu's red-light district.

"This place is even better than I remembered," says Earl.

"That's the beauty of dives," I say, "they improve with age."

"Just like you and me, my friend."

We toss back our shots and chase them with cold beer.

"To the Ding Dong," says Earl.

"Long live the Ding Dong."

"Fuck. I'm amazed it lived this long."

After Earl heard what happened in sudden death, he felt duty bound to get me hammered as quickly as possible, and after five shots of Jameson and four cans of Primo, which I'm told is the Pabst Blue Ribbon of Hawaii, we're making solid progress. And since neither one of us sees any benefit in being photographed stumbling onto the curb at closing time, he thought we'd be better off in an obscure hole-in-the-wall than one of the glittering tourist traps near the hotel. Then he remembered the Ding Dong Lounge, first visited almost thirty years ago on an R&R trip during his second tour in Vietnam.

Despite my gloom, the Ding Dong had me from aloha. From the gentle, murky light to the pleasantly dank aroma to the scarred wood surface of the horseshoe bar, everything about it is imperfectly perfect. Halfway through my fourth Primo, even the name starts to grow on me.

"I know it was a sad occasion," says Earl, "but it was great to spend a little time with Sarah and the kids. You're one lucky motherfucker. And not just for being born white."

"Luck has nothing to do with it," I say with a straight face.

"Oh, really?"

"Survival of the fittest. Natural selection. It's science, really. But speaking of luck, I've got to say, I didn't feel so goddamned fortunate four hours ago when that putt caught the lip on eleven and..."

Earl puts down his Primo and points an admonishing finger. According to the ground rules for this excursion, clearly laid out on our walk from the hotel, any reference to "ancient history," as in what happened on the golf course this afternoon, is strictly off-limits. "The goal," he said, "is not to understand it, which would be impossible anyway, since it's golf, or even to learn from it, but to forget it, or at least dilute it."

"You're right," I say, getting back on script. "I'm a very lucky Caucasian. Lucky. Lucky. Lucky. Although I'm not sure Sarah feels the same way."

"How could she, under the circumstances? But let's take your kids. You know how many turn out to be assholes? A lot. Yours are smart, decent, and fairly good-looking."

"Thanks, Earl."

Earl reaches for his Primo, and in mid-sip, his eyes go slack, like he just saw the ghost of an old army pal who didn't make it home.

"You okay?"

"Not really," he says and, with the same blank expression, mumbles more to himself than me, "Motherfucker...of all the joints, in all the towns, in the whole motherfucking world, this motherfucker walks into mine."

When I swivel in the direction of Earl's empty gaze, I see that three large, beefy men have joined us at the bar, and that the one in the middle is wearing a red lei.

"Hey, Travis," says Peters. "Hey, Earl."

Although his greeting could not be more innocuous, it causes his two friends to double over with laughter. All three are at least as intoxicated as me and Earl. Why shouldn't they be? They have something to celebrate.

"Hi, Hank," responds Earl for both of us.

"Travis," says Peters, "I got to say something. For the record. What happened on eleven was the worst piece of luck I've ever seen." And when I don't respond, he adds, "No shit."

"I know, Hank. I was there. Remember?"

"We're grown men here, give or take. We've seen lipouts and power lipouts. But this was another level. A tsunami to a hurricane. Your ball came out the other side like Dale Earnhardt coming out of the five turn at Daytona."

Peters, to my surprise, has a gift for simile.

"It was like one of those putting machines some asshole executive has in his office where the ball goes up a little ramp and when he makes it, there's a bit of a pause before the thing spits it out. Then the ball rolls down the little ramp back to his loafers, the kind with little tassels on them. And then his hot secretary sticks her head in the door and goes, 'I got Chandler on the horn. What should I tell him?' 'Tell him what you always tell him, doll face—I'm busy.' You know the kind?"

"Yeah, Hank, I think I do."

"Why am I telling you? You were in advertising. You probably had one."

In the last couple of minutes, his friends have managed to regain their composure, but now beer comes flying out of their mouths and they slap the bar.

"Could we talk about something else? Believe it or not, I'm actually trying to forget it. As a matter of fact, that's why we're here."

"I mean, what the fuck was in that hole, Travis? A snake? A frog? And one other thing, what was your putter doing in the air?"

I still hear their laughter, but now it seems far away, as if reaching me from a distant room, because at this point I'm out of my chair and flying through the air toward the red lei and his giant jug head. Even in midair, I'm aware of having crossed a line from which there is no graceful retreat. As soon as I reach Peters, I have no choice but to start punching, and Peters has no choice but to punch back.

14

THE SPORTS BAR BETWEEN Gates 7 and 8 in the American Airlines section of the Honolulu International Airport is no Ding Dong Lounge. There's the antiseptic airport smell and the barrage of highlights and scores blaring from overhead TVs—does a twenty-seat bar really need four televisions?—but my biggest issue is with the light. There's so much glare bouncing off the tarmac, I'd need sunglasses even if I didn't have a black eye.

A respite from the noise induces me to glance upward. ESPN has gone to a commercial and there's Earl, three miles outside of Hanoi, walking in his new Reeboks, over terrain he used to hump in combat boots. Now he's talking to some elders in a village, sharing photographs of himself as a young soldier, and now he's standing beside some rice paddies doing a clinic for the kids as a water buffalo looks on. I hope it doesn't end up as a pair of golf shoes.

When *SportsCenter* resumes, I take a sip of my Bloody Mary and assess the damage. In addition to my shut right eye, which is more purple than black, all the ribs on my left side are sore, and one may be cracked, because when I raise my left hand to push my Ray-Bans back on my nose, there's a piercing pain. That must be why I'm drinking with my right. In addition, my head hurts in a way that can't be explained entirely by a hangover.

Nevertheless, I don't feel bad. On the contrary. Sixteen hours after the fact, the thrill of having survived and almost held my own in a brawl with camo-wearing, tobacco-juice-spitting Hank Peters hasn't worn off, and my niggling list of injuries seems a small price to pay for glory. As I'm nursing my drink and my memories, the bartender, a brunette in her late twenties, pauses in front of me.

"Want to see something hilarious?" she asks.

"Sure."

"Then check out these two clowns."

I peer up gingerly (my neck) and see a man who looks a lot like me flying at a man with a lei around his neck. Then the two flail at each other in a highly undignified manner. When they cut back to the anchor, there's a reference to a security camera at a Honolulu bar.

"How often have they been showing this?"

"A lot. Apparently, they're both professional golfers … on the *Senior* Tour."

I'm resisting the urge to ask her which of

these two clowns, in her estimation, won the fight, when a call comes in on my cell from Ponte Vedra, Florida.

"Is this Travis McKinley?"

"Yes."

"This is Tim Finchem." The commissioner of the PGA tour. "I need to see you in my office tomorrow afternoon."

15

THE NEXT AFTERNOON, PETERS and I are side by side again. Instead of being perched on bar stools, our butts are nearly scraping the broadloom in a pair of low-slung leather chairs. The chairs are facing PGA Commissioner Timothy W. Finchem, who looks down at us, in every sense, from behind his brilliantly polished mahogany desk. Despite the quality of Finchem's furniture, suit, and haircut, the scene reeks of high school, specifically that doomsday moment when you're summoned to the principal's office.

For a couple of minutes, Finchem lets us twist in the over-air-conditioned breeze. As we endure the silent treatment, I notice that Peters is as banged up as me, with a badly swollen lower lip and a shiner of his own. I'm struck by how young Finchem looks. On paper, Peters and I may only have him by about five years, but he has spent a lot less time in the sun and a lot more in the gym, and it shows.

Then again, we work for a living. Kind of.

I'm also puzzled by the three black plastic cassettes on his desk. Presumably they contain the surveillance footage ESPN has been wearing out on *SportsCenter,* but why three? Has Finchem made duplicates so we can each take one home and study it before we write our essays on how we will never get caught fighting on camera in a dive bar again?

Finchem takes the top one off the stack and feeds it into the VCR, which along with a monitor has been wheeled into his office. By now I've seen the footage half a dozen times, but it doesn't get any easier. This version, which picks up the action about a minute sooner, is even more damning than the one they've been airing. A camera mounted on the far wall shows Earl and me bent over our drinks as Peters and his friends take the empty spots beside us, then captures our awkward surprise as we discover we're sitting next to each other. Finchem winces at the monitor, as if the seedy interior of the Ding Dong is desecrating his immaculate office, and seems baffled that anyone, let alone three members of the Senior Tour, would choose to be there.

For the next thirty seconds or so, the tape shows Peters attempting to engage me in conversation. While Peters's posture is upright, expansive, and friendly, I look down at the surface of the bar. Then, without any apparent provocation, I spring from my stool and attack him.

"This is from last night," says Finchem as he ejects and replaces the tape.

The screen fills with color bars, which give way to a stage on which Jay Leno is in the midst of his *Tonight Show* monologue.

"I guess you've all heard about those two palookas McKinley and Peters? Did you know HBO's doing a rematch—McKinley and Peters II? It's going to be on pay-per-view for nineteen ninety-five. Sounded pricey to me, too. Then I realized they're going to *pay us* to watch."

As Peters mimes a burlesque drummer providing a rimshot, Finchem switches cassettes again, so we can see what Letterman can do with the same material.

"You know where this fight took place?" asks Letterman, fingering a button on his double-breasted blazer. "A very classy watering hole by the name of the Ding Dong Lounge. I'm not making that up," he says, then slowly repeats the name with exaggerated clarity—"the...Ding...Dong...

Lounge. I know what you're thinking—what kind of person goes to a place called the Ding Dong Lounge? Well, now we know the answer: ding-dongs. The Ding Dong Lounge is a place where ding-dongs feel welcome and at home." As the CBS Orchestra plays the theme from *Cheers,* Finchem hits Eject and the audio-video presentation is over.

"Commissioner," says Peters, "I have nothing to say about these last two tapes, except that they remind me how much I miss Carson. As for the first, it couldn't be more misleading. Based on that tape, you, or anyone else, would think Travis started this. In fact, this fight was instigated entirely by me and my big mouth. Without sound, you can't hear me taunting Travis repeatedly about what happened a few hours before in sudden death.

"Commissioner, I didn't say one or two things. I said about five, all unnecessary, all uncalled-for, and at least one came after he

politely asked me to stop. Under the circumstances, I think Travis showed a lot of
restraint."

"You call that restraint?"

"That's what I said, Commissioner. Restraint."

"Hank, I appreciate you standing up for
your fellow competitor, but the video
shows what it shows. You two have embarrassed the tour and tarnished our brand.
You think the banks and investment advisors who sponsor our events want to see
two of our most popular players brawling
in a dive? Hank, you're on probation for
the rest of the year. Travis, you're suspended for six months."

"That's ridiculous," says Peters. "If anyone should be suspended, it should be me."

But this isn't a hearing, and Finchem is
already out of his chair.

"I feel terrible about this," says Peters
when the two of us are alone. "And you
were playing great golf. That shot on eigh-

teen was the best shot I've seen this year.
You need to borrow some money to tide
you over, don't hesitate to ask. It's the least
I can do."

"Thanks, Hank, I'm okay on that score.
And I appreciate what you said."

"It's all true. Not that it did any good.
But what do you expect from a guy who
went to college on a debating scholarship?
And one other thing…my friends call me
Stump."

16

BEYOND THE UNFAMILIAR WINDSHIELD is an empty parking lot illuminated by the last few minutes of daylight. On the passenger seat are a half-eaten turkey sandwich and an empty can of iced tea, and I have no memory of either. The insignia on the steering wheel indicates the car is a Chrysler, and a glance over my shoulder reveals the interior of a minivan. The odometer shows 169 miles, so that explains the new-car smell, but not much else, and the clock, when I finally find it, reads 6:09. It's not until I open the glove compartment and unfold the rental agreement from the Jacksonville Airport Alamo that I remember where I am and why, and realize I've been sitting like this in the deepening dusk for nearly an hour.

For the second time in little more than a year, I've lost my job, but this one I loved and was actually quite good at. Against lotto-like odds, I achieved a lifelong quest to play competitive golf for a living, and in forty-five videotaped seconds screwed it up. A spot on the Senior Tour is fleeting to begin with. Under the best circumstances, three or four years is a pretty good run, so losing six months of my middle-aged prime is a pretty stiff price to pay for a relatively harmless fight.

Yet as stunned as I am by Finchem's harsh penalty, I'm more undone by Peters's generosity. How could I have been so wrong about the guy? I spent thirty years hating a person who didn't exist. Pressed to come up with an explanation for my dislike, I would have cited his good ol' boy routine and his redneck shtick, but I can see that was nothing but a smokeless smoke screen.

The reason I didn't like Hank Peters is because he is a better golfer than I am. And he knows it. That's not the abridged edition. It's the entire volume. You want to earn my lifelong enmity, just be better than me at something I care about, exude a little more self-confidence, and beat me in a college match in which I have you down two with three to play.

Do that, and I'll hate you for life. I promise. And how does Peters respond to all my petty bile and cranky bullshit? How does he repay me for three decades of tight-lipped, phony smiles and bad-vibing? By treating me like a friend.

According to the dashboard clock, another twenty minutes have gone missing as mysteriously as that half a sandwich. If I'm going to make my flight, I need to hustle. I find the keys, start the car, and turn on the lights, and as I reach back for the seat belt, I catch a glimpse of the one person I least want to see.

17

My reception in Winnetka is more in keeping with the return of a conquering hero than a disgraced asshole. As I step through the front door, all three remaining full-time residents of the McKinley household—woman, child, and dog—hurl themselves at me with delight. Sarah plants a fat, juicy kiss on my mouth, Louie paws my legs and crows like a rooster, and in between, Noah wraps his arms around me and says, "Dad, that fight was awesome."

"A brawl?...In a dive bar?...With a guy

named Stump?" whispers Sarah breathily in my ear. "I had no idea you were such a badass."

"Really?"

"Yeah, really."

Although it's almost midnight, I'm hustled from the foyer into the kitchen and seated at the head of the table. Noah hands me a glass of the best red on the premises, and Sarah takes a warm plate from the oven. Artfully arranged on top of it are the best parts of a roasted chicken, surrounded by potatoes simmered in its juices, and ringed by blackened Brussels sprouts.

"I made you your death row meal," says Sarah, and I try not to wince at the unintended irony.

"Everything is absurdly delicious. I only wish I deserved it."

"We think you do," says Noah, pouring himself a bowl of Cheerios.

"You've won tournaments before, Travis. This was different."

"Not in a good way. It turns out I couldn't have been more wrong about Peters."

"You've always disliked him."

"For no good reason. In our meeting with Finchem, he defended me like Clarence Darrow. Insisted the whole thing was his fault."

"Maybe it was."

"And I assume you haven't forgotten the part about me being suspended for six months."

"That's unfortunate and unfair. But you'll come back stronger than ever. We're sure of it."

"You too, pal?"

"No question," says Noah, milk trickling down his chin.

Interjecting reality into this late-night celebration makes me feel like the killjoy I am. Instead, I hoist my Pinot and toast the room. "What a meal! What a wife! What a kid! What a dog!"

"That's more like it," says Sarah.

"By the way," says Noah, "did I tell you that even Mr. Wilmot in gym is treating me better?"

"Big surprise there."

After dinner, Noah trudges to bed and Sarah refuses to be talked out of washing the dishes, so I head to the couch with Louie. When he rests his head on my thigh, farts, sighs, and falls asleep, I'm grateful that at least one member of the household isn't burdened with false illusions.

18

THE NEXT MORNING, I drop Noah at school, and Louie and I take a drive to the Creekview Country Club, which is as deserted as it should be on a Wednesday morning in mid-January. I park in the rear corner, and the two of us set out up the first fairway, following the cart tracks left from my grandfather's funeral. Three weeks later, the ground is still frozen, but the temperature has soared into the high twenties, and the air is heavy with forecast snow.

On the first green, Louie and I find the spot where the first installment of my grandfather's ashes were scattered, my fallible memory confirmed by Louie's infallible nose. Whenever things get shaky, and sooner or later they always do, my first instinct is to go talk to Pop. It's been that way since I learned to walk, let alone swing a 7-iron, and it's not going to change now just because he's dead. Gazing down at the green, I fill him in on what happened in Hawaii, from the last hole of regulation to the only hole of sudden death. Then I get him up to speed on my visit to the Ding Dong and Finchem's office before Louie and I move on.

Over the years I've gotten almost as much comfort from this old golf course as I have from my grandfather. It's not only where I learned to play, it's where over the course of thousands of rounds, I literally grew up. Or tried to. Even here, however, I can't escape the harsh glare of self-scrutiny, set off by Peters's unexpected support. As Louie and I wander in the cold from hole to hole, I rewind as much of my first fifty-one years or so as I can stomach, searching for an occasion, or preferably more, when I behaved as generously.

Ten holes later, I haven't come up with one. There is, however, no shortage of cringeworthy moments, incidents so damning I'm not going to share them now. Whenever I think I've unearthed something I can hold up in my defense — "Your Honor, I refer you to exhibit one A" — I soon see through it for what it was, a transparent attempt to impress a girl, or a friend or a college admissions staff. As far as I can tell, my only genuine acts of kindness have been directed at Sarah, Elizabeth, Simon, and Noah, and they're simply an extension of myself and inadmissible as evidence.

Being back on home turf isn't doing much for me, but Louie is having a blast. I know every blade of grass on these sub-urban sixty acres, but for Louie it's all thrillingly new, and he is beside himself at having the run of such a vast, fascinating tract. Like a canine Columbus wading ashore in the New World, he races from tree to bush to rock, raising a leg and planting the flag of Louie.

On the 14th fairway, Louie picks up the scent of Simon and, barking maniacally, follows it to the portion of the green where my older son tipped Pop's ashes. What, I wonder, did my grandfather see in me? If I were nothing more than a little sawed-off bag of shit, even he wouldn't have loved me. Since he did, he must have detected a crumb of decency. Right? Or was it all just biology, a kindhearted old coot giving his flesh and blood the benefit of the doubt? Unfortunately, that sounds more like it.

As we hover over the fresh memory of Pop's remains, Louie starts barking again, this time skyward, and when I tilt my head back, it looks as if an enormous old pillow has burst open. Like Louie last night on the couch, the sky is letting it all go. Still barking, Louie sprints out into the pouring snow, and after one last aside to Pop, I head after him.

19

IT SNOWS FOR TWENTY-FOUR hours, and when I look out the window Thursday morning, Winnetka has rarely looked better. All the tacky details and worst pretensions of suburban architecture have been whited out. What's left is the snow-topped geometry of rooftops and telephone lines and the poetry of trees.

Just as lovely is the muffled quiet, and so in its own way the rattling and scraping of the first wave of municipal plows. Then the local citizenry wheel out and rev up their snow-moving toys. To escape the din,

I grab my golf bag from the garage and haul it to the basement.

Downstairs, I pull out all the clubs and lean them against the wall of my workshop. It's been almost a week since I've touched my sticks, and I miss them. What happened in Hawaii wasn't their fault. At least, not entirely. Arrayed by height, from my homely Big Bertha to my lovely ancient bull's-eye, they look like the multiple generations of a large, eccentric family gathered for a portrait.

I'd clean the clubs, but Johnny A took care of that before we packed up, and the shaft, grip, lie, and loft of every one have already been tweaked and fitted to within an inch of their lives. I consider adding a couple of degrees of loft to my 4-iron to close the gap between it and my 5-wood, but decide instead to replace the grips on my wedges, which is equally unnecessary but at least not destructive. I've got my gap wedge in the vise and the old grip half off when Louie starts imitating a watchdog.

Upstairs, I open the front door to a tall, pudgy teenager, about seventeen, whose face is scarred with acne. He holds a shovel and, despite the cold, wears only a sweater, scarf, and hat, all three of which are made of the same coarse green wool and are far too sturdy and singular to have been purchased at the local mall.

"Sorry to interrupt your pliering," says the boy, referring to the pliers in my right hand. "I was hoping I could shovel your walks and driveway."

"I'd appreciate that."

"Does twenty dollars seem fair?"

"Not to you," I say. "There's at least two feet of snow, and it's wet and heavy."

"Your points are all well taken," responds the boy with a goofy grin that outshines his acne, and his European accent underlines the arcane diction.

"Let's make it forty dollars."

"Excellent," says the kid, extending a large hand reddened by the cold. "We have a verbal contract and a handshake agreement."

Then he turns his back and starts shoveling, and while he digs his way from the front door to the driveway, I return to my subterranean busy work. In total, I manage to kill almost an hour. I replace the grips on all three wedges (twenty-five minutes), polish and clean my big white Mizuno bag (twenty minutes), then do the same to my golf shoes (ten minutes).

When I climb out of the basement, the sun is blinding and the smell of hot chocolate wafts from the kitchen. Outside, the kid has finished the walk and is attacking the driveway, and as I watch from the living room, Noah, with Louie trailing, emerges from the side of the house bearing two steaming mugs. After the shoveler accepts his, the pair chink cups and sip their warm drinks in the winter sun, chatting like old pals. Then the boy hands back the empty, makes a courtly bow, and returns to work.

"I like Jerzy," says Noah, back in the kitchen. "He's good people."

"I like him, too."

Jerzy shovels for three hours. When he returns to the front door, he holds the plastic bag containing a day-old paper. "An artifact excavated from the base of the driveway," he says. "Perhaps it will be of some interest." More conspicuous than his accent is his delight in his new language, as if every word and figure of speech is inherently amusing.

"Thanks, Jerzy. You did a hell of a job. I'm Travis."

"I know who you are, Mr. McKinley. You're Winnetka's most notorious professional athlete."

"I guess you heard about the suspension."

"It struck me as rather draconian."

"Ditto. You play?" I ask.

"Unfortunately not, but I spectate via television."

I pull two twenties and a ten from my wallet and, as I hand them over, notice that the acne on his forehead camouflages a nasty gash.

"This is too much," says Jerzy.

"Not at all. You earned it. What happened to your head?"

"Tripped on the ice. Unfortunately, both my feet are left ones."

"Well, good luck getting back. And thanks again."

20

I RIP THROUGH THE wet wrapper, and without so much as a glance at the world, local, business, and cultural news, apply myself directly to Sports. An unseemly amount of the first page is devoted to the exploits of Michael Jordan, who led the Bulls to victory last night in Texas, and there's a photo of him throwing one down over San Antonio's rookie center, Tim Duncan.

I'll get back to that in a moment, but first I want to see how Earl is faring in Tampa. Among the box scores and standings, I find the leaderboard for the GTE

Suncoast Classic, where order has been restored. Tied for the lead are Hale Irwin and Gil Morgan, and four strokes back is Earl Fielder. It looks like Earl is going to have to wait another week before getting that first *w,* but back-to-back 69s are nothing to sneeze at and almost certain to lead to his twenty-fifth top ten in a row. There's no sign of Stump. Most likely, he took the week off to enjoy his victory and give his face a chance to look more presentable.

I sip my coffee and study the small type like a tax attorney searching for loopholes. From the box score, I learn that Jordan scored thirty-five points in thirty-three minutes, shooting eight for fifteen from the field, four for nine from three-point range, and seven for seven from the line, and Pippen was one assist and two rebounds short of a triple-double. My scrutiny shifts from the NBA standings to the Blackhawks box score to the college basketball results (Eastern Michigan 68, Northwestern 52) before alighting on "Transactions." If the agate are the crumbs of the sports section, then "Transactions" are the crumbs of the crumbs. But where else would I learn that the Bears have agreed to a four-year contract with outside linebacker Boswell King and waived (football is even crueler than golf) defensive lineman Simon Briggs and placed Ted Keating on injured reserve? Or that Phil Jackson has been fined $10,000 for criticizing the officials after last week's loss in Portland, which strikes me as rather draconian?

What, you may wonder, is so interesting about an endless succession of contrived contests staged day after day, night after night, in gyms, rinks, and arenas? For one thing, they're easy to digest. Someone won. Someone lost. Someone, like yours truly, screwed up, and someone, like Hank Peters, didn't. The rest of the paper is never that clear, and even if you learn what happened, you don't know what it means. Maybe you'll know in a week or a month. More likely, you never will.

I spend over an hour of the only life I'll ever have poring over scores, standings, and minutiae, and just when I think I've extracted every last bit of infotainment from these four pages of newsprint, I stumble on half a dozen paragraph-sized morsels herded under "Briefs." The headline for the golf item reads: CADDIES INJURED IN CRASH.

Two regular caddies on the Senior Tour were injured yesterday afternoon on Route 75 ten miles outside of Tampa, Florida, when their van swerved to avoid a deer. GW Cable of Sarasota, Florida, was treated for a concussion and held overnight and Brandon Fielder of Monroe, North Carolina, was treated for a broken arm and released.

The news that Earl is without a caddy jolts me upright. Suddenly restless, I get up and wash out the saucepan Noah used to make the hot chocolate and place it in the drying rack. Outside the kitchen window a black squirrel clings to the top of the bird feeder. Hanging upside down, he struggles to extract a couple of seeds, an athletic challenge with more at stake than any of those I read about.

As the bird feeder swings back and forth, I recall the fateful day when Earl and I were paired in the second round of Q-School, and how my immediate comfort with him helped me through the round. Then I think of our even more important meeting four days later, after I squeaked through and he fell just short, when he volunteered to carry my bag for my rookie season.

If the situation had been reversed, and he had gotten through and I had narrowly missed out, would I have even considered making him the same offer? I know the answer, but why not? Earl is single, with a pension and an impressive stock portfolio, so I would have needed a job more than him. Is it because I'm a snob who considers caddying beneath him? And is part of that snobbism based on race? More likely, it's because I would have been sulking too much to think objectively.

What I would or might have done years ago is interesting, at least to me. The more pressing question is what am I going to do now? Before I have a chance to chicken out, I grab the phone and call Earl.

21

THREE DAYS LATER, WEARING a white bib with FIELDER pinned to the back, I'm standing like a statue behind the first tee of the Longboat Key Club & Resort, site of the Greater Sarasota Intellinet Challenge. Although my only immediate responsibility is to make sure Earl's bag doesn't topple over in the middle of his backswing, I'm more nervous than if I were the one teeing it up, and as Earl takes his practice swings, I thumb the corner of the index card in my back pocket like a security blanket.

Due to the blizzard, I couldn't get a flight

out of Chicago till this morning and didn't screech into the parking lot till forty minutes ago. That was barely enough time to fill out that index card with the distances Earl hits all his clubs and grab a yardage book, and as Earl settles behind the ball, I tap them both again to make sure they're still there. Then Earl pipes his drive down the center, and I hoist his bag over my right shoulder and hustle after him.

The lack of time to prepare certainly contributes to my agitation. A bigger factor is Earl's reaction when I volunteered my services. Let's just say he didn't jump at the offer. After ten seconds of awkward silence, the best he could come up with was "You sure you want to do this? The bag's pretty heavy."

"I know," I said. "I just carried mine down to the basement."

"Imagine what it will feel like after six miles."

"You didn't have any trouble."

"Yeah. Well, I'm not you."

That night at dinner, Sarah and Noah were just as skeptical about my suitability for hard anonymous labor. An informal poll of best friend and family yielded the unflattering consensus that I was too much of a pussy and too much of a prima donna to happily hump a forty-pound bag with another man's name on it.

I don't say a word as I escort Earl down a tight fairway lined with modest houses and screened-in swimming pools. Pacing off yardages, pulling clubs, and reading greens will be enough of a challenge without engaging in small talk, and I want to make it clear from the outset that I'm not here to hang out but to work.

Despite my determination to exceed everyone's low expectations, I narrowly avoid disaster, and it happens on the very first hole, after Earl follows his perfect drive with a crisp 7-iron that leaves him twenty-two feet below the hole. One of the great perks of being a professional golfer, right up there with not having to work for a living, is that eighteen times a round, you get to flaunt your good fortune by performing a simple ritual permissible only for pros— the mark and toss. Upon finding your ball on the green, you saunter up behind it, mark the spot, then toss the ball to your caddy, who wipes it clean with a damp towel.

Every pro performs this little sequence in his own inimitable fashion, but always with as much nonchalance as he can muster with a straight face. Some players release the ball without even a glance at their caddy, like a look-away pass in basketball. Others lob it like a baby hook. Earl's signature is to put a bit of air under it, and when he flips it to me, perhaps as a joke or perhaps as a kind of initiation, he puts even more than usual, and the height of the toss gives me way too much time to consider the consequences of booting it.

Mainly, I'm thinking about the pond, directly behind me at the base of a closely mown slope, and the fact that the surface is coated with opaque green slime. If I yip the catch, not only will Earl's ball end up in the soup, but there'll be no way to find it, and based on my rereading on the flight down of that page-turner known as *The Rules of Golf*, I know that if Earl has to putt out with a different ball than the one he just threw to me, I'll go down in looping lore as the rookie who cost his player two strokes on his first hole. As a result, I brace myself for this little pop-up as if it were a vicious line drive and, with two hands extended and Earl's clubs bouncing around on my back, am barely able to corral it.

"Nice catch," says Earl.

Six holes later, I find another way to amuse my new boss. Because it's a muggy Florida afternoon, I'm careful to stay hydrated, so careful I'm soon in need of a bathroom. I put it off as long as a man of a certain age can, but when there's a wait at the par-three 7th, I jump at the chance and scurry to the small white stucco structure discreetly tucked among a cluster of shading palms. Unfortunately, a tournament official got there first and tacked a sign to the door: FOR PLAYERS ONLY.

That leaves the plastic Porta-Potty roasting in the sun ten yards away. "Enjoy the facilities?" asks Earl when I get back.

"Immensely. Thanks for asking."

22

EARL SHOOTS 71 IN the first round and 71 in the second. Then again, Earl's rounds often mirror each other. That's why he's the Joe DiMaggio of senior golf, with twenty-four consecutive top tens and counting. The man doesn't make bad swings or hit squirrelly shots.

Earl's got one of the most repeatable swings on the planet. I've always known this, of course, but witnessing it up close and personal is a little disconcerting. Again and again, I pace off the distance to the nearest sprinkler head, do the math, and come up with the same number to the center of the green on Saturday that we had on Friday. Once, I'm quite certain, his ball came to rest on top of his old filled-in divot.

For his caddy, it's as frustrating as it is impressive, because despite his otherworldly ball-striking, we're a whopping two under. He doesn't make bogeys, but he doesn't make birdies, either. He's the human unhighlight film.

So where does Earl drag me after the second round is in the books? The driving range, of course. Like everyone else, Earl likes to practice what he's good at. It reminds me of the greasers in high school who would spend all afternoon waxing and polishing their already gleaming Camaros and GTOs.

"You know how many fairways you missed the first two days?" I ask, after I've seen one too many perfect 5-irons.

"Not a lot."

"One. By six inches. You also missed twenty-four putts inside twenty feet. And guess how many you got to the hole?"

"Not enough."

"Two."

"Wow, Travis. You're actually paying attention."

"That stuff you said about how you would trade all those thirds and fourths for one win. Was that bullshit?"

"No."

"Then put that club away and follow me."

To my relief, he does, and we spend the next three hours on the practice green performing one drill. From anywhere from eight to sixty feet, I drop six balls, and he has to get every one to the hole. If he doesn't, we start over.

Want to know the results of this three-hour master class? I was afraid you might. On Sunday, Earl doesn't make a putt over six feet and leaves just as many short.

Thanks to my meddling, he shoots 72 and finishes out of the top ten for the first time in a year. I violated the caddy's version of the Hippocratic oath, which is not to make things worse. And yet, as I throw my bag in the trunk and motor south, I'm buoyed by an almost giddy sense of optimism.

23

THE REASON I'M SO hopeful is that our next stop, Shoal Creek, just outside Birmingham, Alabama, is the toughest track the seniors play all year. That means Earl, even with me on the bag, has a real chance. Let me explain.

Most of the tournaments out here, like the one we just wrapped up in Sarasota, are held at resorts. Resort courses play easy. They have to, because they're laid out with the hacker in mind. The fairways are wide, the rough anemic, and the hazards so close to the tee they're not really in play, at least not for the pros, who start drooling all over themselves before they get out of their cars. Since keeping the ball in play isn't much of a challenge, these tournaments turn into putting contests, and Earl isn't going to win many of those.

At Shoal Creek, which was carved out of the woods by Nicklaus in '77 and has already hosted two PGA championships, no one's salivating in the parking lot. It's long and tight and unforgiving and there are no houses and swimming pools lining the fairways. To contend at Shoal Creek, you need to be a bona fide ball-striker, someone who can drive it long *and* straight and hit greens from 200 yards out all day. Even on the Senior Tour, there aren't many of these, and Earl is one of them. Once you get to the deep end of his bag, he's as good as any old fart in the world.

In Birmingham, Earl and I have three days to prepare, and the more we see of the course, the worse it looks and the more

I like it. Not only is the course hard, it's set up hard too, with four inches of the juiciest Bermuda rough this side of a U.S. Open. In our first practice round, I drop three balls into it and invite Earl, one of the stronger guys out here, to hack away with his 7-iron. His best carries 85 yards.

"This stuff is horrible," says Earl.

"No, it's not. It's beautiful. Because you're not going to be in it. And a lot of your so-called friends will be."

24

MY BIGGEST FEAR IS that Earl wants it too much. Ever since we rolled into town the press has been all over both of us. A former U.S. Senior Open winner who gets himself suspended, then comes out to caddy for his old pal, is good copy, and part of what makes it intriguing, particularly in Alabama, is that the golfer is black and the caddy white. When Shoal Creek hosted their second PGA Championship in 1990, the club's all-white membership became a national story after Hall Thompson, its founder and president, defended his club by saying "we don't discriminate in every other area except blacks." Since then, Thompson has changed his tune, at least slightly, and added one African-American to the roster, but a black golfer winning the tournament would still be newsworthy, maybe even historic.

In the press tent, Earl insists he couldn't care less about any of that. "Winning my first tournament is all the incentive I need," he says. That's true, as far as it goes, but the racial backstory gives him all the more incentive. Why wouldn't it? And you can tell that it means something to the club's black caddies, who go out of their way to shake his hand, wish him luck, or just make eye contact.

If Earl won't talk about it, maybe I will. In the last three days, I've received dozens of interview requests, including one from ESPN's Stuart Scott, who suggests I might want to be known for something other than the Ding Dong Lounge. I turn them all down—the last thing I want to do is say something stupid that will put extra pressure on Earl—and Thursday night, when there's a knock on my hotel door, I ignore it like all the rest.

After thirty seconds, it turns into banging.

"Travis, open up. I know you're in there."

Annoyed, I hop from the bed and unchain the door. It's Stump.

"I want to wish you good luck," he says. "I think it's great that you're out here with Earl."

"Thanks, Stump. I hope Earl feels the same."

"Believe it or not, he does. I just ran into the Duke of Earl in the elevator. He told me you actually know what you're doing. Surprised the hell out of him."

"I bet. Speaking of surprises, thanks again for what you said in Ponte Vedra. It really opened my eyes. For thirty years I didn't like you very much."

"I kind of deduced that."

"All because you beat me in a college match thirty fucking years ago."

"You mean the one where you had me down by two with three to go?" says Stump with a shit-eating grin.

"Yeah, that one."

"You're a competitive prick, Travis. So am I and so is Earl and every other asshole out here. We wouldn't be here otherwise. If it makes you feel any better, I always thought you were an asshole, too."

"But you were right."

"Yeah, good point."

Then Stump leans forward and points at a spot above my collar, like he can't quite believe what he's seeing. "No doubt about it," he says. "That's raw and pink and angry. It's official, son. You're a redneck now, too."

25

THE FINAL PIECE OF bad/good news is the weather. On Monday, the temperature barely reached sixty, and it has gotten colder and windier ever since. This morning, when we finally tee off for real, it's forty-eight, with twenty-five-mile-an-hour gusts. On this course with this setup and this wind, it's about survival, and who knows more about that than someone who got himself home in one piece from four tours in Vietnam?

For the next four and a half hours, Earl and I keep our heads down and plot our way from point A to B to C, following the routes we mapped out for each hole. Off the tee, Earl keeps it out of the wind with a low, hard stinger even Tiger wouldn't sneeze at. Although the ball doesn't get more than twenty feet off the ground, he gets so much roll that he puts it out there 275/280 every time, and while Earl's playing partners, one of whom is the golf commentator and Senior Tour rookie Gary McCord, are hacking it out of the rough every three or four holes, Earl doesn't stray from the short grass.

I'm not saying Earl makes it look easy. The human unhighlight film isn't endowed with that kind of flair. But he makes it look boring, which is even better, as far as I'm concerned. Fairway, green, two putts. Fairway, green, two putts. After six holes of this, I overhear McCord mumble to his caddy, "I think that motherfucker is an android."

Earl's got things so under control, I can

enjoy the rugged scenery. When I say Shoal Creek was carved out of the woods, I mean real woods, and unlike most courses we play, the wilderness hasn't been utterly obliterated so a bunch of middle-aged guys can play golf. There have been sightings of foxes, coyotes, and bears, and except for a brick chimney high on Double Oak Mountain, which looks down over the 14th hole, the views aren't marred by houses.

The first round is classic Earl—fourteen of fourteen fairways, fifteen greens in regulation, and thirty-four putts. One birdie, one bogey, and sixteen pars. That's just fine, because for once, he's playing a course where par means something. Earl's opening 72 leaves him tied for third, two strokes out of the lead.

26

SATURDAY'S JUST AS RAW and gusty, and now it's raining. By the third hole, it's coming down hard and we all expect play to be suspended, but with no electricity on the radar, the marshals decide to have us slog on. The wet fairways make the course longer and harder, which plays into Earl's strengths, but I'm more than a little worried about holding up my end of the bargain, since the one thing harder than playing golf in the wind and the cold is caddying in the rain.

Add a downpour to the equation and

caddying becomes borderline impossible. Ever try carrying the bag, cleaning and pulling clubs, pacing off yardages, and deciphering the wind and greens while holding an umbrella over your golfer? It's like being a short-order cook at a popular diner on a busy morning, when you've got a grill full of crackling eggs and new orders piling up. There's too much to do, and if you crumble under the pressure, you're toast, as in whiskey down. To keep Earl and his equipment dry, I've got four towels in rotation—two in the bag, one under my jacket, and one hanging from the tines of Earl's umbrella beside an extra glove—and all I'm trying to do is stay calm so Earl can stay calm, too.

"Bearing up okay?" asks Earl as I swap a soaking towel for a semidry one.

"Piece of cake," I lie. "You just concentrate on fairways and greens."

Earl does as instructed. He's like the U.S. Postal Service. Neither wind nor cold nor rain can stop him from delivering pars. On the par-five 10th, he even throws in a birdie, and when the horn blows to stop play with Earl safely on the 12th green, I'm disappointed, because I doubt anyone else is faring as well under these conditions.

Till now, I've been too busy to verify that, but as Earl and I thread our way back to the clubhouse, we get our first look at the leaderboard. At the very top, so high it hurts my neck, is the name on the back of my overalls—Earl Fielder—and beside it the only number in red, –1, because he's the only golfer under par.

"Take a gander at that," I say.

"Let's not get too worked up yet. We haven't even played thirty holes. Speaking of which, as soon as we're done here, you should head back to the hotel and take it easy. Tomorrow's going to be a marathon."

27

I CARRY EARL'S DRIPPING bag through the hotel lobby and into the elevator, and when I get off on the third floor, there's a puddle in the corner. Inside my room, I pull all the clubs and dry the grips with a bath towel. Then I crank the tin heater to 11, lay the soaking bag in front of it, and head back out the door.

When I drive back through the stone pillars, Shoal Creek is empty. After a day like today the players can't get away fast enough, and the only people milling about the grounds are the employees of the beverage companies, who are here to restock the hospitality tents for Sunday. In its soggy way, the course is as lovely in the damp gloaming as in blazing sunshine, and as I walk past the abandoned clubhouse, I can hear the water running down the gutters and dripping off the leaves.

Beyond the clubhouse is the pro shop, the retail outlet tastefully tucked away in a Colonial-style house with an eagle over the front door, and tacked to the rear of it like an afterthought is the low-slung caddy shack. Since the touring pros brought their own and the course is closed to members, there's no work for the regular caddies this week. Nevertheless, a handful have come in to help each other while away a miserable day. Three play dominoes, a solitary tall figure stretches out over a pool table, and a fifth stands between them stuffing kindling into a potbelly stove that glows orange at the center of the room. The man stoking the fire seems the most approachable.

"That little stove throws off some heat," I offer.

"Better than nothing."

"I'm Travis. I'm caddying for one of the seniors this week."

"Lucky you."

"It's going to take more than luck to win tomorrow. That's why I'm here."

"Who's got you on the bag?"

"Earl Fielder."

"Why didn't you say so?" says the man, unlocking a smile and extending his hand. "I'm Vince. How can I help you?"

"I'm looking to talk to someone who knows a lot more about this track than me. Hopefully, someone willing to share what he knows."

"I wouldn't be of much use. As the caddy master, I'm only on the course on Mondays, when they let us play. Those three aren't what you're looking for either. They're what we call bag toters. The person you need to talk to is Ron Bouler," he says, pointing toward the pool table. "Owl's been looping here since the day it opened. He knows every blade of grass on this plantation. I'll introduce you.

"Hey, Owl," says Vince, "someone's here to pick your brain." Bouler, who wears a leather cap, is setting up to bank the six ball in the far corner, and when he swivels his head toward me, I see why he was nicknamed after a bird of prey.

"Travis is caddying for Earl Fielder this week and is looking for an edge, things you can't find in the yardage book." Without taking his eyes from me, Bouler slides his stick forward. The chipped cue hits the evergreen ball dead center, sending it caroming the full length of the table into the corner pocket.

"Travis," says Bouler, "aren't you the one who got into it in Hawaii?"

"'Fraid so."

"And now you're caddying for a brother. How the mighty have fallen."

"I'm just trying to return a favor and help a friend get his first win. Tomorrow, I want every advantage I can get."

"Local knowledge."

"Exactly. As much as you can spare and I can absorb in one night. I want to know how the greens will handle all this water. Which putts are going to look faster than they are and which are going to be slower? Which ones are going to break half an inch less than they look like they will and which ones will break half an inch more? What are the worst patches on every green and fairway? Where are you as good as dead and what can you live with?"

"You bring the chart of where they're cutting the holes tomorrow?" As he puts down his cue, I pull a damp piece of paper from my rain jacket, unfold it, and hand it to him. When Bouler leans into the light, I'm surprised by how young he is, midthirties tops.

"I stopped going to school after ninth

grade," says Bouler as he studies Sunday's pin positions. "You were wondering how I could have caddied here since seventy-seven. Well, that's how."

"Math was never my strong point," I say.

"It was mine, but I couldn't afford to stay in school. Not if I wanted to eat, too. I started here at fifteen, actually before that. I grew up a mile down the road. When they brought in the big earthmoving machines to lay out the course, I rode over on my bike and watched. I saw the greens when they were just mounds of dirt, and when it poured like today, I watched the way the water ran over them. That's the way the putts still roll."

Owl turns his eyes from me and calls back to Vince, who's reading at the desk near the front door. "Vince, any chance you could put on another pot of coffee? Travis and me, we got some homework to do."

28

By Sunday morning, the rain has cleared. It feels more like early September than late February, and that first-day-of-school edge in the air does nothing to ease my tension. Earl's feeling it, too. On the range early, just after dawn, he hits a couple of balls off-center.

For those who didn't complete yesterday's round, there's a shotgun start at 8:16 a.m., and shortly before that our threesome is ferried out to the dew-covered 12th green, where the previous afternoon, Earl marked his ball in the rain. The 460-yard

12th is a brute of a par 4, and reaching the green in regulation was no mean feat. Still, there's a lot of work to be done. If you placed the ball by hand, you couldn't come up with a longer or more difficult putt on this green.

Earl's marker sits on the right edge, and the hole is cut on the far left. In between is a seventy-five-foot travelogue that features two knolls and a steep drop. The first half of the putt is uphill and slow and the second half is the opposite, with a dozen feet of break from right to left. After a couple of minutes to digest it, Earl shakes his head and says, "It's like putting over a camel... that's drinking water."

While Earl walks the width of the green and surveys the putt from both sides, I refer to my notes from last night's cram session at the caddy shack. Before Owl focused on the pin placements for the third round, he spent a good ten minutes breaking down this first crucial, tone-setting putt, and

since I could tell him where Earl had
marked his ball, he could be extremely specific. He even made a little sketch:

"The first key," I say, "is hitting it firm
enough to get it to the top of the second knoll." I make a point of avoiding the
word *hump*. "The second is getting it right
enough to account for the break. Because
of the rain, the first half of the putt is even
slower than it seems. You need to hit it

twenty percent harder than it looks. The second half of the putt will be hardly affected by the rain. The back half of the green always drains a lot better than the front."

I walk to the apex of the putt and point to a spot on the right side of the second knoll. "This is our target. If you can get the ball to die here, the slope will do the rest."

For a second Earl appraises me as coolly as the putt. Although he doesn't say a word, I know what he's thinking: *When the fuck did you become an authority on the drainage of the 12th green at Shoal Creek?*

On the practice green, I had Earl hit a dozen putts of similar length, but there was no way to prepare him for these contours or the pressure of having to deal with them on his first stroke of the day, and when he replaces the marker with the ball and squats behind it, I can see he's still struggling to believe in both himself and me.

"Earl, I did my homework. The line is perfect. You got to trust it." Earl makes three long practice strokes, takes one last peek at his distant target, and gives it a roll. The hit is solid and the ball easily crests the first knoll, slows as it climbs the second, and settles at the top, exactly what I asked for, except that the ball has come to a complete halt. For the next couple of seconds it doesn't budge. It just sits there like Louie refusing to take a walk, and it's not clear if it's going to stay put or roll back to Earl's feet. Instead, it makes a quarter turn forward and then, after a second pause, another, until once again it is on its merry way.

When it stops for the third time, it's three inches from the hole.

"Hell of a putt, Earl."

"No, Travis, it was a hell of a read."

Compared to that, the next six holes are a piece of cake. Earl pars them all, and his 71

keeps him perched at the top of the leaderboard, two up on the only other golfers
who managed to shoot par in the second
round. Hale Irwin and Gil Morgan, who
else?

29

"Let's go, Earl."

"Come on, baby."

"Time to go to work, big fellah."

Earl attracts some of the most boisterous galleries out here, particularly since he laced up his Reeboks and went back to Vietnam. Nevertheless, this crowd is louder, warmer, looser, and funkier than any that we've experienced so far.

"We at Shoal Creek or Soul Creek?" asks Earl with a smile.

"Come on, Travis," says a mellifluous southern voice I recognize as Owl's. "You got to bring it, too."

Hearing my name called out elicits a quizzical look from Earl. "Travis, you got family down here?"

"Not that I know of."

This is Earl's first time going off in the final group on Sunday, let alone with Morgan and Irwin, and the southern hospitality is just what he needs. He comes out of the gate striping the ball with his characteristic precision and gets right back on the par train he's been riding since dawn. Unfortunately, conditions have been steadily improving since then, and by the time we approach the green of the par-five 3rd, a chilly, blustery morning has blossomed into a gorgeous Alabama afternoon without a trace of wind. The perfect weather and receptive greens are not a propitious combination, at least not for Earl, because it means that par isn't going to get it done after all, and as if to emphasize the point, Irwin rolls in a twenty-six-footer for birdie and Morgan rolls his twenty-two-footer on top of it, cutting Earl's precious lead to one.

If Earl's going to get his name engraved in silver, he's going to have to go low too, and as I learned from Earl in Sarasota and Louie in Winnetka, it's not easy teaching a middle-aged dog new tricks. On 5, Earl has an eminently makeable eighteen-footer of his own for birdie, and after referring to my crib sheet, I pass on this wisdom from Owl: two inches right and firm. Earl starts it on line but comes up half a foot short, as usual, and on the next four holes he leaves three more birdie putts in the jaws. When we walk off 9, Earl's lead is gone with the wind (and the cold and the rain) and the Birmingham chapter of Earl's Platoon is as frustrated as his caddy.

Not that Earl lets it affect his ball-striking. He opens the back nine with two more solidly struck shots to give himself yet another legitimate birdie chance. This one is from nineteen feet, not that it really matters, and as Earl looks it over, I return to Owl's notes and diagrams, sickened at the thought of all this proprietary reconnaissance coming to naught.

"Looks like an inch and a half off the right to me," says Earl. "What do you think?"

"I know exactly what it is. But why bother reading 'em if you're not going to get the ball to the goddamned hole?"

Amazed, Earl stares at me hard, and I meet him halfway. "Right edge," I say, and slap the Bridgestone in his palm.

"Jesus Christ," he says. "One forty-five-second fight and you're a certified mother-fucker." Then he bangs the nineteen-footer into the back of the cup.

"You're welcome," I say.

30

WHAT FOLLOWS IS THE rarest of phenomena—an Earl Fielder birdie binge.

Earl follows up his birdie on 10 with three more on 11, 12, and 14. With that last ten-footer, he snatches back the lead at five under, one better than Morgan and two up on Irwin, and the ruckus raised by Earl's Platoon echoes off Double Oak Mountain.

Now it's just a matter of coaxing Earl back to the sprawling antebellum clubhouse, and using my proprietary database of local knowledge, I walk him through three stress-free two-putts. On 15, I get him to play a twenty-two-footer like it's thirty. On 16, I add two inches of break, and on 17, I pass along Owl's instruction to ignore what he sees and hit it straight.

As a result, Earl steps up to the 18th hole with both his lead and his nerves intact, and as he has all day, he pipes another drive straight up Broadway. I walk off the yardage to the nearest sprinkler head and do the math, then do it two more times just to be sure. As I told Owl, math was never my strong point. Three times I get the same numbers—158 yards to the middle, 143 to the hole, but with water in front, I'm only thinking about that second number, the one to the center of the green.

The prospect of delivering Earl his first PGA win has me approximately as worked up as watching Elizabeth be born, and I pull the index card from my back pocket one last time, not for the distances Earl hits all his clubs, which I've long since memorized, as much as for the tactile comfort of its softened edges. In the last two weeks that card has been in and out of that pocket and the rain so many times, it's as faint and frayed as the Shroud of Turin, but the barely legible numbers confirm what I already know—that 158 is a garden-variety 7-iron. If there's half as much adrenaline coursing through Earl as me, 7 is a little too much club and will put him in the back half of the green, but with water in front, there's no way I'm pulling less.

"It's a generic driving range seven," I say. "You're going to be a little pumped, but back of the green is just fine."

"I agree," says Earl. "Got to be the seven. I don't want to be anywhere near that water."

I pull the club and Earl goes through his brisk routine of two practice swings and a waggle. As he slides the club behind the ball, the wind, which has been nowhere to be seen or felt for two hours, picks up, and with it, just as suddenly, comes a light shower. As Earl steps away from the shot, I open the umbrella, hand it to Earl, and toss up a tuft of grass, which blows straight back into my face. After a couple of minutes of discreet stalling, I toss another pinch in the air and it comes back with interest.

"With the rain and wind I'm thinking six."

"I'm with you," says Earl. "It's got to be the six."

I put back the seven and, still holding the umbrella over his head—now the rain is coming down even harder—I hand him the 6.

"Nice and smooth. Nothing fancy."

After two practice swings and a waggle, Earl turns on the ball and hits it just as pure and solid as he does on the range 365 days a year, except in leap year, when's its 366, and it's all over the flag...until it splashes in the back of the pond.

With a horrible sinking feeling, I drop my

eyes to Earl's bag and confirm what I already know. The 6-iron hasn't moved. It's still there. In the wind and the rain and the adrenaline, and whatever other excuses I'll come up with over the next three or four decades, I handed him the 9 instead of the 6.

After a drop, a pitch, and two putts, Earl finishes with a double bogey and adds one more top five to a resume already bursting with them.

31

FOR THE SECOND TIME in a month, Earl feels obliged to take me out and get me hammered. To dilute the misery, he invites Stump to join us, and Stump, a frequent visitor to Birmingham, insists he knows just the spot. Its official name is the Plaza, but to regulars it's the Upside Down because the sign above the door is flipped over, and as we duck beneath it and descend the stairs, I tell myself it's got to be a coincidence and not a twisted reference to the upside-down 6 that I handed Earl on 18.

To be fair, Stump might just as likely

have chosen the Plaza because he likes it. As we discovered in Honolulu, the three of us share a weakness for dives, and the Upside Down is certainly a fine example, right up there—or down there—with the Ding Dong, and after grabbing our three-dollar shots and two-dollar beers, we settle into a cozy corner in the blue glow of the jukebox. Beyond the pool tables and the pinball machines is a redbrick wall festooned with graffiti, including the terse posting GET OVER IT.

Easier said than done.

To my relief, Earl is taking my screw-up better than me. In fact, he seems unfazed, and after my second shot, I can't resist the urge to verify that. "Earl, you're really not mad at me?"

"Travis, why the hell would I be mad? You busted your ass for me for two weeks, and did a hell of a job."

"With one little... I guess not so little... exception," interjects Stump.

"When you called, I thought I was doing you a favor," says Earl. "I was wrong. You lit a fire under my ass. I had four birdies on the back nine! At Shoal Creek! On a Sunday! When was the last time you saw me do that? Never. I don't go that low at my muni back home. I couldn't have done that without you."

"Or Owl," I say.

"Yeah, let's not forget Owl all of a sudden," says Stump, hoisting his mug.

"When you told me to get the fucking ball to the hole on twelve, that was beautiful. Exactly what I needed to hear. And the best part about eighteen is there's no scar tissue... because I can blame it entirely on you."

"Wonderful."

"It really is," says Earl.

"You know what we need?" says Stump, digging a couple of quarters out of his pocket. "Music." He walks to the jukebox, and before he gets back, the unmistakable sound of Hendrix's guitar pours out.

"I wouldn't have thought a redneck like you had any use for Jimi," says Earl.

"There's a lot about me you don't know, son."

"I guess so."

"For example, you probably didn't know I can sing. You're looking at the five-time karaoke champion at the Frog Tavern in Macon, Georgia."

And he can. When Hendrix starts to sing, Stump, clenching his Pabst like a mike, is right there with him, shamelessly adding extra syllables to one-vowel words, like *sun* and *shine,* in the time-honored rock star tradition.

IF THE SUHUNNNNN REFUSED
  TO SHINNNNNNNE
I DON'T MIND.

"Stump, you motherfucking bucket of shit," I say.

32

"WHAT NOW, TRAVIS?" ASKS Sarah two days later at breakfast. "Any plans?"

"Sarah, I've been out of work eight minutes, less if you consider I worked the weekend."

"I know. But we love you and want to keep you out of trouble, so we're just wondering, like I said, if you had any plans?"

"As a matter of fact, I was thinking about it on the flight back, that is when I wasn't seeing Earl's Bridgestone dive into that pond. No disrespect to Jack, but it's kind of a cliché to put water in front of the last green, don't you think?"

Sarah makes a circular motion with her index finger.

"I thought I'd spend a week practicing, then fly back down to Florida and play a couple of events on one of the mini-tours not under the auspices of the PGA. The courses are dog tracks and the prize money worse, but the best players are at least as good as the seniors, and if nothing else, it will give me an idea of what I need to work on. When I'm back, I figure I'll write a long, heartfelt letter to my pal Finchem and try to convince him that I've been re-habilitated. I'll explain that caddying for Earl and slumming on the mini-tours have given me time to take a long, hard look at myself. If he buys it, he may knock a couple of months off my suspension."

"Sounds very reasonable, Travis."

"You seem surprised."

"Not at all."

"And how about you, Noah? Does this meet with your approval?"

"Absolutely," says the kindergartner as he shovels Cheerios into his mouth.

"Good. Because those are my plans, at least my medium-range ones. Short-term, I'm taking Louie for a walk."

33

OUTSIDE, IT'S STILL SUBURBAN Chicago. Still February. Still cold as hell. Although there hasn't been another snowfall, the old snow hasn't gone anywhere, and after lying around for two weeks, it's not nearly as picturesque.

Louie, who has a coat like a woolly mammoth, is undaunted by the chill and as relieved to be out of the kitchen as me. Spewing steam from both nostrils, he struts up the block like a cop walking his beat. As he writes tickets in yellow script to potential interlopers, school buses pick up students and commuters stride purposefully to their cars, and even if it has only been eight minutes, their well-dressed haste makes me feel underemployed.

With nothing beckoning except my frigid stall at Big Oaks, I give Louie the reins and encourage him to take his sweet time. Straying beyond our usual four blocks reminds me how much the neighborhood has changed since Sarah and I moved in twenty-seven years ago. Every other house has been razed, rebuilt, or added to within an inch of its life, and the new construction is bloated and out of scale for the half-acre lots. In many cases, there's no yard left, and what's the point of paying down a mortgage if you can't walk out on a summer evening and have a catch or hit a few chips?

A block away and across the street is a turreted eyesore, and in front of it, a dozen slouching teens wait on their bus. Standing among them—but not with them—is a tall student wearing a green wool cap.

"Hey, Louie, look. It's Jerzy."

I wave but fail to get Jerzy's attention. As he gazes into the distance like an explorer scanning the horizon, three classmates in shiny black parkas saunter over. By way of greeting, the middle one punches him in the stomach. Then the other two, who are bigger, join the fun. As Louie and I look on, pinned to the wrong side of the street by brisk commuter traffic, one knocks the books from Jerzy's hands. The third kicks them down the street.

34

TRANSFORMING BIG OAKS INTO Augusta National requires not only concentration but a certain level of optimism, and after witnessing what happened to Jerzy, I'm not feeling it. Instead of dogwoods and doglegs, I see a school bus rolling down an upscale suburban street, and instead of my line and trajectory, I picture Jerzy trapped inside, doing his best to act like what just happened didn't, avoiding eye contact with his classmates as assiduously as they avoid his.

Unable to float a color-corrected daydream, I lower my sights and aim my 8-iron at the filthy Srixon banner hanging from the wire mesh at the end of the range. I had a feeling Jerzy saw me waving from across the street, and now I'm certain of it. His not wanting to acknowledge me suggests he knew what was about to happen, and that probably means it happens a lot. And so much for that explanation for the wound on his forehead.

After a dozen desultory swings, I abort my practice and walk across the street to a diner, where I nurse a coffee till it's time to pick up Noah. Reflecting on this morning leads inevitably to thoughts of Noah, who, like me, took an instant shine to Jerzy. Let's face it, Noah is a bit of an odd duck himself. Does that mean he's going to have to deal with this crap in a few years?

At Belltown Grammar, three yellow and black buses are lined up in the lot. Manufacturers must make them look antiquated on purpose. In forty years, they've barely changed. Is that why they stir such strong feelings and pop up in so many coffee commercials? This afternoon, they seem sinister in their indifference.

Lost in thought, I don't notice Noah until he opens the front door.

"How was practice, Dad? Bring Augusta to its knees?"

"Actually, I just hit balls."

"Really?"

Now he's the one worried about me.

35

THE NEXT MORNING IS worse, because like Jerzy, I know it's going to happen again.

I had hoped to reach the bus stop sooner, but Louie doesn't take well to being hustled, and by the time the turrets loom, the school bus has made the turn onto Parade Hill Road. Like yesterday, Jerzy is conspicuous for his height, isolation, and attire, which bears little relation to the season or decade. Despite the twenty degrees, he wears a too-small blazer over a white shirt, and his signature green cap. In their dark parkas, his tormentors are easy to spot as well. For the moment, they ignore Jerzy, but even from across the street, I can tell that the reason they're hanging back is to instill dread, which for characters like these is half the fun.

The leader and his backup muscle don't sidle over until the bus is a hundred feet away, and this time Jerzy ends up on his knees on the curb and his books end up in a puddle. Once again, Louie and I are too late, and when we cross the street the bus doors are closing. After it pulls away, I notice a man in a wool tweed suit.

"One of your children on the bus?"

"Two," he says.

"Did you see what those kids did to their classmate?"

"Yes."

"Why didn't you say something? I know Jerzy. He's a great kid."

"That's not what I hear from my daughters. You know those kids from Roxbury Farms are troublemakers. He probably asked for it."

Roxbury Farms, a tiny complex of garden apartments, went up at the edge of
the neighborhood four years ago. It provides exactly seventeen units of low-income
housing, although based on the hysteria
at the planning and zoning meetings, you
would have thought the town had buried
asbestos in our backyard.

"Maybe you should find another place to
live," I suggest.

"Why's that?"

"Because you're an asshole."

I would have thought that someone
who dresses (did I mention the pocket
square?) and behaves like my neighbor
would be accustomed to being called an
asshole, and through time and repetition,
it would have lost the power to offend.
Apparently not. His cheeks flush and he
throws a wild right hook, which I see
coming from a block away. My response
is less telegraphed, at least by comparison.
It knocks his wind out and doubles him

over, and it takes all my restraint not to slip the leather bag off his shoulder into a puddle.

"Whatsa matter?" I ask. "Don't you have cable?"

36

"I saw these kids roughing up Jerzy while he was waiting for the bus," I explain. "Jerzy's the boy who shoveled our driveway. It happened two days in a row. The second time, Louie and I crossed the street. The bus was already on its way, but there was a parent standing there who had witnessed the whole thing and did nothing. In fact, he seemed to approve. He looked like the classic investment wanker—wing tips, horn-rimmed glasses, three-piece suit."

"I really don't need a description of his wardrobe," says Sarah.

"He also had a pocket square."

"Travis."

"Okay. I asked him why he just stood there and didn't say anything. He responded by taking a swing at me and I defended myself. This has absolutely nothing to do with the incident in Honolulu."

"He tried to hit you for asking him a question? That seems unlikely. Are you sure that's all you said?"

This second interrogation is conducted in the front seat of Sarah's Jeep outside the headquarters of the Winnetka Police Department. The first, handled by two of Winnetka's finest, was less intense. Louie sits in the ample space between us.

"I may also have called him an asshole."

Although the car is parked, Sarah lays her hands on the steering wheel and drops her head. Her hands, which have delivered hundreds of Winnetkans, are as beautiful as they are skilled, and I fell in love with them approximately ten minutes before the rest of her.

"Travis, are you having a midlife crisis?"

"It's about time, don't you think?"

She twists in the driver's seat and stares at me, as if forming her own diagnosis, and I convince myself that there's an inkling of a smile in her pale green eyes.

"So what are you going to do about Jerzy?"

"I don't know."

"If you don't do anything for him, this is all macho nonsense."

Sarah's smile, if that's what it is, is subtler than the Mona Lisa's, but there's no ambiguity in Louie's eyes. To Louie, there is no such thing as macho nonsense. To him, *everything else* is nonsense, with the notable exception of food, and since my altercation this morning, I'm convinced he's been beaming at me with newfound respect.

My arrest and release make the afternoon paper and are picked up by the wires, and that evening I get calls from both Earl and Stump. Like Sarah, they suspect that I've gone completely off the rails and they don't seem any more reassured by my version of events. The other call, the one from Ponte Vedra, Florida, informing me that my suspension has been extended for the remainder of the year, doesn't come till 11 p.m.

At least I don't have to write that letter.

37

THE NEXT MORNING, I put on my most presentable blazer and one of my few pairs of shoes that don't have spikes sticking out the bottom and drive to New Trier Township High School. Since Elizabeth graduated a decade ago, I've only been back to vote. In fact, pulling a lever in a high school gym every four years is the sum of my input as an American citizen, and that makes coming here to this well-lit administrative office on behalf of a student I barely know all the more unsettling.

Behind the front desk is a human roadblock, whose placard reads: LAURA SKELL-CHOCK.

"Laura, good morning. My name is Travis McKinley. I need to talk to someone about a student who's being bullied."

"That's Reece Halsey, our assistant dean. She's out of the office till Friday."

"Can't I talk to someone else?"

"I'm afraid she's the one you need to talk to."

"It can't wait that long, Laura. The kid is getting beat up every morning. He could be dead by then."

"How do you know him?"

"That's the thing. I don't, and that's all the more reason why you should take me seriously."

"I am taking you seriously, Mr. McKinley."

"The only thing I know about him is that he shoveled my driveway and he did a good job and he's a nice kid and he was nice to my son. But even if he did a lousy job on the driveway and was a snotty kid and was mean to my son, he still shouldn't get beat up every morning."

Skellchock responds to this last rhetorical flourish with an eye roll.

"Isn't there a way I can get in touch with his parents? The student's name is Jerzy Solarski. I could also help identify the kids who are involved. The incidents occurred at the bus stop at Downing and Parade. Less than a dozen students get picked up there. It shouldn't be hard to figure out who they are."

The way Skellchock's smile congeals tells me there's something impatient in my tone. The shadow that falls across her eyes bears a frightening resemblance to the one I saw at the Department of Motor Vehicles when someone was insane enough to ask why the line was moving so slowly.

"Aren't you the person who got into the fight with one of our parents?"

"That was unfortunate, but there were no charges."

"Lucky for you, Mr. McKinley. And didn't another fight get you suspended from the Senior Tour?"

"That was also unfortunate."

"Sounds like you're the bully, Mr. McKinley." Then, as suddenly as it arrived, the shadow lifts and her smile softens. "Mr. McKinley, as I'm sure you can appreciate, we can't share information about our students to every nut job who waltzes in here. What I can do is pass your number to Jerzy's parents. If they want to reach out, they will."

"I appreciate that, Laura. Truly."

"My husband's a golfer," she explains.

38

SARAH CAN'T BE THAT mad at me, because that night, she roasts another chicken. Later, as I'm gratefully washing the dishes, I get a call from a woman with a strong Eastern European accent. "This is Rodica Solarski," she says. "Thanks so much for coming to the school today. I can't talk now because I'm at work, but if it's not too late, I could call again during my break."

Instead, I offer to come to her, and an hour later, I retrace my old commute into downtown Chicago. It's been a year and change since Leo Burnett *let me go,* and much longer since I've visited midtown at night. After hours, the district exudes the bristling vigilance of a military installation. Even emptied of workers, it throbs like an enormous machine that never gets switched off.

Rodica's address isn't far from my longtime employer's, and out of morbid curiosity, I walk past the darkened entrance, setting loose the bad old feelings. Three blocks south, still regretting the detour, I enter a massive tower that takes up the entire west side of the block and, escorted by the night guard, ride a chrome-filled elevator high above an inner atrium. "Rodica's the only one on the floor," says the guard.

I slip him a twenty, and he buzzes me through the frosted glass doors. Then I follow the corridor that divides the executive offices and conference rooms that look out over the atrium from the green expanse of shoulder-high cubicles. Parked in front of an open office is a cart laden with cleaning supplies, and in the doorway, a surprisingly delicate woman in her early forties. I hand Rodica the coffee I picked up at the corner and follow her into one of the conference rooms, where we sit at a mahogany table.

"The meeting is called to order," says Rodica, and peels the wax paper off a sandwich brought from home.

"Did Jerzy mention he shoveled my driveway?"

"No. Don't be offended. He rarely talks to me at all."

"We didn't talk much either, but his wit made an impression."

"I think the American term is *wiseass*," says Rodica. Her pale face is framed by jet-black hair cut to her shoulders. Like Jerzy's, her accented English is fluent and precise.

"So did the generous way he treated my five-year-old. That's why I was so disturbed by what I saw at the bus stop. Why do you think they target him, Rodica?"

Rodica shrugs, as if the answer hardly

matters. "Because he's too big to be invisible and too soft to fight back," she says. "Because he has an accent and bad skin, and because he's really sweet...."

The mention of her son's kindness causes Rodica's face to crumple. To gather herself, she pries the cap off her coffee and takes a long gulp. "Maybe it's my fault. It was my idea to come here from Bucharest, five years ago—me, Jerzy, and his older sister, Beata. Ironically, I came for the schools. For Jerzy, it's been disastrous from the start, and with Beata graduated, it's much worse. When his sister was here, he at least had someone to sit with at lunch, and she wasn't afraid to confront people."

"Have you spoken to anyone at the school?"

"A waste of time, or, as you Americans like to say—a waste of breath. No one is willing to lift a finger to protect my son. Now his grades have slipped and he's stopped talking. My biggest fear is that he'll do something to harm himself. To be honest, Mr. McKinley, I'm terrified."

Rodica's face crumples again, and now her coffee is finished, so she pushes her hair behind her ears, fits the lid back on the empty cup, and folds the brown paper bag that held her sandwich. "I should get back to work," she says. "Thanks so much for coming and also for the coffee." Before I can respond, she pushes herself away from the table, drops the cup into the garbage bag hanging off the end of her cart, and disappears around the corner.

I head in the opposite direction for a couple of steps, then stop and, for a minute or maybe two, stand there frozen by indecision. Then I head back around the corner and find Rodica in another office.

"Sorry to bother you again. How would you feel if I spent a little time with your son?"

"Doing what?"

"I'm a professional golfer, so I thought maybe I could teach him how to play."

"That sounds wonderful, Mr. McKinley. Golf is all he watches on TV," she says, but her expression is neutral. "I won't mention anything to Jerzy for now. You can surprise him."

On the way to the elevator, I slow to peer into a cubicle very much like the one in which I spent five years. I wonder if Rodica has memorized these snapshots of weddings, babies, graduations, and barbecues.

39

THE BELL IS STILL ringing when Jerzy bursts through a door in the back of the science center and walks with badly concealed haste toward the yellow and black buses lined up on the far side of the parking lot. Although scores of students pour from a dozen buildings, he is as impossible to miss as a giant turtle without a shell. In a sea of affluent preppies, his Eastern European hand-me-downs seem particularly off-kilter, and while Jerzy is certainly uncool, he is also flaunting it. Economic hardship may explain the baggy wool pants and too-small blazer, but not the smiley face T-shirt or Where's Waldo hat. Despite the obvious drawbacks, he can't resist drawing attention to his geeky self. As his own mom points out, he's a wiseass.

If Jerzy hoped to reach the safety of the bus before the Shiny Black Parkas could get a bead on him, it's too late. They're already lying in wait between him and the bus door, and from the front seat of Simon's old pickup, I get my first good look at the brains of the outfit. He's of medium height and wiry, pale and blond, his long bangs cut straight across his forehead. Instead of any outward sign of malevolence, there's something unformed and missing in his features, like the overly symmetrical oval of a child's drawing.

As he waits for Jerzy to get within arm's length, he slips a hand out of his pocket and forms a fist, and as I hop from my truck, I catch myself doing the same. *Be careful. You get in a third fight in a high school parking lot with a bunch of teenagers, Sarah won't be asking any more questions. She'll just put you on meds.*

"Hey, Jerzy," asks the leader softly. "Where you headed?"

As at the bus stop, Jerzy's only resistance is willful denial. He plods ahead as if he doesn't see or hear a thing.

"Over here, you fat fuck."

"Dipshit, he's talking to you."

By now, I'm directly behind the three, and when Buster Blond pulls back his arm, I step in front of him.

"Excuse me, fellas. Don't mean to interrupt, but I need a word with my friend."

For a couple of seconds, the leader stares at me nonplussed, not sure how to react to me or what to do with his fist. When he puts it back in his pocket and steps aside, I guide Jerzy past them to the front seat of Simon's pickup.

40

"You're probably wondering why I'm here," I say.

"Kind of."

"I came to see if you'd like to hit some golf balls."

"Wow," says Jerzy, still digesting his reprieve as his classmates hover nearby. "I guess you really do have a lot of time on your hands."

"As a matter of fact."

"I could probably clear my calendar for the afternoon."

*   *   *

Big Oaks is cold and bleak as Siberia. In every respect, it's the same dreary interior I had to reimagine as Augusta National just to get myself to show up every day, but based on Jerzy's expression you'd think it actually was Augusta. "This place rules," he says, and his eyes delight in every sorry detail, from the ripped Srixon banner advertising a ball they stopped making two years ago, to the corny clock with golf clubs for arms, to the shuddering ball machine.

Once we pick up the clubs and get settled in my stall, I do a quick inventory of what I have to work with. Jerzy, who is at least 6'3" and 220 pounds, is a seventeen-year-old man cub. He has big hands, big feet, and a big head, and the kind of natural size and heft that often translates well to golf. (See: Jack Nicklaus, Craig Stadler, Colin Montgomery, and my old nemesis Stump Peters.) Size gives you ballast that roots you to the ground and, once you learn to shift your weight at the right time, natural power.

I pull the 7-iron from my bag and mold his hands around it until they've glommed into something cohesive. "You want to hold the club very gently," I say. "Whatever you think the pressure should be, it's half that. Okay, now take your hands off and place them back on....All right, now try it again....One more time....That's excellent. Where you've got them now looks really good."

"Thanks, Mr. McKinley. I need to get a grip."

"You and me both...and it's Travis."

I align his feet, tilt him forward into the proper posture, then share a fundamental concept of a good swing, which is to barely swing at all and instead twist your torso back and forth, with your arms going along for the ride. To provide a sense of how it feels when the chest initiates the move, I have him cross his arms and I place my hands on his shoulder, but before I can turn him halfway back, he winces in pain, and when he covers it with a quick smile, I know it's from all the punches he's been taking every morning and afternoon.

"A quarter swing is all we want today. For our purposes, it's better. On the way back, just enough of a turn to get your weight on the inside of your right foot. Then plant the left and turn around it."

I have him rehearse the move several times before I pluck a yellow ball from the basket and place it on the thin mat. Jerzy's first swing is a whiff. So are the second, and the third; and the fourth catches so little of the ball, it doesn't roll off the mat.

The next hour is a blur of shank hooks and shank slices. He hits behind the ball, on top of it, and beside it, and yet, within two thirds of a bucket, I know he has the makings of a golfer. Not because he's flashed an inkling of athletic talent or shown evidence of having absorbed a single thing I've said, but because he is a glutton for punishment. An hour of nonstop frustration and repeated failure rolls off his thick shoulders like rain. Undaunted, he tries as hard on his eighty-eighth swing as his fifty-third and his eleventh. Not only that, he is having fun.

"Keep your grip pressure constant throughout the whole swing," I say, and nudge another Big Oaks rock between his feet. "And try not to get so geeked at the ball. Don't react to it at all. Pretend it isn't there."

"What ball?" he asks.

For the hundredth time, Jerzy pivots and unleashes his abbreviated swing, and for whatever reason (Yahweh, Vishnu, Jesus, grip pressure), the sound of club striking ball is entirely crisper, deeper, and sweeter—and the velocity with which it flies off the face is deliriously disproportionate to the effort put into it.

When it drops out of the air and stops rolling, it's traveled more than two football fields.

"Piece of cake," says Jerzy.

41

JERZY SMILES LIKE THE Pope the whole
drive home. That's the effect hitting it on
the sweet spot has on one's sense of well-
being. It smooths out the edges, even the
jagged ones. It's like Zen meditation, only
better because it isn't bullshit. Although I
couldn't be happier for him and even take
some credit for his beatific glow, my own
state of mind is precarious. I've been up-
tight since we stashed the clubs at the front
desk and headed for Simon's truck, and as I
dodge the potholes on Route 38 my unease
blooms into something closer to panic.

It started when I placed my hands on Jerzy's shoulders and saw the toll of those punches, and his flinch recalled Rodica's half-smile when I asked about spending time with her son. I realized that the reason she didn't want to tell Jerzy was not to preserve the surprise. It was to protect him from the likelihood that it wouldn't happen at all, that I would have a change of heart or "something would come up" and my impulse to help her kid would evaporate as mysteriously as it arrived.

Rodica's pessimistic scenario didn't pan out. I did show up. Not only that, I snatched him out from under the nose of that little vacant-eyed assassin and introduced him to the wonder that is Big Oaks. But what now?

As I turn onto the street that dead-ends at Roxbury Farms, I think about the bruises on Jerzy's arms and wonder how much of a commitment I'm prepared to make for a goofy teenager who shoveled my driveway and was nice to Noah and whose sardonic wit reminds me of my grandfather. Maybe Rodica knows me better than I know myself, and I'm not cut out to be a do-gooder. If her assessment is accurate and I bail after two or three or four sessions, will that be worse than doing nothing?

And then for some inexplicable reason (Yahweh, Vishnu, Jesus, grip pressure), the anxious voices shut up long enough for me to think, Who knows? And besides that— fuck it.

"So, Jerzy, I've been thinking."

"Uh-oh."

"How about we do this every Tuesday afternoon?"

"Really?"

"Yeah. Really. You'll help me get through my draconian suspension, and I'll teach you a little about golf."

I'm not sure which one of us is more surprised. Or pleased.

42

WHEN I PICK UP Jerzy the following Tuesday, I can tell from his eyes it's been a rough week. I don't know how rough until we get to our stall and Jerzy takes two easy swings with the 7-iron, stops, and looks down at his feet.

"Jerzy, what's the matter?"

"My arms, my shoulders, my ribs. I can't do it."

To be here at Big Oaks and unable to hit a shot is devastating to him, and I don't know what to say. I'm still struggling to come up with plan B when Jerzy hands me

185

the club. "Since I'm so useless, why don't you hit a few? Maybe I can learn by watching."

After a few practice swings, I scoop a ball from the plastic basket with the blade and bounce it into my palm. "You're in for a treat, my friend. Bear in mind that what you're about to see is on a whole different level from just hitting balls."

"I'll try."

"When I have to describe to the layman what it is that I do, I often fall back on the language of art. To put it simply, I use my clubs to paint pictures."

"Let me see if I grasp the analogy," says Jerzy. "The irons, woods, and putter are brushes. The ball is the paint, this stall the easel or studio, and the golf course, or in this case Big Oaks, is your canvas."

"Very good."

"And you're Picasso."

"Hey, you said it, not me."

"Paint away, Pablo."

My first two swings are Jerzyesque. I don't whiff—I'm a former U.S. Senior Open champion, for Christ's sake—but like him, I get too amped, hold the club too tight, and the result is two ground balls.

"Maybe you need to loosen up. Or is this your blue period?"

"That's an excellent suggestion. Thank you."

I bend at the waist, windmill my arms, and swivel my hips. "A routine I picked up from my amigo Miguel Ángel Jiménez," I say. Despite the elaborate stretching and Castilian lisping, my third shot rolls harmlessly off-line. On my fourth, I finally make a good pass at it. It produces a hard hook that never gets five feet off the ground and misses my target by inches.

"I get it," says Jerzy, almost smiling, "you're trying to hit the guy in that lunar vehicle picking up balls."

"It's not easy being a role model," I concede. "There's a lot of pressure and responsibility. And, in case you haven't noticed, that thing is moving."

Which is why I consider my next salvo—a vicious slice that bores in on the buggy like a heat-seeking missile before scoring a direct hit on the front door—one of the two or three best shots in my career, and as the driver slams on the brakes, I improvise an understated victory dance, which goes on for minutes and owes heavy debts to the WWF and *Soul Train*.

"Good thing you stretched," says Jerzy.

The guy behind the wheel, who is being bombarded while picking up balls at minimum wage, is less enthused. "McKinley, you do that again," he shouts, "I'm going to come up there and kick your ass."

43

THE CAGED BUGGY, WHICH had drawn perilously close, makes a U-turn and goes back to collecting Big Oaks range rocks.

"Jerzy, I'm sorry you couldn't swing the club today, but we're going to make a golfer out of you, I promise."

"Turn me into a Cheez Doodle for all I care. As long it's something other than Jerzy Solarski—dipshit, fat fuck, pizza face, loser, and one other thing, what is it? Oh, yeah, Polack."

"When I'm through with you, you'll be Jerzy Solarski—dipshit, fat fuck, pizza face, loser, Polack, golfer. How does that sound?"

"Better."

And that should have been enough for me. Thankfully, it's been a while since Elizabeth and Simon passed through the pricklier stages of adolescence, yet not so long that I've forgotten that conversation with a teen is a minefield. If you are able to extract a glimmer of a smile from a seventeen-year-old, you've done a full day's work. Time to go home, crack a beer, and put your feet up, but I'm so relieved about having salvaged the afternoon, I prattle on like a twit.

"I hope you realize that not a single thing those morons are calling you is accurate. You're a big dude, but you're hardly fat. You're no bigger than Jack Nicklaus was at your age, and he's only the best golfer of all time. You're not a loser, your skin issues are minor and temporary, and you're not a dipshit, whatever that is, and the last

I checked, you can't be a Polack, if you're not from Poland. Although I suppose they could make an exception."

"How did you know I'm not Polish?"

"Your mom told me that she and your sister and you came here from Rumania."

"When did you talk to her?"

"A few days ago. I couldn't show up at school and pick you up without running it by her."

"Why didn't she tell me? Was this some plan she dreamed up to boost my self-esteem?"

"The reason she didn't tell you was because she was afraid I wouldn't follow through and then you'd be disappointed. Your mom had zero to do with this. Believe me, she has enough on her plate."

"What is that supposed to mean? What do you know about her plate?"

"Not much."

"Exactly," he says, and lumbers off in the direction of the bathroom. While he's gone I work my way through the bucket with the 7-iron and berate myself for having learned so little in half a century. After ten minutes, he still hasn't returned, and after fifteen, I realize he's not going to. I reach the parking lot in time to see him step onto an eastbound bus.

44

THE FOLLOWING TUESDAY, I'm back in the New Trier parking lot waiting on Jerzy and the bell, and once again, I'm not alone. Till now, I'd never appreciated the commitment, discipline, and punctuality required to be a top-notch high school bully. Less motivated sociopaths-in-training would be in the library reading a muscle mag or carving sinister symbols into a desk. Instead, they're out here freezing their asses off behind the maintenance shed and choreographing their next ambush.

My rivals are conscientious, but I have the element of surprise. This morning I persuaded

Sarah to swap cars, so that while I keep an eye on the boys in black, they take no notice of the green Jeep or the man behind the wheel, his face buried in the afternoon paper.

From my reading, I learn that the Trevian hoopsters dropped their ninth straight last night to archrival West Hill. The photograph shows West Hill's Dave Bond scoring over a New Trier player with distinctive straight bangs named Brune Pickering, and according to the box score, Pickering led the losers with eleven points and seven assists. Is that all it takes to become a total shit?—be the best player on an awful basketball team, and be saddled at birth with the name Brune? Whatever.

When the bell goes off, I close the paper and scan the exits. This afternoon, Jerzy makes his retreat from the study hall. While the Parkas move to intercept him at the end of the walkway, I roll up from the other side of the lot, moving slowly so as not to be noticed.

As I inch along, I study Jerzy's face and body language and am encouraged by what I don't see. There are no fresh wounds on his face or neck, and his gait doesn't favor one side or the other. Wishful thinking, maybe, but I also detect a new bounce in his step and a hint of defiance.

Unaware that anyone else is eyeing their prey, the boys take their time. That allows me to slip in front of them just before Jerzy reaches the end of the walkway. When Pickering spots me, I've already reached across and opened the front door and called out in an urgent whisper, "Hey, Jerzy, it's me. Get in."

Jerzy is so close the front door nearly hits him, yet nothing in his expression indicates he sees me. The blank mask he adopts for his tormentors is now aimed at me. Instead of climbing into the safety of the Jeep and heading to Big Oaks, he walks directly past the car into a whirlwind of flying fists.

45

THREE DAYS LATER, I'm back at New Trier again. This time I park and walk around to the main entrance, where I inform the guard I have an appointment with the assistant dean of students, Reece Halsey. On the way to Halsey's office, I must make a wrong turn, because instead of entering the administrative wing, I find myself in a wide hallway lined with classrooms. The classrooms are empty and so is the corridor, but the tin lockers and low water fountains drum up a parade of ancient memories, mostly lousy.

When the corridor ends, I turn in the direction of the noise, which grows more urgent with each step till I push through a pair of doors into a vast rotunda. The multicolored flags of every nation, presumably including Rumania, hang from the high ceiling, and to my left is a stack of faded green plastic trays. I grab a tray and a plate and watch a woman wearing a hairnet ladle something brown onto something white. Then I slide the tray over the rails, fill a paper cup with something pink, and face the din.

The cafeteria must hold a thousand students. Nine hundred and ninety-nine of them crowd around a hundred tables, and one, his jug head tilting toward the straw in a carton of milk, sits alone, surrounded by empty chairs.

"What are you doing here?" he asks.

"I hear the chef does an amazing beef stew."

"Yeah," says Jerzy. "He opens the can."

As I take my first bite, a wet napkin lands with a splat at the center of our table, setting off a round of laughter.

"There's something I want to tell you, which I haven't shared with anyone in thirty-five years. Not my wife, my kids, or my best friend. Not even Louie."

"Louie?"

"My dog. I believe you two have met."

Half a muffin hits the table, followed by several packets of salt and pepper. I open one of each, sprinkle them on the stew, and take another bite.

"In eighth grade, the same shit happened to me. At that point, I was as tall as I am now, absurdly skinny, braces, glasses, an all-round winning look. This kid named Rudy Laplante, who happened to be the scion of a huge trucking company, decided he was going to make my life miserable, and for several months did a thorough job. At one point, my mother found out what was happening. You know what she said I should do?"

"No."

"I guess you wouldn't, since I haven't told you yet. Take a chair and smash it over his head."

"Did you?"

"What do you think? But I've always been grateful for the suggestion."

"Just as well. You could have fractured his skull. How would your mother have felt then?"

"You know, I've wondered about that. One possibility is that she knew I wasn't capable of it. The other is that she didn't give a shit. Figured that was Rudy's problem. I prefer that one."

"You saying I should smash a chair over Pickering's head?"

"In your case, that probably wouldn't be a good idea, although I'd love to watch, if you did. In fact, I'd pay to watch."

The aerial assault picks up and the incoming turns healthier—grapes, pineapple cubes, an apple core, a banana—and Jerzy

and I ignore it all, having reached an unspoken agreement not to give the assholes
the satisfaction. More miraculous than the
manna from heaven is the arrival at our
table of another student. She is small and
thin and wears a black Smashing Pumpkins
T-shirt over a black vintage dress, with
black nail polish and black lipstick. In addition to being monochromatic and brave,
she's pretty.

"Welcome to Pariahville," says Jerzy.
"Population three. I hope you brought an
umbrella."

"You're funny," says the girl.

"I think you mean funny-looking."

"No, I. mean *funny*," she says with a
touch of impatience. "As in witty. And I
like your blazer. Very Angus in AC/DC. All
you need is the shorts."

You're right, that's all he needs. But I appreciate the sentiment. To me she looks
like a black angel.

"So, Jerzy, we good?"

"Yeah."

"See you next week, then," I say, and wielding my tray like a shield, I head for the exit.

46

THE FOLLOWING WEEK WHEN we return to Big Oaks, Jerzy grabs the 7-iron and swings without discomfort. Pain-free, his move is as long and loose as Sam Snead's.

"Pickering's appendix burst," explains Jerzy. "He's been out all week and could be out for a month." I would rather have heard he's on life support, but I'll take it.

"How about that wonderful girl? Any more interaction with her?"

"Which girl?"

"Don't give me that 'which girl.' The one who joined you at lunch."

"Lyla," says Jerzy. "Of course not. That was a once-in-a-lifetime event, like Halley's Comet."

"She likes you."

"That's a physical impossibility. As far as I know, she's not blind."

"She's not. She commented on your attire. Favorably. In any case, between Pickering's appendix and Lyla's Comet, I'd say things are looking up. I propose we show our gratitude, up the ante, and go to work."

That afternoon, we spend almost four hours in the stall. Jerzy makes so much progress, we decide to come back the next afternoon and Thursday, and in our third session, Jerzy has a breakthrough that most golfers never do. He learns how to "save it for the bottom," as in connect his considerable size and heft to the bottom of his swing where the club meets the ball, the only part that matters. It sounds like a shotgun and turns every head on the range.

"That was stupid long," I say as his

3-wood bounces off that old Srixon banner. "At least thirty yards longer than I hit that club."

"You're not exactly a spring chicken, Travis."

"True. I'm a September chicken."

Over the next couple of days, he tattoos the old banner so many times that it finally gives up the ghost, detaches from the wire curtain, and flutters to the ground. "I can't tell you how long I've been waiting to see that," I say. "Like Berliners when the wall came down."

The bigger revelation comes a week later, when I hand him my old bull's-eye putter and walk him to the green rectangle about the size of three parking spaces which they have the temerity to call a putting green. I don't know if it's up there with Harvey Penick and Ben Crenshaw at Austin Country Club, but I'll never forget the first time I see Jerzy roll it on the Big Oaks cement.

Putting is two things—aim and feel.

Aim is the easy part. With practice, almost any asshole can do it. Feel, sensing how hard to strike a putt to make it roll the desired distance, is more elusive and nearly impossible to teach. After giving him a chance to get acclimated to the speed, approximately like putting on a bowling alley, I drop a tee ten feet away and ask him to stop the ball beside it. When that proves a minor challenge, I drop four more at three-foot intervals, then place five balls at his feet and ask him to roll each one to the next farther tee. When he's done, I realize I've underestimated his potential.

"Jerzy, I got some good news. You can hit it long and you can putt. If you can do both, you can play. As in really play."

47

By now, it's the third week of March, and that weekend a lovely thing happens. It gets warmer. That Saturday and Sunday it soars into the high thirties, causing the snow to lose a bit of its grip and giving the ground a chance to thaw. Monday morning, it's back into the twenties again, but by then it's too late. When I pick up Jerzy at school that afternoon, Louie sits beside me on the front seat.

"I don't think they allow dogs in Big Oaks," says Jerzy.

"They don't allow dogs where we're going, either, but since no one will be there, it's not going to be a problem."

Instead of the haul up 38, we make the shorter trip to Creekview Country Club, where, with half the course still under snow, the lot is empty.

"It's time to go golfing," I say as we hop out of the car. "I got one of my old bags and put together a set for you. I've got literally hundreds of clubs in my basement. It's really no big deal."

"It is to me, Travis. Thanks."

"My pleasure," I say, then reach into the trunk for the Big Oaks caps I bought that morning. "This is so we don't forget where we came from."

"Representing," says Jerzy as we doff our new caps.

With Louie trotting behind us, we make the short walk to the practice range, where we hit and shag a dozen balls apiece. Then we roll a few on the muddy practice green.

"This is your first round of golf," I say. "That's a big deal, so we're going to play for real. Because of the conditions, it's got to be lift, clean, and place, which means we can pull the ball out of the muck, wipe it off, and place it in a playable spot, but we're going to write down every stroke, and when we're done, we're going to add them all up. Golf is a number. That's all it is, and the only way to see if we're on the right track is to keep score. So as my grandfather used to say, 'No gimmes, no mulligans, no bullshit, let's play golf.'"

Despite the twenty-eight degrees, the three of us enjoy a lovely afternoon, and it occurs to me that when it comes to golf, Twain got it exactly wrong. Rather than *a good walk spoiled,* it's a crappy walk made bearable. Golf takes what would otherwise be a tedious eight-mile hump, marred with far too much self-reflection, and makes it interesting. Just because you don't know the name of every tree and bird, and couldn't care less, doesn't mean you don't appreciate being outside, feeling the breeze on your skin and the ground underfoot. And just because you have a little hand-eye coordination, that doesn't make you a lightweight.

Jerzy, it turns out, has more than his share of hand-eye coordination, and although he hits four bad shots for every good one, he takes pleasure in them all, just like that first afternoon at Big Oaks. Pop would have appreciated that, the same with Jerzy's brisk pace of play, which allows us to get around in two hours and finish before the sun disappears. On 18, Jerzy rolls in a twelve-footer for 117, and we tilt our caps and shake hands.

"Thanks, Travis. What a wonderful day. I'm only sorry I didn't get a chance to meet your grandfather."

"You met him eighteen times. His ashes were sprinkled on every green."

We get in two more rounds that week and, with Pickering still recuperating, three more the following. Along the way, Jerzy's scores dip steadily—116, 109, 97, 88, 83, and when I pick him up the following Monday, I feel like he's got a legitimate chance to break 80, particularly with the breeze down and the temperature hovering around forty. Unfortunately, his right eye is swollen shut.

"I take it Pickering has made a full recovery."

"Correct."

"What are you doing Sunday?"

"Watching the Masters, of course."

"Then come over and watch it with us."

In case you're interested, here's the scorecard from Jerzy's first round of golf:

HOLE	PAR	JERZY	TRAVIS	HOLE	PAR	JERZY	TRAVIS
1	4	6	4	10	4	6	4
2	5	11	4	11	4	7	3
3	4	5	4	12	4	8	4
4	4	5	5	13	5	6	5
5	3	4	2	14	4	6	4
6	5	8	5	15	3	5	3
7	4	8	4	16	4	5	4
8	3	7	4	17	3	5	3
9	4	6	4	18	5	9	5
OUT	36	60	36	TOTAL	72	117	71

Creekview Country Club

SCORER: *Travis McKinley* ATTEST: _____ DATE: _____

48

THE HEAVYSET KID WHO knocks on my door Sunday afternoon looks discouragingly like the one who arrived two months earlier. He wears the same heavy green sweater and black wool trousers and, instead of a gash on his forehead, sports a Technicolor shiner from the same source, which in the last couple of days has bloomed purple green. My only discernible influence is the Big Oaks cap.

Inside the entryway, there's the usual stunted male reception—a sniff from Louie, a too-cool-for-school "Hey" from

Noah, and an inspired "Come on in" from the reigning patriarch. Thank God Sarah comes running from the kitchen and throws her arms around the kid, or else he'd never know how glad we all are to see him inside our house.

The initial awkwardness behind us, we head to the den, where, with snacks and beverages at hand, we hunker down for the afternoon. Final-round coverage has just begun, and Jim Nantz, in his third year at the helm, sets the scene. After nine holes, Couples, the leader from day one, is still out in front at eight under par, one better than Mark O'Meara and three better than David Duval, but the story of the morning is Jack Nicklaus, who birdied four out of his first seven holes and at fifty-eight is making yet another run.

"You've got plenty of time," says Jerzy. "He's six years older than you."

"Yeah. And he's Jack Nicklaus. Besides, I don't look good in green."

For the next several hours, we luxuriate in the dependable pleasures and smarmy eccentricities of golf's most polished telecast. With the tinkling soundtrack underneath, Nantz walks us across the Hogan and Nelson Bridges, discourses on the swirling winds of Golden Bell, and points out the Sarazen plaque and the Eisenhower tree, the only thing all afternoon that gets a rise out of Louie. For longtime viewers like us, the familiar bits of lore and language—*Amen Corner, Firethorn, the pine straw, the patrons*—are like the refrains in a secular hymnal. Through it all, there's the stunning seminatural beauty and the blissfully few commercials.

"Ever play Augusta?" asks Jerzy.

"Only in his mind," says Noah for me.

"When I become a member, you and Noah will be my first two guests," says Jerzy.

"Can't wait," says Noah.

After Nicklaus falls back, it's a three-man race to the wire between Couples, Duval, and O'Meara. Couples is the most beloved and Duval the most feared, yet it's the chubby-faced O'Meara, who till now has been best known for his friendship with Tiger, who stands over a seventeen-footer for birdie on the last hole to win it all. No one thinks for a second he'll sink it. Instead, there will be polite oohs and ahhs as his putt slides barely off-line, and the three will head back to 11, aka White Dogwood, for the play-off. O'Meara, however, refuses to follow the script. He hits one of the great putts in Masters history and pours it into the heart.

If this were a normal stop on the PGA tour, it would end right now with a wife and toddlers in his arms, but because it's the Masters, *a tradition like no other,* it's on to Butler Cabin. There, with a fire crackling in the background and Hootie Johnson, the chairman of Augusta National, presiding, last year's winner, Tiger Woods, helps his friend into a 43 regular.

When the telecast ends, I lend Jerzy the book on Augusta that I got from my grandfather and give him a ride home, the two of us still buzzing from the purity and finality of O'Meara's putt.

"I've always been a sucker for underdogs," I say.

"Me too," says Jerzy. "I wonder why."

Fired up by O'Meara's courage and galled by the spectacle of Jerzy's right eye, I blurt out a reckless offer:

"The next time Pickering hits you, you hit him back twice as hard. *Or* you ask Lyla on a date. Do either one, I don't care which, and I'll take you to Augusta."

49

THREE DAYS LATER, I take my place in the New Trier parking lot with even more trepidation than usual. By dangling a round at Augusta as a reward, I put a bounty on Pickering's head, and if by some wonderful chance Jerzy takes me up on it and comes out on top in a big way, I could be an accessory to assault, the point of no return for Finchem, if not Sarah. However, it's the more likely scenarios that have kept me up at night, which are that as a result of my grandiose meddling, Jerzy gets the crap kicked out of him, or his heart stomped. Or both.

You can imagine my relief when I see Jerzy's jug head, looking no worse for wear, bobbing above the stream of students that pours out of the back of the science building. Spotting Lyla nearby further bolsters my spirits. I try not to make too much of this—after all, they're not interacting—until I notice the shorts. He is not wearing golf shorts or tennis shorts or gym shorts but the black wool variety, which Lyla said was the one minor detail separating him from the lead guitarist of AC/DC. As I mull the ramifications of Jerzy taking fashion cues from his Goth classmate, Pickering and his posse zero in.

As always, Jerzy acts as if he doesn't see them, but Lyla, as befits someone in a black jumpsuit, ripped stockings, and army boots, is more combative. She curses Pickering out, and now it's Pickering who looks away, as flummoxed by this outburst of female ferocity as Jerzy was with him. When Lyla gets in his face, he still won't meet her eye, so Lyla, who weighs about ninety pounds with her boots on, shoves him with both hands.

After an awkward shrug toward his cronies, Pickering pushes Lyla back, and although Pickering's response is halfhearted and gentle by comparison, it's not gentle enough for Jerzy, who hauls off and smacks him in the face. I know it's a slap and not a punch because of the sound, which is very similar to one of his flushed 3-woods.

With the sound still echoing in the parking lot, Pickering and his cronies jump Jerzy, and for ten seconds it looks like three dogs attacking a bear. I hop from the truck, but before I get much closer, a tiny ragtag militia races to Jerzy's defense. One sports a tartan skirt fastened with a big brass pin, the other a patriotic Mohawk dyed red, white, and blue, and although neither is much bigger than Lyla, they are enough to turn the tide, and when two teachers and a guard pry them apart, Pickering and company are more relieved than outraged.

To the victors go the spoils, and for several minutes the three beam and strut while accepting the plaudits of a jubilant throng of misfits. Then Jerzy excuses himself from the celebration and wanders over.

"I guess you're wondering why I went with a slap instead of a punch," he asks.

"Based on the sound, I'm glad you did."

"The last thing I want to do is break my hand now," he says with a poorly suppressed grin.

"I gather you had already asked Lyla out."

"Correct," says Jerzy, his face turning approximately as red as Pickering's after impact.

"Well done. Two for two. I'll start making some calls."

50

Two weeks later, Jerzy and I walk out of the sleepy Augusta Regional Airport with our sticks in tow. Parked at the curb is an azure-blue '74 Eldorado convertible, antelope horns sprouting from the grille and Creedence's "Born on the Bayou" blaring from the stereo. Behind the wheel is Stump and beside him is Earl, and both seem to be relishing their morning cigars.

"Are you going to stand there gawking at the man's ride," asks Earl, "or you going to get in?"

We do the latter and desist with the former, or is it the other way around? I can never remember. In any case, we're soon loping down a Georgia two-lane on a perfect late-April day, the wind in our hair, the sun on our faces, and the smoke in our eyes. At the city line, Jerzy taps me on the elbow and points at the large roadside sign: WELCOME TO AUGUSTA, GEORGIA, HOME OF THE MASTERS, but I can't say that it fills me with the same giddy anticipation.

Even before I left Jerzy and Lyla in the parking lot that afternoon, I began to compile a list of people I could call who might be susceptible to groveling. As you might imagine, the list wasn't long and my connection to most of it tenuous. To give you an idea, I even put in a call to my good pal Marcus Azawa, chairman and CEO of Azawa Industries, based entirely on the enthusiasm with which he shook my hand before the play-off in

Hawaii. Unfortunately, with Marcus and everyone else I contacted, my reputation preceded me. Even Stump, who might otherwise have been able to wangle an invite, was tainted by association, and Earl wasn't going to be of much help prying open the gates of an institution that didn't accept its first African-American till 1990 and where until 1983 all the caddies were black.

Stump turns off the main drag, and with the V-8 gurgling beneath the endless hood, rolls up Washington Road. At 2604, he pulls over so we can all peer through what looks like a tunnel but is in fact a canopy of branches formed by the sixty surviving magnolias planted from seeds by Prosper Berckmans a century and a half ago. In the light at the far end, behind a circle of grass and a flagpole, are the steps of a simple white plantation-style house, and walking past it is a man in white overalls and a green cap. Just off our chrome bumper is a

---

sign that reads PRIVATE PROPERTY. NO TRESPASSING.

"Magnolia Lane," says Stump through his cigar smoke, "the most famous address in golf and the object of all hope and desire. We're not going in now—you can't just hop on a track like Augusta National after eight hours in airplanes and rental cars—but I thought you might want to see it from the front as God intended."

What is needed first, according to Stump, is a tune-up, which is why he's taken the liberty of booking a tee time at a course nearby. Stump isn't exaggerating about the proximity, and less than two minutes later he noses the Caddy through the gates of the Augusta Country Club and pulls up to a clubhouse at least as impressive as the one at the end of Magnolia Lane.

Since this is a warm-up, we forgo the range and the putting green and head directly to the first tee, where we take a cou-

ple of minutes to stretch our mostly
middle-aged bodies in the Georgia sun.

"Jerzy, I know it's got to be intimidating," says Stump, "to share the tee
box with two household names and a
journeyman."

"Intimidating?" says Jerzy with a bit of
Rumanian in the vowels. "I feel like I stumbled into an AARP convention."

"Well, let's see how you feel in an hour,
motherfucker," says Stump, but Earl snorts
his approval.

"Where the hell you find this kid,
Travis?"

"In the neighborhood."

"Really?" says Earl. "He seems too interesting for your neighborhood."

With Stump serving as obscene MC, we
enjoy a raucous couple of hours, but when
we reach the 9th fairway even Stump falls
silent. To the left of our carts are a stand
of pines and, beyond them, shimmering in
the afternoon light, the dazzling emerald

of another fairway, a pair of greens, and a sliver of water.

"Jerzy, you know what that is?" asks Stump.

"Of course, Mr. Stump. It's Amen Corner. And why are you whispering?"

51

AFTER WE HOLE OUT, I thank Stump and Earl and let them know we'll see them in three and a half hours. Exactly. Then I walk to the cart and pull off my bag.

"Jerzy, grab your sticks."

"Why?"

"A deal is a deal. I told you that if you stood up to Pickering or asked out Lyla, I'd take you to Augusta National, and you did both. Since I couldn't get us an engraved invitation, we'll have to be a little more proactive. Besides, fuck 'em if they can't take a joke."

"I don't think they can," says Jerzy, un-fastening his bag and following me into the woods, where we soon reach the stone wall that marks the boundary between the two courses. From there, we can hear the water flowing through Rae's Creek and see two golfers and their caddies on the right side of the 11th green.

"Take a joke, I mean," continues Jerzy softly. "I don't think they have a sense of humor about any of this—the patrons, the cabins, the green jackets, the trees, *the tradition like no other*. I don't think they have a sense of humor about one blade of their bent or Bermuda grass. In fact, they might shoot us on sight."

"Which is why we can't get caught."

I remove my Big Oaks cap and stuff it between my irons. Then I unzip the side pocket of my bag and pull out a large manila envelope addressed to me. Jammed into the right-hand corner are more than two dozen stamps, and in the other is a return address in Birmingham, Alabama. "A gift from a friend named Owl," I say.

I run a finger under the flap and pull out an immaculate pair of white overalls. On the right chest pocket is the insignia of Augusta National—the outline of the continental United States with a red flag sticking out of the approximate spot where we are now. Since Owl is a man known for his fastidious attention to detail, the envelope also contains an official green Masters cap, a scorecard, a yardage book, and a pencil.

"Aren't you going to play?"

"Not today, Jerzy."

As I step into my new uniform, I take another look at Jerzy's. The same afternoon I called Owl, who then got in touch with his cousin, a former Augusta National caddy, Jerzy and I took a trip to Brooks Brothers, where I bought him a pair of pink seersucker shorts, a white polo shirt, and a pale blue cashmere sweater, each

preppy item carefully selected to suggest
the social ease of someone who is not only
well off but has been so for generations.
Overall, Jerzy carries off his new look
pretty well, I think. The only thing I
couldn't talk him out of is the Big Oaks
cap, which as far as I know, he hasn't taken
off since I gave it to him.

After two putts apiece, neither golfer on
11 is any closer to the hole, which gives me
time to stash my clubs and confirm that
there is not another group coming up right
behind the twosome. When the golfers and
their caddies clear the green, we clamber
over the wall, take off our shoes and socks,
and wade across the icy stream.

52

UNDER ANY CIRCUMSTANCES, YOUR first
steps on Augusta National are going to be
overwhelming. That ours are heading in
the wrong direction on the 11th fairway
only makes them more so. On one hand,
the scene is achingly familiar, since I've
watched drives bounding down this fairway countless times on countless telecasts.
On the other, there's the shock of actually
being here in person and feeling the sacred
televised sod pushing up through the soles
of our shoes. Then, on top of everything
else, there's the darker thrill of being unin-
vited and being here anyway.

"Jerzy, what do you think?"

"I'm not sure I can."

"Well, to paraphrase Julius, we've crossed our creek. There's no turning back now."

"I assume you mean Caesar, not Boros," he says.

"Correct."

To settle my nerves, I focus on my job, which is to guide Jerzy around this course in as few strokes as possible, and as we head up the fairway, I pull out the scorecard and fold it to the back nine. "We're starting on eleven," I offer, "aka White Dogwood, a long par four. Where we're walking now is about where you want to land your drive." And when we reach the tee box, I pluck a couple of blades of grass, and rather than pocket them as souvenirs, feed them to the warm breeze.

"So what do we got?" asks Jerzy, looking over my shoulder at the card.

"A bit of a dilemma."

"A little late for that, isn't it, Emperor?"

"I mean which tees do we play. From the championship tees, the ones used by O'Meara, Couples, and Duval, the course plays a robust sixty-five hundred yards. For the members, it's a more manageable sixty-one hundred, but as you know, we're not members, and are unlikely to ever be members, so I don't feel quite right playing their tees."

"You saying we should play this puppy from the tips?"

"Why not? We came all this way, inhaled all that airplane air. Let's find out what the fuss is about. Get our money's worth, so to speak."

"Works for me," says Jerzy with a grin.

"Good." I hand him the driver and slap a new Titleist in his palm, the initials *J* and *S* written with a blue Sharpie on each side of the red 3, but as he bends to tee it up, I hear voices, and they're growing louder.

53

WHEN I LOOK OVER my shoulder, a golf cart, containing two large men and no golf clubs, is barreling directly toward us. Rather than your standard E-Z-GO, it has four rows of seats. It's the kind of all-purpose vehicle used to transport golfers back to their respective holes after a rain delay, or, to cite just one more example, to whisk a pair of trespassing miscreants off the premises, and that's where the burliness of the occupants comes in. Both look like they could have played Division I football while moonlighting as bouncers, and one of them has a walkie-talkie in his hand.

Despite evoking Caesar so recently, I look back over my shoulder toward Rae's Creek, but there's no point making a run for it. Not with Jerzy's sticks on my back and them in a cart. *We're going to get kicked off the course while our feet are still damp,* and my last coherent wish is for Jerzy to hit the goddamned ball so that after all the humiliation, career damage, and legal fallout, we'll at least have that one shot at Augusta to burnish in our memories, but now the cart is parked beside us and it's too late even for that.

"My apologies for the interruption," says the driver. "We'll be out of your way in a second." Then he touches the brim of his cap and keeps on going.

54

"THAT WAS AEROBIC," I say as the cart disappears over the hill and the palpitations in my chest subside.

"Thank God for Owl," says Jerzy.

"True. To recap and regroup, we're on number eleven, aka White Dogwood. It looks tight from the tee, but as you saw on the way here, it opens up. It's not as hard as it looks."

This is not entirely true. By the luck of real estate and geography, we're starting our round on the second-hardest hole on the course, but I see no point in sharing that, and my tact is rewarded when Jerzy steps up and pipes his first drive straight down the middle.

"Golf shot, Jerzy. Let's go find it."

When we do, I see why the hole plays so hard. After a perfect drive, Jerzy has 207 yards, from a hook lie to a green with water left.

"Anything right of the flag is great," I say. "Even right of the green. Anything left is in the water. And don't be afraid to take a divot. It's just a golf course. The grass will grow back."

Despite my assurances, Jerzy hits a top, which might actually be lucky, because it takes the water out of play and still rolls within fifteen yards of the green. Before he attempts the chip, we walk up the bank to get our first good look at an Augusta National green, whose contours and color are so dramatic they seem extraterrestrial. Apparently the grass really is greener on the other side.

"It's like walking on the moon," says Jerzy.

"One small step for Jerzy Solarski. One giant leap for golfkind."

Jerzy thins his chip, too, leaving himself a forty-five-footer, straight downhill with at least nine feet of break. But as you may recall, Jerzy can roll his rock. He taps it as delicately as you might nudge a beloved snoring grandfather at the Thanksgiving table, and the ball tracks perfectly end over end, takes the break, and on its last half-turn, topples into the hole.

"These greens are fast," says Jerzy. "But they're not Big Oaks fast."

55

AFTER ONE OF THE better opening pars in the underdocumented history of golf trespassing, we soldier on to Golden Bell, perhaps the most whispered-over 155 yards on earth. If you've ever owned a television, you know too much about this nasty little par 3 with the bank in front that funnels anything short into the creek, the traps and flower beds that catch anything long, and the inscrutable winds that make it so hard to avoid one or the other.

Months of airtime have been devoted to the breeze alone, and while I've learned that Hogan studied the leaves on a certain branch of a certain tree, and Snead looked at some other bit of foliage, while Nelson and Nicklaus looked somewhere else again, none of that is the least bit helpful. Neither is the one thing I can remember with certainty, which is that you can't go by what the flag is doing.

"We just got out of Rae's Creek," I say as I hand Jerzy the 6. "We don't want to be in it again."

As I feared, it turns out to be a club and a half too much, and after chipping out of the azaleas, Jerzy walks off with his first bogey.

56

THAT SETS THE PATTERN of par/bogey golf, which Jerzy somehow maintains for the next hour. On the par-five 13th, he reaches the green in regulation and two putts for par, and on 14, the most wildly contoured green on the course, he rolls in a side-hill twelve-footer to steal bogey. Two putts from fifty feet earn him another par on 16, and despite catching a piece of the Eisenhower tree off the tee, he manages to bogey 17.

I'd describe these holes in more detail, but you know what they look like as well as me. Instead, let me try to convey what it's like to experience them in the flesh. I've mentioned the colors and the contours of the greens, and I'm sure you've heard about the drastic changes in elevation, all of which are impossible to appreciate on television, but the biggest difference, between Augusta today and all those afternoons in my den, between Augusta standing up and Augusta sitting down, is the silence.

You want an idea of what it's like to play Augusta on your own, watch the Masters on mute. With no applause from the patrons, no roars through the pines, no microphones on the tees, and no blather from the tower. When we walk over the Hogan Bridge to the 12th green, we do it without Nantz murmuring sweet reverential nothings in our ears, and when we traverse the Nelson Bridge to the 13th fairway, there's no cocktail music underneath.

It's just the course, the pines, the sky, and...oh, yeah...us, and no offense to

CBS, this is better. So much so that it's all going too quickly, and before I know it, Jerzy has backed up a solid drive through the chute on 18 with an even better iron to the green and tapped in for his fourth par in eight holes.

I know what you're thinking. How can a kid who didn't pick up a club till three months ago par half his holes at Augusta National? From the back tees? Certainly, it's unlikely, and I'm surprised too, but it's not like we haven't all brought home the occasional unlikely score now and then. In any case, let me explain how Jerzy's been getting it done. Some of it might even be helpful the next time you tee it up.

First of all, Jerzy is a big kid with a real golf swing. When he catches it right, it flies as far and high as a top college player's. He only does that about a fifth of the time, but when he does, either off the tee or from the fairway, it gives him a chance for a par. Another twenty percent of his shots

are "good misses," pushes or pulls that fly
within fifteen yards of his target, and at
least today, so far, they haven't led to big
numbers. The same is true with his god-
awful shots, and that's been the biggest key
today. Jerzy's most frequent miss is a hard
top, and on these fairways, they roll forever.

The truth is that in some ways, Augusta
plays surprisingly easy. The fairways are
enormous, there isn't a blade of rough, and
when you hit into the trees, there's almost
always room to advance the ball. What is
hard is the greens, and Jerzy is a Rumanian-
American Crenshaw. After his first day at
Big Oaks, he was a better putter than me,
and after a week, he was better than two
thirds of the guys on the Senior Tour.

Another factor in Jerzy's favor, if I say so
myself, is that he's got yours truly on the bag.
For example, forty minutes ago on 13, after
he pushed his drive into the pine straw. Even
though he only had 201 to the green and a

direct shot, I refused to turn over the 4-iron and made him chip out. With all the chances we've taken to be here, you might think it's odd to be conservative now, but to me the two are unrelated. The only thing that matters in this game is the score, something hackers never quite understand, even when they think they do. If you can't make a shot eighty percent of the time and there's a penalty if you don't, you shouldn't try it. Ever. No matter where you are.

Finally, please bear in mind, you did buy a book with the word *miracle* in the title.

57

THEY SAY THE MASTERS doesn't start till the back nine on Sunday. It may even be true, but it doesn't apply when you play on a Wednesday and start on 11. In our particular circumstances, the critical stretch isn't the back nine or the front, it's the precarious stroll we're about to take now from the 18th green to the first tee. This exposed fifty-yard perp walk, which leads between the practice green and the back of the clubhouse, where a cocktail party is in full bloom, is *our* Amen Corner, and the prayer that comes to mind is the one from Sunday school about forgiving *our trespasses, as we forgive those who trespass against us.*

Lured by this lovely weather, the party has spilled out from the veranda onto the back lawn, the women in summer dresses, the men sporting blazers whose brass buttons catch the late-afternoon sun, and our route takes us right through them. I think I can impersonate a caddy—I *am* a caddy— but can Jerzy project the body language and entitlement of a brat? And will his weight and bad skin work against him? Surely one of the members will notice something amiss in our bearing or breeding and see us for the interlopers we are.

Among those directly in our path is a middle-aged man who looks strikingly familiar. That's not surprising. Augusta's roster is loaded with captains of industry, so perhaps I've seen his face staring back at me from the magazine rack at the dentist or the jacket of a bestseller. But I've been avoiding the dentist for months and haven't read anything except the sports section in years, and I know I've seen this face recently.

Then it all falls into place like that last piece of fruit in a slot machine window. He was the guy sitting next to Nantz in the Butler Cabin, the one who asked Tiger to please place the green jacket on his good friend and new Masters champion, Mark O'Meara. It's Hootie fucking Johnson, chairman of Augusta National, and at the same moment that I recognize him, Hootie reaches out his hand and claps it down on Jerzy's shoulder.

58

"WHAT'S YOUR NAME, SON?"

"Brune, sir. It's a pleasure to make your acquaintance."

"Then call me Hootie, for Christ's sake! How was it out there?"

"Hootie, it was awesome," says Jerzy, the last bit of leftover accent cutting through the molasses of Hootie's drawl. "I don't think I've ever seen the course in better condition. It's so good we're heading back out for another nine."

"Got to make hay while the sun shines. After all, you never know when you're going to get down here again."

"Sad but true, Hootie."

"Your home course?" asks Johnson. Since his right hand is still on Jerzy's shoulder, he refers to the Big Oaks cap with his gin and tonic.

"Correct," says Jerzy, after a slight delay. "Just outside Chicago."

"Why haven't I heard of it?"

"It's still a bit under the radar," says Jerzy, his voice dipping to a whisper. "But not for long, I fear. The next time you're in the vicinity, I'd be honored to give you a tour."

As impressed as I am with Jerzy's performance, astounded even, I'm more than ready for this delightful exchange to be over. I know Jerzy's wardrobe is right, but under such prolonged exposure something is bound to out him, whether it's the accent or the mysterious *home course*. Even after Hootie finally takes his hand off Jerzy's shoulder, the conversational ball keeps going back and forth.

"I just might take you up on that, young man. What's your last name, Brune?"

"Pickering."

"Pickering," repeats Hootie softly to himself. "Brune Pickering?" Then he turns to me. "And how about you? I don't believe we've met either."

"Rudy, sir. Rudy Laplante. I started this week."

"Rudy Laplante? You don't say?"

"Yes, sir."

"Well, Brune, how's old Rudy doing?"

"Very well. And he's not as old as he looks. I believe Rudy has the makings of a first-rate caddy, and you can quote me on that."

"He's got the Brune seal of approval, does he?"

"Correct. Of course, there's been a misread now and then, and a missed club here and there, but not even Hogan always got the wind right at Golden Bell."

"Fair point, Brune."

For a few seconds that seem like a month, Hootie stares at each of us in turn; then he shakes his head and chuckles softly to himself. "Well. I'll let you both get to it, then. Hit 'em straight."

"Thanks, Hootie. I'm so pleased I finally got a chance to meet you."

"Me too, Brune."

When Hootie repairs to the veranda, Jerzy and I continue to the first tee, which, without hundreds of patrons surrounding it, seems oddly naked. "Jerzy, you have any idea who that man was?"

"No idea."

"Me neither."

59

LESS THAN THREE WEEKS ago, sitting in
my den with Louie, I watched Sam Snead
walk onto the first tee and hit the ceremonial first shot of the '98 Masters. Now I'm
watching Jerzy Solarski, a seventeen-year-
old from Bucharest, who three months ago
knocked on my door with a shovel, tee it
up from the same spot. Almost as unlikely,
I've now spent two hours on a course where
I've fantasized playing for forty years,
haven't taken a single swing, and don't seem
to mind.

With Hootie and company sipping their

second or third cocktails, Jerzy and I have Prosper Berckmans's former nursery entirely to ourselves. You could argue that the experience is more rarefied than actually playing the Masters, where you're obliged to share it with the likes of Tiger and Phil, a hundred other pros, and tens of thousands of fans, I mean *patrons.*

Aside from those snippets of an old-timer stooping over on the first tee on Thursday nights on ESPN, the front side is untelevised, and that makes playing Tea Olive, Pink Dogwood, Flowering Peach, and Flowering Crab Apple a lot different than playing Camellia, White Dogwood, and Golden Bell. From our shared reading, Jerzy and I know the approximate layouts, but we haven't witnessed golf history on every hole. That takes the edge off considerably, and as the sun begins its swift descent, Jerzy pars two of them and the par/bogey train keeps chugging through the Georgia pines.

As we walk off 5, Magnolia, the sun dips beneath the trees, and now the birds stop chirping. Engulfed in quiet, it's harder to ignore the question I've been dodging all day, if not all week, which, of course, is "Why?" Why are we doing this? What message am I trying to convey? What, if anything, am I hoping to instill in an impressionable young mind beyond a healthy disrespect for private property and a love for destination trespassing?

Well, here's my answer. To have some fun in this life and avoid swallowing a mouthful of shit per day takes more than luck, and this is a lesson, however ill-conceived, in audacity. If the last year or so has taught me anything, it's that every once in a while you need to take a deep breath, do your best impersonation of a badass, and see where it goes. If nothing else, you might make some new friends as interesting as Earl, Stump, and Jerzy, and what's more precious than that?

On the famous back nine, we felt like a couple of tourists gawking at golf's Eiffel Tower. Finally, we can just play. Hit it. Find it. And hit it again. Do that, good things tend to happen, even to mediocre golfers. Over the next three holes, Jerzy cards two more pars, and when he slides in a six-footer on 8 for the second one, the laid-back quality of our afternoon evaporates. Suddenly, I'm as nervous as I was walking beside Earl up the 18th fairway at Shoal Creek on Sunday.

60

"You know where we are right now?" asks Jerzy.

"Number nine," I say, "Carolina Cherry. Golf course called Augusta National."

"In addition to that?"

"Eight over," I concede.

"Correct. So I need to birdie one of the next two."

"Yup."

If my share of the dialogue seems flat, it's intentional. I appreciate the weight of the moment, at least as much as Jerzy, but I'm doing my best to pretend otherwise.

After sixteen holes, Jerzy has eight pars and eight bogeys. Since Augusta National is a par 72, that means he's sitting on 80, and if he can play the next two holes in 1-under-par, he'll shoot 79.

For every hacker who's ever teed it up in vain, breaking 80 is the Promised Land, and getting there for the first time is like meeting Saint Peter at the pearly gate. In terms of personal significance, it trumps playing Augusta National, Pebble Beach, and St. Andrews combined. It isn't even close. Let's say that on the same day that you eked out an 83 at Augusta National, you drove to a muni on the wrong side of town and shot 79, "no gimmes, no mulligans, no bullshit," to break 80 for the first time. Which round at which course do you think you'll be replaying in your mind all night? I'll give you a clue. It's not the one with the azaleas.

On the other hand, if you're going to break 80 for the first time, Augusta National is a highly auspicious place to do it. In order of magnitude, it would be like losing your virginity to Marilyn Monroe. And having a signed document, suitable for framing, to verify it. People have gone on to become president for a lot less.

Unfortunately, Jerzy's chances of doing one are about as good as the other, and Marilyn, bless her generous soul, has been dead thirty-six years. The problem is the difficulty of our remaining two holes. The 9th, with its signature three-tier green, is one of the hardest on the front nine, and the 10th, a 495-yard par 4, is the hardest hole on the course. The last two holes are so long and tough that playing them even would constitute a minor miracle, but as I guess you know, the name of this book is not *The Minor Miracle at Augusta.*

"So how am I going to get this done?" asks Jerzy.

"Birdieing nine would be a good start."

61

JERZY AND I STAND on the 9th tee and squint at what's left of the fairway. There's so little light, the only way to get an idea what we're facing is to pull out the yardage book. With Jerzy squinting over my shoulder at the diagram, I lay out the challenge. Since we both know he needs birdie, I don't sugarcoat it.

"Carolina Cherry is a dogleg left. Downhill off the tee, uphill to the green. It's all about the tee shot. If you can get it to the bottom of the hill, where you can hit a short iron or even a wedge on your second, you've got a much better chance for birdie. To do that, you need to get all of it, and it's got to be straight, because there are trees on both sides."

Jerzy's tee shot—a low hard top—is on me. Tell a seventeen-year-old, or even a nearly fifty-two-year-old, he needs a big drive, he's going to overswing every time, and despite the lousy light, I know it's nowhere near the bottom of the hill. As we soon discover, it hasn't even rolled off the top plateau, and when I step off the distance to the nearest sprinkler head and do the math, I get 221 to the center of the green.

There's just enough light to make out the flag on the left side, and by referring to the yardage book, I determine that it's cut in the second of the three tiers. When I also see that the green tilts sharply from back to front and, to a lesser degree, from left to right, I can't resist a dark smile. The only shot with a chance in hell to stay on that second tier, where he would have a realistic putt at birdie, is the one I practiced all winter at Big Oaks. And he's got to hit it, not me.

"You're in luck," I say. "This calls for a high draw, and I'm something of an expert on this shot. We could spend a month on it, but here's the fifteen-second tutorial: move the ball back closer to your right foot, close your stance, and think about hitting the inside of the ball."

I feel like a quarterback sketching a play in the dirt on the last drive of the Super Bowl, but I'm not Bart Starr and Jerzy's not Paul Hornung. Or maybe he is, because in his first attempt, with 79 on the line, he hits it purer than I did all winter with nothing at stake, and before the ball disappears from sight, we can see it bend gently toward the flag.

"Congratulations, Jerzy. According to your new friend Earl Fielder, you just hit the suavest shot in golf."

"Who am I to contradict Earl?" says Jerzy.

Now all that's left is the minor technicality of that pesky twenty-two-footer. Jerzy steps up to it as if it holds all the peril of a tap-in and rolls it dead center. Let's see what he's like in thirty years after he's missed a mile of five-footers.

62

"Jerzy, that was sweet. Now all you got left is the hard part—making a four on ten."

Somewhere between the 9th green and the 10th tee, the last bit of light drains from the sky. If this were a tournament, they'd have sounded the horn thirty minutes ago. At least we're on the back nine again, and along with Owl's trusty yardage book, we have the benefit of having seen this hole in Central Time on CBS.

"Another downhill dogleg left," says Jerzy, squinting at the diagram. "Looks like nine."

"Particularly in the dark," I say. "This one is forty yards longer, but there's a speed slot on the left side of the fairway. If you can drop it in there, it plays about the same. Take a three-wood, put an easy swing on it, and let the slope and gravity do the rest."

As a preamble, it's a helluva lot better than what I came up with on 9. Jerzy strikes it solid, gets the sought-after roll, and when we find it just off the left side of the fairway, 185 yards from the center of the green, this absurd pipe dream still seems possible. From here, the green is harder to see than the flag, but by working off the sand on the right and the yardage book, I place the flag back and left.

"You've got one ninety-three to the pin," I say. "It's cooler now, so it's going to play all that. Aim for the right side of the green and don't worry about the bunker. It's much better than being left."

I hand him the 4-iron, and Jerzy delivers

his third pure swing in a row, like he's just getting warmed up. In fact, it's too good, or maybe he catches a flier, or more likely I gave him the wrong club, because he airmails the green. After it soars over the trap, it disappears from view, and as we tilt forward and strain our ears in that direction, we hear it hit a branch and then another and maybe even a third.

Just like Shoal Creek all over again, I think as the pines play pinball with Jerzy's 79. Last hole. Last swing. All we need is par, and I pull the wrong stick. Funny thing about golf acoustics—sometimes a ball hitting a tree sounds exactly like a ball splashing into a pond.

63

WITH THE RESILIENCE OF youth, Jerzy bounds after it.

"Jerzy, wait up. I got to make you hit a provisional. In this light, we might never find that ball."

Even if we don't, and Jerzy limps home with a triple, he still shoots 82, and the last thing I want to do when this is over is hand him a scorecard with a big fat asterisk attached. Whatever he shoots today is going to be legit. No gimmes. No mulligans. No bullshit.

I hand him the 5, and he goes

through the same routine he did with the 4—a practice swing, a waggle, and go. Again he hits it well, and when we get closer, we see that it's rolled onto the front edge. Then we head to the spot beyond the right trap where his first ball disappeared.

In the trees, it's three shades darker, and a glance at my watch shows we're coming up on our appointed rendezvous with Earl and Stump. By now it's a cool Georgia night—all pretense of a late afternoon or early evening is gone—and we spend the next few minutes weaving through the pine straw trying to will a Titleist into view. When that doesn't happen in five minutes, I call off the search and we return to the green.

"All that means," I say, "is that you're going to have to make one last putt. The goal was to get you on the green with a putt for par, and we've done that. Whether his name is Ben Crenshaw or Dave Stockton, there is no one I'd rather see putt this ball than you."

I don't know what makes the putt harder—the distance or the darkness. Between the ball and the flag are over a hundred feet of barely visible green, and a big break from right to left. I wish I could be more specific, but in this light, I can't. The only thing in our favor is that it's up-hill.

I know that in the course of this tale, I've pushed your credulity to the limit. If I tell you Jerzy drains a 110-foot putt with about 20 feet of break in total darkness on the hardest hole at Augusta National to break 80 for the first time, will that be a bridge too far? In any case, all I can do is tell you what happened.

After we've learned all that we can by studying an invisible green, I send Jerzy down to his ball with his magic putter and I head to the hole to tend the flag. At the bottom of the green, Jerzy is a dark shape, and behind him at the top of the hill, the light in the Crow's Nest looks like a low moon. "Don't be afraid to hit it. The one thing you can't do is leave it short."

On opposite ends of the green, Jerzy takes his practice strokes and I reach for the pin. I've already made one gaffe on this hole. I don't want to compound it by getting the flag stuck and then yanking so hard that the entire cup comes out with it. To ensure that the flag will slide out smoothly, I twist it back and forth, and something rattles at my feet. When I look down, I see a white Titleist with a blue *J* and *S* on each side of the 3.

"Don't putt it, Jerzy," I manage to shout in time. "Pick it up. Your first ball is in the hole. You didn't just break eighty. You broke seventy-eight."

Here's the final scorecard after I pencil in his 2 on Camellia. No matter how many times you add it up, it comes to 77.

Hole	Par	Jerzy		HOLE	PAR	Jerzy	
1	4	5		10	4	2 e	
2	5	(5)		11	4	(4)	
3	4	5		12	3	4	
4	3	(3)		13	5	(5)	
5	4	5		14	4	5	
6	3	(3)		15	5	6	
7	4	5		16	3	(3)	
8	5	(5)		17	4	5	
9	4	3 b		18	4	(4)	
Out	36	39		TOTAL	72	77	

SCORER: *Travis McKinley* ATTEST: _____   DATE: *April 25th*

271

64

"How does it feel?" I ask when Jerzy finally reaches the hole and sees the evidence for himself.

"Ridiculous good," he says. He plucks the ball from the hole and holds it in the moonlight. "So ridiculous good, it should be illegal."

"Actually, it is."

"Well, fuck 'em if they can't take a joke."

"That's what I say."

We give ourselves a minute before we vacate the green. Then we walk past the 11th tee, where our round began, and for the first time today, a part of Augusta National is familiar, not because we've seen it countless times on television but because we stood on this very spot three hours before, and that makes for a richer strain of nostalgia.

The feeling of déjà vu is even stronger as we head up the 11th fairway, crest the hill, and gaze out toward the amoeba-shaped shadows that are the 11th and 12th greens. Now the moon is all the way up and crickets have replaced the birds, and as we walk through the dew-drenched grass, I feel the same elation I did as a twelve-year-old, when after *"two more holes"* and *"just one more"* and then *"one more and that's it,"* I raced back through the sudden nightfall toward the Creekview parking lot.

Fifty yards short of the green, I hear Rae's Creek, and then I smell it. We step out of our shoes and socks and wade back across. On the other side, I lay Jerzy's bag on the ground and, from our dry perch on his clubs, stare back across the creek at Amen Corner.

"Jerzy, you know what was your best swing all day?"

Jerzy shrugs, still hauling aboard his birdie/eagle finish.

"The only one that didn't count. After you knocked it into the trees on ten, you stepped up to the provisional with the exact same attitude as the first. That showed a lot of heart. I'm really proud of you for that. There are a lot of pros who couldn't have done that. In fact, you're sitting next to one of them."

"That's because you're a great big baby."

"Correct."

After one last glance across the creek, we turn our backs on Augusta National and make the slow climb through the pines. I should have thought to pack a flashlight, because scrambling over the wall is borderline dangerous, particularly for an exhausted almost fifty-two-year-old. Once we're back on legal ground, Jerzy finds the spot where I stashed my clubs, and we slip through the trees onto the grounds of the Augusta Country Club.

"You think Hootie is going to take you up on that tour?"

"I hope so," says Jerzy. "When I said I'd be honored to show him around Big Oaks, I meant it. It's still my favorite place. Always will be. That reminds me, there's something I've really got to say."

"What?"

"Next time, I'm caddying."

"No shit."

For a couple of minutes, we stand in the dark and smile, savoring a ridiculous good day. Then Earl turns on a flashlight and we see the two carts parked side by side.

"Well?" asks Stump. "How'd our boy do?"

"That's it?" I ask. "No hello? It's good to see you? We were a little worried about you guys? None of that? Just, what did he shoot?"

"That bad, huh?"

"Afraid so," I say. "Seventy-seven...from the tips."

Stump emits a sound only a 220-pound tobacco-chewing redneck is capable of producing without injury. "This calls for a celebration, and I know just the place. But Jerzy's going to need ID."

"For fuck's sake, Stump," says Earl. "After everything they've done today, I think they're capable of getting themselves into your silly-ass bar."

"They better be. Because Wednesday is karaoke night."

Stump motions for Jerzy to take the seat next to him and I get in the cart with Earl and we race beneath the moon to the empty parking lot. The last thing I hear, before their cart slips out of earshot, is Stump telling Jerzy, "You got a nice little game, son, keep it up."

Epilogue

IT'S A LITTLE MORE than two months later, and I'm sitting in the den with Sarah, Noah, and Louie, watching golf on television. For obvious reasons, I've been doing more spectating than competing this summer, and this weekend is particularly rough because it's the U.S. Senior Open, my one shining moment as a pro. That must be why Sarah, who wouldn't normally spend Saturday indoors, has joined me and Noah on the couch.

The good news is that both Earl and Stump are having a great Open. Not only are they tied for third at four under par, they're paired in the second-to-last group, and with Lee Trevino rounding out the threesome, they're guaranteed plenty of airtime. In fact, the broadcast opens with Stump, shameless as ever, waving his cap back and forth and whipping the crowd into a frenzy. When he finally puts the cap back on his head, I can't make out the name on the front, but I can tell it's not Titleist or Skoal, his primary sponsors.

"Noah, can you read what it says on Stump's hat?"

"State," says Noah.

"Must be Georgia State," I say. "Either that, or he signed a new deal with an insurance company."

When Trevino takes the tee, the crowd is even more raucous, and when he doffs his cap, I notice the same unfamiliar white font.

"How about Lee's hat?" I ask Noah. "Can you read that?"

"*Re* something," he says.

Next and last is Earl, and as he goes into his brisk preshot routine, I see he's wearing the same boxy black hat with the same simple white font on the crown, this time a word beginning with *M*.

"Your name is on his hat," says Sarah, stunned. "It says McKinley."

"It does, Dad."

Earl splits the fairway for the millionth time, and after his ball stops rolling, Earl, Stump, and Trevino pose side by side, their hats reading: MCKINLEY, STATE, RE-IN. Then Earl switches places with Lee, and the three hats read: RE-IN STATE MCKINLEY.

The three are still side by side on the tee box and beaming into the camera when my favorite on-course interviewer, Dave Marr, hustles over and asks, "What's with the hats, gentlemen?" and shoves a microphone in front of Earl's face.

"This is for our buddy Travis McKinley," says Earl, "who got suspended for nothing more than a scuffle between consenting adults. He's been out four months now, and that's four months too long."

"Enough is enough," says Stump.

"And how about you, Lee? You feel the same way?"

"These guys were both there. If they think it's ridiculous, that's good enough for me. Besides, Travis is one of my favorite players. I miss him, and I'm sure the fans do, too."

"Dad, can you believe Trevino just called you one of his favorite players?"

"No, I can't...and it's too late to tape it."

It doesn't stop there. On the second tee, Earl's Platoon takes up the chant: "Reinstate McKinley...Reinstate McKinley!" and when they tire of that, switch to the catchier "It can't wait! Reinstate!" often with Stump out front conducting the choir. Earl and Stump must have been plotting this for weeks, because by the back nine, half the field has switched to a black cap with either RE-IN, STATE, or MCKINLEY on it. I don't have to look over at Sarah to know that tears are streaming down her face, but I risk it anyway.

Overwhelmed, I retreat to the backyard with Louie, sip my beer on a lawn chair, and gaze up at the trees. Sarah and I have lived in this house nearly thirty years, and the branches get fuller and lovelier each summer, and for twenty minutes I watch and listen as the leaves move in the gentle breeze. When my cell phone goes off and I see the call is from Ponte Vedra, Florida, I consider not answering, but on the fifth ring I succumb.

"Travis, it's Tim Finchem."

"I had no idea they were planning this. Are you calling because you want me to ask them to stop?"

"No, it's too late for that. I'm calling to eat crow. If your fellow players want you back, who am I to stand in the way?

As of this moment, your suspension is officially suspended. You are once again a member in full standing on the Senior Tour."

I hear the words, but they're more than I can absorb, so I close my eyes and listen to the leaves.

"Travis, you there?"

"Yes, Commissioner. Thanks very much."

"Don't thank me, Travis. Thank Earl and Stump and Lee. You got a lot of good friends out here. I hope you know that.... One other thing, before I forget. A couple of weeks ago, I got a call from Hootie Johnson. You know Hootie, right? The chairman of Augusta National?"

"I know who he is. I can't say I know him."

"Well, apparently he knows you. I don't know what prompted this, and I'm not sure I want to, but he said if you ever want to play Augusta National you should give him a call. Good night, Travis, and welcome back."

I stare at the rustling leaves for another hour before I go back inside and share the news.

About the Authors

JAMES PATTERSON has created more enduring fictional characters than any other novelist writing today. He is the author of the Alex Cross novels, the most popular detective series of the past twenty-five years. His other bestselling novels feature the Women's Murder Club, Michael Bennett, Private, and NYPD Red. Since his first novel won the Edgar Award in 1977, James Patterson's books have sold more than 300 million copies.

James Patterson has also written numerous #1 bestsellers for young readers, including the Maximum Ride, Witch & Wizard, Middle School, and Treasure Hunters series. In 2010, James Patterson was named Author of the Year at the Children's Choice Book Awards.

His lifelong passion for books and reading led James Patterson to create the innovative website ReadKiddoRead.com, giving adults an invaluable tool to find the books that get kids reading for life. He writes full-time and lives in Florida with his family.

PETER DE JONGE is the author of the critically acclaimed crime novels *Shadows Still Remain* and *Buried on Avenue B. Miracle at Augusta* is his fourth collaboration with James Patterson, preceded by *Beach Road, The Beach House,* and *Miracle on the 17th Green.*

BOOKS BY JAMES PATTERSON

FEATURING ALEX CROSS

Hope to Die • *Cross My Heart* • *Alex Cross, Run* • *Merry Christmas, Alex Cross* • *Kill Alex Cross* • *Cross Fire* • *I, Alex Cross* • *Alex Cross's* Trial (with Richard DiLallo) • *Cross Country* • *Double Cross* • *Cross* (also published as *Alex Cross*) • *Mary, Mary* • *London Bridges* • *The Big Bad Wolf* • *Four Blind Mice* • *Violets Are Blue* • *Roses Are Red* • *Pop Goes the Weasel* • *Cat & Mouse* • *Jack & Jill* • *Kiss the Girls* • *Along Came a Spider*

THE WOMEN'S MURDER CLUB

Unlucky 13 (with Maxine Paetro) • *12th of Never* (with Maxine Paetro) • *11th Hour* (with Maxine Paetro) • *10th Anniversary* (with Maxine Paetro) • *The 9th Judgment* (with Maxine Paetro) •

The 8th Confession (with Maxine Paetro) •
7th Heaven (with Maxine Paetro) •
The 6th Target (with Maxine Paetro) •
The 5th Horseman (with Maxine Paetro) •
4th of July (with Maxine Paetro) •
3rd Degree (with Andrew Gross) •
2nd Chance (with Andrew Gross) •
1st to Die

FEATURING MICHAEL BENNETT
Burn (with Michael Ledwidge) • *Gone*
(with Michael Ledwidge) • *I, Michael
Bennett* (with Michael Ledwidge) •
Tick Tock (with Michael Ledwidge) •
Worst Case (with Michael Ledwidge) •
Run for Your Life (with Michael Ledwidge)
• *Step on a Crack* (with Michael Ledwidge)

THE PRIVATE NOVELS
Private Vegas (with Maxine Paetro) •
Private India: City on Fire (with Ashwin
Sanghi) • *Private Down Under* (with
Michael White) • *Private L.A.* (with Mark

Sullivan) • *Private Berlin* (with Mark
Sullivan) • *Private London* (with Mark
Pearson) • *Private Games* (with Mark
Sullivan) • *Private: #1 Suspect* (with
Maxine Paetro) • *Private* (with Maxine
Paetro)

NYPD RED NOVELS
NYPD Red 3 (with Marshall Karp) •
NYPD Red 2 (with Marshall Karp) •
NYPD Red (with Marshall Karp)

SUMMER NOVELS
Second Honeymoon (with Howard
Roughan) • *Now You See Her* (with
Michael Ledwidge) • *Swimsuit* (with
Maxine Paetro) • *Sail* (with Howard
Roughan) • *Beach Road* (with Peter de
Jonge) • *Lifeguard* (with Andrew Gross) •
Honeymoon (with Howard Roughan) •
The Beach House (with Peter de Jonge)

STAND-ALONE BOOKS

Miracle at Augusta (with Peter de Jonge) • *Invisible* (with David Ellis) • *First Love* (with Emily Raymond) • *Mistress* (with David Ellis) • *Zoo* (with Michael Ledwidge) • *Guilty Wives* (with David Ellis) • *The Christmas Wedding* (with Richard DiLallo) • *Kill Me If You Can* (with Marshall Karp) • *Toys* (with Neil McMahon) • *Don't Blink* (with Howard Roughan) • *The Postcard Killers* (with Liza Marklund) • *The Murder of King Tut* (with Martin Dugard) • *Against Medical Advice* (with Hal Friedman) • *Sundays at Tiffany's* (with Gabrielle Charbonnet) • *You've Been Warned* (with Howard Roughan) • *The Quickie* (with Michael Ledwidge) • *Judge & Jury* (with Andrew Gross) • *Sam's Letters to Jennifer* • *The Lake House* • *The Jester* (with Andrew Gross) • *Suzanne's Diary for Nicholas* • *Cradle and All* • *When the Wind Blows* • *Miracle on the 17th Green* (with

Peter de Jonge) • *Hide & Seek* •
The Midnight Club • *Black Friday*
(originally published as *Black Market*) •
See How They Run • *Season of the Machete* •
The Thomas Berryman Number

FOR READERS OF ALL AGES

Maximum Ride
*Nevermore: The Final Maximum Ride
Adventure* • *Angel: A Maximum Ride Novel*
• *Fang: A Maximum Ride Novel* • *Max: A
Maximum Ride Novel* • *The Final Warning:
A Maximum Ride Novel* • *Saving the World
and Other Extreme Sports: A Maximum
Ride Novel* • *School's Out—Forever: A
Maximum Ride Novel* • *The Angel
Experiment: A Maximum Ride Novel*

Daniel X
Daniel X: Armageddon (with Chris
Grabenstein) • *Daniel X: Game Over* (with
Ned Rust) • *Daniel X: Demons and Druids*

(with Adam Sadler) • *Daniel X: Watch the Skies* (with Ned Rust) • *The Dangerous Days of Daniel X* (with Michael Ledwidge)

Witch & Wizard

Witch & Wizard: The Lost (with Jill Dembowski) • *Witch & Wizard: The Kiss* (with Jill Dembowski) • *Witch & Wizard: The Fire* (with Jill Dembowski) • *Witch & Wizard: The Gift* (with Ned Rust) • *Witch & Wizard* (with Gabrielle Charbonnet)

Middle School

Middle School: Save Rafe! (with Chris Tebbetts, illustrated by Laura Park) • *Middle School: Ultimate Showdown* (with Julia Bergen, illustrated by Alec Longstreth) • *Middle School: How I Survived Bullies, Broccoli, and Snake Hill* (with Chris Tebbetts, illustrated by Laura Park) • *Middle School: My Brother Is a Big, Fat Liar* (with Lisa Papademetriou, illustrated by Neil Swaab) • *Middle School:*

Get Me Out of Here! (with Chris Tebbetts, illustrated by Laura Park) • *Middle School, The Worst Years of My Life* (with Chris Tebbetts, illustrated by Laura Park)

Confessions
Confessions: The Paris Mysteries (with Maxine Paetro) • *Confessions: The Private School Murders* (with Maxine Paetro) • *Confessions of a Murder Suspect* (with Maxine Paetro)

I Funny
I Totally Funniest: A Middle School Story (with Chris Grabenstein, illustrated by Laura Park) • *I Even Funnier: A Middle School Story* (with Chris Grabenstein, illustrated by Laura Park) • *I Funny: A Middle School Story* (with Chris Grabenstein, illustrated by Laura Park)

Treasure Hunters
Treasure Hunters: Danger Down the Nile
(with Chris Grabenstein, illustrated by
Juliana Neufeld) • *Treasure Hunters* (with
Chris Grabenstein, illustrated by Juliana
Neufeld)

Other Books for Readers of All Ages
Public School Superhero (with Chris
Tebbetts, illustrated by Cory Thomas) •
House of Robots (with Chris Grabenstein,
illustrated by Juliana Neufeld) •
Homeroom Diaries (with Lisa
Papademetriou, illustrated by Keino) •
Med Head (with Hal Friedman) • *santaKid*
(illustrated by Michael Garland)

For previews and information about the
author, visit JamesPatterson.com or find
him on Facebook or at your app store.

WEATHER

Also by Lee Bennett Hopkins

I Can Read Books®

Surprises

More Surprises

Questions

Picture Books

Best Friends

By Myself

Good Books, Good Times!

Morning, Noon and Nighttime, Too

The Sky Is Full of Song

Books for Middle Grades

Mama and Her Boys

Click, Rumble, Roar

Professional Reading

Pass the Poetry, Please!

Let Them Be Themselves

WEATHER

Poems selected by

Lee Bennett Hopkins

Pictures by Melanie Hall

HarperCollins*Publishers*

WEATHER
Text copyright © 1994 by Lee Bennett Hopkins
Illustrations copyright © 1994 by Melanie Hall
Printed in the U.S.A. All rights reserved.

Library of Congress Cataloging-in-Publication Data
Hopkins, Lee Bennett.
    Weather / poems selected by Lee Bennett Hopkins ; pictures by
Melanie Hall.
        p.   cm. — (An I can read book)
    Summary: A collection of poems describing various weather
conditions, by authors such as Christina G. Rossetti, Myra Cohn
Livingston, and Aileen Fisher.
    ISBN 0-06-021463-5. — ISBN 0-06-021462-7 (lib. bdg.)
    1. Weather—Juvenile poetry.   2. Children's poetry, American.
3. Children's poetry, English.   [1. Weather—Poetry.
2. American poetry—Collections.   3. English poetry—Collections.]
I. Hall, Melanie, ill.   II. Title.   III. Series.
PS595.W38H66   1994   92-14913
811.008'036—dc20   CIP
                                                                      AC

2   3   4   5   6   7   8   9   10 ❖

To my great-niece
ToniLynn Christine Yavorski
In all kinds of weather!

LBH

To my teacher
Fred Brenner
with great affection

MWH

ACKNOWLEDGMENTS

Every effort has been made to trace the ownership of all copyrighted material and to secure the necessary permissions to reprint these selections. In the event of any question arising as to the use of any material, the editor and the publisher, while expressing regret for any inadvertent error, will be happy to make the necessary correction in future printings.

Thanks are due to the following for permission to reprint the copyrighted materials listed below:

Curtis Brown, Ltd., for "A Week of Weather" by Lee Bennett Hopkins. Copyright © 1974 by Lee Bennett Hopkins; "Thunder" by Lee Bennett Hopkins. Copyright © 1994 by Lee Bennett Hopkins. Used by permission of Curtis Brown, Ltd.

Farrar, Straus & Giroux, Inc., for "Sun" from *Small Poems* by Valerie Worth. Copyright © 1972 by Valerie Worth. Reprinted by permission of Farrar, Straus & Giroux, Inc.

Lillian M. Fisher for "Weather Together." Used by permission of the author, who controls all rights.

Isabel Joshlin Glaser for "On A Summer Day." Used by permission of the author, who controls all rights.

Harcourt Brace Jovanovich, Inc., for "Fog" from *Chicago Poems* by Carl Sandburg, copyright 1916 by Holt, Rinehart and Wintson, Inc., and renewed 1944 by Carl Sandburg; "Grayness" from *Everything Glistens and Everything Sings* by Charlotte Zolotow. Copyright © 1987 by Charlotte Zolotow. Both reprinted by permission of Harcourt Brace Jovanovich, Inc.

HarperCollins Publishers for "Looking Out the Window" from *Out in the Dark and Daylight* by Aileen Fisher. Copyright © 1980 by Aileen Fisher; "Icicles" from *Cold Stars and Fireflies: Poems of the Four Seasons* by Barbara Juster Esbensen. Copyright © 1984 by Barbara Juster Esbensen. Both reprinted by permission of HarperCollins Publishers.

Margaret Hillert for "Listen." Used by permission of the author, who controls all rights.

SUN

NO~SWEATER SUN

by Beverly McLoughland

Your arms feel new as growing grass

The first No-Sweater sun,

Your legs feel light as rising air

You *have* to run—

And turn a thousand cartwheels round

And sing—

So dizzy with the giddy sun

Of spring.

THE SUN

by Sandra Liatsos

Someone tossed a pancake,

A buttery, buttery pancake.

Someone tossed a pancake

And flipped it up so high,

That now I see the pancake,

The buttery, buttery pancake,

Now I see that pancake

Stuck against the sky.

MISTER SUN

by J. Patrick Lewis

Mister Sun

　　Wakes up at dawn,

Puts his golden

　　Slippers on,

Climbs the summer

　　Sky at noon,

Trading places

　　With the moon.

Mister Sun
  Runs away
With the blue tag
  End of day,
Switching off the
  Globe lamplight,
Pulling down the
  Shades of night.

13

ON A SUMMER DAY

by Isabel Joshlin Glaser

Noon's lion-faced sun

shakes out

its orangy mane.

Its tongue

scorches

leaves.

Even the bugs

want

rain.

SUN

by Valerie Worth

The sun

Is a leaping fire

Too hot

To go near,

16

But it will still

Lie down

In warm yellow squares

On the floor

Like a flat

Quilt, where

The cat can curl

And purr.

17

AUGUST

by Sandra Liatsos

The desert sun of August

Is shimmering my street

And turning houses into dunes

That glitter in the heat.

One tree is my oasis.

I need the ice cream man!

His truck comes just as slowly

As a camel caravan.

WIND AND CLOUDS

GO WIND

by Lilian Moore

Go wind, blow

Push wind, swoosh.

Shake things

take things

make things

fly.

Ring things

swing things

fling things

high.

Go wind, blow

Push things

wheee.

No, wind, no.

Not me—

not *me.*

21

CLOUDS

by Christina G. Rossetti

White sheep, white sheep,

On a blue hill,

When the wind stops

You all stand still.

When the wind blows

You walk away slow.

White sheep, white sheep,

Where do you go?

FOR KEEPS

by Jean Conder Soule

We had a tug of war today

Old March Wind and I.

He tried to steal my new red kite

That Daddy helped me fly.

He huffed and puffed.

I pulled so hard

And held that string so tight

Old March Wind gave up at last

And let me keep my kite.

THE MARCH WIND

by Anonymous

I come to work as well as play;

I'll tell you what I do;

I whistle all the livelong day,

"Woo-oo-oo-oo! Woo-oo!"

I toss the branches up and down

   And shake them to and fro;

I whirl the leaves in flocks of brown

   And send them high and low.

I strew the twigs upon the ground;

   The frozen earth I sweep;

I blow the children round and round

   And wake the flowers from sleep.

SPILL

by Judith Thurman

the wind scatters

a flock of sparrows—

a handful of small change

spilled suddenly

from the cloud's pocket.

RAIN AND FOG

TO WALK IN WARM RAIN

by David McCord

To walk in warm rain

 And get wetter and wetter!

To do it again—

To walk in warm rain

 Till you drip like a drain.

To walk in warm rain

 And get wetter and wetter.

GRAYNESS

by Charlotte Zolotow

Fog on the river

fog in the trees

gray mist moving

the golden leaves.

Willow bending,

dancelike,

long arms trailing

trancelike.

Gray morning

gray light

gray mist

gray night.

from

INSIDE TURTLE'S SHELL

by Joanne Ryder

Rain

bends

the tall grass

making

bridges

for ant.

34

RAIN

by Myra Cohn Livingston

Summer rain
is soft and cool,
so I go barefoot
in a pool.

But winter rain
is cold, and pours,
so I must watch it
from indoors.

THUNDER

by Lee Bennett Hopkins

Crashing

     and

Cracking—

Racing

     and

Roaring—

36

It
whips
through
a cloud.

Why
must
thunder
come
rumbling
this
      LOUD?

37

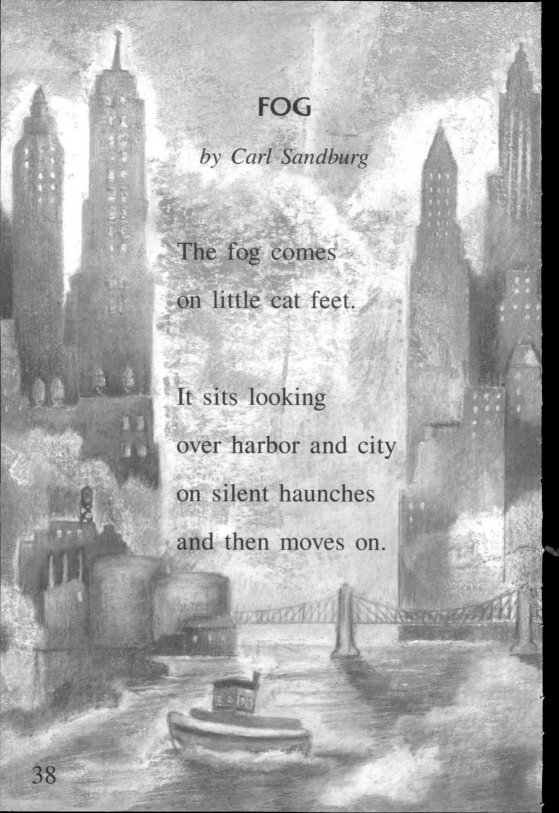

FOG

by Carl Sandburg

The fog comes

on little cat feet.

It sits looking

over harbor and city

on silent haunches

and then moves on.

38

SNOW AND ICE

LISTEN

by Margaret Hillert

Scrunch, scrunch, scrunch.

Crunch, crunch, crunch.

Frozen snow and brittle ice

Make a winter sound that's nice

Underneath my stamping feet

And the cars along the street.

Scrunch, scrunch, scrunch.

Crunch, crunch, crunch.

ICICLES

by Barbara Juster Esbensen

Have you tasted icicles

fresh from the edge

of the roof?

Have you let the sharp ice

melt

in your mouth

like cold swords?

The sun plays them
like a glass
xylophone   a crystal
harp.

All day they fall
chiming
into the pockmarked
snow.

LYING ON THINGS

by Dennis Lee

After it snows

I go and lie on things.

I lie on my back

And make snow-angel wings.

I lie on my front

And powder-puff my nose.

I *always* lie on things

Right after it snows.

SNOWFLAKE SOUFFLÉ

by X. J. Kennedy

Snowflake soufflé

Snowflake soufflé

Makes a lip-smacking lunch

On an ice-cold day!

You take seven snowflakes,

You break seven eggs,

And you stir it seven times

With your two hind legs.

Bake it in an igloo,

Throw it on a plate,

And slice off a slice

With a rusty ice-skate.

47

WINTER MORNING

by Ogden Nash

Winter is the king of showmen,

Turning tree stumps into snow men

And houses into birthday cakes

And spreading sugar over lakes.

Smooth and clean and frosty white

The world looks good enough to bite.

That's the season to be young,

Catching snowflakes on your tongue.

Snow is snowy when it's snowing,

I'm sorry it's slushy when it's going.

WINTER SWEETNESS

by Langston Hughes

This little house is sugar.

Its roof with snow is piled,

And from its tiny window

Peeps a maple-sugar child.

WEATHER TOGETHER

A WEEK OF WEATHER

by Lee Bennett Hopkins

Monday/Muggy-day

Tuesday/Tornado-day

Wednesday/Windy-day

Thursday/Thunder-day

Friday/Foggy-day

Saturday/Soggy-day

Sunday

    At last!

SUN

    day.

RAIN SONG

by Leland B. Jacobs

Spring rain is pink rain,

   For petals sweet and fair,

Summer rain is rainbow rain,

   With colors everywhere.

The rain of fall is brown rain,

   With leaves that whirl and blow,

And winter rain is white rain,

   But we call it snow.

LOOKING OUT THE WINDOW

by Aileen Fisher

I like it when it shines

on the oaks and pines.

I like it when it snows

and a white wind blows.

I like it when it tinkles

with sprinkles of rain

that crinkle the face

of the windowpane.

UNDERSTANDING

by Myra Cohn Livingston

Sun

and rain

and wind

and storms

and thunder go together.

There has to be a little bit of each

to make the weather.

WEATHER

by Anonymous

Whether the weather be fine,

Or whether the weather be not,

Whether the weather be cold,

Or whether the weather be hot,

We'll weather the weather

Whatever the weather

Whether we like it or not.

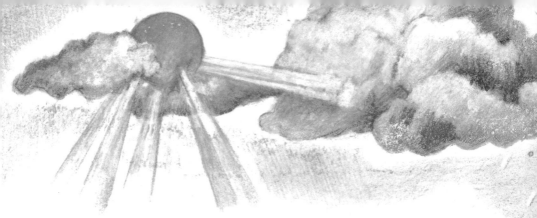

WEATHER TOGETHER

by *Lillian M. Fisher*

There are holes in the clouds

   where the sun peeks through,

Patches of sky,

   scraps of blue.

It's raining rain

   and bits of ice

Bounce down like

   tiny grains of rice.

This weather together

changes by the minute

And I can hardly wait

to walk out in it!

INDEX OF AUTHORS AND TITLES

Those Who Trespass

Those Who Trespass

A Novel of Murder and Television

BILL O'REILLY

bancroft
press

BALTIMORE, MARYLAND

Published by Bancroft Press
P.O. Box 65360, Baltimore, MD 21209
(800) 637-7377
www.bancroftpress.com

Library of Congress Catalog Card Number 97-77343
ISBN 0-9631246-8-4
Printed in the United States of America

First Edition

1 3 5 7 9 10 8 6 4 2

Distributed to the trade by National Book Network, Lanham, MD

This book is dedicated to the women in my life:
Maureen, Mom, Makeda, and Janet.

*"Anger is brief madness and,
unchecked, becomes protracted madness,
bringing shame and even death."*

Petrarch

CHAPTER ONE

MARTHA'S VINEYARD
SEPTEMBER, 1994

As Ron Costello saw it, the night-time media party in Edgartown provided him a wide-open window of opportunity—one he could make the most of. For he was frustrated and fed up, and what he badly needed was to satisfy a basic human need, the need for some kind of physical release. Chasing the Clintons around the resort island of Martha's Vineyard, looking on as a cracker First Family acted out its vacation in front of millions, was not just tiring for him, but unnecessary. When a family—even the First Family— went golfing, boating, and horseback riding, it was hardly newsworthy. And Costello was, after all, the chief White House correspondent for the powerful Global News Network, not some travel narrator, for Christ's sake. But here he was, on a GNN assignment he hated, reporting on President Clinton and family eating barbecue.

The jazzy voice of the singer Sade wafted through the humid night air, and Ron Costello pursed his thin lips and sized up the situation. Already in his sights was a pretty camerawoman light-headed from too much vodka. Costello felt he had a real chance with this young woman, who was now walking toward the makeshift bar located in the corner of the front porch. Surely this babe was impressed with his résumé. He had been a correspondent with GNN for twenty-six years. The power and prestige of his job brought him big-time perks, like the attention of young women eager to advance in the arbitrary world of television news. That Costello's wife and kids usually stayed in D.C. during his presidential travels heightened his risk-reward ratio considerably.

Perhaps fifty people attended the party, which was being tossed in an old Colonial home overlooking Edgartown harbor. GNN had rented the house for the summer and it was the perfect executive retreat. For thirty years, Martha's Vineyard had attracted rich and powerful media personalities. Walter Cronkite owned a multi-million dollar home on the outskirts of Edgartown. Mike Wallace had a summer house on the island, as did Katharine Graham of the *Washington Post*.

Scores of lesser known writers and television reporters also owned small beach houses, usually on the Vineyard's south side. It was considered a prestigious place to be, and to many in the media, prestige was an intoxicant more powerful than opium.

Ron Costello himself suffered the prestige addiction, but his judgment was not entirely clouded by it. With his extended belly and thinning hair, he knew he was no Tom Cruise, and therefore no threat to GNN anchorman Lyle Fleming, a man who held serious power. Costello got plenty of coveted air time on GNN's daily broadcast of "The News Tonight," chiefly because he was competent and bland—a perfect journalistic soldier who did exactly as he was told, and kissed the butts of the executives who did the telling.

All of that made Ron Costello an angry, bitter man. Despite his obvious limitations, he thought he deserved to be in the first echelon of broadcasting stars. He wanted a lead role, more fame and, especially, more power. Because he had not achieved any of those three ambitions, Costello vented his frustrations upon the rank and file below him at the network. That they universally loathed him bothered Costello not at all. In fact, he never even thought about it. His energy was directed toward getting as much as he could of what he wanted. And tonight he wanted this freelance GNN camerawoman named Suzanne. He wanted her in a big way.

So he turned his gaze toward Suzanne, who was slowly meandering back toward him, her hips discreetly swaying. His intense sexual hunger was apparent to anyone who bothered to notice. And someone *was* noticing. From the shadows across the street, a man dressed in dark clothes stood perfectly still. Had he entered the party, many would have known him. But he did not want to be recognized. The man staring at Costello wanted complete anonymity.

The ferry from Woods Hole, on Cape Cod, had carried this observer to Vineyard Haven just three hours prior. He checked into a small bed and breakfast house a few yards from the ferry terminal and, soon after, took a cab to the media center, located in an elementary school just outside of Edgartown.

Telling the cabby to wait, the man circled the media center while staying close to the wall. He wanted no one to see him. Then he was handed his first stroke of luck. On the door outside the center, a posted sign told of that evening's party in Edgartown. Knowing how Ron Costello operated away from home, he suspected Costello would be there.

The man now lurking in the shadows was about to do something he had never done before. It had taken him more than a year to decide to act. But, now, he was both determined and apprehensive.

Costello himself had no idea he was being stalked. The thought would never have occurred to him. He knew he had enemies, but he lived in a world of rules and entitlement. He was protected by law and position. Never in his life had he personally felt the horror of violent crime.

The man in the shadows watched patiently as Costello began speaking to a well built brunette. Though much too far away to hear the conversation, he sensed what was going on.

"Let's get out of here. I have some really good weed back at the hotel."

"Ron, you know I don't smoke. Besides, what would your wife say?"

"We're separated."

"Bullshit, Ron."

"She's in D.C. and I'm here. That's separated, Suzanne."

The young woman silently sighed, her brown eyes darting to the floor. She wanted no part of the disagreeable Ron Costello. Her friends at GNN had warned her about the lecherous correspondent. His wire-like lips gave him a perpetually cruel expression. And that belly hanging over his belt! No way she was buying into this. Lyle Fleming—that might be another matter.

Costello, armed with a predator's instinct, sensed it wasn't going well. So he did what he usually did when gratification eluded him—he got unpleasant.

"Listen, luv, I'm giving you a great opportunity here. You could be back in New York doing ambush interviews for the tabloid shows. Instead, you're on this beautiful island with the First Family. But that could end very fast."

"Are you threatening me, Ron?" the woman asked, suddenly a bit more sober.

"Not at all—just reminding you of your good fortune."

"Excuse me, Ron." And with that Costello's fantasy girl for the evening walked away for good.

Ron Costello's posture now changed considerably. As the brunette briskly left the front porch and headed inside the house, his shoulders slumped and he grew agitated. For his stalker, this was good. The bastard would be preoccupied.

Costello's night was ruined, and he was royally pissed off. 'Goddamn bitch. She'll be sorry. Goddamn Clinton and his stupid family. What the fuck am I doing here?' With those black thoughts ricocheting around his brain, Costello drained his beer, said a few insincere goodbyes, and headed for his hotel. From a safe distance, the man watching Costello followed.

He knew exactly where the correspondent was going. For years, the stalker had been coming to the Vineyard. He could thoroughly describe the island—from the wilds of Chappaquiddick, where Edward Kennedy had abandoned a trapped and struggling Mary Jo Kopechne in a car filling with sea water, to the stately homes of Chilmark, the chic area where the self-destructive John Belushi was buried. The stalker knew that Ron Costello was heading back to his suite at the Whaler's Inn, where most of the network correspondents stayed while on assignment.

The streets of Edgartown were done up in the colonial style. White-shingled homes lined both sides of the main avenue, many adorned with lanterns and elaborate gables. Picket fences surrounded some of the larger homes, giving the small town the traditional New England look that tourists love. Although a chill was rolling in from the sea, it was an easy, comfortable stroll following Ron Costello as he wove his way toward the hotel.

All the rooms at "the Whaler," as it was known, could be reached from outside terraces overlooking Edgartown Harbor. As Costello climbed the stairs to his room, the man below slowly removed a pair of surgeon's gloves from the pocket of his denim jacket and put them on. He then took a long-stemmed spoon from his back pants pocket, checking it closely. The spoon was stainless steel, the kind used for stirring drinks in tall glasses. The stem of the spoon was exactly eight inches long. The man put it back in his pocket.

In the last moments of his life, Ron Costello did the following: flicked on the TV, stripped off his clothes, urinated, and donned a bathrobe with a blue crest on the chest pocket. Then he heard the knock.

'What the fuck?' Costello thought. 'It's almost midnight.'

"Mr. Costello, this is the night manager. We have a hand-delivered message from a young woman for you. I thought it might be important."

Ron Costello's eyes lit up. 'Maybe the little bitch has come to her senses.'

Costello opened the door and immediately felt excruciating pain. Something hit him in the chest, taking his breath away. As he doubled over, he felt a blunt object smash into his nose, breaking it. Stunned by what turned out to be a blow from his assailant's knee, Costello hit the floor, bleeding profusely.

The assailant quietly closed the door and stood over the prone correspondent. As with most assault victims, Costello was completely disoriented and terribly afraid. Everything had happened so fast. The correspondent was having so much trouble breathing he couldn't have screamed if his life depended on it. And it did.

The man knelt beside Costello, careful not to get any blood on his clothing. He was outwardly calm, but inside he was raging. He hated Costello. Hated him beyond words, beyond reason.

"Look at me, Costello. Do you know me?"

The struggling correspondent looked up, trying to focus his eyes. Because breathing through his broken nose was now impossible, he gasped for air through his mouth.

"You do know me. For a lot of years, remember?"

A glint of recognition shone in Costello's eyes, but he still wasn't sure who his attacker was. His hearing was intact, but his broken and swelling nose blurred his vision.

"No network can help you now," he heard a deep, soft voice say. "Nobody can help you, Costello. You are an evil person. You hurt and use people. And now you are going to leave us in a rather painful way."

Costello knew he was in mortal danger, but he wouldn't accept the thought that he could lose his life. His mind struggled to find words that might save him. He believed someone would intervene. 'This is absurd,' he thought. 'This can't be happening.' He was Ron Costello, GNN's chief White House Correspondent. Costello tasted the salty flavor of blood running into his throat. He gagged, struggling to speak. Finally, the correspondent's last words on Earth left his mouth: "Why, why are you doing this to me?"

The intruder responded by savagely grabbing Ron Costello's windpipe with his left hand and squeezing hard. Costello gasped, his mouth opening wide, blood trickling down his chin. The assailant's right hand, now holding the oval base of the spoon, rocketed upward, jamming the stainless steel stem through the roof of Ron Costello's mouth. The soft tissue gave way quickly and the steel penetrated the correspondent's brain stem. Ron Costello was clinically dead in four seconds.

Finally came the response the White House correspondent had asked for: "For Argentina, that's why."

CHAPTER TWO

The policemen were clearly frightened. Their fascist powers were being brazenly challenged. Standing directly in front of the police were nearly ten thousand very angry Argentine citizens screaming curses and revolutionary slogans:

La Gente Unida Venceramos!
Muera la Junta!
Muera Galtieri!

GNN News Correspondent Shannon Michaels translated the chant and wrote it into his notebook: "The people, united, will never be defeated! Death to the Junta! Death to the dictator Galtieri!" Shannon and his video crew stood behind the police, five hundred strong crowded together in a massive show of force. Their assignment was to guard the presidential palace, called the Casa Rosada—the Pink House—and to protect President General Leopoldo Galtieri. But the crowd was getting more and more aggressive, pushing towards the large metal gate that provided access to the palatial grounds. Shannon saw that The Plaza de Mayo, the huge square in front of the Casa Rosada, was now filled to capacity. Something very ugly was going to happen, Shannon thought, and happen soon.

The sky was clear, but clouds were assembling in the west. Shannon ran his fingers through his thick mane of wavy brown hair. His teal blue eyes were locked on the agitated crowd. It was his eyes that most people noticed first—a very unusual color that some thought materialized from a contact lens case. But Shannon, the product of two Celtic parents, didn't go in for cosmetic enhancements. His 6'4 frame was well toned by constant athletics, and his pale white skin was flawless—another genetic gift. Shannon's looks, which he thoroughly capitalized on, made him a natural for television.

As the mob continued its boisterous serenade, Shannon slowly shook his head. Most wars were foolish, he thought, but this one was unusually idiotic. The Argentine Junta, a group of military thugs led by General Galtieri, had ordered an invasion of the British-administered Falkland Islands on April Fool's Day, 1982. The government claim was that the islands, which the Argentines called the Malvinas, became a part of Argentina through a Papal declaration in 1493. The British disagreed. So, nearly five hundred years after the grant of land, the Argentine Army swarmed ashore, startling eighteen hundred British subjects and tens of thousands of bewildered sheep.

A small British garrison of sixty defenders put up a spirited fight for three hours, killing seven Argentines and wounding fifteen others. But on April 2, 1982, the Argentine flag finally flew over the rocky, wind-whipped islands in the remote, freezing South Atlantic.

The islands, of course, were of importance only to the Junta. Things were not going well in Argentina. Inflation had destroyed the economy and the only way the military government could control the disenchanted population was to brutalize dissenters. Argentine citizens were routinely kidnapped and murdered by the Junta's German-trained secret police. So that no evidence could be found, some of the murdered bodies were tossed out of military planes flying over the Atlantic.

Argentine dissatisfaction with the government grew unabated, so Galtieri and his cutthroats needed a major nationalistic diversion—and preferably a big win—to bring the population to their side. They thought the invasion of the Falklands might provide it.

During his seven-year career as a TV news correspondent, Michaels had seen rank stupidity, but this moronic government strategy boggled the mind. Anyone who read a newspaper knew that the British Parliament, and especially Prime Minister Margaret Thatcher, would never allow British honor to be besmirched. It took the Brits just three months to thoroughly humiliate the Junta, further angering the Argentine citizenry. No wonder they were now filling the streets in passionate demonstration against the Galtieri government.

Two weeks after the Falklands War began, GNN ordered Shannon Michaels to fly from his base in Miami to Montevideo, Uruguay. It was in this South American port city, located where the Rio de la Plata meets the Atlantic Ocean just east of Argentina, that wounded British military were removed from transport ships and flown to London for treatment.

Shannon's orders from GNN were to hit the ground running.

• • •

The Pan Am Clipper from Miami landed in Montevideo early in the morning and, by noon, Shannon Michaels was standing on a cold, windy dock as wounded British sailors were carried off the transport ship "Herald" on stretchers. The casualties were from the British destroyer "Sheffield," which had been sunk by an Argentine Exocet missile. Shannon was not easily shaken, but his stomach became queasy on seeing two dozen badly burned sailors, some scorched from head to toe, whisked away in ambulances. Wrapped like mummies, only their eyes visible, many of the men would be grossly disfigured for life.

Shannon Michaels took a moment to pull himself together. He had witnessed death and destruction in El Salvador, but nothing like this. One Argentine high tech missile had destroyed an entire British ship, killing twenty and wounding hundreds. Shannon blew on his hands to warm them and then began writing in his notebook. His words emphasized the intensity of modern warfare. A few minutes later, he spotted a group of British officers walking down the plank of the ship. He signaled his cameraman and soundman, and the three met the officers on the dock below the ship. Shannon's best soundbite came from a British medic who had been aboard the "Sheffield."

"The lads never had a chance," said the medic in a quiet voice filled with emotion. "The bloody Exocet came in low in the dead of night. The explosion was deafening and sheets of flame flashed through a section of sleeping quarters. The lads were burnt within seconds, screaming with pain. I still hear those screams every night. I can't get 'em out of my mind."

Shannon asked a few more questions but knew he had what he needed for a first-rate report—one deserving a prominent position on GNN's "The News Tonight" with Lyle Fleming. He and his crew returned to the GNN office at the Excelsior Hotel, edited the video tape in just two hours, and sent the three-minute story by plane to Buenos Aires, where it would be fed back to GNN's headquarters in New York via satellite. Later that evening, Shannon and his crew went out to dinner to celebrate a job well done. A good story always overrode the tragedy that spurred it. Shannon hoped his friends in the states would see him on the air that night. But Shannon's story never made air.

Instead, GNN news managers in Argentina electronically took Shannon's voice off the video and inserted a voice-over done by Ron Costello. The veteran correspondent then did an on-camera stand-up in Buenos Aires that was edited onto the end of Shannon's battle casualty piece. Many of the words Costello used were the exact ones Shannon Michaels had written, but to GNN's worldwide audience, it looked as if Costello had written and reported the entire story himself.

The next morning, without any knowledge of what had happened, Shannon Michaels called a GNN producer in Los Angeles to get some feedback on his story. The producer, a friend of Shannon's, was confused. Ron Costello, he told him, had filed the story. What was Shannon talking about?

Fury gripped Shannon like a tourniquet. Costello wasn't even in Uruguay. What the hell was this about? In Montevideo, Shannon's GNN colleagues told Shannon to be cool, advising him not to bitch until he found out why his report had been co-opted. But Shannon's anger blocked out reason. His disposition turned chillingly quiet. Two days later, when street demonstrations erupted in Buenos Aires, he was summoned to Argentina.

During the Falklands War, GNN's headquarters was located inside the Buenos Aires Sheraton Hotel, where all the networks had offices. The competition was fierce. Each network tried to one-up the other, vying for exclusive combat footage, dramatic interviews, and the latest intelligence information.

The Sheraton was a typical rectangular high rise—no charm, but very functional. GNN had rented the entire fifteenth floor, installing editing facilities in some of the guest rooms, using others as offices and lounges. Technicians were constantly scurrying around, pushing hotel beds against walls and installing microphones, TV monitors, and recording equipment. Some rooms looked like giant spider webs, with mazes of wire running up and down walls and into closets. Bathtubs were often filled with videotapes, equipment boxes, and various war souvenirs such as flags and leather flight jackets. Telephone lines were patched in almost everywhere. The fifteenth floor of the Buenos Aires Sheraton looked like the Jersey Turnpike north of Newark.

Shannon Michaels was new to all this. He had joined the network just three months before the Falklands War broke out, having been hired by GNN after a successful six and a half year career in local television news, where he had piled up four Emmy Awards for excellence in reporting. He had already spent time at the GNN bureau in El Salvador, and felt confident he could handle the work in Argentina. But upon his arrival in Buenos Aires, he remained troubled by what he considered the theft of his work by Ron Costello, and the fraud he and the network had perpetrated on the viewing public.

"Michaels, good job in Uruguay," said GNN South American bureau chief Robert Solo as Shannon walked into his office, a large suite overlooking the hotel courtyard. "Welcome to B.A."

Shannon shook Solo's hand. The GNN administrator was about 5'8, and very thin, with a pallid face and blue veins crisscrossing his nose. 'A drinker,' Michaels thought. 'No question.'

"Bob, I need to talk with you about my casualty report," Shannon said, his face tense. "What happened?"

Solo knew immediately what Shannon Michaels was referring to. Network gossip travels fast, and word had gotten to him from Uruguay that Michaels was pissed off. "Shit, you know how New York is," Solo said with a casualness that rankled Shannon. "They wanted Costello on the air that night, so we decided to fold him into your package."

"But that," Shannon said slowly, "is plagiarism." He was angry but trying to remain in control.

Solo's eyes narrowed into a ferret-like squint. "That's network news, Michaels. We're all team players here, not glory boys. If New York wants Costello, we give them Costello. There will be other stories, Michaels. Let this one go."

Instinct told Michaels two things: that Solo was not a sympathetic audience, and that he should end the discussion. But his ego overrode his instinct. Shannon was used to having the final word. "Well, I think it's bullshit," he said with a harsh edge in his voice.

Solo shrugged and walked away, thinking Michaels might need to be taught a lesson someday.

Shannon, still quite upset, walked out of Solo's office and nearly tripped over a cable lying on the hallway floor. Cursing to himself, he rode the elevator down to the hotel lobby. The three small children in the elevator with him apparently sensed the anger in the air, backing away from the big, Anglo man, then practically sprinting out of the elevator as the door opened. Shannon quickly strode into the lobby and then into the hotel coffee shop off to the left. As Shannon walked in, he recognized a face from television sitting alone at a corner table. David Wayne was a long-time GNN correspondent. In his early forties, Wayne was a reliable reporter who backed up the featured players. Michaels introduced himself.

David Wayne stood up and shook Shannon's hand. His grip was one Shannon would remember. Wayne himself was over six feet tall and powerfully built. He had the physique of someone who trained seriously with weights.

"Have a seat, Michaels. First time in B.A.?"

"Yeah, I've been here about six hours and I've already been screwed." David Wayne did not respond. The older correspondent took a sip of coffee and measured Shannon Michaels. He saw a twenty-eight-year-old man with piercing blue eyes, a swagger, and a blunt manner. Immediately, David Wayne knew that Shannon Michaels would be in for it. His good looks made him a threat to other correspondents and his hard attitude would make assaults against him easy.

Wayne put down his coffee cup and said in a soft voice, "Getting screwed is part of network news, Michaels. You've got to do it their way. If you're not up for that, grab the first plane north."

Shannon sighed and looked at the older correspondent. He had heard the old "their way or the highway" line throughout his professional life. He hated it. For the moment, however, he needed information and David Wayne might be able to provide it. "So what's the landscape around here?" Shannon asked.

"B.A.," said Wayne, "is boring, Michaels. They destroyed most of the old, charming parts and built a modern city that looks like Paris without the attractions. Good leather, good steaks, some good-looking women, but they won't talk to you. People who live in B.A., the Portenos, are overwhelmingly anti-American because they think we're siding with the Brits. Oh, and one more thing—don't go out by yourself at night. Three days ago, the police picked up Doug Stein—you know, that New York local reporter, and took him for a ride. They roughed him up a bit and then stripped him naked and dumped him in the middle of a busy street. The message was, 'We don't like American reporters—they're not real men.'"

"Sounds ugly," Michaels said.

"It's just beginning. Word is the Brits have control of the islands, and the Junta will have to surrender pronto. Most of the Argentine pilots have been killed and those guys were the only ones fighting for the Junta anyway. Forget the army. They won't fight."

"So what happens when the Argentines pack it in?" Shannon's voice was eager. He felt like Wayne knew what he was talking about.

"My guess is that all hell will break loose here. The Argentines are a lot like the Chinese—they can't stand to lose face. And the people hate the government anyway. So the mob might try to remove the Junta by force, and the fighting could shift to here."

"Lots of action for us, then."

David Wayne, fidgeting with his coffee cup, watched Shannon Michaels size him up. Wayne was cautious, but sensed that Shannon resembled what he had been fifteen years before: a young journalist intent on telling good, truthful stories.

Wayne scratched the back of his dyed brown hair. His deeply set brown eyes wandered around the room while he calculated exactly how much information to give Shannon Michaels. It was a tough call, but he decided to take a chance. "Here's some advice, Michaels. Stay out of the line of fire. You can get killed on the streets here real easy. They gunned down Bill Stewart in Nicaragua for absolutely no reason. He was a veteran reporter for ABC. A lot of Latin soldiers and police despise reporters; to them, we're the enemy. And if you're ever confronted by idiots with guns, do not, I repeat do *not*, show any fear. South of the U.S. border, showing fear means you are not macho.

"If these thugs think you're afraid, they're more likely to shoot you —in their warped minds, you're someone worthy of respect. Somoza's thugs made Stewart go down on his knees. That, I believe, was his fatal mistake. As soon as he did that, he lost macho. It wasn't his fault, of course. Put a gun to my head and I'd drop down too. But he might have had a better chance if he had defied the order and kept his feet. Anyway, it's not worth taking any chances down here. Stay low and out of the way."

"But what about covering the action?" Shannon asked.

Once again David Wayne paused and pondered his response. Shannon returned his gaze, now noticing the well defined lines in the older correspondent's face. They were lines not only of fatigue, but also of frustration.

"Michaels, the action *will* get covered. And now I am going to tell you something important. But if you tell anyone what I am about to say, I will deny it, and I will come after you. Understand?"

Seeing the intense expression on David Wayne's face, Shannon nodded assent. Even though he had just met Wayne, he knew that this was not a man he wanted to cross.

"I saw the story you filed from Uruguay," Wayne said, "and it was damn good. But the bigfoot got you. Costello liked your report and stole it. This happens all the time. Some genius at GNN has decided that a few big-name correspondents should get all the important stories, whether they personally report them or not. The thinking is that the audience will remember these reporters and more readily identify with GNN. Fleming is going along with it because he wants the most recognizable reporters on the evening news. He thinks it makes the broadcast stronger."

Shannon Michaels sat enthralled hearing Wayne lay out the way things worked at GNN, but he was having trouble believing it all. He had never heard this stuff before.

"So what you've got here," continued Wayne, "is a caste system. And it doesn't matter if you develop a good story. There's a chance these bastards will order you to do the work, and then let Costello or some other fraud get the glory. This bullshit's called bigfooting and it's been around in various forms since Vietnam. I was over there and I saw a lot of reporters build up big reputations sitting around the bar at the Rex Hotel in Saigon.

"Other journalists risked their lives in the jungle and highlands, only to see these fucks take their video and voice it over. They would run over to Tan Son Nhut Airport and do a stand-up in front of a burned out tank or something. Back home, everybody thought they were the big, brave war correspondents. Total bullshit. Yeah, some gutsy people like Hillary Brown actually did the dirty work and got the praise they deserved. But there were a lot of frauds. So why take the chance, Michaels? Why get killed if you're just going to get stepped on by a bigfoot? Do your job, but don't do it too well. The system will fuck you in the end."

Shannon Michaels stared hard at David Wayne. He saw a very bitter man who, by the look of his red face, eased his frustration with the help of a filled glass. "How come you guys don't complain to the brass?"

Shannon asked. "Isn't there anyone at GNN who's appalled by this?"

"Apparently not," the older correspondent said. "Everybody knows what's going on. That fuck Costello stole my interview with Galtieri just last week. I spent a month wining and dining that idiot's PR people, went out with them three times a week and picked up the tab. Sat through the most incredibly boring conversations you have ever heard. Finally, they produce El Supremo, but just as I'm about to walk out of the hotel to do the interview, fucking Solo calls me back and tells me New York wants Costello to do the interview. They're all bastards, Michaels. Remember that and remember you didn't hear any of this from me."

"One more question, David," Shannon said. "You seem like a smart, honest guy. Why do you put up with this?"

"It's simple and it's pathetic," David Wayne answered. "Money and prestige. We're fucking GNN correspondents. We're paid six figures. We travel the world. We stay in fancy hotels and eat and drink on the company. We're big shots. The elite at the top of our field. Flash that gold-embossed GNN business card and watch the doors open."

David Wayne's face took on a look of sadness. "Where 'm I gonna go? Some local station in Houston? Covering fucking city council meetings? This is it, Michaels, the big time. Most of us struggled to get here and we know there are thousands who would take our place in a second. Yeah, it's not what everybody on the outside thinks it is, but what's the alternative?"

The older correspondent paused, drumming his fingers on the table. His face was pale, his worry lines now more noticeable—no amount of dye could cover them.

"GNN sells us prestige," Wayne continued, "and that's what we're buying. Love it or leave it. And believe me, few leave it willingly. We take the abuse and come back for more. As Cronkite used to say before they killed him off, 'That's the way it is.'" And with that, David Wayne got up, smiled cynically at Shannon, and walked away.

• • •

The call came early, about seven a.m. Shannon was already awake, but still in bed. He reached over groggily and picked up the hotel phone. "Michaels, this is Solo. The Argentines just surrendered. Get

17

down to the Casa Rosada as fast as you can. Francisco Alonzo will be your cameraman, Juan Lopez will do sound, and Carlos will be your driver. The van is out front."

Eight hours later, as Shannon Michaels stood behind the nervous Argentine palace guard, he wondered why he did not see David Wayne or Ron Costello or any of the other three GNN reporters assigned to Buenos Aires covering the action there in front of him—the thousands of people demonstrating against the government. Throughout the day, the crowd had been building and Shannon had interviewed a number of Argentines, all of whom had told him essentially the same thing: Argentina has been disgraced and the Junta must go.

Shortly after three in the afternoon, Michaels heard the sound of sirens coming from behind the presidential palace. The Casa Rosada was surrounded by a seven-foot-high iron fence anchored by two huge gates, one in the front of the building and one in the back. The protective police line was behind the fence, but now a dozen brown transport trucks escorted by police cars were roaring into the courtyard through the back gate. Immediately, soldiers began jumping from the trucks—combat-ready shock troops dressed in full battle gear and armed with machine guns.

The crowd's chanting got louder:

Nunca La Derrota! "Never surrender!"

The mob began pelting the troops and police with rocks and coins. To Michaels, it looked like a scene out of the middle ages: a castle under siege—the sky full of arrows raining down on the inhabitants.

And here in "Castle Buenos Aires," the "arrows" were finding their targets. Scores of soldiers and police were hit. Blood flowed down their faces. Tempers on both sides flared. Shannon knew he had to get away.

"Francisco," Michaels yelled to his cameraman, "take Juan and go to the left side of the palace. Remember, Carlos is waiting for us behind the palace in the van. If we get separated, meet me there at 6:30 sharp. We've got to make the 7:30 feed to New York."

Heeding their orders, cameraman Francisco Alonzo and soundman Juan Lopez took their gear and ran. Shannon followed closely behind, detailing the worsening confrontation in his notebook. His crew had already shot great video from the front lines. Now they would get another perspective by shooting from the side.

The afternoon sun was setting and the air was growing chilly—the cool Argentine winter was just beginning—but the crowd in front of the Palace continued to grow, both in number and in passion.

Hijos de putas! shouted the crowd, spitting obscenities at the soldiers. "Sons of bitches." The army was unrattled. Shields were being used to deflect the accompanying rocks and coins. But now, the agitators began throwing cans full of beer and soda, and bricks, and the military shields offered less than full protection. That did it for the troops.

Without warning, they began firing directly into the crowd. Shannon was stunned. Hundreds of people immediately fell onto the cement of the Plaza de Mayo.

Madre de Dios ayudanos! a woman screamed. "Mother of God help us!"

Shannon saw one man take a bullet squarely in the right eye. He was killed instantly. The mob panicked. Ten thousand tightly packed demonstrators were now desperately trying to get away from the gunfire any way they could.

Shannon and his crew held their ground, continuing to tape the scene from a side street. Francisco and Juan stood in the middle of the road, getting shots of the fleeing mob. As hundreds of Argentine citizens fell, the stampede intensified and hundreds of helpless people were trampled on the cobblestone road. One prone woman, who tried to get up, was knocked back down in a heap. She curled into a fetal position and vanished under a sea of legs.

Shannon was standing in a doorway scribbling notes when a pack of fleeing young men smashed into Francisco and Juan, knocking both men down. The camera bounced into the street, where it was kicked away and lost. Shannon, fighting his way through the panicked mob, ran to help his fallen colleagues. Francisco, the cameraman, was dazed from a kick in the head, and blood ran from his ear. Juan, the soundman, was shaken but okay. He had managed to right himself and to hang onto the tape deck and video tapes.

"Juan, get those tapes to the car. I'll take care of Francisco. Tell Carlos not to move till I get there."

"But what about the camera?"

"Fuck the camera, it's gone. Get moving," Shannon ordered.

"But that camera cost twenty-five thousand dollars. New York's gonna be pissed," the soundman screamed.

"Get the fuck out of here, Juan," Shannon screamed back, his voice hard, his look murderous. He then helped Francisco to his feet, all the while continuing to stare at Juan. The soundman finally got the message and moved out.

Francisco was in bad shape but could move his legs. Shannon half carried him off the street and over to a courtyard, away from the fleeing mob. Scores of people were still running by. Gunfire and screams filled the air. Michaels gently put the cameraman down and leaned him against a stone wall. For the first time, Shannon noticed how bad the bleeding really was. He knew he had to get Francisco to a doctor soon.

But movement of any kind would not be easy. The army had emerged from behind the palace gates and plunked itself down in the Plaza de Mayo. The crowd was in complete disarray. Scores of dead and wounded lay on the cold concrete. Soldiers were bending over, checking the casualties. Some of the troops were actually laughing. Shannon couldn't believe it.

Just as he began escorting Francisco to the GNN car, Shannon heard a sharp, metallic, clanking sound. He looked back and saw a canister of gas rolling in the street about twenty feet away. The mob was already completely routed, Shannon thought, so why were these idiots firing gas canisters? Shannon looked toward the Plaza and saw soldiers donning masks. Then came the familiar hissing sound. Shannon, gassed once while doing a story on Delta Force training, knew he had about thirty seconds to get away before the burn in his eyes would make it impossible to see.

He boosted Francisco up and the two lurched down the street toward the prearranged meeting place with Carlos, the driver. After walking about two hundred yards, Shannon suddenly heard a command in Spanish: "Halt."

Turning toward the commanding voice, Shannon saw an M-16 pointed directly at his head. The young soldier sighting him stood about ten yards away.

Periodista! Por Favor, no dispare! Shannon used the phrase that every Latin American correspondent was required to know: "Journalist. Please, don't shoot."

Shannon was frightened but looked directly into the soldier's face. He had the high cheekbones and dark brown eyes of an Indian. 'Probably a poor kid from the countryside,' Shannon thought.

The soldier stared back at him, then looked at Francisco. It was obvious to anyone that the Gringo was helping this man, this Latin man. The young soldier, his gun still raised, began to gently rock back and forth. Shannon didn't move. 'The guy is thinking things over,' he surmised.

Shannon continued to watch the soldier. He tried desperately to remain perfectly still but felt his legs shaking. 'Show no fear,' Shannon thought. 'Show no fear.' Finally, after what seemed like hours, but was really about twenty seconds, the soldier lowered his automatic weapon, and briskly walked past the correspondent and cameraman without even a glance.

Shannon Michaels felt a surge of relief, but also a strange sense of anger and humiliation. He had been powerless in front of that soldier— no longer in control of his own life. He even thought he might cry—something he never did—and maintained his composure only when he heard a deep moan from Francisco.

It took Shannon ten minutes more to get Francisco back to the car. Juan had made it back with the video tapes, and Carlos was already behind the wheel. Shannon quickly assessed the situation: it was five minutes before seven and the bureau was a ten-minute drive away. Shannon had been told that there was a doctor at the hotel, so Francisco could be treated right there—no need to divert to the hospital. Argentine time was one hour ahead of New York time, giving them a good shot at transmitting their video tape to New York just when the evening newscast was opening. For the first time all day, Shannon felt a bit of optimism.

As Shannon was about to get into the car, he heard a voice: "Excuse me, sir. I am a courier for GNN and Mr. Solo wants me to take your tape back to the bureau." The man spoke perfect unaccented English.

"That's okay," Shannon said, "we're going to the bureau. I'll run the tapes back."

The man smiled. He was small and well dressed in a dark suit and white starched shirt. "But Mr. Solo sent me, and if I don't bring back the tapes I will be fired."

"I'll cover for you," said Shannon, who now noticed a change in the man's facial expression. His smile went from good-natured to cruel with astonishing speed.

As the man reached into his suit jacket, Shannon's right fist swung forward, smashing into his jaw. It was pure instinct, pure adrenaline from the violence Shannon had just experienced. The man dropped to the ground, a handgun falling from his jacket. Secret police. Shannon wanted to kick the man as he lay there. He wanted to hurt him badly. He had been warned in Uruguay that Argentine security people tapped all hotel phones and watched the foreign press very closely. But Shannon controlled himself and resisted further violence.

As he jumped into the GNN van, Shannon yelled, *Carlos, vamonos! Apurate!* "Carlos, let's go! Hurry!" The driver sped down the Avenida San Martin, ignoring stop lights and dodging dazed pedestrians. The van made it to the hotel in eight minutes. Hotel personnel helped Francisco into the lobby while Shannon took the video tapes and raced toward the elevator. The feed point was on the top floor of the Sheraton and Shannon burst into the transmission room ten minutes before Lyle Fleming was to go on the air.

"Tell New York I've got four tapes of riot footage," Shannon breathlessly told a startled technician. "Incredible stuff. No time to edit. Lyle will have to voice-over the raw footage."

"He doesn't like to do that," the tech said.

"Any other suggestions?" Shannon asked sarcastically. "We've got a good chance of beating the competition if Lyle can voice-over the action as the video comes in."

Shannon Michaels was right. GNN led the broadcast with vivid scenes of the violence in Buenos Aires. Lyle Fleming explained to the audience that the dramatic video tape had just been shot, and the anchorman heightened the drama by telling GNN viewers that they were seeing the first pictures of the chaotic Argentine situation. As the video images rolled by on the TV screen, in all of their brutality, Fleming ad-libbed facts about the Falklands War and the Argentine surrender. With the help of some Associated Press wire copy placed in front of him, Fleming pulled off a compelling piece of broadcast journalism for which he would subsequently take an enormous amount of credit. None of the other networks had any video from Buenos Aires until twenty minutes later. It was a stunning victory for GNN.

Shannon Michaels, riding the elevator from the feed point down to the GNN Bureau on the fifteenth floor, was elated. He knew his work had given GNN a huge victory. Now he would finally get the recognition he deserved.

GNN producers, correspondents, and technicians, hyper from a mutual adrenaline rush, gathered around telephones listening to "The

News Tonight" broadcast live from New York. Everybody knew GNN had been first with the story. As Shannon Michaels entered the large suite, he expected his colleagues to greet him warmly. Instead, they completely ignored him. He couldn't believe it.

Sitting down at an empty desk, he turned his body outward toward those sitting nearby. Still no reaction. As he looked around the room, it became clear to him that something was up. And that something walked into the room about five seconds later.

"I need your tapes and notes, Michaels." The harsh voice belonged to Ron Costello, a man Shannon still had not met despite the previous bigfooting incident.

"Why? And nice to meet you, too, Ron," Shannon answered as he stood up. He had been back in the hotel for less than an hour, and his emotions were still raw from what he had experienced. He was in no mood to be treated disrespectfully.

"Why I need them is not your concern, Michaels. Just hand over the tapes and notebook."

Shannon Michaels was not ready for this confrontation. He was instantly annoyed at the unpleasant man now standing before him. Then, his annoyance quickly turned to intense anger. Nobody was going to take his story away from him this time. As the fleshy face of Ron Costello glared at him, Shannon broke eye contact and looked over at the group of GNN people who stood silently watching. He sensed the group was hoping something would happen. Then he turned back and softly said: "Fuck you, Costello."

"What? What did you say to me?" Costello's face dissolved into a grotesque mask of hate. He moved closer to Shannon, who could now smell his alcohol-tainted breath.

"Use your own notes," Shannon said, looking down into the man's pinched face, "and you can have the tapes after I screen them. Now get away from me."

"Is there a problem?" A secretary had alerted Robert Solo to the developing confrontation, and the bureau chief now walked quickly into the room from the adjacent suite which housed his office.

"Yeah, we got a big problem, Bob," said Costello, still staring up at Shannon. "This hot shot won't cooperate. I've got a piece to do on the riots for the special tonight, and he won't give me the tapes."

Shannon was stunned. 'What special? What's going on?' he

wondered to himself.

"Michaels, GNN is doing a half-hour special to compete with 'Nightline' about the situation here. Ron will be anchoring from B.A., Lyle Fleming will be in New York. So we need your notes and tapes to get Ron up to speed."

Shannon Michaels looked around. The crowd of GNN employees in the room had grown substantially. Like rubber-neckers at a bad accident, they were looking for blood. Shannon realized that he had no allies in the room, but it didn't stop him from exacerbating the situation.

"Well, if Ron had covered the story like he should have, he wouldn't need my tapes and notes, would he, Bob?" Shannon then took a step toward Costello. "Where were you anyway, Ron?"

"That's none of your fucking business..."

"Hold it, Ron." Robert Solo's authoritative tone silenced the snarling correspondent. Solo then turned slowly in Shannon's direction and calmly stated: "Listen, Michaels, we needed Ron here to handle the diplomatic end of the story. We were trying to get an interview with Galtieri and we couldn't have our top guy running around on the street if and when it came through."

Costello smirked at Michaels. Shannon's throat was suddenly dry. He swallowed and said: "Then let Ron do the diplomatic angle tonight and let me do the riot piece. I was there when it all went down, Bob. I was in the best position to report the story. I am the GNN correspondent who actually covered this thing, who almost got killed doing so. Doesn't that mean anything?"

"It means you don't know what the fuck you're doing, Michaels," said Ron Costello, his right index finger jabbing into Shannon's chest. The younger correspondent's left hand shot out and locked onto Costello's wrist. With his right hand, he bent Costello's hand sharply downward. The older man gave a cry of pain.

"You're fucking crazy," Costello screamed. "You're through in this company. I'll see that you never work again. Do you hear me, you fucking incompetent jackass?"

Shannon Michaels released Costello's hand and shoved him backwards, the whole day's emotions fueling his thrust. With a stunned look on his face, Ron Costello crashed into the wall, and slumped to the floor, his face drained of all color. No one said a word. Robert Solo looked at Shannon Michaels and shook his head. It was all over for Shannon. Everybody knew it. Shannon glared at the fallen Costello and walked quickly out of the room. He did not appear on the GNN special that night from Argentina. In fact, Shannon Michaels never appeared on any GNN broadcast again.

CHAPTER THREE

MARTHA'S VINEYARD
SEPTEMBER, 1994

His breathing labored, his mind trying to sort out his feelings, the assassin now stepped away from Ron Costello's corpse. He felt strangely detached from the grisly scene around him. Ron Costello's lifeless body looked to him like a painting to be curiously evaluated. He felt no remorse. He knew he was at war. People had hurt him badly, and one of them had just paid the price.

Still staring at Costello, whose eyes were opened wide, the killer listened for any sound. He heard none. He slowly walked around Costello's bloody body, looking for any potential clues he might have left behind. Finding nothing, he opened the door and put the "Do Not Disturb" sign on the outer handle. He then removed his surgeon's gloves and put them in his jacket pocket. It would be many hours before anyone missed Ron Costello. By that time, the assassin, having carried out his well-developed getaway plan, would be off the island.

Leaving the hotel quickly but inconspicuously, the assassin pulled his collar up, walked with his head down toward the Edgartown dock area, and caught a cab back to his small hotel in Vineyard Haven, which was about a fifteen-minute drive from Edgartown. It was approaching midnight and the bars were still hopping, music and laughter filling the air. As he walked, the killer heard one bar band playing an old song by the group Asia:

It was the heat of the moment,
telling me what my heart felt.
The heat of the moment, shone in your eyes.

The song had been popular in 1982. Ironically, it had been a big hit then in Argentina.

As he expected, a line of cabs flanked the docks. The killer approached one cab and, as he slipped into its back seat, he saw someone staring at him from the porch of the Barnacle Bar above him and to the right. A feeling of danger enveloped the assassin, but there was nothing he could do but look quickly away. The cabbie drove off.

A slightly tipsy woman watched as the taxi headed out of Edgartown. She knew that man's face, but what was his name? She shrugged, dismissing the question as unimportant, and headed back inside for another Sam Adams.

CHAPTER FOUR

MANHATTAN
SEPTEMBER, 1994

On the night Ron Costello was murdered, Detective First Class Tommy O'Malley was hard at work. The big policeman sat in a city-owned 1990 Buick LeSabre parked outside a dilapidated tenement building on 124th Street, just off Third Avenue. He and his partner, Jackson Davis, were hunting a career criminal named Edgar Melton, known on the street as "Robo." Associates had pinned the nickname on him because he did everything, including murder, like a robot—without emotion.

Both Tommy O'Malley and Jackson Davis hated this kind of stake-out. Robo was a true psycho—so extremely unpredictable that he'd have to be handled with maximum force and maximum caution. 'Civilians have no idea what the police have to face these days,' Tommy thought. An onslaught of babies born addicted to drugs, or severely abused as children, were now young adults, and many had absolutely no respect for life. They were true sociopaths. The Rodney King incident had put the police on the defensive, but there was a new saying going around the precinct houses: "Better to be tried by twelve than carried out by six." Cops knew that violence on the streets of America had never been more brutal, nor more unfathomable.

Trying to run down and apprehend dope dealers like "Robo" Melton was dangerous, time consuming, and a major pain in the ass, mostly because of their network of safe houses. As soon as a cop appeared on the street, some kid would sound the alarm and criminals like Robo Melton would disappear into the bowels of urban decay. Chasing punks over rooftops and through cruddy basements was not something Tommy O'Malley relished. That's why he had Jackson, who was quick and fearless.

Tommy and Jackson had been partners, or "married" in police parlance, for ten years. Both were members of the NYPD's elite Specialized Homicide Detective Squad, and their territory was Manhattan North, from 59th street to the Bronx. It was a huge beat that comprised some of the most crime-infested neighborhoods in the United States. O'Malley and Davis investigated scores of murders each year, clearing or solving about seventy-five percent of them—an efficiency rate ten percent above the department average.

As a cop, Tommy O'Malley knew he had at least one thing going for him. Though forty years old, he remained the favorite in just about any street fight he was forced to participate in. A long time ago, at Boston University, he had played halfback on the varsity football team, and his physical strength was still feared on the streets. With his reddish-brown hair, lopsided grin, and slight paunch, Tommy looked like a guy who would buy you a drink and solve your problems. Which was often true. But O'Malley was, by nature, an intense man, sometimes quick to anger. And he hated the fact that brazen young criminals controlled some of the city's poorest, most vulnerable neighborhoods.

These thugs killed with a casualness that O'Malley could not comprehend. They lived their lives deep in the recesses of evil: selling drugs to kids, prostituting their own sisters, gunning down trusted friends for money. He had seen all that and more. And he had also seen a criminal justice system that did not want to deal with the brutal reality of what was happening. On the ghetto streets where Tommy O'Malley spent a large part of his days and nights, the lives of American citizens were cheap, and America didn't seem to care. But Tommy and Jackson Davis did care, dealing with the situation in their own sometimes brutally efficient way.

• • •

As Tommy O'Malley impatiently sat in his unmarked police car, Edgar "Robo" Melton was partying a half block away. He felt he deserved an extended binge, and had enough crack to last him and his girlfriends the entire night. Robo used his "product" only occasionally, but tonight was special. He had two fifteen-year-old girls who would do anything for the drug, and he was determined to exploit the situation.

"Say, baby, put that pipe down and get my pipe up," Robo said to one of the girls. She was so intoxicated she had trouble standing, but Robo was her sugar daddy, and as he sat in a filthy, imitation leather couch, there in the living room of a run-down three-room apartment, she obediently performed oral sex on him.

Five feet away, the other teenage girl sat on a mattress on the floor and watched, greedily sucking on the crack pipe Robo had passed to her. Edgar looked over and grinned, showing yellow, decaying teeth. Obviously, he preferred oral sex to oral hygiene.

"You're next, girl, and I want you to do her too," he ordered.

As Robo took the crack pipe back, the teenager groggily nodded her consent. Inhaling deeply, Robo blew the cocaine smoke out through his nose and mouth. The bitter taste left him feeling powerful, energized, and free of worry. He was bad and he was flush.

Two weeks earlier, Robo caught up with a burnt-out thief named Ramone, to whom he had sold, "on credit," two thousand dollars worth of drugs. Ramone, an addict for a decade, was weak from shooting heroin, and in no condition to fight, when Robo and his two enforcers, Petey and Dread, dragged him to a tenement basement, tied him up, gagged him, and cut off his fingers one by one. Robo then shot Ramone in the back of the head. The next day Robo mailed individual fingers to ten other "customers" who owed him money.

Of course, word about Robo's brutal escapade got around quickly, and that's exactly what he wanted. Gave him a big rep in the hood. Made collections a lot easier. By the end of the week, he was considerably richer.

What Robo did not count on was Tommy O'Malley.

Robo had made the mistake of killing Ramone on O'Malley's turf. An informant told Tommy about the incident and identified the block where Robo lived, though not the exact address. So Tommy and Jackson were now stuck waiting for Robo to show his ugly face.

Tommy O'Malley knew he had no case against Robo Melton. No witnesses except for Robo's two henchmen, who would be dead within hours if they ever decided to testify. But Tommy also knew that he had to make life miserable for Edgar "Robo" Melton for having the gall to commit this vicious crime on O'Malley's beat. This was the power game that the police and the criminals played on the streets of New York.

"He's three buildings down," Jackson Davis said upon returning to the car, his blue windbreaker covered with dust. "Some little kid saw him go up the stairs about three hours ago with two young ladies. Looks like a party. Should we crash?"

"Nah, no warrant," Tommy said. "Makes life too hard. All that paperwork. Lawyers screaming. Let's wait a little while. The hump has to eat. I bet he ain't exactly Chef Boyardee in the kitchen. He'll go out for a pizza. Wait 'n see." O'Malley looked at Jackson, "Wanna bet on the time?"

"Ten bucks says it'll be one hour from now," Jackson Davis said.

"Thirty minutes—and whoever is closest wins," replied Tommy.

"Wait a minute, what if he calls for home delivery?" Jackson looked concerned. It was a put-on.

Tommy knew it but took the bait. "Yeah, right. And the Domino guy will drive right up here to Harlem and climb all those stairs to deliver the pie to Robo in less than thirty minutes. Can't you just see it? The only people who deliver in this neighborhood, Jack, are dope dealers and they don't take coupons. Jesus, Jackson, where d'you think you're at? Garden City?"

Jackson Davis laughed and the two men settled in to watch the street which was full of swirling litter but nearly empty of people. Dense inner-city neighborhoods are places where two men who look like cops are quickly identified (and avoided) by the populace. Tommy glanced in the rearview mirror. Across Third Avenue, looking sullenly at the car, was a group of young men standing around on the corner. 'Tough home boys. Could be street dealers. And we're bad for business,' Tommy thought. The business was drugs, prostitution, and illegal gambling.

According to the city Health Department, which had studied this section of East Harlem, nearly twenty percent of the residents were intravenous drug users. One out of every thirty-five adults had AIDS. Twenty percent of the buildings were abandoned. It was Third World poverty and desolation in the richest city on the planet.

Jackson Davis lit up a cigarette, one of ten he allowed himself each day. A neatly groomed man, he was just under six feet, with a slender build, closely cropped jet black hair, and an earring that Tommy ragged him about every day. But Tommy O'Malley loved Jackson; the bond between the two men was unspoken but unbreakable.

Jackson had been raised in a high-rise apartment project on the lower east side of Manhattan, a few miles south of where the two policemen currently sat. Originally, the projects had been designed as temporary way stations for minority families just starting out—low rent shelters to allow people to save money for homes of their own. But many of the projects had degenerated into moral sinkholes, filled with every human indignity imaginable. A few criminals had moved in, realized there was little supervision, and opened for business, selling dope, women, and gambling opportunities. And God help the tenant who complained. It wasn't long before the housing projects became combat zones.

Such living conditions may have turned some children into unfeeling predators, but Jackson Davis and his two little brothers still turned out to be solid citizens. Their mother ran off with a gambler and abandoned the family when the boys were very young. Jackson hadn't heard a word from his mother since he was ten years old, and he never talked about her. They were raised solely by their father and paternal grandmother

His father accepted the situation stoically, working as an usher in various sports arenas and stadiums around New York City. Lionel Davis' hours were long and irregular, so his three boys were often left pretty much on their own in the tough neighborhood. The up-side was they got to see a lot of ballgames on weekends. Jackson loved that, and loved his father immensely. Tommy O'Malley once asked Jackson why he and his brothers hadn't turned to crime or dope. Jackson just grinned and said the Davis brothers all had a strong prejudice against death, meaning their father would have killed them if they had headed in that direction.

Jackson Davis had to struggle for everything he'd ever gotten in this life, and, for that, Tommy respected him greatly. Growing up in Levittown, out on Long Island, might have been hard for Tommy, but compared to Jackson's upbringing, it was like a trip to Tahiti. Small three-bedroom house and one bathroom for five people. Lots of screaming and hitting by his frustrated father and his rambunctious brother and sister.

As they waited in the car for "Robo" Melton to appear, the police radio transmissions kept Tommy and Jackson amused. A nude man had been seen running down the middle of The Harlem River Drive and police units were responding. A screaming woman had to be removed from the Lexington Avenue multiplex by uniformed officers after she began caressing Mel Gibson's image on the big screen. The usual New York City craziness had momentarily taken Tommy's mind off Robo, but now he refocused.

According to his rap sheet, Robo was just twenty-three years old, but had been arrested fourteen times. Three convictions. One was for robbing a seventy-five-year-old widow and pushing her down a flight of stairs.

Despite a broken hip, the woman survived. But because she lived alone in a three-story walk-up, leaving her apartment to go to church— her only source of solace—became extremely difficult. Tommy and Jackson had visited the woman a couple of times, bringing her groceries and perfume. But Tommy knew her spirit had been crushed. No matter how hard he tried, he couldn't make her smile. She died six months after the mugging. "Natural causes," the doctor said. When the case finally came to trial, "Robo" was able to plea down to simple assault because the sole witness against him was dead. He served three months on Riker's Island. 'Three months for murder,' Tommy thought.

From that time on, O'Malley had Robo Melton on his radar screen. Tonight, he sensed something would happen. He wanted something to happen. Tommy wanted to hurt Robo Melton for crimes against humanity. Of course he could never say that aloud, but that's exactly how he felt. He was going to make Robo Melton pay for taking an elderly woman's life.

Up in his dirty apartment, Edgar "Robo" Melton was getting bored. A scrawny man, he had a badly trimmed black goatee that made him look as mean as he was. On his skinny left bicep was a tattoo that said "rock hard." His fingernails were clogged with dirt, and he used them often to scratch his light brown face, especially when he was high.

When the crack cocaine began to wear off, Robo began to feel the pangs of hunger. One of his female companions had passed out, and the other kept talking to herself about angels. He needed a break.

"I be back, girl, don't you go nowhere," he said. The intoxicated young girl on the mattress stared blankly at Robo, seemingly incapable of putting together a sentence.

In a semi-hazy frame of mind, Robo threw on his light green Philadelphia Eagles warmup jacket, failing to remember that he had secreted five white rocks in the side pocket. He then left the apartment in a hurry. When Robo had a need, he had to fulfill it immediately. His need now was to get food.

"Our man dead ahead," Jackson announced. "Damn, only forty-two minutes. You win."

"And Edgar loses," Tommy said as he watched Robo approach the

Buick.

Ordinarily, Robo Melton, out on the street in his own neighborhood, would have been alert to his many enemies. But on this night, Robo was feeling no pain. The feeling wouldn't last much longer.

As Robo walked near their car, Jackson Davis quickly threw open the heavy, passenger-side front door, slamming Robo into a backwards fall. Perfect timing.

Tommy O'Malley was out of the driver's side with surprising quickness for a forty-year-old. He grabbed the collar of Edgar's jacket and roughly pulled him to his feet.

"Edgar, how nice to see you again," Tommy said, his voice low and hard-edged. "Please put your hands on top of the car." Before Robo could comply, O'Malley savagely pushed him into the side of the Buick. The thug's eyes darted around wildly. He realized he was trapped.

With Robo's hands now on the roof of the car and his legs spread, Jackson Davis patted him down and quickly discovered the rock cocaine in his jacket pocket.

"Well, well, Edgar. What have we here?" Tommy was speaking directly into Robo's right ear, and could smell the man's unwashed body. "Looks to me like a controlled substance. Isn't that what this looks like, Jackson?"

"Definitely."

O'Malley yanked Robo's hands off the car and pulled them behind his back. Jackson snapped handcuffs on him.

For the first time, Edgar "Robo" Melton spoke to the policemen: "Fuck you, motherfuckers."

"Edgar, Edgar, Edgar. Those sentiments are so distasteful," Tommy said menacingly. He could feel the veins pulsating in his neck. He knew the man in front of him enjoyed hurting people. "You know, Edgar, I hear you have a thing for fingers."

"Motherfuckin' pig asshole," Robo Melton replied. And then the dope pusher made another of his many mistakes in life. He spat at Tommy O'Malley.

The white-gray phlegm caught Tommy on the shoulder of his blue blazer (on-duty homicide detectives were required to wear business clothes). He slowly turned his head, looking down at the insult. Jackson Davis glanced at Tommy, and gave him a knowing shrug. With that, Tommy O'Malley grabbed the cuffed man's right thumb, bending it

35

back hard. The snap was loud and clear. His scream pierced the night. Robo Melton's thumb was broken.

O'Malley watched as Robo's hand swelled up. 'That must really hurt,' he thought, giving in to a feeling of sadistic pleasure. The man's cries of anguish were beginning to attract attention from people living in the surrounding buildings, so Tommy and Jackson decided to leave the area and drive back to the station house. But before putting Robo in the unmarked car, Tommy O'Malley leaned over and whispered in the whimpering thug's ear, "How'd ya like that crack, Edgar?"

CHAPTER FIVE

The page one headline in the *New York Globe* was designed for maximum consumer impact: TV BIG MURDERED COVERING CLINTON. The article that followed was taken from an Associated Press wire report, and concentrated mainly on the mystery surrounding the death of Ron Costello.

The Massachusetts State Police, who were handling the investigation, weren't saying much. On an island that heavily depends on tourism, any crime is subject to damage control, and facts about Costello's murder were being kept very closely guarded by the authorities.

Sitting in her office along the east wall of the gigantic *New York Globe* newsroom, which was located in a newly built high-rise building on Manhattan's swanky upper east side, Ashley Van Buren read the AP dispatch for the fifth time. 'Something unusual was going on here,' she thought. 'Where is the information? Was this a robbery? How exactly did Costello get it? None of these questions was answered in the wire report. How strange.'

At age thirty-one, Ashley Van Buren was climbing quickly in the make-it-any-way-you-can world of newspaper reporting. After just four years on the street, she had been promoted from general assignment reporter to featured crime columnist. Her position gave her an office with a view, and caused much jealousy among some *Globe* reporters, who considered her too young to have such a prominent byline. But her "Crimetime" column was building up quite a following.

And, office politics being what they are, Ashley knew she had to do two things: watch her back *and* do extraordinary work. So, she spent sixty hours a week on the job. And she loved it. Everything moved very fast. Working for a newspaper had not been expected of her when she was sorting out possible jobs and careers after college. Her family thought that, after Ashley graduated from Vassar, she would go to law school or at least become a psychologist. Instead, she was running around a ruthless city writing about the dregs of the earth. And those were just the cops! The criminals were even worse.

Ashley Van Buren knew her good looks were partly responsible for her rapid rise. She had the face, though not the body, of a fashion model: a small, straight nose, vivid green eyes that were deeply pene-trating when offset by black mascara, and natural blonde hair that featured short bangs cascading onto her forehead. Just 5'2, she had a rather large bust that both helped and hurt her depending on the situ-ation. Ashley knew the newspaper could market her somewhat wholesome appearance. Her picture appeared atop her column, and the Globe's public relations people regularly trotted her out to the TV talk shows. In the brutally competitive media arena of New York City, she was becoming a star.

Opening her compact, Ashley checked her face for debris. It was a humid day and the air in the newsroom wasn't exactly imported from the Alps. Ashley cared about, but didn't obsess over, her looks. She did take good care of her fair skin, staying out of the sun and using mois-turizer every night. But that was about it. Not much makeup, never any provocative clothing except in private, and a shoulder-length hairstyle that was easy to dry and brush in the morning.

Right now, Ashley was cultivating a look of innocence. She consid-ered a non-threatening appearance an important psychological tool when trying to convince people to tell her things they didn't want to tell her. Last week she had even tied her hair in a short ponytail, some-thing she hadn't done since high school. She liked it, but the rest of the *Globe* newsroom started singing Olivia Newton John songs when she passed by, so that was the end of that.

As Ashley Van Buren watched a rusty barge float past the decaying docks of Long Island City, she decided to take on the Ron Costello story. TV guys don't usually wind up getting murdered and, even if it had just been a robbery gone bad, there might be some social implications here. If she got lucky, Ashley thought, there could be much more.

Placing the Costello wire story in the center of her desk, Ashley picked up her phone and speed-dialed one of the press flacks at the NYPD's public information office, located in lower Manhattan at One Police Plaza. After two rings, a man with a thick New York accent answered.

"Jerry? Ashley. How ya doin'?" To bond with the guy, Ashley

slurred her words in the New York tradition. "Didja read about this guy Costello? What happened?"

"How the hell should I know, Ashley? It went down in Massachusetts." Jerry sounded more impatient than usual, something of an accomplishment since his average concentration span hovered around ten seconds.

"Do you have any contacts up there?"

"No."

"You're a real Boy Scout today, Jerry, you know that? Helping a citizen in need and all."

"Listen, Ashley, we got five killins a day here. I got no time to think about some TV bigshot on a slab in Martha's Vineyard."

Ashley switched to a mock hysterical voice: "Jerry, help me! I'm a lady in distress. Jerry, Jerry..."

"OK, OK, geez." Jerry began to chuckle. 'The charm had worked again,' Ashley thought.

"Tommy O'Malley went to Boston U. He might know somebody up there. Go torture him. He deserves it."

"Thanks, Jerry, I owe you one."

"Ashley, you owe me a lot more than one."

Ashley Van Buren knew Detective Tommy O'Malley, but only slightly. He had a major two-pronged reputation: one, for clearing murder cases, and two, for being murder on newspaper reporters. Ashley had written a nice column on him about a year ago and the guy had never even called to thank her. She wasn't looking forward to asking him for a favor, but dialed the Manhattan North Homicide unit as quickly as she could. A secretary answered and transferred the call.

"Detective O'Malley?" Ashley used a deep, sexy tone.

"Speaking."

"This is Ashley Van Buren from the *Globe*. Do you remember me?"

"Certainly, Ms. Van Buren," O'Malley remembered her very well— about 5'2 and great looking. "What can I do for you?"

"My, aren't we a bit formal today, Detective," Ashley said in her teasing voice. "You can call me Ash."

"That's swell, Ms. Van Buren. Now if you don't mind a lot, whaddya want?

Ashley thought she heard O'Malley actually growl the word "swell."

"Well, Detective, I'm working on this Costello case. The TV guy who was murdered up on Martha's Vineyard while covering the president?"

"Yeah."

"And I was wondering if you have any contacts up in Massachusetts. We can't get any specifics from the state police."

"Let me get this straight," O'Malley said. "You want me to call the cops up there and get you a story about how this guy got whacked? Is that what you're asking me?"

"Uh, I guess so."

"Look Ms. Van Buren, I'm busy. I got guys shooting other guys here. I got paperwork. I got court appearances. I got an ex-wife calling me all the time asking for stuff, just like you're doin'. Give me a break."

"Detective, I will owe you a big favor. I will never forget this."

"Never forget *what*? I'm not doin' anything."

"Please, just get me some basic info. I'll take it from there. If you do this for me, I'll take you to dinner at Elaine's. That's where the Commissioner eats all the time."

O'Malley laughed sarcastically right into the receiver. "Oh boy, Elaine's, you promise?" He couldn't believe this woman.

"I do promise, Detective. Please help me out on this one."

Tommy O'Malley leaned back in his chair picturing this small, cute blonde and thought to himself, 'There are worse people to have dinner with.' He really didn't want to be bothered, but knew that having a newspaper columnist owing him a favor was a good thing.

"Okay, I'll make one call. Get back to me in two hours."

"Thank you, thank you..." said Ashley. After the first "thank you," Tommy O'Malley had hung up.

Precisely two hours later, Ashley Van Buren called the detective back.

"Well, somebody didn't like this Costello," Tommy began. "No robbery, no break-in. Somebody just walked into this guy's hotel room and shoved a stainless steel spoon into his brain."

"What?" Ashley was writing notes as fast as she could.

"Yeah, had to be a pretty strong guy. The cops on the Vineyard are under a lot of pressure. There's been only one murder on that island in the past twenty years. The Chamber of Commerce is panicked that this story will hurt tourism, so the lid is on tight. That's why no press conference or anything."

"Do they have a suspect?" Ashley asked.

"They have *nada*. They discovered the body eighteen hours after the hit. The room was clean. No prints, no nothing."

"But a spoon, what kind of spoon?" Ashley was almost breathless.

"A long-stemmed spoon, and get this, the perpetrator jammed it through the roof of the guy's mouth. Hell, that must have hurt."

"A silver spoon in his mouth," Ashley said thoughtfully. "Do you think that has some symbolism, Detective?"

"Yeah it does," Tommy O'Malley replied. "It symbolizes that the guy is dead."

CHAPTER SIX

Shannon Michaels put down the *New York Globe* and reached for the glass of freshly squeezed orange juice taking up space on his butcher-block kitchen table. Ashley Van Buren's column on the murder of Ron Costello had fascinated him. It was very well written and, to him, rang true, except for the part about Costello being "well respected and liked by his colleagues." Her story was the only one to provide details on the murder weapon. The other papers had zilch. Shannon was impressed. The woman was a good reporter.

In the hard news story next to Ashley's column, the *Globe* ran a GNN statement that it had no idea why anyone would want to hurt Costello or any of its newspeople. GNN speculated that the murder was the work of a deranged person, and that Costello had just been in the wrong place at the wrong time. The statement didn't surprise Shannon. If GNN had done the unthinkable—and told the truth—its spokesperson would have said that Costello was such a despicable character that suspects were legion. Shannon Michaels was sure he was not alone in his loathing for the late Ron Costello. His thoughts turned to David Wayne, who also truly despised Costello. Shannon wondered how Wayne was reacting to the news.

Shannon got up from the table and walked through a huge center hallway into his living room. Filled with excellent interior workmanship, his colonial-style house had been built in 1928, when the wealthy in Sands Point were making all kinds of money in the stock market. It had five large bedrooms, three baths, hardwood floors, and a brick fireplace in the living room and another one in the master bedroom. Shannon had looked specifically for a home with Old World charm and had found it, along with five acres of land, on the north shore of Long Island. And he could walk to the beach. His house was his sanctuary, a place of sanity in the midst of an insane career.

After being forced out of GNN in the early eighties, Shannon

Michaels had received a gift of good luck: A television station in New York City hired him as an anchorman because he came cheap and could write quickly and with considerable skill. That saved the station the salary of a newswriter. When Shannon arrived at Newscenter Six, the station was mired in fourth place in the news ratings. Three years later, the station's six o'clock broadcast was on top, and Shannon's down to earth, tough guy broadcast style was widely credited for the turnaround.

As the ratings for Newscenter Six grew, so did Shannon's salary. In 1990, he signed a contract that paid him more than one million dollars a year, so he could afford the $950,000 price tag on the house in Sands Point. Always good with money, Shannon invested wisely. He bought into the Hong Kong stock market early and made hundreds of thousands of dollars in 1992 when things were hot over there. When his career crashed a year later, Shannon had enough money to live well for a long time.

Shannon Michaels walked out his door and began his daily run. The Long Island Sound bordered the wealthy enclave of Sands Point on three sides. Shannon moved quickly down his long driveway to the street virtually unnoticed by neighbors or passersby. He had plenty of privacy; his house was hidden from the road, sheltered by an abundance of tall oak trees and surrounded by shrubbery.

As Shannon jogged on the beach, his thoughts drifted to the present. His television career lay in ruins, the victim of a classic setup and back stab by his nemesis at Newscenter Six, Lance Worthington. He should have seen it coming, but his termination had taken him by surprise.

That was a year ago, but Shannon's bitterness still tasted fresh. His dismissal from Newscenter Six was a terrible humiliation. It had shattered him emotionally when the newspapers ran major articles parroting the Newscenter Six line: "Shannon Michaels was losing popularity among younger viewers. He wasn't worth his million-dollar-plus salary in these days of economizing. He was also difficult to work with. An out of control ego. An anchor monster."

Everywhere Shannon went in the New York area, he was reminded of his ordeal. Because his TV anchoring had made him a famous face, many were aware of his dismissal. Some even walked up to him asking why he had been fired. New Yorkers are not shy about confronting the

famous. His firing was replayed over and over in daily social inter-
course. He could not leave his property without an unpleasant
intrusion by the public. On the verge of emotional collapse, Shannon
decided to get some help.

His therapy sessions turned into monologues with his hundred-
dollar-an-hour therapist. Shannon told her in great detail about the
events that led to his departure from Newscenter Six. She was the only
person on earth to whom he could unburden himself. One story, in particular, had the therapist scribbling notes as fast as she could.

In addition to being the main anchorman, Shannon also served as
story editor for the top-rated six o'clock broadcast. That meant that he
looked over and approved the words that he and other Newscenter Six
reporters would say on the newscast. One day, shortly after a new news
director, Lance Worthington, arrived from Dallas, Shannon walked into
the cluttered newsroom to check the story lineup for that evening's
broadcast. He noticed that two of the writers—men with too much
nervous energy from drinking gallons of coffee every day—were snick-
ering and looking in his direction. He soon saw why.

Shannon sat down in his black swivel chair and stared hard at his
computer screen, where Newscenter Six's evening lineup materialized.
Shannon's first perusal brought a deepening of the frown lines on his
forehead. Then his eyes shrank into a menacing squint. "What the hell
is this?" Shannon said, loud enough for most in the newsroom to hear.

"That's what *we'd* like to know," one of the writers answered.
"Lance put in the rundown today. Kessler is out sick." The writer was
referring to the regular six o'clock producer, Barry Kessler. "Are we really
going to lead with that animal story?"

"No, we're not," Shannon said harshly, and immediately bolted out
of his chair, heading for the news director's office.

The Newscenter Six newsroom, called "the floor" in news slang, was
a disgraceful dump. The lime green carpet was frayed and stained with
endless beverage drops. The tan walls were filthy, full of grimy fingerprints and handwritten signs advertising everything from studio
apartments to unwanted cats. Phones rang constantly. Many went
unanswered because management was constantly laying off secretaries.

Even though Newscenter Six made close to three million dollars a
year in profits from advertising, its parent company allocated little
money for the comfort of its employees. In one of their unending series

of cost cutting measures, corporate bean counters had reduced the newsroom cleaning service to thrice weekly. That decision led to an infestation of tiny, crawling insects, one of which Shannon had just crushed under his tasseled loafers while walking over to speak with Lance Worthington.

Through the walls of his glass-enclosed office, Lance Worthington saw Shannon Michaels coming. He despised the anchorman, whom he saw as a distinct threat to his power. He strongly suspected that an unpleasant confrontation was about to occur. Even though Worthington's phone call had just ended, he did not hang up. Instead, he listened to dial tone rather than appear available to talk with his agitated anchorman.

Shannon Michaels didn't bother to knock; he just walked into Lance Worthington's office and sat down in front of his desk. "What's the lead story tonight, Lance?" Shannon asked, his voice already tinged with accusation.

"Jay Walker is going to be live in Astoria. We've got some dead animals in a pet shop out there." Lance Worthington kept his voice calm, but his hands tensely gripped the sides of his chair.

"What kind of animals, rare Bengal Tigers?"

"Not funny, Shannon. People care about dead pets. In this case, five gerbils died after a gas leak."

"Let me get this straight, Lance," Shannon said, his voice dripping with sarcasm. "We've got two thousand murders a year in this city and you want to lead the broadcast with dead hamsters? Is that what you're telling me?"

"This discussion is over, Shannon."

"We're not leading with dead hamsters, Lance."

"Yeah, we are. You're out of line, Michaels. You don't run this newsroom."

"Didn't you learn anything from the last fiasco, Lance?" Shannon was referring to the recent and highly embarrassing "Rico the Dog" incident. Shortly after Lance Worthington had assumed the news directorship at Channel Six, he ordered a full court press on a feature story about a collie named Rico. It seemed that Rico had sniffed out an abandoned infant who had been left under some debris in a Brooklyn alley. The infant was saved because of a quick call to 911 by Rico's owner.

The next day Newscenter Six devoted seven minutes to the story, a huge block of time on a TV newscast. Lance Worthington even ordered a high tech news van to the scene so that Shannon Michaels could interview Rico's owner live via satellite. Shannon had recognized the merit of the story but advised Worthington against overdoing it. His advice was ignored.

Unfortunately, all the attention over-stimulated Rico the collie and, as the Newscenter Six van was leaving the scene of the story to return to the broadcast center, the dog bolted into the street. As onlookers watched in horror, the news van accidentally ran over Rico, breaking the heroic dog's left hind leg. The New York City newspapers went nuts, dubbing the story: "Dog Day Afternoon at Newscenter Six." For weeks afterward, everywhere Newscenter Six reporters went, other newspeople started to bark. Shannon Michaels was not amused.

Lance Worthington deeply resented Shannon Michaels for throwing the dog incident in his face. Trained as a bloodless bureaucrat, Worthington held his temper and spoke in a calm rational voice, "Look, Shannon, research shows our viewers react strongly to emotional stories about animals. My concern is directed toward what our viewers want, not what you want." The news director swept his right hand through his sandy hair. Shannon noticed Worthington's skin reddening ever so slightly. Good. He liked pissing this loser off.

"Yeah, and I react strongly to irresponsible, manipulative TV news programs," Shannon answered. "And my concern is directed toward valid news. Remember this, Lance. It's my face out there, my reputation. We're number one in the biggest market in the country because we have credibility. Because we cover important stories the right way. Because I know the difference between what's important and what's crap."

Lance Worthington leaned back in his chair and smirked. "If that's true, then why did they bounce you out of network news?"

Shannon Michaels' teal blue eyes turned cold and his jaw tightened with anger. He stared hard at Worthington who, in turn, faltered and looked down at his overly neat desk. It was a hateful remark and both men knew it. Silence circled the room like a starving turkey buzzard.

"Okay, Lance, here it is. We are going to lead this evening's newscast with Sheila Smith's report on violence in the homeless shelters. Then we'll update the Iraq situation. The pet thing can play right after the first commercial break. If we had any integrity at all, it would play after the weather. If you have a problem with that, my agent will take it upstairs."

Lance Worthington didn't like being dictated to, and this insubordination would not go unpunished, but right now might not be the time to strike. The ratings were too high and he was too new as the station's news director. Shannon Michaels had power. A confrontation could get messy. Worthington would bide his time.

"This bullshit isn't worth the trouble," Worthington said finally. "We'll change the lead. But I'm running this newsroom, Michaels, understand?"

"Just run it responsibly, Lance. And one more thing: you don't know shit about what happened to me at the network, so don't ever bring it up again."

The two men stared at each other. Each knew their working relationship would not last much longer. Each was confident of winning the ultimate showdown.

After listening to that and many other TV sagas, Shannon's therapist told him the obvious: that he was a deeply angry man who needed to work out his anger. Shannon smiled and paid his bill. Therapy, he decided, was just like local news: a recitation of the obvious.

• • •

The Manhattan restaurant Le Cirque is one of the best in the world. Its habitués include some of New York's most powerful residents—like Henry Kissinger, Barbara Walters, and Liz Smith. By New York tradition, it is a place to be seen.

Ashley Van Buren's father, the respected corporate attorney Francis Van Buren, favored Le Cirque for dinner whenever he came to town from Boston, where he had his practice. Ashley herself thought the restaurant a bit too stuffy, but if her father called, she'd always join him there for dinner.

Ashley loved her father, but he drove her crazy. He lectured rather than discussed, and he often talked down to her. At least that's how she heard it. Ever since her mother had passed away a decade before, her father had become increasingly critical of Ashley and everything else. To hold one's own with Francis Van Buren, advance mental preparation was definitely required.

Underneath her composed exterior, Ashley was an affectionate and vulnerable woman who took after her mother. Her years of therapy had taught her that she craved her father's approval, but would rarely receive it. Therefore, she needed to be strong and in control when she saw him—"empowered," the shrink had called it—and not take his brusque manner personally. Easier thought than done, as Ashley knew from experience.

Francis Van Buren stood up as Ashley walked across the crowded restaurant. As usual, Mr. Van Buren had been seated at a power table against the far wall—a prime position from which to view the entire room.

Ashley looked striking in a black suit by Ann Taylor, and an ivory blouse opened at the neck to show the perfect string of black pearls from Tahiti that her father had given her last Christmas. Her entrance was dramatic, and Ashley realized that many of New York's elite were staring as she kissed her father and sat down.

"Good column today, Ash. I can't believe somebody got killed on the Vineyard and Teddy Kennedy wasn't involved."

Ashley smiled at the joke. Her father was a bedrock Republican. As the waiter took their drink orders, Ashley's maternal instincts kicked in and she began examining her father closely. Though Francis Van Buren was in uniform—dark gray flannel suit, white starched shirt, red and black striped tie—she thought he looked tired and pale. Ashley worried about her father. In his late fifties, he lacked close friends in Boston. He spent most of his time working or at home alone. He did focus on Ashley but, like many fathers and daughters, the two had severe lifestyle disagreements.

As a child growing up in Newton, Massachusetts, an affluent Boston suburb, Ashley felt a constant pressure from her father. Francis Van Buren had extremely high expectations for his daughter and her younger brother, Peter. The children received the best education possible, and enjoyed the many privileges of wealth. Peter graduated from Stanford Law and then migrated south to Los Angeles, where he practiced entertainment law for a large talent agency. In the materialistic environment of L.A., Peter had quickly succumbed to a severe dependency: an addiction to himself. Ashley and her father rarely heard from him. He was always busy "taking meetings." As for the holidays, well, Peter's girlfriend didn't like to fly.

So it was left to Ashley to monitor her father's welfare. Her mother's early death from breast cancer had caused the family tremendous heartbreak. Ellen Van Buren was a sunny spirit, kind and down to earth—the perfect compliment to her sometimes stern father. It had taken Francis Van Buren years to recover from his wife's death and even now, ten years later, he was still prone to bouts of depression. Ashley knew that she alone could cheer him up, at least most of the time.

Because she saw her father only once every several months, there was much to talk about. Francis Van Buren ordered for both of them and did his usual excellent job: Escargot, sole with a lemon sauce, and an artery-clogging but delicious soufflé. Then came the question that usually arrived with the appetizer:

"So, how's the social life, Ash?"

"Pretty boring, Dad, if you want to know the truth."

"Why is that?"

"I guess I'm just too busy to find Mr. Right."

"Maybe you need some help."

"Dad. Please. This is so predictable. Let's call Peter. He'll get us parts in a sitcom."

Francis Van Buren ignored his daughter's sarcasm. "Listen, Ash, how are you ever going to meet anyone decent running around this corrupt city writing about criminals?"

Before Ashley could reply, her father continued: "If you want, I could put a word in at the *Times*. The metro editor over there owes me a favor. It's a much more prestigious venue, you know, and you'd meet a much higher caliber of person."

"Dad, they don't cover crime at the *Times*."

"Precisely, my dear. You could become involved with the arts, maybe medicine, religion."

"Religion? I'm already well on my way toward becoming a nun."

Again no response. Ashley thought her father might not even be listening to her. He continued his monologue. "They write about all kinds of things at the *Times*, Ash, and they write well."

"No, thanks Dad, I like the *Globe*.'"

Francis Van Buren gave up. He knew his daughter would not allow him to pull strings to help her. "Okay, Ash, but do me one favor. A young attorney in my firm is coming to New York next week and I want you to go out with him. He's very bright, Yale Law, a member of the

Algonquin Club, and all the girls in the office are mad about him. He'd really like to meet you."

Ashley looked at her father. He had tried this before and the dates had been disasters. But if her social life got any worse, it would qualify her for the cloisters, and this guy sounded like he might have potential. Besides, she was getting tired of sitting at home on Saturday nights watching "Sisters" on the tube.

"What's this guy's name, Dad?

"Stanford. Stanford Williamson."

"Don't you know any guys named Vinnie, Dad?" interjected Ashley, smiling. "Okay, have old Stan call me, but tell him no club ties on the first date. Now let's eat, I'm famished."

What Francis Van Buren did not discern from the crack about club ties was that his daughter was fed up with preppy men. She had not had sex for eight months, and was running out of patience with the steady stream of bland guys who wanted to date her.

Her most recent disaster had been a guy named Brad. On her fourth date with this Ivy League stockbroker, Ashley decided to make her move. Though she knew Brad was definitely not "Mr. Right," he was handsome enough to be "Mr. Right Now," so Ashley decided she would get up close and personal with him that evening.

While they shared a huge bowl of pasta primavera in a small Italian restaurant on the Upper East Side, Brad's end of the conversation centered around his experiences on the Princeton crew. For the umpteenth time in her dating career, Ashley found herself enduring a lecture on the merits of rowing. It was a great sport, she thought, but she'd heard more than her fair share about it growing up in Boston.

Still, Ashley invited Brad back to her large one bedroom apartment, which was a designer's dream; she had decorated it herself in early Martha Stewart. A floral patterned couch filled with fluffy dark green pillows dominated the living room and faced a large screen TV. Ashley flicked it onto VH-1, got Brad a beer, and excused herself for a moment.

Standing at the foot of her queen size bed, Ashley Van Buren removed her sky-blue silk blouse and unsnapped her bra. Her unrestrained breasts were full and firm and she slipped a tight, white tee shirt over them. It was the kind of shirt that skinny models wore in the Victoria Secret catalogues. Ashley's breasts swelled the cotton fabric, and her nipples were clearly outlined underneath.

Next, she took off her jeans, replacing them with blue silk shorts. Her freshly waxed legs reflected light in the full-length mirror nearby. Ashley checked her teeth, smoothed her blonde hair, and licked her lips. If old Brad didn't like this package, she thought, he must have taken an oar to the head at Princeton.

"Would you like another beer, Brad?" Ashley said as she walked back into the living room. Brad was playing around with Ashley's personal computer, which stood on a small wooden table in a corner of the room.

"No thanks, hon," Brad said smiling. "I don't want to get out of control."

"That might not be so bad," Ashley replied with a forced giggle that almost made her gag. She felt slightly uncomfortable. She was standing there in a very provocative outfit, and Brad had this vague look on his face.

"So what do you want to do, Ash?" Brad said while looking around the apartment. Ashley thought he should be looking at her.

With an inaudible sigh, Ashley walked over to the couch and sat down, crossing her legs so that her shorts rode high up her legs. She'd break this guy yet, she thought.

"Sit here next to me, Brad."

Brad walked over and sat down. Ashley got ready for the broker to make a move. He was staring at Ashley, smelling her expensive perfume. She turned her head to him and heard him ask, "Aren't you cold in that outfit, Ash? You hardly have anything on."

Ashley looked at her date in amazement. The guy truly didn't get it. And wouldn't be getting it. She leaned back on the couch and looked up at the ceiling. What was going on? Why was she continually striking out? A wave of insecurity enveloped her, but she fought it off. Smiling insincerely, Ashley looked at her date, platonically patted his hand, and thought, 'If this keeps up, I'm calling K.D. Lang.'

• • •

When the phone rang, Tommy O'Malley was lying in bed staring at the ceiling. It was Saturday morning, his day off. He didn't want to answer the damn thing, so he let the answering machine click on. "You have reached the man who could be your worst nightmare. Think carefully before leaving a message." Tommy was getting tired of his poor attempt at wit. The beep annoyed him, as it always did. The voice after the beep annoyed him even more.

"Tommy, I know you're there, pick up the phone."

O'Malley put his large hands over his face. It was his beloved ex-wife. Talking to her would be a major mistake, he knew, but he lifted the phone off the receiver anyway. "Hi, Angela, how's it going?"

"Not good, Tommy. You owe me money."

"Yeah, well, I've been working my butt off. I'll mail the check today."

"One more time and we're back in court."

"That will make your lawyer very happy, Angela, and probably you too."

"Don't be a wiseass, Tommy. I can't believe I married you."

"I can't believe it either, Ange. How lucky can one guy be?"

"You better hope I get the check by Friday."

"I'll hope and I'll pray." Without saying goodbye, Tommy put the phone back on the receiver.

Tommy O'Malley knew his last remark would rankle Angela Rufino. When they had first met five years before, Angela was a dark haired Italian-American princess with a thick Long Island accent and the largest brown eyes Tommy had ever seen. She was a selfish woman, but great fun. The two of them went out to expensive restaurants and clubs three times a week. And the sex afterward was the best Tommy had ever experienced. Angela was passionate and wild. Then they got married.

Tommy's mother was not thrilled with the union but went along with it because her son could do little wrong. The fact that Angela was twenty-six and immature worried Dorothy O'Malley, but Tommy had always known what he was doing. Tommy was the strength of the family and had taken care of her and his sister ever since his father had died two years earlier. Tommy's older brother, Brendan, was a drinker and therefore not much help.

Three years into the marriage, Tommy called his mother and broke the bad news. Angela had been born again. Had found Jesus in a Roman Catholic Church on Long Island. Had become a "charismatic Catholic."

Tommy knew nothing about charismatics but quickly learned that they take Jesus very seriously. He is on their minds at all times and they make that fact known to whoever is around them. Angela Rufino

O'Malley attended church five times a week, quit her job in public relations because it interfered with her mission, and began donating ten percent of Tommy's take-home pay to the church.

Tommy did not entirely understand. It wasn't that he objected to religion. Having been raised an Irish Catholic, he respected the Church. But he was wary of some of the clergy, and fanaticism on any level disturbed him. He wanted the immediate return of the woman he had married. That woman, Angela told him, was dead. By the grace of God, she had been born again.

Their defining battle took place in the bedroom where Angela informed Tommy that she would "perform her duties as a wife" as Jesus had instructed. But forget about any of the kinky stuff. In addition, Tommy should let her know well in advance when her "wifely duties" would be needed so that she could "mentally prepare" herself. Tommy digested that piece of information and moved out three hours later. The marriage was over.

Tommy O'Malley got out of bed this Saturday morning and walked into the bathroom. He lived in a crummy one-bedroom apartment on 88th Street, between Second and Third Avenues. It cost him $950 a month, and the bathroom was so small he could hardly fit into it. The apartment featured charming extras like paint peeling off the ceiling and a toilet that cleared only after three flushes. He loathed everything about the place.

His ex-wife, on the other hand, lived in a fairly nice house in Westbury, Long Island. Not a palace, but considerably better than the dump where he was currently residing.

The divorce had left Tommy feeling like a failure. He was resigned to being alone, and to putting up with Angela's weekly calls from hell. But he did hold out some faint hope. Maybe if the Pope finally allowed priests to marry, Angela could find the man for her. He figured the Church would give Angela an annulment on the grounds that Tommy and Satan were best friends.

If Angela didn't remarry soon, Tommy thought, he would be bankrupt. With lots of overtime, he made about eighty thousand dollars a year, but had exactly $1,438 in his checking account. As his father had told him over and over: "You pay dearly for any mistakes you make in this world."

As Tommy stepped out of the shower, the phone rang again. It was his boss, Lt. Brendan McGowan.

"Tommy, I know it's your day of rest but we got two stiffs down at the East River and 125th. Can you get right over there? I'll authorize the overtime."

"Cause of death, Mac?"

"Shots to the head. How unusual, right? By the way, the assistant D.A. stopped by yesterday. Bad news. They don't want to prosecute this Robo Melton. Say it's not worth the city's time and money for five rocks of crack. It'll be a merry-go-round. The jerk-off will be assigned to drug rehab. You know the drill. And Tommy, the guy is screaming you broke his thumb."

"He was putting the gorilla on me, Lieutenant, and we had trouble cuffing him," Tommy replied. (To "gorilla" someone on the streets of New York is to be disrespectful to them. The term derives from the eight hundred pound gorilla who can do whatever he wants.)

"Well, I know how troublesome that can be. Anyway, get that Melton paperwork cleared by tonight, okay, so I can get this lady prosecutor off my back."

"The guy is a killer, Brend."

"Prove it, Tommy, and we'll break his balls as hard as his thumb. See ya later and thanks for helping me out."

"No problem," said Tommy. And it wasn't. He didn't have anything better to do anyway.

CHAPTER SEVEN

The Global News Network had its international headquarters in a Japanese-owned high rise just a few blocks up Sixth Avenue from Rockefeller Center, the home of NBC. Personnel for GNN's nightly newscast, "The News Tonight," took up the building's entire fifth floor, with the rest of the network's apparatus on the sixth and seventh.

Anchorman Lyle Fleming's magnificent office—complete with large bathroom, shower stall, massage table, and refrigerator—looked out over the Avenue. Just outside Fleming's door was a huge room which contained "the oval," a large round table where the anchorman sat with the producers and writers who worked on "The News Tonight."

Mounted on the white walls surrounding "the oval" were framed, color pictures chronicling GNN's long history of reporting. Winston Wilcox, the legendary anchorman whom Fleming replaced, was featured in three of the photos. Lyle himself could be seen in ten of them. The wall of fame, as it was called, never failed to impress visitors who gazed admiringly at Lyle Fleming's various poses: Lyle atop a camel dressed in Arab robes. Lyle with Gorbachev pointing out over Red Square. Lyle scrutinizing a captured Scud missile. Lyle had apparently seen it all.

Sitting on built-in shelves above the photo gallery were two dozen fifteen-inch television monitors. Half of the monitors were programmed to display videotape being transmitted to GNN by satellites from all over the world. The other dozen TV screens were tuned to the competing networks and cable stations so that nothing on the American airwaves would escape the attention of GNN news personnel.

At the far end of the room, about fifty feet away from the oval desk, was the secretarial pool. The men and women there took all calls coming into "The News Tonight," passing along information and messages to the producers and correspondents. Lyle Fleming had his own personal secretary, Lanie Sharp, whose desk was right outside his office.

If you wanted to talk with Lyle for more than thirty seconds, you had to see Lanie. That was the unwritten rule.

The actual set of "The News Tonight," where the show was broadcast each weekday at 6:30 eastern standard time, was upstairs on the sixth floor. Outsiders were often surprised when they saw just how small the set actually was. On television, with the anchorman holding court, it looked large and bright. In reality, it was a small blue desk with just Lyle's chair, and God help anyone who sat in it. Lyle was superstitious. His chair was for him and him alone.

The background of "The News Tonight" set was an actual newsroom, where assignment editors, researchers, and production assistants sat and worked. Bulletin boards lined the walls displaying maps from all over the world. Wire machines, devices that print and transmit news reports, were stationed throughout the floor and were closely monitored around the clock. The people at GNN were determined that nothing should happen in the world without their knowing about it.

Directly behind the newsroom were fifteen comfortable offices for the New York based news correspondents and field producers. These were the men and women who traveled outside the building, actually witnessing and gathering the news. Competition for the best stories was extremely intense among the correspondents. As a result, there was not a lot of camaraderie going on in the corridor outside their offices. Most of the field people preferred to keep to themselves.

The seventh floor of GNN headquarters was reserved for the *News* executives, with the largest office inhabited by William Foster, the President and virtual dictator of GNN's worldwide news organization. Foster was rarely seen outside his lavish suite. He was not a man to mingle. This strategy helped make Foster a mystery figure: feared and inaccessible. Few knew what Foster was thinking, and that was just fine with him.

GNN's Vice President of News Personnel, Hillary Ross, had her office five doors down from Foster's. Hillary was also right next to the office of her best friend, Northeastern Bureau Chief Randi Klein, who supervised news-gathering from Philadelphia to Boston.

Ross was a tall, thin, unattractive woman whom her detractors—just about everybody working at GNN—nicknamed "Olive Oyl." Like the character in the Popeye cartoons, she had long limbs and huge feet. Her face, which was dominated by a weak chin, was elongated. Mousy brown hair completed the look.

In addition to Hillary's physical shortcomings, she was mean. She had risen rapidly through the executive ranks at GNN because she was willing to do the dirty work. Which is exactly what she was doing when Randi Klein walked into her office.

"I'm just about finished, Rand. Wait 'till you hear this one."

"Patrick Downey's obituary?" asked Randi Klein. Downey was an older correspondent based in Chicago. GNN was not going to renew his contract even though he had worked for the organization for more than twenty years. Downey was fifty-five years old and making $250,000 a year. Too much in GNN's opinion. He was expendable.

"Yeah. Here it is, see if you like it. 'Dear Mr. Downey,' I can't use Patrick, it's too informal. 'The executives of The Global News Network have decided not to renew your contract, which expires on the first of next year. As you know, times are tough, and there are cutbacks in every department. I am writing to you personally instead of going through your agent because it is the proper thing to do. GNN appreciates the loyal service you have rendered and will, of course, continue to pay you until the end of your contract. We would, however, appreciate it if you would clean out your office as soon as possible. We will be doing renovations in the Chicago Bureau. If you have any questions, please feel free to contact me.'"

"Wow, that *is* cold, Hillary."

"The moron deserves it. Do you realize we've been carrying this guy for years? He's lucky if he gets on the morning news once a month. When was the last time you saw him on Lyle's broadcast? Lyle hates the guy."

Randi Klein giggled. She was a short woman with large brown eyes and a mole above the right side of her lip. "If we fired everybody Lyle hates, we'd be awful lonesome."

"Well, he loves *us*. I know that for sure," Hillary Ross replied. "And that's what matters these days. So what do you think, Rand? Should I fax this to Downey so the whole bureau can see it, or should I FedEx it?"

"Give him a break, Hil. FedEx it."

"That'll cost the company more money. No, I think I'll fax it. By the way, are we still on for dinner tonight?"

"That's what I came to tell you. My husband is sick. I've got to go home early."

"Rand, when are you going to get rid of him?"

Randi Klein laughed and walked out.

Hillary Ross began finishing up her paperwork. She was a neat freak, her desk uncluttered and organized. She buzzed her secretary and handed her the fax for Patrick Downey. The secretary, who knew better than to glance at it in Hillary's presence, quickly left the room. Hillary Ross proceeded to watch that evening's newscast, and to make a few phone calls. At seven p.m., "The News Tonight" wrapped up its second feed, the satellite transmission sent to its affiliated stations. Lyle Fleming and William Foster usually left for the day by 7:30. Hillary wanted to be available if either of them needed her, so she always stayed late, and left about 7:45.

The evening was chilly when Hillary stepped onto Sixth Avenue. Though her fax to Patrick Downey would have a profoundly negative effect on the man's life, she had not given the matter another thought. He was out now, officially a non-person in her mind. End of story.

Hillary buttoned up her black leather coat and hailed a cab, giving the Pakistani driver her address at 88th and Central Park West. The cabbie had trouble understanding English, and Hillary became annoyed when asked to repeat it. Sulking in the back seat, she was unaware of the black car that had pulled out from an illegal parking space and was now following close behind.

The car's driver had not seen Hillary Ross in years, but spotted her immediately. Not too many 6'1, homely women come out of the GNN building. The man followed Hillary's cab into Columbus Circle, up Central Park West, adjacent to the Park itself, and northward, passing the Tavern on the Green restaurant, and the Dakota apartment building where John Lennon was shot to death. Finally, her cab stopped in front of an elegant high rise.

Hillary Ross paid the cabbie but did not tip him. He said something unintelligible as she closed the back door. 'Screw you,' Hillary thought. 'Learn the language.' A doorman opened the door for her and Hillary walked through the building's rather bland lobby toward the elevator.

Outside, the man driving the black car double-parked, peering into the lobby of Hillary Ross' building. He was not pleased. 'This is going to be tough,' he thought.

Expensive New York City apartments almost always have sophisticated, around-the-clock security. The man who was following Hillary

Ross knew that two doormen would always be on duty in her building, that there would be cameras in the elevators, that each tenant would have a button in the apartment to push for emergencies.

Besides that, the building itself was huge and he had no idea what apartment or even what floor Hillary Ross called home.

But Hillary Ross' stalker had a good idea of GNN's inner workings, and that provided him an advantage. He knew, for example, that all the networks had drastically cut manpower on the overnight shifts. Both the foreign and domestic news desks were now run by just one person.

Helping the overnight news manager was a bunch of young, unpaid interns from local colleges who answered the phones, checked the news wires, and got sandwiches and coffee for the boss of the grave-yard shift. Sitting in his car, the stalker mulled over various strategies that might help him exploit these naive kids to get the information he needed. After about ten minutes, a plan crystallized. He quickly drove to a public phone on Columbus Avenue.

"GNN foreign desk, Melissa speaking." The young woman who answered the phone spoke with a Valley girl accent, overemphasizing the letters A and R, and ending declarative sentences on an up note as if they were questions.

"Melissa, this is Trevor Langley, your stringer in Beijing." The man spoke with a British accent. Melissa was impressed by a call from China. She vaguely remembered being told that stringers were freelance pro-ducers, and that she should accept their collect calls. Only this guy wasn't calling collect.

"How can I help you, Trevor?"

"Well, Melissa, I've got a big problem. I promised Hillary Ross that I would send her a Chinese vase in time for her mother's birthday. It seems I have her home address, but I don't have her apartment number. And overnight delivery won't take it out of here without the complete address. So could you punch up her address in the computer and give me the apartment number?"

"You could just send it here, Trevor."

"Melissa, can I tell you something in the strictest confidence?"

Melissa felt a tingle of excitement. "Sure."

"The company disapproves of us sending personal things like this. I'm doing Hillary a discreet favor by sending it to her home. I'm sure she'd appreciate the fact that you are helping in this."

Melissa had heard only bad things about Hillary Ross, and didn't want to run afoul of her. She gave Trevor Langley the information.

"And one more thing, Melissa. Don't tell anybody about this, okay? I don't want to get Hillary in trouble, and I sure don't want to get me in trouble. So be a love, will you?"

"Okay, Trevor. By the way, what's the weather like in China?"

The man calling himself Trevor Langley looked down Columbus Avenue, put his finger into the air and said, "A little windy, Melissa, a little windy."

CHAPTER EIGHT

MANHATTAN
JULY, 1982

The early eighties were a great time to be young and single in New York City. The disco era was still alive, the nightclubs of Manhattan throbbed with energy, excitement, and daring, no one had heard of AIDS and, apparently, few had heard of sexual restraint. Not since the late twenties had young men and women been so available to each other. In such a period, a young, affluent, handsome TV guy like Shannon Michaels might have been a prince of the city. He could have partied as hard as he wanted.

But Shannon was miserable. Three days after the blowup in Argentina, he had been recalled to New York for "consultations." GNN provided him with a temporary office, booked him into the Warwick Hotel, and told him to "sit tight." After ten full days of sitting around doing absolutely nothing, he was finally summoned to a meeting with anchorman Lyle Fleming and then-News President Darren Darwin. He knew his career was on the line.

During the meeting, Shannon got his chance to explain what had happened in Buenos Aires. He spoke passionately about nearly being killed, about bigfooting, about journalistic ethics. Fleming and Darwin appeared to listen, although Darwin kept glancing at a clock on his desk. After hearing Shannon out, both promised to appoint someone to investigate the matter. It turned out to be a bright young woman just hired by GNN from Barry Goldwater's senatorial staff—a woman named Hillary Ross.

Shannon left the meeting feeling somewhat better but, as the days went by, reality once again slapped him in the face. No one at GNN would talk to him. When he walked the company corridors, his coworkers avoided his eyes, mumbling "how ya doin" and little more. He received no assignments, and couldn't even eat lunch in the company cafeteria because no one would sit with him. 'I'm a leper,' Shannon thought. 'I should carry around a little bell warning people to stay away.'

Finally, feeling he had nowhere else to turn, Shannon picked up the phone, punching in David Wayne's extension. His office was right across the hall, and Wayne had just returned from Argentina.

"Jesus, Michaels, I can't believe you're calling me."

"I need some help, David."

"The understatement of the millennium."

"David, I'd like to know what's really going on. You gave me solid advice in Argentina. I've got no one else to go to now."

"Look, Michaels, I can't talk here. The walls have ears in this place. If they find out I'm talking to you, they'll figure out some way to punish me." Wayne paused. Shannon thought he could almost hear him thinking.

"There's a bar, a dive, on the corner of First and 58th. Near the bridge. No one at GNN would be caught dead there. I'll stop in about eight tonight. If you're there, you're there. See you."

It was a hot, humid evening in Manhattan, the kind of night when the heat hits with double intensity: dank, murky air from above; scalding asphalt from the street below. A New York City night in midsummer heat is a dream of which only Dante would approve.

Shannon Michaels was extremely depressed as he walked east on 57th Street toward his rendezvous. He had been through tough times before, working his way up to the network by reporting in places like Scranton, Pittsburgh, and Detroit. Moving to a strange city every year or so was a lonely way to live, and the competition in each workplace was stiff. But Shannon's aggressive reporting style had made him valuable. Finally, his dream was realized when GNN hired him as a network correspondent, a very prestigious job for someone only twenty-eight years old.

But the dream was evaporating and he knew it. Getting fired from a network post six months after being hired was a career killer. For one of the few times in his life, Shannon simply didn't know what to do. He felt powerless, the same way he had felt as a child when his father came home drunk and out of control. He hated that feeling more than anything on earth.

Shannon rounded the corner onto First Avenue. The 59th Street Bridge loomed high in front of him. It was falling apart. Shannon felt like he was, too.

David Wayne already had a beer and a shot in front of him when Shannon sat down at the table. The bar was Irish, with paper Shamrocks on the wall flanked by Aer Lingus travel posters. A song by The Chieftains played on the jukebox. The air conditioning was on full blast and there was condensation on the inside of the front bay window.

"David, thanks for meeting me. I really appreciate it." David Wayne rose to shake Shannon's hand. He didn't smile.

"I really must be nuts to talk to you, Michaels," David Wayne said. "You really fucked up. Costello is on a relentless campaign to ruin you. Solo and just about everybody else in B.A. is backing him up. You're outnumbered, and help is definitely not on the way."

Shannon actually appreciated the candor. He looked at Wayne sadly. "I had a meeting this morning with Fleming and Darwin."

"Oh, and let me guess. They told you they would look into the matter. And they appointed Hillary Ross to investigate."

"How did *you* know?" Shannon said, his voice laced with surprise.

"Because Ross is going around telling everyone you are history. She and her little girls' club had a big laugh about it at lunch today. There are no secrets at GNN, Michaels. Everybody knows everything."

Shannon Michaels clenched his jaw. Wayne's knowledge of his "private meeting" stung him badly. He stopped feeling sorry for himself, and began feeling angry. "So what's going to happen, David?"

David Wayne did not answer. Instead he drained his beer, knocked back the shot, and signaled the waitress for another round. Shannon ordered a Coke.

"That's your problem right there, Michaels. You don't drink. You need to drink in this business. A lot. Everybody does."

The drinks appeared with impressive speed. As the young, heavyset waitress laid them down, David Wayne looked at Shannon Michaels. He felt sorry for him. He knew Shannon was about to be taken down by a bunch of bastards. The kid just wouldn't play the game.

"Here's the way it is, Michaels. Hillary Ross will issue a report that says you are not ready to be a correspondent for GNN, or some bullshit like that. The report will cite your immaturity, blah, blah, blah. Bottom line: you're gone.

"Now, they probably won't fire you outright because then you could file a grievance with AFTRA" [the American Federation of Radio and Television Artists] "and they don't want to deal with union bullshit. That could get 'em bad publicity, and they might be forced into embarrassing testimony in court. So they'll suggest that you resign. In return, you'll get some money and a letter of recommendation. If you don't resign, they'll bad-mouth you so much not even Fargo, North Dakota will hire you, and you'll sit on your ass on the overnight shift until your contract runs out."

Shannon stared hard at the veteran correspondent. "Is there any chance this Hillary Ross will talk to Francisco and Juan? Those guys were on the streets with me. They know what really happened down there."

"None. Hillary Ross was hired by GNN to be a hatchet person. And she had a great teacher. Did you know she was Goldwater's top staff person in his Arizona office? And Barry loves her. She beat the hell out of the press, threatening and blackmailing reporters so that nothing bad about her boss got into print or on the tube. Ross has no respect for journalists at all. We're all scum to her. She couldn't care less about 'journalistic ethics' because to her it's an oxymoron. Her entire career has been based on using and abusing the press, and to her you're just another rag reporter on his way out."

David Wayne paused for another swallow. His face was red and his eyes bloodshot. Suddenly, he became agitated. It was as if something had caused him unexpected physical pain. "I hate that Ross bitch," said Wayne, spittle actually flying from his mouth. "She's a fucking Nazi. No feeling for anyone but herself. People like us, people with skills, with a profession, have to fear her 'cause she can kill our careers. Taking someone's job in this business is like taking someone's life. That woman never once covered a news story, yet she's a GNN vice president. What the fuck is that? I despise her in a major fucking way."

Wayne's vehement outburst surprised Shannon Michaels. He watched the older correspondent closely. Both men were silent for a time and then Shannon began to massage his temples with the palms of both hands. He couldn't believe what was happening. He was being set up. The meeting with Fleming and Darwin had been a complete farce. Hillary Ross was his executioner. His foot began tapping on the floor. Nervous energy flowed through him like water from an open hydrant, but he had no outlet for it. "So Hillary Ross is going to bring me down." Shannon said it as a statement, not a question.

"Yeah, she will," Wayne said, calmer now. "And here's why. Ross knows that Ron Costello and Lyle Fleming are buddies. She also knows that Darwin doesn't give a damn about anyone, or anything. You're an annoyance to him, nothing more. He doesn't give a shit about what happened in Argentina. He cares about his GNN stock options, his bonus payments, his golden parachute. Your life means nothing to him. Add it all up and there's no reason for the bitch to help you."

"So it's hopeless," said Shannon, looking down at the table, his rage barely under control. He was clenching and unclenching his fists.

"Look, Michaels, here's what I would do. Take their shitty deal. Get six months pay and a letter. Then tell your agent to get you a local anchor job. You've got the stuff for that. Successful local anchors make big money and have power. In this business, you need power to do good work and to get it on the air. I know it stinks, but that's what I would do."

Shannon looked at Wayne and shook his head. "I can't believe I'm going down for this. I can't believe it."

David Wayne lit a cigarette and blew the smoke straight into the air. "It isn't only you who's getting screwed. Most of us eventually get it. Just a matter of time. But things have a tendency to even out. What goes around can definitely come around." Wayne leaned back in his wooden chair and looked slyly at Shannon Michaels. 'Enough said,' the veteran correspondent thought, 'enough said.'

The two newsmen talked casually for a few minutes longer, but nothing meaningful was said. Shannon then picked up the tab and walked out into the humid night. He thought about Wayne's advice, but it did not comfort him. For one of the rare times in his life, Shannon Michaels knew he was defeated.

Two weeks after his bar conversation with David Wayne, Shannon's agent negotiated his resignation. Hillary Ross's report had come back saying that Shannon had endangered the lives of two GNN crew members, had been responsible for the destruction of a $25,000 camera, and had committed an assault on Ron Costello, which could be construed as criminal behavior. Everything Wayne predicted had become reality.

CHAPTER NINE

For the man who called himself Trevor Langley, following Hillary Ross for a week had been easy. The GNN vice president led a boring life. Out to dinner with friends one night, a movie by herself another. No dates, no trips. Having established her pattern of movement, Langley now had the raw data for a plan, but it relied heavily on luck, and it was strictly a one-shot deal.

On Halloween night, Ross left work at 7:45 and, as was her custom, took a cab home. Trevor Langley followed in his black car, and was pleased when she proceeded directly up to her apartment on the eighteenth floor of her high-rise.

Langley then drove into an underground parking lot ten blocks north on 98th street. He could not risk getting a parking ticket on the street, because that could be traced. He also figured that while investigating the demise of Hillary Ross, the police would question parking lot attendants within a five square block radius of the crime scene.

Before handing over his car keys to the lot attendant, Langley took a knapsack out of his car. He was careful not to look the attendant in the eye. He did not want to be remembered.

It was a half mile walk back to Hillary Ross' building, which overlooked Central Park, and Langley took his time. Small children in Halloween costumes raced by him, their parents struggling to keep up. There was a festive feeling in the air along Central Park West. Langley approached the high rise and stopped directly across the street. There he waited, leaning against the stone wall that surrounds Central Park, patiently watching the apartment lobby in the cool of the evening.

About an hour later, Langley saw a group of adults in Halloween costumes enter the lobby of Hillary Ross's building. He quickly darted across the street, pulled a Richard Nixon mask from his knapsack, and placed it over his face. Seven people in costume were now standing in front of the doorman, who was sitting behind a circular wooden guard's desk to the right of the revolving doors. Apparently there was a Halloween party on the fifteenth floor. The guard called up to the apartment, got the okay to let the partygoers in, and directed them to the elevator. Discreetly and silently, Langley joined the group in his Nixon disguise.

The ride up took only seconds. The revelers chatted and laughed, but no one paid much attention to Richard Nixon. He smiled underneath his mask, pleased to have surmised correctly that at least one Halloween celebration would be going on in a building with so many residents.

On the fifteenth floor, Langley did not leave the elevator along with the rest of the group. Instead, though he knew somebody might be monitoring the security camera in the elevator, he continued up to 18, stepping into a dimly lit hallway. Looking around, it reminded him of a Holiday Inn. He smelled onions—somebody was cooking a potent dinner. But he saw no one. He removed a blunt object from the knapsack, putting it in his back pocket. Then he approached apartment 18 D and rang the bell.

"Who is it?" Hillary Ross called as she got up from watching CNN, GNN's competition, and walked to her door.

"Ms. Ross, my name is Trevor Langley. I'm your new neighbor down the hall. We're having a Halloween party. Would you like to join us?"

Hillary Ross peered through the peephole in her door and saw a tall man wearing a Richard Nixon mask. She didn't know many of her neighbors, but a well built man was a well built man, and she had always liked a British accent. She opened the door.

"That's very nice of you, Mr. Langley, but I don't think I have a costume." Hillary was smiling, showing a considerable amount of gum above her front teeth.

"Well, you can have mine." Langley's left hand moved up to the top of his mask. At the same time, his right hand reached into his back pocket for a police-style nightstick, hidden by the untucked-in tail of his flannel shirt. Hillary never saw Langley's right hand move at all, so intent was she on watching him unmask himself.

With lightning quickness, Langley raised his hand and viciously clubbed Hillary Ross above the left ear. She saw white, then black, and fell backward, unconscious.

Langley quickly looked around. The hallway was still deserted. He removed his backpack and pulled out a pair of latex surgeon's gloves, donning them so he wouldn't leave fingerprints. Then he entered the apartment, quietly closing the door behind him.

Hillary Ross was lying on her side, her legs bent at a slight angle. Her breathing was shallow but steady. Her assailant stepped over her, walked into her bedroom, found some panty hose in a drawer, and brought them back to where she lay.

Stuffing the hose in her mouth, Langley noticed a slight trickle of blood coming from her ear. Ignoring it, he removed from his sack a roll of adhesive tape and a short strand of thick twine. Ripping off a long piece of the tape from the roll, Langley placed it over his victim's mouth. He used the twine to tie her thumbs together behind her back. Within three minutes, Hillary Ross was immobilized for as long as the intruder wanted her to be.

A surge of adrenaline swept over Langley. He put his hands on his hips to calm himself. He concentrated on his breathing. He needed to be clear-headed, steady. Then the phone rang, and he almost jumped. On the second ring, the answering machine clicked on: "You have reached me, but I cannot come to the phone. Please leave a message and I'll get back to you." Beep.

"Hillary, it's Randi. You'll never believe who's in deep trouble at GNN. You'll die when you find out. Call me right away."

Langley looked at the phone. 'She'll die before that,' he thought.

Walking to the end of the sumptuously furnished living room, he opened the sliding glass doors leading to the terrace. Despite the protection of the mask, the brisk breeze chilled his face. Winter was in the air. Behind him, he heard a low moan. Ross was reviving.

Looking out over the four-foot-high balcony railing, Langley realized he was in a corner apartment. Directly in front of him was 88th Street. To the right, he could see the park. To the left was another high rise. But between the two buildings was a small space containing an alleyway—blocked off from the street by a metal fence—covered with barbed wire. Part of Hillary Ross' balcony overlooked the alley.

Langley saw the opportunity immediately and walked quickly back into the apartment. Hillary Ross was now semiconscious, so he grabbed the collar of her white shirt from behind, roughly pulling her up into a sitting position and dragging her across the hardwood floor. When he reached the terrace, his powerful hands lifted her to her feet. Then he pushed her out to the railing overlooking the alley, forcing her to stand upright.

Hillary Ross felt the cold wind in her face. She opened her eyes and nearly fainted; she was dizzy, her head throbbing with pain. She also felt something soft and gauzy on her tongue, but couldn't open her mouth. Instinctively, she tried to move her hands, but her thumbs were locked behind her back. Completely disoriented, Hillary heard a low voice say, "Why would a person want to be in a position to end so many careers? Why would someone take a job doing that?"

The GNN executive turned her eyes toward the voice, which she didn't recognize. Gone was the English accent. She shuddered with fear and shook her head violently back and forth. The movement caused a rush of pain, and red dots danced before her eyes. She tried to scream, but could make no sound. Panic took hold. She jerked her body up and down, trying desperately to escape.

Had Hillary Ross been able to confront the face behind the Richard Nixon mask, she would have seen Langley's narrowed eyes staring at her with a hatred that caused his temple to throb. Langley looked into Hillary's eyes and saw they were wild with fear. He felt a surge of power. He reached out, grabbing her belt with both hands. He lifted her long, thin body with ease and momentarily held it in the air over the top of the terrace wall.

Panic consumed Hillary Ross. She convulsed her body, trying in vain to kick her assailant. She remembered how, as a child, she had been locked inside a small closet by her friends. She screamed and pounded on the door and finally was set free. But now she couldn't scream. In fact, she couldn't think. Suddenly, she felt herself being lifted again and heard a voice say: "You were always over the top, Hillary." Then she was falling. The wind lashed against her face. She couldn't see. It was dark. Should she pray? Then a total, instantaneous pain. Then, nothing.

Trevor Langley did not watch Hillary Ross's plunge to death. As the woman fell to the ground, he was on his way out of the apartment. Once out in the hallway, he took off the gloves, put them in the knapsack, walked to the elevator, and hit the down button with his elbow.

In two and a half minutes, he was out of the apartment building. There were no complications. No one heard or saw Hillary Ross fly off the balcony or hit the pavement in the isolated alley. It all happened too quickly.

Langley moved quickly in implementing his escape plan. He retrieved his car from the parking lot, then drove north up Broadway. In Harlem, he stopped at a restaurant dumpster where he deposited his knapsack containing the Richard Nixon mask, surgeon's gloves, and the nightstick. His hands were shaking, but his mind was clear. Two of his enemies were finished, and his strategy had been perfect. They would never catch him. He took a deep breath of the cool autumn air, got back in his automobile, and calmly drove away.

CHAPTER TEN

MANHATTAN
NOVEMBER 1, 1994

At 6:53 a.m., approximately ten hours after Hillary Ross' death, her body was spotted by Patrolman Luis Ortiz, who was walking his beat on West 88th Street. It was an overcast morning in the city and traffic was just beginning to pick up. Usually, Ortiz covered his beat quickly. He was just twenty-three years old and had a lot of energy. But after arguing with his girlfriend the night before, he was depressed. So he took his time this morning, stopping frequently, preoccupied and sad.

Ortiz never would have seen the streams of blood that had seeped underneath the alley gate if he had not stopped to lean against it. The gate was locked but, after seeing the dried blood, Ortiz shined his flashlight through the bars of the gate and saw clearly someone lying in an extremely awkward position behind it. Immediately, the policeman radioed for an ambulance, radioed for backup citing a possible "jumper," and gained access to the alleyway through the back door of Hillary Ross' apartment building.

What Ortiz saw sickened both him and the doorman he took along for security purposes. The body was like rubber, not a bone intact. Ross' eyes were open and bulging. Ortiz also noticed something strange—tied to her left thumb was a small piece of cord. The policeman did not touch anything, and quickly returned to the lobby, where he used the doorman's desk phone to call the Manhattan North Homicide Squad. He didn't want the conversation overheard on the police radio.

Tommy O'Malley was working the seven to four shift and had just arrived at his cluttered desk. Munching on a chocolate-glazed donut, he noticed that his stomach was beginning to protrude somewhat majestically over his black leather belt. 'Damn,' he thought, 'gettin' old, gettin' fat.' For not the first time, he made a mental note to cut out the junk food. Then the phone rang, as it did constantly, all day long.

"Detective O'Malley speaking."

"Detective, this is Patrolman Luis Ortiz callin'. We have a possible jumper down here on West 88th, sir, but I found somethin' you should know about."

"Go ahead, Ortiz."

"The deceased is layin' in an alley below her apartment. She coulda jumped, but I don't think so."

"Why's that?" asked O'Malley, only mildly interested.

"Well, sir, people don't usually jump into alleys. They go for the big statement. The street, ya know. And I found some string or somethin' on her thumb. Looks to me like she coulda been tied."

"Who is this woman, Ortiz?"

"Lady by the name of Ross. Works for GNN, the doorman tol' me."

O'Malley bolted upright. The connection registered immediately: GNN. Shit. "Listen to me Ortiz. Seal everything right away. Crime scene, her apartment, elevators, the works. And no radio. The media is to be kept away. No access. Got it?"

"Yeah, Detective."

"Play this as a suicide. Low key. Get the names of everybody who works in the building, and all the neighbors. We'll be right down."

"Okay, Detective."

"Good work, Ortiz." Tommy hung up and looked at his watch. Jackson Davis was ten minutes late. No big deal, but O'Malley knew he would need Davis and a squad full of top homicide investigators to handle this bitch of a case.

• • •

The city desk at the *New York Globe* was usually a chaotic place—a constant wail of people demanding immediate attention— and making the early morning the journalistic equivalent of rush hour. Things were little different today at the *Globe*. A parade of scruffy reporters was passing in front of Assignment Editor Bert Cicero and his three assistants (two women and one man), all seated at a long desk that looked like a lunch counter. In front of the assignment desk, at least sixty obnoxious, aggressive newspaper people milled around, all assessing what their career needs might be in the very near future. The phrase "this assignment sucks" had long since replaced the traditional "good morning" as the standard greeting to Bert Cicero and his staff.

Bert Cicero's daily headache started at five a.m., the moment he sat down at his computer terminal. The phones in front of him rang every few seconds and, as the newspeople began to filter in, the gripes and suggestions became more annoying than the phones. The *Globe's* fashion editor "simply must" fly to Milan. The Brooklyn bureau chief's wife called in to say that her husband was sick, that he might have an ulcer. The legendary columnist Larry Miskin had been charged with DWI the night before. Cicero could not believe he actually reported for work every day knowing the chaos and demands he would encounter.

In between sorting out mini-emergencies, Bert Cicero was listening to the police radio, which was always monitored. Shortly after seven, he heard a police transmission asking for an ambulance to be sent to Central Park West. Then he heard the word "jumper."

The *Globe* would not ordinarily cover a suicide, but Central Park West was a ritzy neighborhood, and Cicero felt his face twitch a little and his news instinct kick in. Hell, it could be Madonna or someone. He looked around and saw rookie reporter Nancy Hall sitting at her desk. "Hey, Hall, go check out some police activity on 88th and CPW. Take Lenny, just in case there's a gory photo-op. Give me a call if it's anything and try not to screw up, will ya?"

• • •

Thirty minutes after the call from Officer Luis Ortiz, Tommy O'Malley and Jackson Davis were staring at the dead body of Hillary Ross. "Geez, they're gonna need a blotter to pick her up," Jackson said as he circled the body, careful not to step on the dried blood that was splattered in all directions.

"Jack, she bounced," Tommy said as he knelt down next to the body. "She bounced in the air after impact. Here's the spot where she first hit." Tommy pointed to a place about three feet from the body. "Then she went back up and landed over here. Eighteen floors straight down will do that. Christ."

Tommy and Jackson couldn't take their eyes off the limp corpse. Hillary Ross had been protected by the best apartment security that money could buy. Yet here she was, dead in an alley. Both detectives were thinking the same thing: who the hell would do something like this to this kind of woman?

As the officer in charge of the crime scene, Tommy would oversee a seven-member team of detectives for the investigation. He was quickly putting things together in his mind. Because Hillary Ross held a powerful position at the Global News Network, he knew that this would be a major case, and that the Commissioner would be all over it. He also suspected that if somebody was killing GNN personnel, it was very possible that Hillary Ross would not be the last victim. Tommy quietly cursed. "The goddamn print media will go wild."

The detectives combed the alley for clues. They found one piece of string tied to the woman's thumb, but they did not find any more twine. If there had been any adhesive tape, it must have blown away during the night.

Tommy O'Malley knew a few things about the case right away. First of all, the woman had landed too close to the building to be a suicide. People who jump from high places almost always leap forward before gravity takes over. It's instinct, to push off a ledge. This woman was dropped from the building, her hands probably tied behind her back.

Also, Tommy suspected that the killer was a strong man who had thought the crime out carefully. Dropping the woman into the alley was deliberate. This was not a crime of passion where somebody got crazed and flipped their lover into the street.

The eight-man homicide team was quick and efficient. Divided into twos, the four units methodically examined the alley, Ross' apartment, the elevators, building, and surrounding neighborhood. They canvassed the doormen and neighbors, asking who had seen what. They called the night shift people, arranging for them to go to the precinct for questioning. By the time the Crime Scene Unit took over four hours later, they had done a textbook job of gathering information.

The incoming C.S. unit would gather any physical evidence, like blood, dirt, fiber, fingerprints, skin under fingernails, and bring it to the police laboratory for analysis. The coroner who responded with the C.S. unit would examine the body. Tommy wanted no mistakes, and made this very clear to Detective Luke Murray, whom he assigned to monitor the C.S. unit. Everybody involved with law enforcement knew that O.J. Simpson's lawyers were going to tear the Los Angeles police apart for sloppy investigative work in the upcoming trial. Tommy would not subject himself to that if the GNN case ever came to trial in New York.

As Tommy took one last look at the body of Hillary Ross, he felt anger welling up inside him. Whoever did this was a brutal bastard.

First a spoon through a guy's brain. Now killing a woman in this unspeakable way. How could someone do these things? Tommy had heard many confessions by killers. He was well aware of the terrible fear that the victims go through, especially when they know they are going to die and can do nothing about it. Tommy's jaw tightened. He strongly believed he was looking for a revenge killer. Probably a highly intelligent one. A man who firmly believed he could get away with murder because the police were too stupid to catch him. A man with no conscience, no compunction.

Walking a few paces behind Jackson to their unmarked car, Tommy sighed deeply. He believed that he personally would have to bear the burden of catching the GNN killer. Making an investigation personal went against all training. But Tommy realized that his career would be riding on this case. It was, in effect, catch the killer or be killed.

• • •

Despite her *Globe* credentials, Nancy Hall couldn't get anything out of the "uniforms." That in itself was unusual because cops, almost always off the record, love to talk about gory crimes. She also knew something strange was up because the street cops wouldn't let her near the crime scene or any of the investigating detectives. Plus, Mike McAlary, the high profile columnist for the competition, *The New York Daily News*, had shown up. And it looked like he wasn't getting anything either. She decided to check in with Bert Cicero.

"Bert, this is Hall. Something's going on, but I can't tell you what. They got everything sealed. Nobody's talking."

"Come on, Hall, turn on the charm."

Nancy Hall rolled her eyes and spoke into her portable phone. "Bert, even McAlary's getting zero on this. I've been watching him every step."

"Shit, McAlary's there?" Bert Cicero knew it was serious. And he knew that if the *News* beat the *Globe* on the story, he'd never hear the end of it.

"Hall, keep at it. I'll send some reinforcements. But get something. Be a pain in the ass."

'Just like you,' Nancy Hall thought, but simply responded: "Okay, Bert." And then she hung up.

Bert Cicero, fearing a situation he could not tolerate, immediately called his most experienced crime reporter, Ronnie Kramer. Then he called Ashley Van Buren. Both were at the scene within thirty minutes with orders to get the story any way they could.

Ashley Van Buren could tell by the sound of Bert Cicero's voice that this was no ordinary murder. She was toweling off from her shower when Cicero had called, practically screaming into her answering machine. Ashley quickly picked up the phone, took down the address from Bert, and got moving.

When she arrived at the crime scene, it was already a zoo. TV satellite trucks surrounded the apartment building, and print reporters swarmed around maniacally. But nobody seemed to have any hard facts. Ashley began to get anxious.

Dressed in her usual street outfit—a brown leather jacket, an oversized denim shirt, khaki pants, and brown leather boots—Ashley broke away from the police line on 88th Street, and strolled around to the front of the building on Central Park West. There she spotted a small man leaving the building, walking rapidly south. He looked as if he was late for something.

Ashley ran after the man, quickly catching up to him. "Excuse me, sir, could you tell me what all the commotion is about?" Ashley, walking abreast of the man, did not identify herself as a reporter.

The man glanced sideways at the woman. Her good looks grabbed his attention. "Somebody got killed. A woman on the eighteenth floor. The doorman said she worked for the Global News Network. But I didn't know her."

"Did the doorman say how she died?" Ashley was now almost breathless, the GNN reference having startled her.

"Jumped off the terrace."

"That's terrible." Ashley thanked the man, did an about-face, and walked quickly back to the apartment building, where she approached the cop stationed by the main entrance.

"Only residents allowed in, lady."

"Can you tell me who the detective in charge is, Officer?"

"Can't tell you nothin', lady."

"Officer, I'm Ashley Van Buren from the *Globe*. I'd really appreciate just that little piece of information." Ashley smiled. The young cop smiled back. He was black, in his mid twenties. A good looking guy.

"You're better lookin' than your picture," the cop whispered shyly. "O'Malley's in charge, but you didn't get that from me."

Ashley nodded, thanked the cop, and turned toward Central Park, which was right across the street. It was still cloudy and windy and brightly colored leaves were fluttering to the ground. Ashley quickly thought it through and decided to take a chance. She stepped onto the street and hailed a taxi: "119th Street between Park and Lex," she said to the cabbie.

The elderly driver looked back at Ashley as she got in the cab. "That's Spanish Harlem, sweetheart. You sure you want to go up there?"

Ashley paused, leaned forward, and looked at the cabbie's dashboard license where his name and hack number were listed. "Hector, I'm real sure. And if you get me there in under fifteen minutes, there's an extra five for you."

Muy bien, senorita. And Hector sped away.

• • •

Sitting on metal folding chairs in a circle in Lt. Brendan McGowan's tiny office were Tommy O'Malley, Jackson Davis, and five other detectives who had responded to the Ross crime scene. Detective Murray remained at the apartment building watching the coroner go through his paces.

McGowan's office was on the second floor of the twenty-fifth precinct. It featured one small window with a view of the decrepit apartment building next door. The detectives barely had enough room to situate their chairs around the lieutenant's cluttered desk, which bothered Brendan McGowan not at all. He did not care that his current office looked like the interior of a body shop. What he absolutely did care about was his future office, the one downtown in Police Headquarters. The one with the blue carpeting, leather sofa, and private bathroom.

McGowan was third generation NYPD. His grandfather had walked a beat in Brooklyn in the thirties. His father had risen to Detective First Class, and now Brendan's self-imposed mandate was to improve on that. Lt. Brendan McGowan wanted the four stars on his shoulder: he wanted the job of Chief of Detectives.

To get that position, McGowan had to play the game. That meant joining the right organizations: The Knights of Columbus, The Ancient Order of Hibernians, The Police Athletic League. It also meant keeping his squad efficient and clean. There could be no corruption allegations, and at least sixty-five percent of all homicides had to be solved.

Thanks mainly to the team of Tommy O'Malley and Jackson Davis, the murder clearance rate was easily achieved, and there had not been a single corruption investigation on his watch. But now Brendan McGowan saw trouble. The minute Tommy had told him about the GNN connection, McGowan knew the case would be personally monitored by the Mayor and the Police Commissioner. Solve it and McGowan was golden. Blow it, and this crummy office was his for the next decade.

As he always did before speaking, McGowan cleared his throat. He was a balding man of medium height and weight. His one distinguishing physical characteristic was a flat nose, broken in a Golden Gloves boxing competition as a teenager. "I just talked with the C.O.D," McGowan told the group, "and he's meetin' with the Commissioner in about an hour. Obviously, this case is priority number one. Tommy, what are we looking at?"

"It's a clean job, Mac. Nothing visible in the apartment. No sign of forced entry. No obvious suspect. It looks like he tied the woman up, dragged her across the living room, and tossed her. The perp didn't leave any prints or any calling cards. The problem is that this is the second dead GNN person. Remember that reporter who got whacked in Massachusetts? We may be looking for a serial killer with a grudge."

"That's all we need," said McGowan, whom Tommy considered a dead ringer for Kojak's boss on TV—the one who was always exasperated at Telly Savalas. "Did we bring in the Laser?" McGowan asked. He was frowning heavily. The specter of a political nightmare was getting stronger.

"The crime scene boys are still out there," Tommy said. "As soon as they finish the prelims, Murray will call and we'll bring in the Laser."

McGowan let loose an audible sigh. The laser system was an infrared, high-tech gizmo that could pinpoint fiber or skin or blood not apparent to the human eye. It was a clue magnet. But Brendan McGowan hated to rely on machines.

"Well, this just sucks," said McGowan, his agitation rising in intensity. "Absolutely sucks. GNN. Goddamnit." Tommy thought Brendan

McGowan might pop a blood vessel.

"We'll get the guy, Mac," Tommy promised softly.

"But not before I'm out on the heart bill, Tommy." The other detectives smiled. If a cop was diagnosed with chest pains, he could retire on three-quarters pay, tax free. Some cops prayed for this; others, like McGowan, were lifers. Everybody in the room knew the lieutenant had upper brass aspirations.

The rest of the meeting was spent batting around theories and dividing up the investigation. Tommy and Jackson would handle the GNN interviews; the other detectives would talk with the apartment people. Information would be pooled, and a daily update would be written for Lt. McGowan's eyes only.

Just as the meeting was breaking up, Rosa Gonzalez, the office secretary, walked into the office to tell Tommy he had a phone call.

"Detective O'Malley."

"Detective, this is Ashley Van Buren. Do you have a minute?"

"Can't talk to the press, Ms. Van Buren."

"Detective, I'm right across the street at Ragg's. I may have some information about the GNN investigation." Ragg's was the corner bar that catered to off-duty cops. Owned by two former policemen, it was a small oasis in the middle of the dangerous, decaying neighborhood where the twenty-fifth precinct and O'Malley's homicide unit were located.

"What kind of information, madam?" asked Tommy, sounding a bit testy.

"Well, Detective, what I have in mind is a little trade. I'll give you what I have, if you give me some background on the case."

Tommy O'Malley hesitated. He knew this kind of quid pro quo was dangerous. But he had nothing. He badly needed anything he could get. "Okay, Ms. Van Buren, walk on over here to our offices. I'll meet you by the side door."

Ashley Van Buren crossed the street at the corner of 119th and Park. A train rumbled above on the elevated track. Looking at the dilapidated exterior of the old precinct building, she quickly reached the conclusion that the city should provide better housing for its police.

Ashley had been inside the "Two-Five" a couple of times, but had never gone upstairs to the second floor offices of the Manhattan North Specialized Homicide Squad. Now she walked through the police parking lot adjacent to the building, and up to the metal door where Tommy O'Malley was waiting. He did not look happy. After his curt greeting, she followed him up the stairs.

The place reminded her of an old high school. The walls were painted yellow, the floor was brown linoleum, and even though the overhead lighting was dim, it was clear the whole place badly needed to be cleaned.

Tommy O'Malley ushered the reporter into his office—the one he shared with three other detectives. Ashley couldn't believe it. The place looked like something out of the old TV show *Dragnet*. There were four metal desks in the room, each with an old manual typewriter on top. Looming over the typewriters were cheap desk lamps in various stages of disrepair. Steel gray filing cabinets lined the walls and, in the back of the office, crooked venetian blinds hung at an angle, exposing a window that was home to dirt from the Truman era.

Ashley took it all in, and then sat down on a wooden chair, crossing her legs. "Quite a showplace you've got here."

"Well, we don't do much entertaining," Tommy shot back. He was in no mood for small talk.

Ashley continued to glance around, fascinated by the notices tacked to the walls. One of the larger signs featured a skull and crossbones. Underneath the emblem were the words: "For quick service, call the Manhattan North Homicide Squad: when it absolutely, positively has to be destroyed over night." Another official-looking sign read: "Corruption Must Be Reported To The Internal Affairs Division." And finally, a handwritten note was taped to a cabinet: "You Don't Have to Go it Alone: Alcohol and Gambling Counseling is Available."

"So, Ms. Van Buren, now that we're comfortable, whaddya have for me?" Tommy looked the reporter straight in the eye. It wasn't hard. A few cops had gathered outside Tommy's office and were glancing inside. It didn't take a detective to figure out why.

"Well, first of all, Detective, please call me Ash. Enough with the Ms. Van Buren stuff. The deal I'd like to make is that after I tell you, you tell me."

"Tell you *what*?"

"What you have."

"No way."

"Well, at least give me something I couldn't get from the uniforms."

"We'll see. What have you got, uh, Ash?" Tommy kept to his gruff mode, but he was definitely attracted to the gorgeous blond reporter.

Ashley uncrossed her legs, leaning forward, all the while keeping eye contact with O'Malley. "Well, after I wrote my first column on the Costello murder, I got a call on my voice mail. Some woman left me a message saying that she worked for GNN, and was on Martha's Vineyard when Costello got it. She said she saw two former GNN correspondents on the island, both of whom had reason to hate this guy Costello. She also said that maybe it wasn't a big deal because a lot of people despised Costello. I think the word she used to describe him rhymed with 'brick.'"

Tommy looked at Ashley and nodded. Sensing his approval, she continued.

"Anyway, the woman wrapped up her call by leaving two names on the tape: David Wayne and Shannon Michaels. Now, I know Michaels. He used to anchor the Channel Six News. I met him at an awards ceremony one year. It doesn't seem possible for a guy like that to be a killer, so I didn't put much stock in the information, especially since the caller was qualifying everything she said and didn't seem convinced that these guys were dangerous."

"Where can I get in touch with this woman?" said Tommy, removing a notebook from his jacket pocket.

Ashley stammered and looked away from O'Malley. She didn't know why, but she was nervous. "Uh, well, uh, that could be a problem. The source didn't leave her name or number on the voice mail, said she didn't want to get sued or anything."

Tommy stared incredulously at Ashley. "You mean to say that you're a news reporter and people can't call you directly? They have to talk to a machine? Don't you realize how much information you can lose that way?"

"I know, Detective, but the paper doesn't want to hire secretaries. Voice mail is a lot cheaper. So everybody has voice mail."

"Jesus Christ, how stupid. So, there's no way we can find this woman? Did you save the taped message?"

"Sorry, Detective."

"Damnit. So, really Ash, you've given me nothing solid."

Ashley stiffened. "I've given you two names, Detective O'Malley. And you know as well as I do that the information is worth checking out. What is it now, about eighty percent of all murders get solved by tips? I've given you a good lead. Two GNN killings. It isn't a stretch to think it might be somebody from the inside."

"Thank you, Agatha Christie." Tommy's voice was still harsh but he allowed himself a slight smile. It wasn't great information but it wasn't worthless either. "There are probably plenty of people who hated Costello and Ross. I hear TV news is a bitch of a business."

Now it was Ashley Van Buren's turn to take out a notebook. "Ross?"

Tommy O'Malley looked again into Ashley Van Buren's green eyes. Hell, she was going to find out anyway. "Hillary Ross, some kinda VP at GNN. Single white female, thirty-nine, fairly affluent. Lived alone on the eighteenth floor. Somebody tossed her off the balcony."

"How awful." Of course, Ashley knew that already, but wanted O'Malley to keep talking. She began taking notes. "Who did it?" Ashley smiled. O'Malley smiled back, again just a little.

"Only the Shadow knows."

"Anything to go on?" Ashley was beginning to notice O'Malley noticing her.

"No comment on the investigation. You know it's policy. The C.O.D. will be updating you."

"Oh, the Chief of Detectives won't say anything everybody else in the world doesn't already know." Ashley opened her eyes wide. "Can't you give me anything, Detective?"

Tommy bit his lower lip. "I don't want to see my name in your column, Ash, so this is from an unnamed source. Got it?" Ashley nodded, and Tommy continued. "Whoever did this crime knew what he was doing. It was a very clean hit. That's all I can say."

"So you're saying it was a professional who did this?" Ashley asked.

"The guy could bat cleanup for Murder Incorporated."

Ashley wrote that down. It was a great line, and the *Globe* would love it. "Okay, Detective. Now, about the dinner I owe you. You thought I'd forgotten, didn't you? Here's my home number. Call me and we'll do it. That is, if you still want to."

O'Malley didn't reply but reached out and accepted Ashley Van Buren's home number, which she had written on the back of her business card. He tucked the card in the inner pocket of his sports jacket. She knew he would call.

"By the way, Detective, are you going to speak with Shannon

Michaels and David Wayne?"

Tommy shrugged. "Don't know."

Once again, Ashley knew that he would.

CHAPTER ELEVEN

The murder of Hillary Ross was page one news in every New York news-paper except *The Times*, which ran it on the first page of the Metro section. The city's three all-news radio stations ran the story every twenty minutes, and one needed a calculator to add up all the TV live shots that originated in front of the murder scene.

But a full twenty-four hours after the discovery of the body, hard information was still elusive. Of course, that didn't stop the reporters. They just speculated.

Shannon Michaels got up early, and as soon as he heard the story on WINS radio, he went out to buy all the papers. As in the Costello case, Ashley Van Buren seemed to have the best take on the situation. She tied the two killings together, emphasizing the lack of evidence left at both crime scenes. Shannon was sitting in his library digesting the news accounts when the phone rang.

"Shannon Michaels speaking."

"Mr. Michaels, my name is Ashley Van Buren, I'm a reporter for the *Globe*."

"Quite a coincidence, Ms. Van Buren, I was just reading your column. What a terrible situation." Shannon kept his voice cool, but his mind was racing. Why was this reporter calling *him*?

"I'm glad you're aware of the case. I wonder if I could ask you a few questions, just for background."

"Why me? I haven't worked for GNN in twelve years." Shannon's voice remained calm, but he was becoming concerned. How did this woman get his number?

Ashley was used to people not wanting to talk to her and sensed Shannon's anxiety. She tried to put him at ease. "I won't use your name or anything. I'm just trying to get an idea as to why somebody would kill these two people. Nobody currently working at GNN will say any-thing. The network flack has no comment, and everybody else is scared."

"But, again, how did you come to me?"

"Off the record, one of my sources at GNN told me that you knew both Costello and Ross. Also, that you were an outspoken guy."

"But how did you find me? I have an unlisted number."

Ashley Van Buren laughed. "The *Globe* often reaches out and touches someone at the telephone company, Mr. Michaels. Most everybody likes to go to the theatre."

Shannon Michaels thought back. He remembered meeting Ashley Van Buren. He remembered that she was extremely attractive. It might be interesting to see her again. He decided to take a chance. "I may be outspoken but I'm not a fool. I'll speak to you off the record. But not on the phone. I was planning on coming into the city today. If you'd like, we could meet for a drink."

"Great, where and when?"

"The bar at the Carlyle Hotel. Four o'clock."

"Fine. I'll see you then. And thank you."

"You're welcome," said Shannon Michaels.

• • •

Tommy O'Malley and Jackson Davis walked into the huge executive conference room on the seventh floor of GNN Headquarters, escorted from the lobby by a young man with an overpowering smell of musk cologne. When asked if they would like coffee, Evian, or a soft drink, the detectives politely declined, and the man departed saying that William Foster, the news president, would be with them momentarily along with his assistants.

The two detectives looked over the conference room. The centerpiece was a beautiful twenty-foot-long mahogany table, polished so finely it reflected the soft overhead lights. The walls were paneled with light brown wood. The carpet was a rich, thick beige.

Along the walls hung an assortment of awards GNN had won. At the far end of the room was a wide screen TV, complete with VCR. A well stocked bar flanked the television on the left side. Two long floor-to-ceiling windows, each draped by heavy curtains matching the carpet color, gave an onlooker an exceptional view of the wide avenue below. The curtains were pulled back, allowing some natural light to stream into the room.

"Looks just like our office," Jackson cracked. Tommy rolled his eyes.

After five minutes, the GNN executives had not yet appeared.

Tommy walked out into the hallway, spotting the young man who had ushered them to the conference room. The man was standing, talking to a secretary.

"Excuse me, sir. Would you remind Mr. Foster that we are here?"

"Mr. Foster is very busy, Detective, but I'm sure..."

Tommy cut him off. "Listen son, if Mr. Foster isn't out here in sixty seconds, my partner and I will be joining him in his office. Is that clear?" O'Malley's tone was condescending.

"Yes, Detective," said the escort as he scampered away.

"Two can play these fuckin' power games," Tommy said to Jackson as they walked back into the conference room. Jackson just yawned. He was not nearly as impatient as his partner.

Less than a minute later, William "Big Bill" Foster and his deputies Myles Romney and Greta Brink walked into the room.

"Sorry to keep you waiting, Detectives. We had a mini-crisis in Japan." William Foster forced a smile as he shook hands and made the introductions. Tommy noticed Foster discreetly checking his appearance. As usual, the detectives were dressed in bland blue business suits bought on sale at Macy's. Foster's appearance was impeccable—dark blue pinstriped suit, blue and red club tie on a blue shirt with a white collar, and black wingtips, freshly polished. Tommy noticed that Foster's fingernails were shiny. Some kind of gloss was on them.

"Please sit down, gentlemen. This is a terrible business and we are here to cooperate in any way we can." Foster was smiling again, smiling even though it was a "terrible business." Tommy instinctively didn't like the guy.

Jackson Davis led off the questioning: "Any idea why somebody would kill two GNN employees?"

Foster responded so automatically it was clear he had anticipated the question. "Detectives, we're not entirely sure these dreadful crimes are related. Both Ron Costello and Hillary Ross were well respected professionals. GNN has absolutely no idea why anyone would want to do them harm."

Tommy directed the follow-up question at Foster: "What did Ms. Ross do here?"

"She was Vice President in charge of News Personnel, which means she oversaw and evaluated the work of our news gathering employees."

"Did she fire people?" asked Tommy, bluntly.

"On occasion. But that wasn't her primary function."

"Well, Mr. Foster, firing someone can cause very hard feelings." As Tommy made his statement, he looked quickly at Jackson. Tommy could read his partner, and it was obvious that Jackson didn't like Foster either.

"I'm sure that's true, Detective O'Malley, but it's a necessary part of the business of television news as well as most other businesses, as I'm sure you know."

Jackson Davis spoke quietly: "How many people have been fired here in, say, the last five years?"

"Myles?" William Foster turned toward his male deputy, a small, thin man with bushy eyebrows and thick black hair. Tommy could smell the man's cologne from across the table. 'What's *with* these guys?' he thought.

"Because of changing economic times," Myles Romney began, "GNN has downsized considerably over the past few years. Unfortunately, we've had to let many employees go."

"How many?" Tommy sounded impatient.

"Hundreds." Myles Romney sounded sheepish.

"But many received very generous settlements," Foster cut in. His voice was smooth, controlled. 'The perfect company man,' Tommy thought.

"Mr. Romney," Jackson Davis said, "we would like a list of everyone who has left GNN in the past ten years, together with their social security numbers." Davis knew how embarrassing that information would be for GNN.

"But that would be thousands of people!" said Romney.

William Foster broke in again, saying, "We'll get you that information, Detectives. What else can we do?"

"Tell us about Ron Costello," Tommy said.

"Well, I've only been President of News for two years, but in that time, Ron was one of our primary correspondents. An excellent reporter."

"Was he an excellent human being?"

"We had the highest regard for Ron Costello." William Foster, his forehead starting to shine with perspiration, looked away from O'Malley. Tommy felt Foster growing a bit uneasy. The man wasn't used to answering tough questions.

"Is there anything else you can tell us? Anything unusual happen before the Ross incident?" Jackson Davis asked.

"Well, there is one thing," Foster said, looking over at Greta Brink. "Greta?"

Foster's female deputy was well tailored in a dark green suit complemented by a light green and white scarf. Her hair was tied back, a generous amount of makeup carefully applied to her face. She looked to be in her mid forties.

Greta Brink cleared her throat and smiled a nervous smile. "Yes, well, one of our interns on the overnight desk told us that she received a call from a stringer in Beijing wanting Hillary's home address. This young woman says she thought it strange, and didn't give him the information. But we can't know that for certain. The name of the stringer does not coincide with anyone working for us."

"Did this young woman come forward before or after the death of Ms. Ross?"

"After."

Immediately, Tommy and Jackson both knew she had given up Ross' home address. "We'll hafta speak with her," Tommy said. "We'd also like to talk with Lyle Fleming."

William Foster looked concerned. "Why?"

Tommy O'Malley looked at the spiffy news executive, with his expensive clothes and shiny nails, and said softly, "Because we want to."

• • •

The Carlyle Hotel on Madison and 76th Street was an old money depot. Its lobby was the very picture of understated elegance—the floors were marble, the wall furnishings were fabulously expensive tapestries that featured scenes of fox hunting, and the flowers flanking the check-in area were always freshly picked.

Ashley Van Buren sat in the bar off the lobby nursing an eight-dollar glass of white wine when Shannon Michaels walked in and approached her. Michaels was wearing a blue suede jacket over a starched white, button-down shirt, jeans, and boots. Black-framed glasses covered his penetrating blue eyes. His brown hair was tousled. Ashley thought he looked dashing.

Shannon bowed slightly and gently shook Ashley's outstretched hand as he sat down. He smiled. 'A shy smile,' Ashley thought. 'A nice smile.'

"What are you having, Mr. Michaels? It's on the *Globe*."

"Just a mineral water, thanks. And please call me Shannon."

"What an unusual name," Ashley said as the waiter went off to get Shannon's drink. "Is it your birth name or a TV thing?"

"I'm named after the river in Ireland. That's where my parents went on their honeymoon, and that's where I was conceived. In a little bed and breakfast place with a view of the Shannon River."

"How romantic."

"The name has really served me well," Shannon continued. "It's trendy for anchormen to have unusual names. Look at Stone and Forrest." Shannon smiled again. Ashley smiled back.

"So what can I do for you, Ashley?" Shannon felt a surge of excitement as he looked into the woman's green eyes. It was probably foolish of him to talk to this reporter. But what the hell. The riskier the situation, the more Shannon was attracted to it.

"This GNN thing is very tough to break down," Ashley said. "I've called dozens of people at GNN, but I'm getting nothing. Nobody will talk about Costello or Ross."

"Everybody's scared," Shannon said.

"Why?"

"We are completely off the record here, right Ashley?"

"Well, I'd like to use what you say, but I won't mention your name. Okay?"

Shannon thought it over, keeping eye contact with the reporter. "Right now, I'm out of TV and writing a book. But I may want to get back in the game sometime. And if you burn me, that will never happen. Nobody in television can speak with candor about the industry because there are always reprisals. It's a small world and talking out of turn is never rewarded."

"Why did you leave Channel 6?" Ashley asked.

"Surely you know I was fired. Your paper ran the story on page one."

"Yeah, and it was strange. You were on top in the ratings. Everybody thought there was something funny going on behind the scenes."

"Then why didn't one of your crack reporters look into it?"

Ashley had no answer, but saw the pain in Shannon's eyes. She immediately felt sorry for him. "Well, if it means anything, I thought you were great on the air. That station hasn't been the same since."

"Nice of you to say. Now let's go over this one more time, because I don't want any misunderstandings. I am trusting you. My words are not for direct attribution. You can use 'a source says.' What I say is not to be taken out of context, or used to debate anyone else. My words stand alone, and you protect my identity. No one is to know that we have spoken, including your editor. Agreed?"

"Agreed." Ashley opened her notebook and felt oddly excited. "First off, tell me about Ron Costello."

"Scum of the earth." Shannon's blunt answer took Ashley Van Buren aback. She stared at him. No smiles now. Shannon Michaels' look was very intense.

"How so?"

"Costello was a fraud. He was a dishonest individual who committed the worst journalistic sin of all: He stole the work of other reporters."

"Can you give me an example?"

"I could, but I won't...because that would lead directly back to me. However, if you do a little leg work, you'll find plenty of GNN people who will privately tell you the same thing."

"So Costello wasn't liked at GNN?"

"The old guard liked him fine. Lyle Fleming and those guys. Costello was a yes man. Fleming knew he was no threat to him as an anchor, but he had been around a long time. The GNN tradition and all that. Remember, Fleming came from local news. He anchored in D.C. Unlike Jennings, Rather, Brokaw, and Shaw, Fleming didn't have network reporting experience before becoming a network anchor. He needed guys like Costello who had so-called credibility. Who had been to Vietnam. Who had covered summits. Fleming is just a reader. He's insecure about his news background. He needs to surround himself with veteran correspondents to jack up GNN's prestige."

"Why did you so dislike Costello?" Ashley asked.

"I despise dishonesty. And Costello was as dishonest as they come. He masqueraded as a reporter. Yeah, he covered big stories. But he didn't actually do much reporting. Others did that. Costello would sit around drinking while GNN producers and reporters were in the field gathering information and shooting videotape. Then he took their work and made it his own. Stole it outright."

"Hard to believe," Ashley said, hoping her skepticism would lead him to say more.

"Check out the term 'bigfooting,'" Shannon answered.

"Can't you be more specific? I'm having trouble with the concept that a news organization like GNN would allow that to happen. Nobody would steal stories at the *Globe*."

Shannon did not reply. He stared at Ashley. The silence grew uncomfortable for her. She changed the subject. "What about Hillary Ross?"

"A hatchet woman who ruined scores of lives and enjoyed doing it." Shannon bit off his words.

Once again Ashley was surprised by Shannon's terseness. She continued taking notes. She knew she was getting great stuff.

"Hillary Ross," Shannon continued, "is, I should say was, one of those people who shows up on the network payroll with absolutely no news experience. Yet, she comes in as an executive. The woman never covered a news story in her life. Had no journalistic skills. But there she was, passing judgment on how veteran correspondents were doing their jobs."

"How did she get in that position?" Ashley asked.

"Two reasons. First, she was an informer. I've lost track of how many Presidents of News GNN has had in the last ten years but, believe me, Hillary Ross was passing along information to all of them. The kind of information that damages people's careers. Maybe an indiscreet remark made in a fit of anger. Maybe a rumor about an affair. Hillary Ross could hurt anyone she wanted to hurt."

"But why would network executives allow something like that to go on?" Ashley's pen was skipping, its ink going dry. She fumbled in her purse for another pen.

"The suits need and want information," Shannon answered. "They aren't trusted, so they don't have direct access to what their employees are thinking. The office politics are intense and the agendas are different. The reporters and producers want to make as much money as they can for themselves, but executives stand in the way of that. Their charge is to keep salaries low, and to make people fear for their jobs. So there's distrust and little interaction. Let's just say there are two separate camps."

"So the executives have to plant somebody in the workers' camp so they can know what's going on."

"Sure," Shannon Michaels said. "They need somebody who will pass along the dirt and that's what Ross did. She had her spies on the floor, and information flowed. But all the time Ross was ratting on those around her, she also protected herself by filling Lyle Fleming in on what was going on in the executive chambers. She knew that Fleming would probably outlast the suits, and she wanted to cover her butt. Wanted some powerful person at GNN, Fleming, to rely on her and protect her just in case a News President came in who was perceptive enough to see what kind of person Hillary Ross really was. So, in effect, Ross was a double agent. And she did very well for herself."

Shannon, looking at Ashley Van Buren, was becoming very attracted to her. He hadn't been with a woman for a long time.

"Are you ready for reason two?" Shannon asked Ashley, her eyes still widening.

Ashley nodded, her pen at the ready.

"Ross was valuable to GNN because she enjoyed firing people. She got off on it. It was like sex to her. Most executives are non-confrontational. They want deniability. They hatch their plots in private. They never want to be associated with a public firing just in case the person they fire winds up winning a Peabody or an Emmy after going over to the competition. So they gave the dirty job to Hillary. And she loved the power it brought her. She loved the fact that people feared her."

Ashley put down her notebook and took a sip of wine. Then she took another sip. She was trying to decide how to phrase a rather delicate question.

"So, you're glad Costello and Ross are dead?"

"No, I'm not," Shannon said warily. "I feel no emotion at all. I wouldn't waste my emotions on those people. But I understand why they died. I believe somebody they knew killed them. I know at least five people who could have done this. But it would be wrong of me to direct suspicion onto someone who may be innocent. That's what the cops do." Shannon's lips formed a wry smile.

Ashley looked at Shannon Michaels and saw something she

couldn't quite define. She was very attracted to him. He was powerful and direct and intelligent. He had presence. But he unsettled her.

Shannon, sensing he was being evaluated, softened his voice. "I'm sorry to come on so strong. It's just that Costello and Ross were two very bad people in my judgment. You should check further. Maybe they had some good qualities I've somehow overlooked." Ashley wasn't sure if Shannon was being sarcastic or not.

"You're an interesting man, Shannon," Ashley said, smiling just a little. "I appreciate your helping me out, and I have just one more question. What do you know about David Wayne?"

The question took Shannon by surprise, but he recovered quickly. "Good guy. GNN fired him in a downsizing slaughter a few years ago."

"Was he bitter about it?" Ashley asked.

"You'd have to ask him. I haven't seen David in years."

"Do you know where he is?"

"No idea. But if I see him, I'll tell him of your interest." Shannon smiled and looked away from Ashley's eyes. Turning back, he added: "You're a beautiful woman, Ms. Van Buren, but probably spoiled as hell." Shannon then gave her his best smile. It worked. She was intrigued.

"Now, I have a question for you, Ashley," Shannon said. "How about having dinner with me Saturday night?"

CHAPTER TWELVE

Lieutenant Brendan McGowan looked like he was either going to cry or throw up. Tommy and Jackson couldn't decide which. Their boss had deep circles under his eyes and his comb-over was coming apart. As he nervously rubbed his head, large portions of pink scalp reflected the overhead light.

"So what you guys are tellin' me is that we don't have shit? Is that what you're tellin' me?"

Tommy nodded. He and Jackson had briefed him on the bad news. Nobody at the apartment building saw anything. It was Halloween. Plenty of people were running around in costumes. Forensics had very little—only a couple of rubber fibers from the sole of a sneaker. The Laser got that. The coroner said the woman had been knocked unconscious before being tossed over the balcony. She had also swallowed some panty hose. That was how the perp gagged her.

There were hundreds of suspects, including all the people Hillary Ross had fired. Somebody with some inside knowledge of GNN, and an English accent, had inquired about her shortly before the murder, at least according to the frightened intern who took the call. But with no physical evidence, and no witnesses, the case was ice. McGowan was distraught.

"Do you guys realize the Commissioner has called me twice? It's my ass on the line here. We've got to clear this thing. Where do we go now?"

"I've got a couple of ideas, Mac," Tommy said. "Both Jack and I think the same guy did both hits. It's probably somebody who feels he was fucked by Costello and Ross. It's definitely very personal. And personal things always unravel."

"I'm going to tell the Commissioner we got leads." McGowan had a faraway look in his eye.

"Yeah, fine. Just give us a little room," Tommy said. "We'll get this guy."

Tommy and Jackson walked out of McGowan's office, sat down at their desks, and worked out strategy. Three individuals remained to be interviewed: Lyle Fleming, who had agreed to meet them in his apartment the following morning; Shannon Michaels, whose address they had gotten from his union, AFTRA; and David Wayne, who was also an AFTRA member. Michaels lived out on Long Island someplace. Wayne lived in midtown.

It was almost eight p.m. and the coffee pot was empty. Tommy and Jackson decided to head over to Ragg's for dinner and maybe a drink or two. Tommy needed a drink. The GNN killer was very professional, very slick, and very arrogant—a thug who figured he could murder with impunity. He was probably laughing at the police right now.

"We're gonna fucking nail this guy, Jack," Tommy said as he walked across the street toward the bar. "I don't know how yet, but we'll get him."

Tommy O'Malley looked over at his partner, expecting a response. But Jackson Davis just kept on walking in silence.

CHAPTER THIRTEEN

The clock radio clicked on at seven a.m. with Billy Joel singing about honesty. A prone Tommy O'Malley, trying desperately to change the station, almost knocked the radio off the nightstand. On came the nasal voice of Howard Stern, the outrageous shock jock whose primary mission in life was to make famous women admit they had had lesbian affairs. O'Malley could never figure out why Stern was so popular, but most of the young cops he knew listened to the guy religiously. This morning Stern was ranting about Michael Jackson seducing little boys, and about Jackson's wife, Lisa Marie Presley, daughter of the King.

Tommy got out of bed and headed into the shower. Forty-five minutes later, Tommy was walking on West 79th Street toward Millie's Coffee Shop, where he was to meet Jackson Davis. Even at this early hour, a legion of beggars was working the streets. 'Mostly crack heads who haven't been to bed yet,' Tommy thought.

"Hey, bro, got change?" Tommy O'Malley stared the blade-thin man down and brushed past him. He couldn't believe that the streets of New York had been turned over to the hustlers. Five years earlier, the cops would have never permitted it. But Mayor Dinkins hadn't seen anything objectionable in having beggars hanging out on every corner, so that's what evolved. The new police commissioner, William Bratton, was changing things for the better, but taking back the streets, if only from the beggars, was a slow process.

When Tommy walked into Millie's, Jackson Davis was already sitting in a booth, shaking his head while reading the *New York Globe*.

"Did you see this Van Buren piece?"

Tommy had not seen it. Jackson brought him up to speed as Tommy ordered coffee and scrambled eggs. Ashley Van Buren had written a column saying that Ron Costello and Hillary Ross had something in common: they were both despised by many of their coworkers. Ashley quoted blind sources—unnamed people—to make the accusations. GNN had no official comment. Yet, Lyle Fleming not only said he had the highest regard for both of the deceased, but practically insisted in the column that anyone saying otherwise was a lying coward.

"Gutsy column," Tommy said. "Had to come from the inside. Maybe former GNN people who got screwed. Could be Shannon Michaels or the other guy, David Wayne. Van Buren has a line on them."

"You going to see Michaels?" Jackson asked.

"Yeah, soon. I gotta see my mother anyway. They're both on the Island."

Jackson smiled. "How *is* she?"

"Busting my chops as usual. Every time she calls, I know it's gonna cost me. The St. Anthony Fund, St. Jude, St. Elsewhere, it never ends. Between her and my ex-wife, I'm going to heaven for sure. And if I don't, I want a refund."

Jackson laughed. "You tell her she owes me a big corned beef and cabbage dinner for saving your ass time and time again. Surely she knows who the brains of this operation is."

It was Tommy's turn to laugh. "Jack, that earring is cuttin' off circulation to your brain. Gimme the ketchup, will ya?"

"I can't believe you dump ketchup on everything. God, don't pour it right on top of those runny eggs. That is gross, my brother. Is there anything you don't put ketchup on?"

"Lobster," Tommy said with a grin. "But I haven't ruled it out."

• • •

Lyle Fleming was one of the most powerful men in America. His forum as GNN's nightly anchorman ensured that twenty million people saw his face each weeknight. The influential and the famous— from the President on down—courted him with vigor. Whatever Lyle wanted, Lyle got. America had rejected royalty, but eagerly embraced media stars and professional athletes, bestowing adulation on them that was almost frightening in its intensity. For Lyle Fleming, the opportunities for immediate gratification were everywhere.

Tommy O'Malley and Jackson Davis arrived at Fleming's Park Avenue apartment precisely at nine a.m. They parked their unmarked car in front of a fire hydrant, checked in with the doorman, and rode the elevator up to the twenty-fifth floor.

Fleming lived in what New Yorkers call a "prewar" building—a structure that was built before World War II. The appointments were impressive: hand-carved stone gargoyles on the building's facade and crystal chandeliers in the lobby. And the entire building was spotlessly maintained. It was exactly what one would expect of Manhattan's upper east side, one of the wealthiest neighborhoods in the world.

Fleming's three-bedroom apartment faced Park Avenue. His young wife answered the door, graciously greeting the detectives. Tommy thought she looked Middle Eastern: brunette, tanned skin, dark exotic eyes with a hint of the Orient in them. A beautiful woman, immaculately dressed in a white blouse and black slacks.

"Lyle will be out in a minute. He's just finishing up a call. Would you gentlemen like an espresso? Perhaps a cappuccino?"

Tommy and Jackson looked at each other. "Sure," Tommy said.

Fleming's wife smiled patiently. "Which will it be, Detectives?"

"Cappuccino," Jackson answered diffidently. "Cappuccino's good."

After keeping the detectives waiting for five minutes, Lyle Fleming finally emerged from his bedroom. He was smiling as he shook hands. His delayed entrance signaled his sense of self-importance. He was used to appearing when he felt like it. Nobody was going to rush Lyle Fleming.

"Sorry to keep you waiting, Detectives, I had to monitor the daily conference call with all our bureaus." Fleming looked to see if his explanation impressed the policemen. He was disappointed.

Fleming walked over to a black leather easy chair and motioned for Tommy and Jackson to resume sitting on the white couch. Although the apartment was built in the twenties, the Flemings had furnished it in a high tech, modern style. Impressionist paintings were hung on the eggshell colored walls. Shiny black tables flanked the chairs and sofa. And the large Persian rug covering the hardwood living room floor was red and black. Tommy was no expert, but he sensed that the interior had been decorated with too much money and too little thought.

"Did you see the *Globe* today?" Fleming asked. Jackson answered yes.

Tommy took in the GNN anchorman. About 5'9, 175 pounds, black, wavy hair—probably colored— and a lined face indicating that Lyle Fleming would never see fifty years of age again.

"Just a terrible, irresponsible piece of journalism," said Fleming, sounding like he was delivering a speech. "These tabloid papers will print anything. Respect for the dead? Forget it. I'm sorry I even talked to the woman."

Tommy and Jackson did not react to Fleming's statement. They did not want the anchorman to get comfortable. Controlling the interview was the detectives' job. To do that, Lyle Fleming would have to be put a bit off balance. The less confident an interview subject was, the more likely he or she would speak candidly.

"Mr. Fleming, our information is that both Costello and Ms. Ross had enemies inside GNN. Is that true?" Tommy's peremptory tone of voice told Lyle Fleming to pay attention.

"Network news is a rough business, Detective. We all have enemies."

"Didn't Hillary Ross fire people?" asked Jackson Davis.

"Well, yes."

"So we can assume that some GNN employees, perhaps those who were fired by her, did not think as highly of Ms. Ross as you seem to?"

Fleming didn't let it show, but he was surprised that Jackson Davis was so well spoken. "Perhaps so, Detective, but, as I told the *Globe*, both Ron Costello and Hillary Ross were valued members of the GNN family."

Fleming's wife appeared with the cappuccino, and just in time. Tommy O'Malley was already losing patience with the interview, especially Fleming phrases like "the GNN family."

"Okay, Mr. Fleming, let's not waste your time. Any ideas about who might have killed these people?" Tommy asked.

"I have no clue, Detectives."

"Do you know Shannon Michaels and David Wayne?"

Lyle Fleming's eyebrows shot up. "Are they suspects?"

"At this point, there *are* no suspects, Mr. Fleming. I am asking you about these men in confidence. I don't want their names splashed all over the news. Or even talked about in the newsroom. That would be 'terrible and irresponsible,' to use your words." Tommy was staring hard at Fleming.

"I quite understand, Detectives. And anything I say is off the record as well. There are so many libel and slander lawsuits these days. Now about your question. Shannon Michaels reported for us for a brief time in the early eighties. He just didn't work out. Got into some trouble in Argentina during the Falkland conflict. After that he went back to local news. Much better suited to that world."

Lyle Fleming took a sip of cappuccino and resumed his monologue. "David Wayne was with us for more than twenty years. Unfortunately, he was let go a few years back when GNN downsized the correspondent corps. I argued against that, you know. I liked David, but GNN commissioned a study by an outfit in Los Angeles, I believe. Its research showed that GNN viewers preferred to watch younger correspondents. So David and four other reporters were let go. I made certain the company gave him and the four others a nice settlement."

'Sure,' O'Malley thought.

"Was Ross the one who fired him?" Jackson asked.

"Hillary was involved in the downsizing, yes."

"And how about Shannon Michaels? Did she ax him too?"

Fleming sipped his coffee and looked at Tommy O'Malley, choosing his words carefully. 'The detective isn't too impressed with me,' Fleming thought. 'Somewhere down the road, he might say bad things to the press about GNN, and worst of all, about Lyle Fleming.'

"I believe Hillary had something to do with Shannon's departure as well. But that was a long time ago. I could be wrong."

"Was David Wayne in Argentina along with Shannon Michaels?" A possible scenario was beginning to form in O'Malley's mind.

"I believe so, yes."

"Was Ron Costello down there?"

"Yes, he was the primary correspondent."

"Any bad blood between Costello and Wayne or Michaels?"

Lyle Fleming was thinking hard now. And both Tommy and Jackson saw his hesitation. "You know, Detectives, there is often intense competition among correspondents for airtime. Sometimes disagreements occur."

"Let's drop the diplomacy, Mr. Fleming." Tommy's voice was low and hard. "Did Ron Costello piss off David Wayne and Shannon Michaels?"

"Yes, Detectives. Now that I think about it, I believe he did."

Tommy O'Malley sat back on the couch, putting his hands behind his head. "Why don't you tell us about that, Mr. Fleming? And please try to recall every detail you can."

CHAPTER FOURTEEN

It had cost Shannon Michaels a crisp fifty-dollar bill, but the restaurant captain had come through on a very busy Saturday night. The table at the Rainbow Grill could not have been better. Shannon and Ashley Van Buren were seated against the window looking south over the towers of Manhattan. The Grill, at the top of 30 Rockefeller Center, more than one hundred stories up, afforded spectacular views of the city.

Ashley's appearance matched the stunning surroundings. Her black silk dress was low cut but elegant. She wore a pearl choker around her slim neck. Shannon had known many beautiful women in his life, but Ashley Van Buren had a natural grace to go along with her beauty. A very rare combination.

Ashley smiled at Shannon, appraising him differently in a social situation than she had on the job. He was very well dressed in a navy blue blazer, gray trousers, and powder blue shirt. His tie was a Hermes. To Ashley, Shannon looked like a *GQ* model without the hair mousse.

Shannon realized he was being measured and it pleased him. Another challenge had presented itself. If he could charm this woman, if he could rise to the challenge, it would be a huge ego boost. He decided to quickly distract Ashley with an offbeat bit of conversation.

"Here's a very personal question for you. Are you related to the political Van Burens?"

Ashley smiled. "I heard somewhere that we are distant cousins of the Van Burens of Kinderhook."

Shannon was impressed. The woman had an historical frame of reference—the eighth President of the United States, Martin Van Buren, was from Kinderhook, New York, on the Hudson. "I don't want to bore you, but did you know that President Van Buren is responsible for arguably the most frequently used word in the modern world?"

Ashley shook her head no, her blonde hair flaring out just slightly. Her lipstick, Shannon noticed, was a subtle shade of light red. 'Just right,' he thought. "Well, here's the scoop. In 1835, Van Buren was Vice President and Andrew Jackson was President. Jackson was a rough guy. John Quincy Adams once said that he was a barbarian who could hardly spell his own name. Anyway, Van Buren was a smooth, slick politician whom Jackson relied on to articulate the policies of his administration. And Van Buren did his job well. In fact, he was so obsequious that he agreed with everything Jackson said. 'Yes, General, you're right, General,' and so on. He was the Ed McMahon of eighteenth century politics."

Shannon paused, looking at Ashley. "This is really boring, isn't it?"

"Not so far, and I'm really looking forward to the payoff." Ashley laughed.

"Well, here it comes. Martin Van Buren's nickname was, logically enough, 'Old Kinderhook,' because he came from Kinderhook, New York. The nickname was eventually shortened just to O.K. And since Van Buren agreed with everything Jackson said, those living in Washington started using O.K. as slang, meaning 'right you are.' And now nearly everybody in the world says okay when things are, well, all right. Is that story *okay* with you?"

Ashley's green eyes shone. She laughed with genuine feeling. "So my great, great, great Uncle is responsible for the word okay?"

"You bet."

"What a great story." Ashley was having fun.

"Thanks," Shannon said and shyly looked down at the table. The move was calculated. Shannon had learned a long time ago that being coy was an essential part of flirting. Women liked confident men, but they also liked little boys. For men, the trick was to combine the two qualities.

The waiter arrived and took their orders: shrimp cocktail, house salad, and baked salmon for her; Caesar salad, filet mignon, and baked potato for him. Ashley was beginning to relax. The wine and table candles helped ease her apprehensions about Shannon Michaels. She was beginning to feel comfortable with him, even though she still sensed a hidden intensity. 'Overachievers are always like that,' she thought.

For his part, Shannon was happy with the way the evening was progressing. He steered the conversation to Ashley to learn more about her family and career plans. She was very open, admitting that she and her father did not see eye-to-eye on some important issues, and she confessed her fears about *Globe* coworkers who might be out to get her. Shannon waited until dessert to ask the obvious question.

"So why aren't you involved with someone?"

Ashley was prepared for the query. She heard it all the time. In truth, the question annoyed her. Nevertheless, she smiled. "Well, probably because I can't find Mr. Right. Most of the guys I meet are either intimidated by my job, looking for a quick conquest, or looking for someone to take care of them. Plus, there are a lot of creeps out there. You have to be very careful in this city. I could tell you stories."

"Go ahead," said Shannon.

"I really shouldn't but...okay, just one. We'll dedicate it to Martin Van Buren." They both laughed. "There was this guy I met at the gym about a year ago. He seemed nice, didn't come on too strong. I talked to him for weeks before I went out with him. Finally, we had a few dates. We had fun. He was always viewing himself in the mirror, but, hey, nobody's perfect. He was very into his body. I once told him he had skinny legs and he sulked for hours.

"Anyway, the guy sold advertising time on TV. Had a lot of money. So he asks me to go away with him to the Berkshires for the weekend. Now, I usually don't do that. I'm always working and I had never spent more than a few hours at a stretch with this guy. But my girlfriends were all for it, saying you have to spend time with someone in order to get to know him. Makes sense, right?"

Shannon nodded.

"So, off we go to Lenox, Massachusetts in his brand new Saab. Unfortunately, I happen to spill some moisturizing lotion in the front seat as we're driving on the Taconic Parkway. No big deal. It comes right off. Well, this guy has a meltdown. He whips the car off the highway. I have to get out while he makes an inspection. For fifteen minutes, the guy is rubbing a cloth on the seat covers. I swear there was nothing there. I'm trying not to laugh, but finally I say, 'Come on.' He gets mad. The weekend went downhill from there. We didn't even sleep together because I made fun of him. I told him if he would rub me like he rubbed the car, I would get very turned on. He didn't see the humor. So, that's what women like me are dealing with these days. Guys who are *Saab*ing."

Shannon laughed. "Great story. You should write it up for *Cosmo*."

"So, how about you?" Ashley asked. "Why aren't you married?"

"Nobody wants to marry me. I guess I've been selfish in my life. I always wanted an adventurous career and I put that first. Relationships are not compatible with running around the world covering war and pestilence."

"Didn't you ever come close? I mean, you *are* in your forties," Ashley asked.

"Never even went steady. I think my mother, before she died, thought I would never get married. I always told her I was gay. She didn't believe me."

"Maybe you are gay and don't even know it." Ashley was teasing him, testing his reaction.

"I hope so. Then maybe somebody will buy me dinner." They both laughed. Ashley was enjoying the parrying. Shannon sensed she liked him, and continued talking about himself for another few minutes. Finally, the check appeared on a sterling silver tray. For what the dinner cost, Shannon could have bought the tray. But he wordlessly paid the tab, and the couple took the elevator down to the real world.

Though it was only early November, the ice skating rink at Rockefeller Center was filled with skaters. Ashley and Shannon leaned over the railing above the oval rink watching a little Oriental girl perform flawless spins in the middle of the ice. After each success, she waved to a man who looked like her father. He was videotaping her performance.

"Do you skate, Ash?"

"Haven't in a long time."

"We'll have to get you out there."

"Not dressed like this you won't." And Ashley Van Buren smiled her break-your-heart smile.

The couple walked over to Fifth Avenue and hailed a cab in front of St. Patrick's Cathedral. During the taxi ride to the Upper East Side, Ashley debated in her mind whether to invite Shannon up to her apartment for a drink. She liked him, but knew she had to be careful. He was charming but somewhat mysterious. She finally decided that she could handle the situation. The cab dropped them in front of a modern high rise building, and the two took the elevator to her apartment on the fifth floor.

Shannon smiled as he glanced around Ashley's place. She was changing in the bedroom, and he was sitting on the sofa holding a glass of Diet Coke and listening to the Polish jazz singer Basia on the stereo.

The apartment was typical upper east side, Shannon thought. Probably fifteen hundred a month. Dotting the walls were a packed bookcase and pictures of Ashley's family and career highlights: Ashley with Rudy Guiliani, and Mario Cuomo, and Bryant Gumbel. The woman had an impressive pictorial résumé. The sofa where Shannon was sitting faced a large TV surrounded by videotapes of every description. On top of the set sat a stuffed teddy bear wearing a button that said: "Get in Dutch with the Dutch."

Ashley emerged from her bedroom wearing a man's white dress shirt untucked over blue jeans. As she stood in front of him, Shannon thought she looked incredibly sexy.

"I can't stay long, but before I go, I want to show you something I learned in Thailand," Shannon said. He knew his statement would pique her curiosity.

"Oh, I've heard that line before," Ashley replied laughing.

"Okay Van Buren," Shannon smiled. "Pull up that Ottoman and sit in front of the couch with your back to me."

Ashley hesitated but, out of curiosity, did as Shannon asked. Sitting on the edge of the couch, he leaned forward and faced her back. "Now, close your eyes and relax your muscles. Let me know if the pressure is too hard." Shannon then placed his thumbs on the top of Ashley's neck, at the base of her skull. Using a circular motion, he kneaded her skin, at first slowly, but then applying more pressure and speed.

Ashley felt the tension dissolving from her neck and shoulders like an ocean tide receding from the sand. Shannon was using all his fingers now, massaging the back of her head lightly.

"I'm messing up your hair. I hope you don't mind."

Ashley shook her head no. She was concentrating on his firm touch against her skin. It felt great.

Working his hands down each side of Ashley's spine, Shannon was careful not to apply too much pressure. Deep massage was the Japanese way. His technique was to continually knead and lightly stretch her skin through the soft cotton shirt. Taking off her shirt had entered Ashley's mind, but she rejected it, deciding it would get her into major trouble.

In a few short minutes, Ashley's chin almost touched the top of her chest, her mind was floating, and she was seriously relaxed. Then

111

Shannon's hands encircled each of her biceps, lightly squeezing them. At the same time, he bent his face forward, softly placing his tongue on the right side of her neck. In an upward motion, his tongue advanced on her skin to just below her earlobe. Goose bumps appeared on Ashley's body. She involuntarily shivered. 'This guy really knows what he's doing,' she thought.

Shannon decided to accelerate the foreplay. He lightly bit Ashley's earlobe, ran his tongue back down the length of her neck, and continued across the top of her shoulders, all the while massaging the top half of her arms. He then quickened the pace, massaging and licking her neck with more pressure. She shuddered again, closing her eyes and trying to control her breathing, which was becoming increasingly labored.

Moving his hands forward, Shannon cupped Ashley's breasts over her shirt. He felt her taut nipples and was surprised at the fullness of her breasts. From rubbing her back, he knew that she wasn't wearing a brassiere.

Ashley was excited, but not ready to go any further. "I think we should stop now," she said in a husky voice.

"Don't worry, I'm almost finished. Just stay relaxed." Shannon's voice was low. He was enjoying himself immensely.

Ashley's shoulders sagged into a passive slouch and she felt Shannon gently tweak her nipples with his thumbs and forefingers. He then began to move his fingers in a light circular motion. Her breasts strained against her shirt. It felt so good. It had been so long since she made love. Shannon then lightly bit the back of her neck while continuing to massage her breasts. "That's all for tonight," he said. "But if you want to learn more about Thailand, I'm available next Saturday."

Ashley remained silent, not wanting to appear anxious.

After the massage, the two kissed passionately and things grew heated once again. But Shannon, believing things would be better if they didn't rush, told Ashley he was staying at his rented house on the North Fork of Eastern Long Island that coming week. It was where he did much of his writing. Very private, no phones, no interruptions. But he would be back in the city next weekend. Ashley agreed to see him then.

After a final kiss, Shannon walked into the night, feeling powerful and in control. It was a feeling he valued above all others.

CHAPTER FIFTEEN

Ashley Van Buren's phone rang at ten a.m. on Sunday morning. She was still in bed, memories of the night before drifting through her mind. Thinking the caller might be Shannon, she immediately picked up the phone.

"Ashley, Tommy O'Malley. How ya doin'?"

"Detective, how nice to hear from you," said Ashley, smiling.

"Call me Tommy. Listen, if you're not busy tonight, maybe we could grab a bite. Something casual."

"That would be great, Tommy, but I'm treating, so let's go someplace nice."

"I don't know anyplace nice," Tommy said laughing.

"Bella Vita. Corner of 75th and York. Seven o'clock. Be there or else." Ashley laughed softly. Tommy liked the sound.

"See ya then."

Ashley got up from her queen-sized bed still wearing the same white shirt and blue cotton panties from the night before. The wine from the restaurant had caused a slight puffiness under her eyes. 'Last night...' she said to herself. 'Last night was nice.'

Because it was overcast, Ashley decided it was the perfect day to run errands. She packed up her dirty laundry, two large sacks full, and took it down to Chin's on Second Avenue. Then she went for a jog to Central Park and back. Finally, she picked up the Sunday papers and devoted the rest of the afternoon to reading. It was rare that Ashley got this amount of quiet time.

• • •

Tommy O'Malley rose from his corner table to greet Ashley Van Buren as she entered the restaurant. His huge frame loomed over her.

"Hey, you better sit down before I get a neck ache. I'm only five two,

113

and, what, you're bigger than Patrick Ewing, right?" Ashley smiled broadly. Her green eyes twinkled.

"Us big guys fall very hard, you know," said Tommy, who thought the reporter looked better every time he saw her.

"Somehow, Detective O'Malley, I cannot see you falling. I just can't picture it. Maybe it would be like a Gulliver thing, and I would be one of the Lilliputians."

"We better stop there. If you're gonna talk literature to me, I'll panic."

The restaurant was nearly empty. Tommy and Ashley looked out the window onto York Avenue. This area of New York City had long been a haven for Northern and Eastern Europeans. Yuppies had recently moved into the neighborhood in force. 'Ashley is certainly one of them,' Tommy thought. But it didn't matter. If he could court and marry Angela Rufino, he could handle anything.

She didn't know him well, but Ashley wasn't guarded with Tommy O'Malley. She instinctively trusted the big detective. There was something about his face. It was open and honest, and Tommy didn't look like he was hiding any dark secrets. He was kind of good looking, not classically handsome like Shannon Michaels. He could lose a few pounds but, with his large frame, he looked stocky rather than fat. Very masculine.

The evening had gotten off to a nice, light start and the couple spent the first half hour of their date talking about themselves, their jobs, and the media. Even though she had just gone through the same drill with Shannon Michaels, Ashley wasn't getting bored. It felt good to talk about herself. Tommy, on the other hand, hated talking about himself but would do it if that's what Ashley wanted. He tried not to stare at her for too long at one stretch, but thought that Ashley was the first woman he had ever known who looked sexy even while chewing a mouthful of food. He was seriously turned on. Finally, Ashley brought up the GNN case.

"So, what's the situation?"

Tommy was comfortable with the reporter now, so he didn't hold back. "Well, we still don't have much. Jack and I went over to interview David Wayne. Strange guy. Divorced, lives alone. Has a thirst that he quenches quite often, if you know what I mean. Doesn't do much. 'A little consulting,' he says. But he works out, and his grip is a crusher. By the way, your tipster was right. Wayne admits to being on Martha's Vineyard when Costello went down. Says he goes there a lot to visit reporter-type friends."

"How did he react to you and Jackson?" Ashley asked.

"Well, he was nervous, but didn't ask for a lawyer or anything. No squawking about his rights. And I didn't get any sense of menace from him, although he does admit to despising Costello and Ross. Actually, he hates just about everyone at GNN. They fired him after twenty-something years, tellin' the guy that research said he was too old to appeal to their audience. Pretty damn ruthless, if you ask me. Anyway, we're gonna watch the guy but we've got nothin' hard on him. I'm sending his picture up to the Massachusetts State Police. They'll show it around the island. Maybe somethin'll pop. Now we gotta talk to this Shannon Michaels."

"He's not your killer," Ashley said, matter-of-factly.

Tommy was instantly on alert. "How do you know?" he asked, more emphatically than he meant to.

Ashley noticed the edge in Tommy's voice but was not put off. "I spent some time with him yesterday. There's no way this guy's a killer. He's establishment all the way, plenty of money, big house. He seemed very genuine and nice. Not the criminal type, in my humble opinion, and I am the 'Queen of Crime,' you know." Ashley smiled, trying to keep things light.

Tommy O'Malley frowned. "Be careful, Ash. Some guys are real hard to read. I have no evidence against this Michaels, but that doesn't mean anything. Remember Ted Bundy? Law student. Had girlfriends in six states. His own mother swore the guy wasn't capable of hurting anyone, and to this day she still can't believe he was a crazed killer. The guy's mom didn't even know what he was capable of! Some of these psychos are really clever. They lead double lives."

"Shannon Michaels," said Ashley, "would have far too much to lose to get involved with anything like this." Ashley was getting more intense in her defense of Michaels, and it annoyed Tommy.

"Are you gonna see this guy again?"

"Maybe."

"Geez, Ash. Let me talk to him first, okay? I've left a couple of messages on his answering machine, but he hasn't called back."

"He's out on the far end of the Island. He's rented a place on the

115

water. A writer's retreat—you know, no phone, lots of privacy, no distractions."

'How convenient,' Tommy thought. "Do you have an address?"

"No, but he's supposed to call me during the week. I'll ask him to check in with you."

"Ash, I really mean this. Be careful with this guy. Both he and David Wayne seem to have motive and opportunity in the case."

"Detective, are you genuinely concerned for my welfare?" Ashley smiled.

"Yeah, I guess I am."

"How nice," Ashley grinned, licking her bottom lip. "My therapist says I need somebody who will be totally devoted to me."

"Your therapist?"

Ashley saw a bit of caution in Tommy O'Malley's eyes, and she instantly regretted the remark about her therapist. She rarely mentioned that relationship to anyone. But she felt so open with this guy. "Yeah," she continued, "she's been a big help to me."

"Why do you need a therapist? You seem like you know how to handle yourself." Tommy was genuinely curious.

"Sometimes things get complicated. Everybody needs someone to talk with. After my Mom died, I didn't have anyone who would sit there and listen to me ramble on. My father would have a heart attack. My girlfriends always have their own agendas. And forget about guys. Tell me the truth: Which would you rather do, listen to me talk about how confused I am, or watch the Knicks?"

"Who they playing?" Tommy said smiling broadly.

"You see. You men are all alike. Well, you're a bit different. You're bigger."

"And smarter, don't forget that."

Ashley laughed. "I don't know, Detective. If you were really smart, you'd have said you prefer me to the Knicks no matter what. Then I'd be yours forever."

"Yeah, but under false pretenses. I'm a man of integrity, you see."

"Oh, that's quite obvious." Ashley laughed, her eyes full of mischief. Tommy was beguiled. He was used to hard-edged women, not someone like Ashley, who was playful and spontaneous. "Now, enough of this," Ashley said. "I want to talk about sex. Tell me everything about your sex life, Detective O'Malley, and don't leave anything out."

O'Malley shook his head and laughed out loud, something he rarely did. Ashley sensed the guy really liked her, and there was something very sweet about him. 'Great,' she thought. 'Last week there were no guys. This week, two show up. Why is life always so complicated?'

CHAPTER SIXTEEN

LOS ANGELES
NOVEMBER, 1994

In Los Angeles, a man using the alias of Peter Grant walked off an American Airlines flight that had originated at JFK airport in New York. Grant was feeling tired and stiff. Though he had paid twelve hundred dollars in cash for his one-way ticket, it had only bought him an uncomfortable seat in coach class. Walk-up airline prices were absurdly high, he knew, but paying them in this case was the smartest move he could make, even if he had to sit in a seat designed for a jockey.

After foolishly going undisguised on Martha's Vineyard, he was now taking major precautions. He had purchased a Nevada driver's license bearing the name of Peter Grant from an outfit that had advertised in the classified pages of *Merc* magazine. The firm was called "What's Up, Documents," and its display ad promised to provide "facsimile" documents of all kinds at reasonable prices.

It was a simple transaction. "Peter Grant" had his picture taken wearing a false mustache and brown contact lenses. He sent the picture, along with one hundred dollars in cash, to the document company with instructions to send the "facsimile" driver's license to a post office box in New York City. His phony license arrived in two weeks. The workmanship was excellent. The day after receiving the license, he canceled the p.o. box, which he had rented for cash under the alias of Peter Grant.

After arriving in L.A., Grant immediately took a taxi to "Ray's Rapid Rent-a-Car" on Airport Way, about two miles from the terminal complex. Over the phone a week earlier, Ray himself had assured Mr. Grant that paying cash in advance would be fine. Fifty dollars a day for a '92 Nissan Maxima, plus a five-hundred-dollar deposit. At check-in, Ray noticed that Peter Grant was from Nevada and asked if he got to Vegas much. Mr. Grant shook his head no. Within forty-five minutes, Peter Grant was driving north toward Malibu. Since he was paying cash for everything, there would be no paper trail that could ever place him in California.

•••

At their New York desks, the paper was piling high as Tommy O'Malley and Jackson Davis went over computer printouts of everyone terminated from GNN since 1980. The list seemed endless and the work was tedious, so they almost felt relief when the "hello phone" rang across the room. The "hello phone" was a private number that informants were to use—it was always answered by a cop who said "hello" rather than "Manhattan North Homicide." The phone also could not be traced to the police department.

All this was necessary because, in the past, some bad guys had bribed corrupt phone workers for the records of suspected informants. More than one had been murdered when a police phone number was found on his call sheet.

Jackson Davis answered the phone, and Tommy noticed Jackson's expression growing solemn. After conversing for about five minutes, Jackson returned to his desk.

"I think we might have Robo Melton."

Tommy sat up straight. "Really?"

"Yeah, that was KY"—a code name the cops gave to this particular informant because the guy thought he was slick. "He says our pal Robo roughed up one of his girlfriends, a stripper named TZ Monroe, really bad. TZ is really pissed and out for extreme retribution. KY says she knows where some of Robo's secrets lie."

"So let's go see TZ. That does have a lyrical ring to it." Tommy grinned at Jackson. "And in what first class establishment can we find the lovely and charming Ms. Monroe?"

"Bare Essentials on 33rd and Fifth."

"A downtown girl. How fortunate for us. You drive, Jack. I'm too excited."

Bare Essentials was one of the girlie bars that were springing up throughout America's larger cities. In the age of AIDS, watching replaced doing in many quarters, and nude dancing in a so-called "upscale atmosphere" became big business. It was also the perfect setup for members of organized crime to launder money. In these clubs, cash flowed freely.

Tommy and Jackson drove downtown on the FDR drive, a construction nightmare that, on a daily basis, horrified drivers from all over the world. It took the detectives forty-five minutes to travel eight miles. They arrived just in time for the advertised happy hour and the lap dancing special.

The doorman greeting them at Bare Essentials was quite a human specimen: a neck that looked like a milk box, a small head, and—not surprisingly—even smaller, beady eyes. "Can I help you gentlemen?" The guy slurred his speech, making his question sound like one jumbled word.

"NYPD, fella. We need to speak to a lady named TZ Monroe." Jackson said the words with authority as he flashed his gold shield.

"I'll have to talk to Richie about that."

"Ah, Richie," Tommy said. "Nice to hear he's gainfully employed. You run along and get Richie. Meantime, we're going in to look around. It's getting cold out here."

"Can't letcha."

Tommy and Jackson looked at each other. They lived for moments like these. "Listen, sonny. We're going in and you can't stop us. And if you try, very bad things will happen to you." Tommy was moving closer to the doorman. In this kind of confrontation, his size always worked for him.

The doorman blinked nervously and backed away. "Richie ain't gonna like this."

"Oh, he'll get used to it," Tommy said as he and Jackson walked past the frustrated bouncer. "By the way, pinhead, lay off the steroids. They shrink your dick."

The inside decor of "Bare Essentials" was crushed black velvet and gold chrome. Upon entering, there was a long bar on the left, floor-to-ceiling mirrors on the right, and beyond, in the center of a long, rectangular room, an elevated stage. Around the stage were scores of round tables surrounded by velvet-covered chairs. About sixty men and perhaps a half dozen women sat around the tables watching naked female dancers writhe. Two dancers were on the main stage, five others atop individual tables.

As they slowly strolled through the club, Tommy and Jackson discussed what kind of a person would shell out the twenty dollar cover charge, pay $7.50 a drink, and another twenty bucks for one of the ladies to dance on top of his table. For a "lap dance," where a woman squirms around on one's upper legs and groin area, the price went up to thirty-five dollars plus tip. Tommy and Jackson agreed that most of the guys in the place were horny businessmen on expense accounts.

There were now six young women dancing with no clothes on—one of the table ladies had called it quits. Five of the dancers were obvious recipients of breast implants. Their unmoving chests were massively mounted, way out of proportion to the rest of their bodies. No matter how hard the naked ladies danced, their breasts stood firmly at attention. The sixth of the dancers was Latin, petite, and all natural.

Tommy and Jackson sat at a table about thirty feet from the stage where a nude woman with extremely long legs was swaying, her back to them. Keeping decent time to a song by Anita Baker, she bent forward and looked back at the audience through her parted legs. Spotting Tommy and Jackson, she waved. They waved back.

"Lovely, girl, don't you think, Jack?"

"All the right qualities," Jackson answered.

"Excuse me, gentlemen. Can I be of service?"

Tommy and Jackson looked up to see a bulky man, about 5'9, with slicked back hair, a ponytail, and diamond studded earrings looking down at them. The man was wearing an expensive, black silk suit. He looked like a dark closet.

"I bet you're Richie," Tommy said, boredom lacing his voice. "We would like to talk with one of your employees, lady by the name of TZ Monroe." Both Tommy and Jackson produced their shields.

"She's on a break right now. Can I ask what this is about?"

"No you can't, Richie. We just need a few moments of Ms. Monroe's time. It has nothing to do with the fine establishment you're running here. So we'd appreciate it if you would go get TZ and then, when we're finished speaking with her, if you would not ask her any questions. Am I making myself understood?" Tommy's severe look bore into the strip club manager. He knew the guy was a low-level thug who didn't like taking orders. He hoped the guy would make a mistake.

But like a feral animal, Richie sensed danger. He didn't want to have to explain a cop-altercation to his boss and brother-in-law, Carmine. He decided to cooperate.

"I'll get TZ. Would you like to use my office?"

"What a kind gesture. Thank you, Richie," Tommy said. And the detectives followed the pony-tailed man to the back of the club.

A few minutes later, Theresa "TZ" Monroe walked into the small office wearing very little but a well practiced scowl. She was actually tiny. Slender legs, slim hips, small waist, and enormous breasts. Tommy and Jackson stared—all of TZ was visible through her see-through top, including a pierced nipple and a small red tattoo of a devil just below her navel.

TZ sat down and the interview began. She wore a black wig, teased high, and had big brown eyes—the hard eyes of someone who hustles money for a living. When the detectives told her they were after Robo Melton, her eyes opened wider. She hated Robo, she said. He had beat her up because she wouldn't screw one of his friends. She couldn't dance for two weeks. That cost her more than three thousand dollars. Before that incident, she had been tight with Robo. He told her everything. Would the detectives like to know where he hid his murder weapons? Yes, the detectives would. Well, then, said TZ Monroe, if she could get paid, she would pass along the information.

• • •

Set back about sixty feet off the Pacific Coast Highway, the Surf's Up Motel on the outskirts of Malibu was one of those places where commerce is conducted one hour at a time. The perfect place for Peter Grant. The check-in guy at the seedy inn gladly took the tired-looking man's cash, in advance, for a three-day stay—an extended period of time for Surf's Up clientele. The guest asked for a room in the back— one that was more private, less noisy—and was checked in within ten minutes. The clerk, a young surfer dude, took little notice. Just another middle aged guy with a mustache and a baseball cap, probably on the prowl for a hooker.

Peter Grant suspected that the man he was interested in, Martin Moore, lived in the Malibu area, but he wasn't completely certain. Moore's company, News Resources, was headquartered in the upscale suburb of Brentwood on San Vincente Boulevard, very near to where O.J. Simpson lived. Moore's home number was unlisted so, using the name of a television executive in New York, Peter Grant had called Moore's office from a public phone saying he wanted to send Moore an "emergency Federal Express package." He hoped the secretary would give him Moore's home address. She would not, saying only that Moore had left for the beach, and wouldn't be available until tomorrow. The secretary asked if the caller wanted to send the package to the office.

Peter Grant politely declined, saying he would call back. As he hung up the phone, Grant figured that the beach the woman had referred to was probably Malibu, about ten miles northwest of Brentwood. Malibu was a prestigious area. Martin Moore coveted prestige.

The following morning, after a restless night's sleep on a mattress that sagged like a hammock, Peter Grant drove to the address of Martin Moore's News Resources Company. The television research firm was located on the fifth floor of a modern brick building, just down the block from Brentwood's most famous bookstore, Dutton's. Moore's building featured underground parking, which was a break for Grant. He guessed that an ego like Moore's would have a private parking space with his name prominently displayed on the wall.

He was right. It took Grant just four minutes of walking around the garage to locate a well-polished silver Jaguar. Written on the grimy white concrete above it in yellow block letters was the name of its proud owner: "Mr. Moore."

At about 6:15 that evening, Moore's silver Jag pulled out of the underground garage's driveway and turned right on San Vincente. Traffic was heavy as the car moved slowly along, taking a right on Bundy and then a left on Sunset heading toward the Pacific Ocean. Martin Moore did not notice the black Nissan following a half block behind him. He was far too busy talking on his car phone.

"Gordon, how are you? How are the overnights?" Moore was talking to the general manager of a Denver TV station. The station was slipping in the news ratings and Moore was being paid fifty thousand dollars plus expenses to find out why. Overnight ratings data provide instant analysis of how a station is performing on a daily basis.

After listening impatiently to the general manager's tale of woe, Moore got right to the point. "I've got in some initial research and it looks like you're going to have to make some changes with the on-air talent. That weatherman, Len Weaver, has no demographic appeal at all. He's skewing very old. Every time someone in Colorado dies, your ratings go down." Moore laughed. It was a line he used often. He turned right at Sunset, heading north onto the Pacific Coast Highway.

"I know he's been at the station for fifteen years, but your core audience is bored with him. My advice is to put him on the early morning shift, and let him go when his contract is up. You need some hot babe doing the weather. Got to get those male viewers up, pardon the pun."

Peter Grant had no trouble weaving through the evening traffic, keeping about three car lengths behind Martin Moore. The sun was already down, and dusk was rapidly turning to darkness. He was glad Moore was on the phone. His reconnaissance and subsequent plan would rely heavily on surprise. All distractions aided the predator.

The silver Jag headed up the highway doing about sixty. As he neared Malibu, the land of mudslides and sprinting brush fires, Grant reminded himself that this was one of the most expensive places on earth to live in. Thus, it was quite a shock when he encountered an atmosphere only describable as honky-tonk. Rundown beach shacks lined the west side of the roadway overlooking the ocean. On the right side, strips of low rent motels and fast food joints stood in front of eroding hillsides. Grant shook his head and grinned as he passed a giant revolving KFC chicken bucket.

Next came a twenty foot statue of a Mexican waiter complete with sombrero holding a tray full of south of the border cuisine. Finally, the electric blue sign for Alice's Restaurant appeared, signaling the heart of Malibu Beach.

Martin Moore exited the highway at Webb Way, taking a right on Old Malibu Road. Grant was relieved. If Moore had taken a left and driven into the famed Malibu Colony, where the likes of Johnny Carson and Tom Hanks lived, Grant's task would have been impossible. The Colony is carefully guarded around the clock.

After seeing that the two-lane road was uncrowded, Grant slowed his vehicle, staying well back as Moore drove north. A pickup truck swerved in front of him, its back bumper emblazoned with a sticker reading "Suicidal Tendencies." About two miles down the road, Peter Grant saw the Jaguar's brake lights illuminate. He accelerated, wanting to see where Martin Moore was turning.

Having finished his phone conversation, Moore wheeled into the driveway of his rented house. He paid eight thousand dollars a month for the three-bedroom home, owned by an Iranian businessman, which overlooked the beach. Moore hit the garage door remote and eased the Jag down the narrow driveway and into the small, attached garage. He was in for the night.

Grant passed Moore's home as the automatic garage door descended. He leisurely drove by, noting the house and its surroundings. Moore's place was the last one on the road, perched on a small cliff. The lot south of him was under construction. When it was finished, that new house would be just a few feet away from Moore's rental. To the north was nothing but rock.

About a hundred yards up the road, Peter Grant stopped, got out of his car, and looked back. Moore's house had direct access to the beach. Moore could walk out his back door and reach the water in seconds. The house was two stories high, and highlighted by a large patio filled with hanging plants and wrought iron furniture. The structure itself was weather-beaten and ringed by a white fence about seven feet high. Moore had plenty of privacy.

Peter Grant's eyes swept the landscape. He realized that the well-secured house would be a formidable opponent—much tougher to crack than the fat, out-of-shape Moore would be. He would need a little time to come up with a suitable strategy.

• • •

Jackson Davis was finishing up the paperwork on the informant KY and the stripper TZ Monroe. Each was to receive one thousand dollars in cash, courtesy of the City of New York, once Robo Melton was taken into custody, and evidence linking him to murder was seized. Davis made sure everything was in order in case the "cheese-eaters," a derogatory name used to describe the NYPD's internal affairs investigators, ever came sniffing around. Both KY and TZ were assigned code numbers, and photocopies of the cash vouchers and receipts were filed in triplicate.

TZ Monroe had spun a great tale. After a few drinks in a quiet bar away from the strip club, TZ told Jackson and Tommy how Robo Melton, after smoking a pipeful of crack, would brag about his murders. Rock cocaine made him feel powerful, TZ said. Robo was so proud of his "hits" that he kept each murder weapon as a trophy, stashing seven guns in the basement of his mother's house in Teaneck, New Jersey. Robo also hid drugs and cash there. He would visit his mother every Tuesday night for a home-cooked meal.

Now that the information was supplied, Tommy and Jackson dealt with the bureaucracy. Jackson called the Teaneck Police, asking the assistant chief to help him get an emergency search warrant. To put it on alert, Tommy called the Bergen County District Attorney's office. Tommy, Jackson and two other NYPD detectives then drove over the George Washington Bridge, met up with their peers from Teaneck in a coffee shop on Queen Anne Road, and planned the raid. Robo's mother lived in a small house just north of Route Four, off Teaneck Road. Eight policemen would surround the house and take Robo down.

The detectives parked their vehicles a block away from the Melton house and made the rest of their way on foot. In front of the white, nondescript home stood a red Mercedes. The New York license plate read "ROBO." 'Subtlety was never Robo's style,' Tommy thought.

Wearing Kevlar vests and armed with shotguns, the police fanned out around the house. Tommy and Jackson Davis walked up to the front door. Jackson rang the bell.

Still wearing a cast on the thumb that Tommy had broken, Robo Melton answered the door. His bloodshot eyes opened wide when he saw Tommy and Jackson standing in front of him with pistols drawn. "Why, hello Edgar," Tommy said. "We've just dropped by for dinner. And we brought a warrant with us."

Before Robo Melton could react, Jackson Davis grabbed his arms, spun him around, and viciously kicked Robo in the back of the knee. Robo collapsed. "Stay down, Edgar," Jackson said. "I mean it."

Tommy and three other detectives walked through the small, neat living room, nearly running into Robo's mother, who had hurried out of the kitchen on hearing the commotion.

"What you doin' to my boy?" The woman was small and round. She wore thick glasses and had her silver-gray hair tied back. Her brown eyes were slightly crossed and they stared at Tommy. She looked very frightened.

"Mrs. Melton," said Tommy, his voice soothing and sympathetic. "I'm Detective O'Malley from the New York City Police Department. We have a warrant to search your home. I'm very sorry for the intrusion, but please remain calm and sit down. We'll try not to be long."

"Oh Lord, oh my sweet Lord! Why are you here? My boy ain't done nothin'! Oh, Lord, please!" Mrs. Melton collapsed into a chair crying. Tommy sat down next to her as the other detectives found their way to the basement. The remaining two policemen in the squad stayed outside, one in the front yard, the other in the back.

Jackson Davis stood over Robo Melton, who lay prone on the

ground. He bent down and whispered, "Take a good look, scumbag. See the pain you're puttin' your mother through? See your mother over there, punk? How you think she's gonna feel when they put you away for life? You're a disgrace to your community."

Robo Melton didn't respond.

It took the detectives just ten minutes to find seven semiautomatic pistols, two small gym bags full of cash, and a brown paper bag that contained scores of tiny white rocks. Crack. The stash was hidden beneath a floorboard behind the oil burner. Edgar "Robo" Melton was arrested, read his rights, and dragged out to a police car. The entire operation took less than thirty minutes to complete.

Tommy was the last to leave the house. Before departing, he phoned Mrs. Melton's minister, asking him to come over immediately. He then gave the sobbing mother his card, promising to call her with more information. He despised Robo Melton, but realized Robo's mother probably knew nothing about her son's activities—in fact, she thought Robo owned a liquor store in Harlem. He saw a woman whose heart was breaking. He imagined how his own mother would look if something this calamitous happened to him.

• • •

The beach was cold. A chilly wind blowing in off the Pacific Ocean kept all but a handful of beachcombers away. The man calling himself Peter Grant didn't mind the brisk conditions. He was completely immersed in putting together his plan. Walking the beach in front of Moore's house, Grant saw signs warning of a silent alarm system. Because a Los Angeles County Sheriff's substation was just a few blocks away, the warning had to be taken seriously.

Under the circumstances, Martin Moore would have to be taken by surprise and in private. Because Moore drove just about everywhere, as most did in L.A., the place to confront him would be in his home. But there seemed to be no easy entry. Peter Grant continued his walk, evaluating various scenarios in his mind. None of them worked. Moore drove to work, drove to lunch, drove to dinner, drove home. He was either in the car or in a public place all day. Grant did not have time to stalk this man for weeks, hoping he would make a mistake. He needed to move fast.

• • •

"Susan, get Phil Lane on the phone for me, quickly please." Susan Oliver rolled her eyes. She had been looking for another job for months. Martin Moore, her boss, was an obnoxious, corrupt slob. She couldn't stand being his secretary. "And while I think of it, Sue, order me some sushi. And tell them it wasn't fresh last time. I want it fresh."

Martin Moore leaned back in his leather chair, his large belly forming a natural handrest. That morning, he had already spilled coffee on his tie, but he didn't care about his personal appearance. He was making six hundred thousand dollars a year, and plenty more in expenses.

Moore, now fifty-two years old, had been married three times. He had two teenage daughters living in Atlanta whom he saw twice a year. He sent them checks every month, so his conscience was clear. He couldn't help it if he thought their mother was a bitch.

Life for Martin Moore centered around television news, and life was good. He had been smart enough to figure out that although the industry was a huge money-making machine, it was very subjective, filled with insecure, frightened executives unsure about what would attract an audience and what would not. In professional sports, performance could be measured quickly in wins and losses. On TV, effectiveness was a matter of opinion. It could take months, sometimes years, to see if an anchorperson or news reporter was really attracting viewers, or to know if the tone of a local or network news broadcast was appealing to the mass audience.

A prime example of this was the CBS anchor partnership formed between Dan Rather and Connie Chung. Chung was given the job of co-anchor because CBS research showed two things: Dan Rather was losing popularity, and Connie Chung was liked by many viewers. Two years later, when the anchor changes failed to hike the ratings and there were all kinds of editorial problems, CBS sacked Chung. There was no word on whether the company fired the research outfit that had recommended the pairing in the first place.

Despite this and similar such failures, many television companies continued to rely heavily on audience research to make business decisions, and Martin Moore had set himself up as a "consultant" to feed off of that. He charged big money, but collecting and analyzing data was relatively cheap and easy. Moore would randomly call people on the phone, asking them what newscasters they liked and why. If the station were paying him a substantial amount of money, he might even pay people a small stipend to watch videotapes of news programs. Afterward, he would ask them to fill out questionnaires. That was called putting together a "focus group."

Moore would then tabulate the responses, which he would provide to the television executives. In his presentations, he used words like "quantitative," "qualitative," and "imagery." These words were soothing to executives because they sounded credible and scientific and, above all, gave management concrete reasons for making difficult decisions. "You can't argue with the research," the executives could say.

Moore had worked for some of the biggest corporations in television, including the Global News Network and Newscenter Six in New York City. His presentations were crisp and easy to understand. He also was a master at detecting the prevailing wind. His research results rarely went against the preconceived ideas of those responsible for hiring him.

Another highly appealing aspect of his job was the power. When he walked into a newsroom, people took notice. His interpretation of research could take their jobs away, and they knew it. Moore was treated with the utmost respect by the biggest names in the television business. He had come a long way from being called "fat boy" as a kid on the streets of Chicago.

• • •

It came to Peter Grant suddenly. Again and again his mind had replayed his surveillance of Martin Moore's Jag pulling into his garage. Grant pictured movement. The automatic garage door. Slowly going up. Slowly going down. Why hadn't he thought of it before? He had his way in.

Quickly, Grant put together the pieces of his plan. He drove to a hardware store in Santa Monica, purchasing a shovel, tape, twine and a large canvas bag. From a martial arts supply store, he bought just the right truncheon. He then phoned the Santa Monica surf and tide information line. Light winds, cloudy conditions, and low tide was the prediction for eleven p.m. that night.

•••

For Martin Moore, it had been yet another good business day. A New Orleans station wanted to change its anchor team and Moore had been hired to find out just what the Louisiana audience wanted. With any luck, he could schedule a trip to New Orleans to coincide with Mardi Gras.

After work, Moore dined at a Greek restaurant on Wilshire Boulevard with a couple he had met on a trip to Hawaii. The woman had chided him about his appearance, saying he'd never get another wife if he didn't clean up his act. His hair was dirty and his tie replete with coffee stains! She was appalled. But Moore didn't give a shit. He ordered more ouzo.

Not wanting any breathalyzer hassles with the police, Martin Moore took his time driving home. A cassette played James Taylor—Moore still relaxed to the music of icons from the sixties and seventies. Though he pulled into his driveway a thoroughly relaxed man, he became briefly agitated. 'Christ,' he thought, 'that garage door is opening awful slowly. I'll have to tell my bastard landlord Revi to fix it, that is if I can learn enough goddamn Farsi to make him understand.'

Moore finally drove his way in, slipped the Jag into park, and opened the car door. The garage door descended slowly, much as Moore expected, and he didn't notice the shadow pass beneath it. When he heard the door suddenly stop in midair, he walked back toward it, saying to himself, 'Goddamnit, that thing is ridiculous. I'll have to call Revi tomorrow.'

Unknown to Moore, an intruder had tripped the door's safety sensor, and was now crouched out of sight behind the Jag. Moore hit the garage door button located on the far wall, saw the door resume its downward path, and turned to enter the house. After taking two steps, he heard a slight rustling noise behind him, but before he could turn around, a flash of pain rocketed through his head. Martin Moore instantly lost consciousness and fell forward.

Peter Grant looked at the truncheon he had used on Moore and returned it to his back pocket. He quickly removed the consultant's shoes and socks, stuffing one of the socks in Moore's mouth. He placed heavy black tape over Moore's mouth and eyes. Flipping him over onto his stomach, Grant tied Moore's thumbs together behind his back. He also tied his ankles as tight as possible, the twine cutting into Moore's flesh. Grant checked his watch: it was 10:30, and there was quite a bit more to do.

Grant dragged Moore's heavy body into the house and placed it in a hall closet. Moore was breathing slowly. He would regain consciousness soon. Grant closed the closet door and pushed the heaviest piece of furniture in the living room, an oak desk, in front of it. Even if Martin Moore managed to break the twine, he probably wouldn't be able to push himself out of the closet.

After shutting down the house alarms and spotlights, Peter Grant unlocked the back door, walking swiftly out onto the patio. A couple of hours before, he had left his canvas bag there. Now, he picked the bag up and, within seconds, was on the beach, digging in the sand with his recently purchased shovel.

It took thirty minutes of intense work to hollow out a four foot hole a few feet above the low tide line. His surgeon's gloves chafed his hands. Wet sand was heavy, and Grant's arms ached. Even though it was cold, he was perspiring freely.

His task completed, Peter Grant stood up straight, cooling down and looking around. Apart from the surf, there was no sound and little light. In accordance with the weather predictions, low clouds were blocking the moon. Grant's back was stiff from his digging, so he tried to work out the kinks by twisting his torso. He saw the ocean beginning to creep back up. It was past eleven. He had to move. The tide was turning.

Careful to make just one narrow footpath in the sand, Grant walked back into the house. He pushed the desk away from the closet door and opened it. After hearing the sounds, Martin Moore began to wiggle, his heavy body flopping up and down. He was moving strenuously but was still secured. Peter Grant inhaled deeply and pulled Moore savagely from his confinement onto the hallway floor, where he then fiercely kicked him in the stomach.

He wanted to kick Moore a second time—seeing the man close up had ignited his rage. But Grant resisted the urge. Instead, he grabbed the back collar of Moore's sport jacket with two hands and pulled him across the living room, onto the porch, and down the stairs to the beach. It wasn't easy work. Moore was a load.

Breathing heavily, Peter Grant dragged Moore in a straight line, obliterating the footprints in the sand that he had made earlier. The fat man tried to struggle, but quickly lost his breath. The sock in his mouth made it hard for him to breathe. His chest was heaving and he was making low grunting sounds.

The freshly dug hole was barely deep enough to contain Moore. Grant forced the bound man into the space in a kneeling position, Moore's head facing toward the ocean. Since Moore was still blindfolded, he could only feel the wet sand filling up around him. He had no idea where he was or what was actually happening.

It took just a few minutes to bury Martin Moore up to his neck in the heavy, wet sand. When satisfied that Moore could not free himself, Grant turned to look at the ocean. The water was now about six feet away and coming in quickly. Grant turned, and again walked back toward the house.

Martin Moore knew he was in trouble, but little else was clear to him. His head throbbed and his stomach hurt badly. Bile rose in his mouth but was blocked by the cotton sock that filled it. Moore heard waves crashing, but in his disoriented state, had yet to put the crisis together. He had no idea who had accosted him. He wondered if he was being robbed.

Moving slowly and meticulously through Moore's house, Peter Grant made sure he left no clues behind. He scattered the sand that had fallen from his sneakers. Using gloves had prevented fingerprints, but his sneakers might have left an impression somewhere. He carefully examined the garage, the living room, and the porch, the only spaces he had occupied. Feeling confident, he returned to the beach, dragging his canvas bag behind him to wipe out any tracks.

The first splash of water touched Martin Moore's chin lightly. It was cold. It sent a chill through his entire body.

"How does that feel, Martin?" asked a low, menacing voice from above. Moore shuddered. He wanted to see who was speaking. When the adhesive tape was ripped away from his eyes, he got his wish.

In the darkness, Moore tried to look upward, rotating his neck in the sand. Another splash of salt water caressed his face. His eyes opened wide, his pupils trying to adjust after being forced shut for more than an hour. He saw a man with a mustache standing over him. He didn't recognize him. He saw the white foam of the ocean coming toward him. The cold water hit him in the face again, this time reaching his lips.

"The tide is coming in, Martin. And it will not detour around you," came the chilling voice. Immediately, Martin Moore knew his fate. He desperately tried to move his hands and feet, but he couldn't. The heavy sand pinned him down. The only thing he could move was his head. He twisted it back and forth, trying to shake the tape off his mouth in order to scream. Another ration of seawater slapped him in the face. Some of the water ran into his nose. Then the voice spoke again, this time with intense authority.

"You are vermin, Moore. Scum. You got me and scores of other people fired. You destroyed lives. But then again, Martin, you did get that nice house on the ocean out of it. Well, the ocean can cut both ways."

Martin Moore fought to control his panic. 'Oh, Christ,' he thought. 'Oh, sweet Jesus. Who is this guy?' But Moore had instigated so many dismissals, he had no idea who his assailant was. He began to feel nauseous. With his eyes, he pleaded for mercy. The man who called himself Peter Grant saw his victim's desperation, but it didn't calm his rage. He turned, looked out to sea, and made a final decision.

"Goodbye, Moore, you malicious bastard. You're in over your head this time. Your worthless life is over." Grant turned away from the trapped consultant, picked up the bag containing the shovel, and, as planned, walked north along the water line. After about a hundred yards, he scaled the short cliff that met the ocean. He then jogged back along the road until he reached his car, which was parked in the construction site next to Moore's home.

Martin Moore struggled furiously under the sand, but could not free himself. The desperate exertion made him short of breath. The oncoming tide now covered his nose. He tried to breathe deeply once the seawater receded for a few seconds. But it kept coming back and enveloping him. Moore's mind raced. His head swiveled from side to side. His eyes stung as the salt water reached forehead level. White foam went up his nose. He gagged on the sock in his mouth. His throat burned as his lungs filled with water. Then, a few seconds of precious air.

But again the salt water came, deeper this time, submerging his head. It took thirty minutes for the consultant to die, but in that time he never bothered to examine his life. To the end, he kept hoping that someone would come along to save him. No one did, and as Martin

Moore's lungs overflowed with water, his last thoughts on earth were pure self-pity: 'Dear God, how could this be happening to a guy like me?'

• • •

As he drove south toward the L.A. airport, Peter Grant tried to remain focused on his situation. He knew the high tide would cover his victim until daybreak. So he took the usual precautions. He deposited everything he had brought to Moore's house into a Santa Monica dumpster, including the dark clothing and sneakers he wore. Once back in New York, he would destroy his disguise and all documents relating to his alias, Peter Grant.

As he thought back on the execution, Grant's head throbbed with a migraine-like pain. This was the third time he had killed, and a strange feeling swept over him. He felt no remorse over the fate of Martin Moore, but he felt dirty and badly wanted to take a shower. He didn't know why. 'These people deserved what they were getting. If they weren't stopped, they would just go on hurting others.'

Peter Grant fought off his discomfort and continued driving south, staying in his car until the auto rental place opened at six a.m. He boarded the seven a.m. American Airlines flight back to New York, arriving home at four in the afternoon. During the journey, he was extremely preoccupied. He thought he would feel nothing from his completed missions but pure satisfaction. And initially, he had. But now his feelings were changing, and try as he might, he couldn't figure out why. Grant struggled with his emotions, trying to fend off the doubts that were creeping into his mind. Finally, he focused on his next victim. He pictured the man's face. Gradually, a quiet rage replaced the gnawing doubt.

Toward the end of the flight, another thought intruded on Peter Grant's consciousness—that of Detective Tommy O'Malley. Annoyed, Grant tried to strike all thoughts of O'Malley from his mind. But it was impossible. O'Malley's voice resounded in his mind over and over, and Peter Grant realized that, at some point, he was going to have to deal with that voice. Intuitively, one thing became very clear: Detective O'Malley was the only person on earth who could possibly stop him from achieving his goal.

CHAPTER SEVENTEEN

MALIBU BEACH
NOVEMBER, 1994

The jogger's scream pierced the thick morning fog. Shortly before nine a.m., Denise Hom, a twenty-five-year-old Pepperdine University graduate student, nearly fell over something protruding from the sand. Then, looking down, she saw Martin Moore's blue and grossly distorted face; his eyes were staring up at her and tape still covered his mouth. Denise Hom immediately vomited, and then ran faster than she had ever run in her life. She reached her car within minutes and drove to a phone booth to call 911.

The two L.A. County deputies who answered the call realized that they had only a short time before the tide would cover the crime scene again. They alerted Homicide Squad criminologists, so they would gather evidence, and the coroner's office, so they could conduct an autopsy. Within forty-five minutes, the murder investigation was well under way. Morbid onlookers were kept at a distance. The media were not contacted. This was Malibu, bastion of wealth and power. As at Martha's Vineyard, things would be kept as quiet as possible.

• • •

David Wayne was feeling both tired and stressed. The Jersey Turnpike was as packed as usual, and it seemed like he had been on it forever. And he had to make a decision. In two miles, he would exit and drive his rental car onto the Garden State Parkway, heading south. The question was: Would relaxation have to be induced? Could he make it to Atlantic City without stopping for some liquid? Or should he buy a refreshment and drink it while driving? He opted for caution. If the cops stopped him and found booze in the car, he'd be toast. His identification would be run through the computer within seconds. Besides, it was only two more hours until Bally's. 'I can make it,' Wayne thought, licking his lips. 'Then, the cocktails will flow.'

• • •

Less than thirty-six hours after being taken into custody, Edgar Robo Melton sang. Faced with strong ballistic evidence and an unknown witness whom the cops said was ready to testify, Robo's lawyer, Manuel Fernandez, made a deal. Robo gave up those who had helped him commit the murders. He also volunteered his drug connections. In return, the police guaranteed that he'd be placed in a protected cell at Riker's Island. Robo also plead guilty to murder, saving the state big money on a trial, on the condition that the maximum sentence, life without parole, was not imposed.

Ordinarily, Tommy O'Malley would have been elated with such a deal. He and Jackson Davis had cleared five homicides in the City, and two others upstate. It was a major coup for them. But Tommy was focused almost entirely on the GNN case. He had not yet made contact with Shannon Michaels, and he strongly suspected that Ashley Van Buren would not follow his advice—and soon see Michaels again.

• • •

As Ashley walked across the newsroom heading for the coffee pot, Bert Cicero bellowed from the city desk, "Hey, Van Buren! There's somethin' on the wires 'bout another TV guy gettin' whacked. In California this time. Check it out, wouldja? Let me know if I should order Morrison to get off his butt and outta the buildin'. The guy makes a livin' out there gettin' a tan." Craig Morrison was the Los Angeles Bureau Chief for *The New York Globe*.

Ashley smiled at Cicero and nodded assent. She actually liked Bert. He was an old fashioned New York newspaperman who worked fifteen hours a day. The last of a dying breed.

The wire report didn't say much. A man by the name of Martin Moore was found drowned on Malibu Beach. Police were investigating, but no official statement had been given. Moore worked as a television consultant. His company could not be reached for comment.

Ashley picked up the phone, dialing Tommy O'Malley. "Hi, keeping the city safe for people like me?"

Tommy smiled. Since their last meeting, he had thought more than once about Ashley. It was rare for him to dwell on his dates, as he was usually wrapped up in his work. Now, he was uncomfortable with his emotions, unwilling to deal with the possibility that he might be smitten. But even if he was, he damn well wasn't going to show it. So Tommy barked into the phone, "I'm keepin' the city safe *from* people like you. And tell me, to what do I owe this honor? The lovely and famous Ashley Van Buren callin' me?"

"Well, I'm looking out for you. There's a wire story from L.A. that says some guy in the TV business was found dead. Drowned. Not much else in the report. He wasn't a famous guy or anything. Didn't work for GNN."

"What did this guy actually do in television?" Tommy asked.

"Says here he was some kind of consultant."

Tommy frowned. 'Consultant. L.A. Lyle Fleming had mentioned a consultant, hadn't he? Downsizing. David Wayne. Presto.'

"Tommy, are you there?" Ashley wasn't used to silence from this cop, especially given his Irish ancestry.

"Yeah, I'm thinkin'. Whenever I do that, it hurts." Tommy opened his notebook and turned to the Fleming interview. There it was. Downsizing. Some consultant from L.A. That's how David Wayne got fired. 'Shit, I think we got another one,' he thought.

"What's going on, Tommy?" Ashley said impatiently.

"In our interview at his place, Lyle Fleming mentioned something about an L.A. consultant being in on a bunch of firings at GNN. I gotta go, Ash. I'll talk to ya later."

"Wait, Tommy..." she began, but he was already gone. Frustrated, Ashley hung up the phone, thinking, 'With yet another murder, this story is getting bigger by the minute. I better go write something.'

• • •

It took Tommy O'Malley four hours to get a call back from the Los Angeles County Sheriff's Department—despite his message saying it was vitally important that someone get back to him as soon as possible. Tommy knew he was lucky to get his call returned at all. Responding to phone messages was often not part of the L.A. lifestyle, even in law enforcement.

What Tommy got from the Public Information Officer was this: Middle-aged white man found buried up to his neck in the sand.

Drowned approximately at midnight. Body discovered nine hours later. No house break-in. No prints. Not much to go on. Criminologists and investigators were still on the job. Bizarre way to die, and we thought we'd seen everything. Keeping the media out of the case in deference to the neighborhood bigshots, and because of the brutal nature of the crime. Don't want to cause panic. Okay to talk to the lead investigator tomorrow.

Tommy and Jackson then decided to drop in on David Wayne, unannounced. They drove to Wayne's midtown apartment in heavy rush hour traffic and were immediately disappointed. Wayne had left on a trip, they were told. No, the doorman didn't know where, but he'd call the detectives the moment Wayne got back.

Tommy and Jackson drove back uptown debating whether a full-blown surveillance on David Wayne should have been ordered. Surveillance was time consuming and difficult to get approved because of the overtime pay costs. But now they had lost Wayne and they badly needed to find him. He had motive in all three killings. And, on this last one, he might have had opportunity. He was out of New York when the L.A. consultant was hit.

With quick action needed, Tommy decided to fly Jackson out to L.A. the next morning to investigate the Malibu killing himself. Lieutenant McGowan would have to approve the trip, but that shouldn't be a problem. Jackson agreed to head right over to Audits and Accounting, where he would pick up plane ticket money and some petty cash. "Petty" was the right word. When NYPD detectives traveled, their per diem was just twenty-five dollars. One hundred dollars per night was the absolute maximum for a hotel room.

While Jackson traveled, Tommy would stay in New York, trying to find David Wayne. He ordered checks on all planes, trains, and buses to see if Wayne had bought a ticket. Then he called an old friend.

• • •

"You're shitting me? Buried to his neck? God help him." Professor Patrick Larkin, a Professor of Criminology at the John Jay School of Criminal Justice, was intrigued by Tommy's description of the Malibu homicide, so much so that he took comprehensive notes. Tommy wanted to know if his friend had any theories about the killing, if there were any clues to be found in the strange method of the latest murder. Larkin said he had a few ideas and would call him back in twenty minutes.

Powerful men are often not patient men and Tommy O'Malley fit that profile. He was angry that he could not stop whoever was doing these killings. Hell, he couldn't even locate one suspect, or get the other one on the phone. And he certainly didn't have enough evidence to bring anybody in. In fact, he didn't have *any* evidence! The case was mocking him, the killer or killers thwarting his every effort. Tommy felt his frustration turning into low-level rage.

• • •

Ashley Van Buren hunched over her Macintosh computer. Beside her was a tuna sandwich, Fritos, and a diet soda—all untouched. She didn't have much information, but still managed to bang out a column concentrating on the third killing of a person connected with television news. She explained who Martin Moore was and what he did for a living, information provided by a girlfriend of hers who worked at ABC News and knew all about consultants. Because she didn't have any of the gory details about the Malibu murder, the column was flat. Nobody really cared what a TV news consultant actually did.

In the space of her eight-hundred word column, Ashley had asked fourteen questions. All of them added up to crap. Her editor was going to hate the piece, but would probably let it slide. Both of them knew that a columnist is supposed to *answer* questions, not ask them.

When the phone rang in her office, Ashley sat, unmoved and in a very bad mood. It was BCS: Bad Column Syndrome. Her voice mail kicked in and she sat back in her chair listening.

"This is Shannon Michaels and I'm tempted to leave a very obscene message." Ashley reached over and picked up the phone—a tad too quickly, she thought later on.

"Hi, where are you?"

"At my house in Sands Point."

"I thought you were locked away writing."

"Finished up this morning and drove in. You're my first call. Are we still on for tomorrow night?"

"Sure. Where and when?"

"Do you want to come out here? See how the landed gentry live?"

Ashley paused. If she went to his place, she knew *he* would have control. But if she turned him down without a reason, that would be rude. Her basic good nature prevailed. "I guess I could drive out there in a news car. But I have to be back here pretty early." She was setting up the possibility of a quick exit if she needed or wanted one.

"No problem. I'll fax you directions."

"By the way, Shannon, Tommy O'Malley wants to talk with you."

"Really? It seems you and he are becoming increasingly close." Shannon laughed softly, but was not amused. "The detective has left three messages for me. The last two didn't sound cordial. I'll have to call him."

"One more thing," Ashley said. "Did you hear there was another media murder?"

Shannon Michaels paused. "No, I didn't. Tell me about it."

• • •

"Here's the deal, Tommy, and it's pretty wild." Professor Patrick Larkin had kept his promise, calling O'Malley back practically within the hour. "What we have here is a killer who apparently knows a bit about history. His method of murder reflects it. To explain, I have to take you back to the Dark Ages."

"That's no problem, Paddy," Tommy said. "I'm very comfortable thinking in Dark Ages terms. Just ask my ex-wife."

Patrick Larkin smiled to himself. Typical Tommy. "Okay, Detective, listen up. Around the turn of the ninth century, the Vikings were creating a ruckus all along the Atlantic coast of Europe, especially in the British Isles. Their long ships usually set out from Norway with forty to sixty warriors along for the ride. These guys were brutal killing machines. Their mission was to pillage, rape, and cause as much chaos as humanly possible. In those days, most of the organized governments had broken down and it was every fiefdom for itself. People lived without the protection of large armies or legal systems."

Tommy took a sip of coffee—his seventh cup of the day. He was listening intently to Larkin and taking notes.

"Because of its monasteries, Ireland was a favorite destination of the Vikings. The Irish monks were educated and sophisticated, often hiding gold and precious stones in their abbeys. The Vikings knew this and attacked the abbeys whenever they could. Sometimes the monks fought back. Sometimes they ran. But it didn't matter what they did. The plunder was so good that the Norsemen came back time after time, eventually establishing colonies in Ireland. That's where you got your red hair. And probably your temper as well."

"Cute, Paddy," Tommy said.

"Anyway, as I said, the Vikings were primitive. Total barbarians. They destroyed just about everything they couldn't carry away. Their destruction of the Iona Monastery, where great literature and culture were kept alive, is talked about in Ireland to this day. Are you still with me, Tommy?"

"Paddy, am I gonna have to write an essay about this?"

Larkin laughed. "Pay attention, good son, here comes the kicker. Killing was recreation for the Vikings. They had no mercy. And if they were bored, they thought up very gruesome ways of ending lives. One of those ways was to bury their captives in the beach sand, allowing only their heads to be uncovered. Our friends from the North would then eat and drink and take bets. Would the crabs cause the demise of their captives by dining on them, or would the tide cover them before the crabs could finish their work? It was great sport for the Vikings."

"Goddamn," said Tommy O'Malley. "So what you're tellin' me, Paddy, is that our killer is a Viking? I should be looking for a guy wearing a steel hat with horns?"

"What I'm telling you is that you're looking for a guy who is probably highly intelligent, as oblivious to the suffering he causes as the worst villain in a Norse fable, and out for major revenge. This type of killing takes planning and guts, like a Viking conquest. Obviously, it would be a lot easier to just shoot somebody. By the way, you didn't tell me if the killer left any calling cards."

"Nothin' we know of, Patrick. I think this is the same guy who killed the two GNN people, but keep that to yourself," Tommy said as he put his pen down.

"No clues in the other hits?" Patrick Larkin asked.

"Nada."

"Damn. Looks like you're up against it. A guy like this will probably kill again. At least that's the pattern of serial revenge types. They like the power. How are you going to get this guy, Tommy?"

"Damned if I know, Patrick. But I'll get the son of a bitch." Tommy's jaw tightened as he spoke. "And when I do, there's a good chance he'll be taught a history lesson he'll never forget."

"Be careful, Tommy," Patrick Larkin said. "A guy like this isn't going to lie down easily."

"Then we'll have to knock him down. Thanks for the lesson, Paddy, I owe you a pint."

"Let's drink it at the arraignment, Tommy."

CHAPTER EIGHTEEN

Driving a car from New York City through the borough of Queens and into Nassau County is the root canal of automotive experiences. Traffic is usually heavy from six in the morning until well past midnight, and the road surfaces are pockmarked with a variety of pot holes, debris, and pavement defects—all capable of coaxing blue language from a nun. But Ashley Van Buren was lucky. On a windy, late autumn Saturday evening, it took her less than an hour to drive to Sands Point in one of the *Globe*'s company cars, a 1994 Oldsmobile. Ashley had signed the car out saying she needed it to do some investigating into the GNN case, which was true in a way.

Ashley was a city girl and didn't drive much, but she felt good getting out of the claustrophobic confines of Manhattan—at least until she hit the claustrophobic confines of the Long Island Expressway, a roadway that has been under construction since the Revolutionary War. Encountering a slowdown just outside the Midtown Tunnel, Ashley caught a break. Police and emergency road maintenance workers, earning triple overtime pay on the weekend, had just finished removing thirty wooden crates of frozen shrimp that had fallen off the back of a graffiti-scarred delivery truck and onto the road. The pickup operation took three hours, but was just about completed when Ashley came upon the mess. She was delayed for only a few minutes.

Shannon Michaels' stately home in Sands Point was exactly twenty-six miles from Ashley's apartment, but it was certainly a world away. Turning into his long driveway, Ashley couldn't believe all the land the man owned. And the house was huge, painted white with dark green shutters and trim. 'This guy lives in style,' she thought.

Shannon greeted his guest with a chilled glass of white wine. Predictable, but effective. A wood fire danced in the brick living room fireplace, and soft jazz played on the stereo. It didn't take long for Ashley to unwind.

The two seemed to have a lot in common. Both favored the preppy look. Ashley wore a navy blue blazer, white cotton shirt, and a tartan skirt over hose that matched the blazer. Shannon wore a forest green Shetland Wool sweater over a white shirt and neatly pressed tan jeans.

"Beautiful ride out on the Expressway, isn't it?" Shannon said smiling.

"You know, it doesn't get any better than passing the Elmhurst Gas tanks in the moonlight," Ashley answered. She was sitting with her legs crossed on Shannon's burgundy couch, sipping her wine.

Shannon laughed softly and Ashley stared at him. She liked his smile very much, but noticed that it did not quite reach his eyes. Unlike Tommy O'Malley, who could be genuinely playful when he let his guard down, Shannon Michaels never seemed totally at ease. In control, yes. But never completely caught up in the moment. Something important always seemed to be on his mind.

As the couple made light conversation, Ashley was consciously comparing Shannon to Tommy. It was interesting to put one up against the other because both possessed strong personalities. But there the similarities ended. Shannon was much more intense. He was also better looking, though both were attractive men. Ashley noticed that Shannon was beginning to look at her strangely. She abruptly stopped the evaluation.

"Are you okay, Ash? You look distracted."

"I'm fine, just getting adjusted to the new surroundings."

"How about a tour, to make your adjustment easier?" Shannon had a very subtle way of mocking her, Ashley thought. She didn't mind. Her father and brother used to do it all the time.

Shannon led his guest through the mansion—through much of its fifteen rooms and five thousand square feet. Ashley was impressed that all the original woodwork was restored. The hardwood oak floors were highly polished, the dark brown stair banisters shined. There was even a working fireplace in the master bedroom. The kitchen was enormous. A custom-made chopping block table divided the room, which was filled with every appliance and utensil a cook could hope for. As she thought of her one-bedroom apartment back in the city, Ashley became momentarily depressed.

Shannon Michaels wanted to impress Ashley Van Buren and guessed he was succeeding. He liked the woman. She was good company and emitted a powerful, understated sexuality. Shannon had planned the evening carefully. He wanted to accelerate his relationship with Ashley.

Having worked for years in New York City, Shannon knew that a country atmosphere had a powerfully seductive allure to many single women living and working in the chaos of Manhattan. Space, trees, clean air, and flowers were aphrodisiacs to New Yorkers. From experience, Shannon knew that his house was a place most women found comfortable and appealing.

Ashley Van Buren proved no exception. She wandered around the house for a full thirty minutes visualizing what touches she would install if it were hers. The closet space was amazing. The library, stunning. Four large bathrooms. 'But,' she thought, 'this place badly needs a woman's touch.'

Shannon regretted not cooking dinner himself—he now didn't want to leave the house. Instead, he had made reservations at a seafood restaurant overlooking the Long Island Sound. He finally persuaded Ashley to leave the library, where she was examining his collection of first edition historical books. In Shannon's black Buick Park Avenue, the two drove off to the restaurant.

The Old Salt was a typical informal fish house, filled with nautical wall prints and overhead fishnets. The lobster was great and so was the fresh bluefish. The couple ordered and gazed out at the harbor lights of Port Washington.

"What is it with you?" Ashley asked. "Every time we go to dinner, we have a table with a view."

"It's just my discerning aesthetic sense," Shannon said with a smile.

"Wow, great vocabulary for a TV guy. That library is really paying off." Ashley was enjoying the repartee.

"Well, I don't want to seem meretricious," Shannon quickly shot back. "I really do enjoy the views. They calm turbulent souls."

"*Meretricious*! My God. You're lucky I have the perspicacity to understand that, Buster."

They both laughed. Shannon was impressed with the woman's wit. After a few more minutes of light banter, the conversation turned serious. Ashley wanted to talk about the GNN case. She asked Shannon what he knew of Martin Moore.

"I made a few calls about him," said Shannon, and then hesitated.

He really didn't want to talk about the case given how gruesome it was. He preferred that Ashley concentrate on the romantic side of the evening. After a short pause, however, he continued, "I actually met this guy one time, and didn't remember it until a friend of mine reminded me he had done some work for Channel Six."

Ashley was on her second glass of wine, but that piece of news put her on alert. "What kind of work?"

"The guy was advising our news director. Very hush-hush. Consultants usually get people fired."

"Do you think he had anything to do with your dismissal?"

"Maybe. They told my agent that their research showed my popularity declining. This Moore could have done the research. But, listen, Moore was behind the purges at GNN and a couple of other networks as well. The guy did a lot of damage."

"So he deserved to die," said Ashley in a probing tone. Shannon picked right up on it.

"Didn't say that. What I am saying is the guy had a lot of enemies, just like Costello and Ross. This is really becoming a fascinating case because the three victims fall into the same category. They were all workplace terrorists."

Ashley's eyes opened wide. She had never heard that term. But it was a great headline for a column. "Workplace terrorists?" she repeated quizzically.

"It's funny. Here in America we think about terrorism in the context of Arabs or the IRA or right wing militia nuts. Fanatics with bombs. But terrorism comes in many forms. Terrorism can be defined as 'coercing by intimidation or fear.' How often do we see that done in life? All the time. In many corporate environments, people are defenseless because there is no due process. If your boss is a workplace terrorist, then you're gonna get terrorized and there's little you can do about it except quit. And well paying jobs aren't easy to find. So few of us quit." Shannon looked at Ashley, who was listening attentively. "I'm sorry, I guess I sound like I'm lecturing."

"No, it's an interesting take. But how does it relate to GNN?" Ashley asked.

"Are you kidding? The media is the worst. Journalism, as you know, is a profession that requires its participants to be aggressive, skeptical, and persistent in pursuit of the truth. Yet, the moment you enter your own newsroom, you've got to drop all that. The managers want total conformity. They want you to play the game, to do what you're told to do. If you don't, or if you raise annoying questions, there's a good chance you'll be terrorized by administrators or others who've been given a semblance of power. People like Costello and Ross."

"So you think somebody in the press is killing these people?" Ashley asked, staring intently at Shannon.

"I think somebody snapped. Costello, Ross, and Moore all had one thing in common: They terrorized people. And they got away with it. Somebody just said, 'Enough.'"

"You sound like you're justifying it."

"No, I'm trying to understand it, Ash. I'm simply theorizing about why it happened. I'm trying to figure out who would do something like this."

"Are you going to share your thoughts with Detective O'Malley?"

Shannon smiled, but inside, he was unhappy with himself. He was shooting his mouth off. First murder theories, now questions about O'Malley. How was he ever going to get Ashley back in the mood? Unable to think of a conversational diversion, he pushed ahead. "You like this O'Malley guy, don't you? Well, he's coming out here tomorrow. He wanted me to come into the city, but I only do that for special people like you." Shannon Michaels smiled again, his best smile. 'Not a bad segué,' he thought.

Ashley looked into his blue eyes. So far, she thought, the guy made a lot of sense. She knew O'Malley suspected him, but maybe Tommy was jealous. Besides, he hadn't even met Shannon yet. Ashley trusted her instincts about people, and her instincts told her that this man was not psychotic. He seemed very grounded in reality. His career trauma had made him bitter, she believed, but not homicidal.

After dinner, the couple drove to the northern tip of Sands Point. It was a clear night and, looking back toward the city, Manhattan glowed in the distance like a candlelit procession. At this distance, the dark of night always had the effect of airbrushing the city, covering all its visual flaws with an attractive, sparkling gauze.

As she contemplated the view, Ashley knew she would soon be forced to make an important decision. When they returned to his house, Shannon would undoubtedly invite her in for a drink. Caution dictated a polite decline. 'Better not to get any more involved with this man until the whole picture became more defined. After all, even though she didn't believe it, Shannon Michaels could be a killer.'

For his part, Shannon Michaels sensed Ashley's doubts about him. And as they drove back to his house, he made a major effort to ease those doubts.

"So, Ash, I know you have to get back to the city, but I can't let you go without some coffee to keep you alert during the drive. Wouldn't want you falling asleep at the wheel and missing the Utopia Parkway exit. It's really something."

Ashley laughed but remained noncommittal, mulling things over as the two drove silently toward Shannon's house. Only when they pulled into Shannon's long driveway did she conclude that it was still early, and that coming in for one cup of coffee couldn't hurt.

Shannon Michaels stoked up the fire in his immense living room. Luther Vandross played softly on the stereo. Ashley was again sitting on the couch, her slender legs curled up under her skirt. Since the conversation about the murders, her mood had changed. She was quiet now, staring at the fire.

"I'll write you directions so you can drive out of here. It's pretty confusing in the dark," Shannon said, speaking as placidly as he could. He did not want to appear anxious to have Ashley stay, although that's exactly what he wanted.

"Are you trying to get rid of me?"

"Well, it is slightly after eleven. And only you know how much beauty rest you require." Shannon's eyes gleamed. He was teasing her.

"I guess I should be going, really," Ashley said, but made no move to get up. The house was seductively cozy.

"Tell you what. Let's play a little game before you go." Shannon very subtly licked his top lip. Ashley noticed.

"Shannon, the last time we played your game, I almost got into trouble. I can't do that tonight."

"This game requires no physical contact," Shannon said.

Ashley was wary but curious. "What are the rules?"

"Okay. We sit across from each other. About ten feet apart. Then each of us gets a turn. You can ask me to do anything that doesn't require me to get up. Then I can ask *you*. Pretty simple, right? Oh, and one more thing. You can stop the game at any time by refusing to do what you're asked. So if the game is boring or you feel uncomfortable, you can quit, and so can I."

Ashley continued to look skeptical. "I don't know. To be honest, it doesn't sound like such a great game."

"We'll see." And Shannon smiled, daring her with his eyes. "What have you got to lose? You can quit at any time. Ready?"

"All right. But you're right on the edge, Mister."

Shannon's smile remained steady. He picked up a small chair and moved it directly across from Ashley. "Okay, I'll go first. Take off your shoes."

Ashley rolled her eyes. "What is this, strip poker without the cards? Don't tell me! Next we'll be spinning the bottle!"

"The shoes."

Ashley slipped off her ankle high black shoes and wiggled her toes. "Happy?"

"Thrilled," Shannon said. "Now it's your turn."

Ashley paused, thinking it over. "Mess up your hair," she said, sticking her tongue out at him.

Shannon shook his head and smiled. "No problem, but you just wasted a turn." He ran both hands through his thick, brown hair.

"Now, Ash, take your right hand and rub your left thigh from the hip to the knee four times. Make sure you do it very slowly."

"Oh, I see where this is going. You men are so predictable." Ashley hesitated, and Shannon thought she might quit, but she looked him straight in the eye and began moving her right hand up and down her dark stockings. She took her time. For some reason, she enjoyed teasing him.

"My request," Ashley said. "Take off your shoes."

Shannon slipped off his brown loafers, thinking she was getting bolder. Good. "Okay, Ash, take your right index finger and put it in your mouth. Then slowly move it in and out of your mouth five times."

Ashley grinned and said, "You are very ill." Then she did what Shannon wanted in a way that almost made him shudder. He knew she was beginning to enjoy the game.

"Unbutton your shirt." Shannon was surprised by Ashley's quick command. It was obvious he was not wearing an undershirt. "Now—"

"Only one request at a time, Ash," Shannon interrupted. Slowly he opened his shirt. His dark chest hair stood out against his white skin. Sitting directly across from Ashley, Shannon was backlit by the fire. His build, Ashley could see, was medium but solid, and his chest well developed.

"Unbutton your shirt." Shannon's voice was low. He smiled at Ashley when she looked at him. He didn't want her to quit.

Ashley paused and thought about it. "No touching, right?" Shannon nodded, and she slowly undid the buttons of her white shirt, careful to keep the fabric close together. She was resisting, but the truth be told, she was becoming increasingly excited.

"Take off that shirt," came Ashley's next order—this one with a slightly huskier voice.

Shannon removed his shirt and threw it behind him in the direction of the fire. Thank God he had gotten rid of the sweater when he came in from the restaurant, he thought. He wanted this woman to see his body almost as much as he wanted to see hers.

Shannon's stomach, Ashley noticed, was flat. 'The man must be doing his situps,' she thought. His posture was also good. Straight back. Even shoulders.

"Here's where the game gets really interesting, Ash," Shannon said, looking straight into her eyes. "I would like you to unhook your bra and let it slide down your arms. You can keep your shirt on."

Once again Ashley paused, but not for long. She felt a tingle of excitement. Thinking that she must be crazy, she nonetheless did as Shannon asked.

Shannon's eyes took in Ashley's round breasts. Her shirt partially concealed them, but their shape was evident. He gazed intently, spotting nipples that seemed taut as they pushed up against the fabric of her shirt. The last time he and Ash had been together, he had felt her breasts. But this was the first time he had actually seen them. He was acutely aware that his blood flow was gaining speed.

Acting on a powerful impulse, Ashley decided to push the game up a notch, to abandon her usual caution. She didn't really know why, but the words that kept ricocheting around in her mind were: 'Why not? Don't I have a right to have some fun once in a while?' Finally, she dictated the course of the evening. "Okay, Shannon Michaels, off with those pants."

While still sitting, Shannon undid his belt and the button on his jeans. Very slowly, he lifted his hips, sliding the jeans down his long legs. When they reached his feet, he deftly kicked them off.

Ashley took it all in. He was wearing Calvin Klein briefs. Black. Her eyes moved downward from his slim hips to his legs. She tried not to stare at his crotch, even though she saw movement there.

"So, Ash, now that you have me at a disadvantage, I want you to do a small exercise. Cup your hands under your breasts and hold them up for ten seconds."

Ashley knew that to do this would leave her completely exposed from the waist up. But she did it anyway.

Shannon stared at the woman in front of him. Not only was she holding her breasts aloft, she was gently caressing them. Teasing him. His eyes swept over her. She was beautiful. Her light skin was growing slightly red. He knew she was getting extremely aroused.

Shannon Michaels ended the game with two words: "I quit." He then dropped to the floor kneeling before Ashley, pushing her skirt up to her waist. Using a fair amount of pressure, he kissed her inner thighs, using his lips and tongue. His hands reached the waistband of her hose. Shannon gently gave a tug and Ashley lifted her hips. He slipped the hose down to her ankles, all the while continuing to knead her skin with his tongue.

Ashley was now wearing only brief white panties. By removing her shirt and skirt, and by leaning back on the couch, she had signaled her desire. Now, she closed her eyes, concentrating on nothing but Shannon's tongue and lips. He gently teased her by licking the areas around her most sensitive erogenous zone. Then he slipped her panties down her legs and, within seconds, his tongue was inside her, moving rapidly. Ashley felt intense pleasure building. Doubts briefly surfaced, but she quickly dismissed them. She had not felt physical pleasure of this kind for a long time. Maybe it had never been this good. Why should she deny herself? There wasn't any concrete reason why she shouldn't enjoy the moment for a change.

Ashley climaxed twice before the two got up from the couch and climbed the stairs to the master bedroom. Shannon ignited the logs in the fireplace as Ashley nestled in, under the down comforter. She could see Shannon outlined against the fire, still partially erect. When he joined her on the king-size bed, Ashley made a move toward his waist. He stopped her. Putting his large hands on both sides of her waist, he gently lifted her up.

She followed his lead and assumed the dominant position while he lay on his back. Ashley moved slowly, savoring the friction inside her. Shannon caressed her body all over, and after a few minutes, she came once again, leaning forward to heighten the sensation. Her body shuddered. 'I need this release,' she thought. 'I've waited so long.'

Shannon Michaels felt energized. He had accomplished his goal—giving Ashley Van Buren a night she would long remember. His physical pleasure was secondary. His primary euphoria came from knowing that Ashley was enjoying every bit of his expertise. He knew it was somewhat clinical, but he was good at disguising his detachment. He was getting off on controlling the situation. He would delay his physical gratification as long as possible.

Shannon lifted Ashley off of him and quickly knelt behind her. His presence was forceful but not demanding. It felt so good that Ashley thought she would lose control. He was speaking in hushed tones, telling her how much he enjoyed her body, using words that in polite conversation would have been vulgar, but in this context were extremely erotic. His hands firmly gripped her buttocks. Ashley could feel his rhythm. First quick, then slow, then quick again. He brought her right up to orgasm, then pulled back. Without warning, he would quicken the pace again. When Ashley climaxed, Shannon finally let himself go. Ashley's knees were shaking. She dropped onto her stomach, completely spent. She silently marveled at Shannon's stamina.

After more than an hour of love making, the couple fell asleep. As the flaming shadows danced across the walls, all their thoughts of tomorrow were put to rest.

CHAPTER NINETEEN

Tommy O'Malley was in what he called "a black mood"—an emotional condition that visits some Irishmen often, but troubled Tommy only occasionally. The depression's cause was his unanswered phone call to Ashley Van Buren earlier that morning. Tommy suspected she was visiting Shannon Michaels, whom he was to question in-person later that day.

A man of force and action, Tommy did not like feeling out of control. But his thoughts about Ashley were now becoming incessant, and uncontrollable. He knew he was falling in love. Worse yet, he suspected his feelings might be unrequited.

Tommy was also distressed over progress in the GNN case. At least on paper, David Wayne was suspect number one, but he was still missing. According to a computer check, he had rented a car from Hertz for a full month. Tommy had sent a heads-up to police in the five states closest to New York saying that Wayne was wanted for questioning in a murder case. Wayne, he hoped, would get pulled over on some interstate. But nothing with him had yet materialized.

While not discounting Wayne, Tommy knew that Shannon Michaels had good reason to despise both Ron Costello and Hillary Ross. 'But,' he asked himself, 'is my negative bias toward Michaels born out of jealousy?' The very question made him angry.

'Three goddamn murders. One missing suspect. What else can happen?' Tommy thought. 'Oh I know: by the middle of next week, I'll be as bald as Michael Jordan.'

Disgusted with feeling sorry for himself, Tommy shifted his thoughts to his immediate environment. The Sunday morning traffic was light as he drove east from Manhattan toward the suburban enclave of Levittown, where he would visit his mother. Growing up, Tommy had had no idea that he lived in a ghetto. Levittown was a huge subdivision of identical, cheaply made houses sold en masse to veterans returning from World War II. Tommy's neighborhood was a mixture of Italians, Jews, and Irish—all of whom had one thing in common: not much money. Dermot O'Malley, Tommy's father, had been a New York City fireman. Providing for a family of five had exhausted every cent Dermot O'Malley ever earned. Luxuries did not exist in the O'Malley household. Life was very basic.

In hindsight, Tommy thought that Levittown closely resembled both the Bronx and Brooklyn—only with lawns instead of apartment stoops, and a few more open spaces. Whites had begun leaving the outer boroughs of New York City around 1950, when greedy real estate agents, called blockbusters, started buying apartment buildings in mostly white working class neighborhoods. Turn of the century buildings were then subdivided, often illegally, and rented to minority families. A building that had housed four poor Irish families, for example, was now home to eight poor black families.

Overcrowding then caused the buildings to deteriorate, and callous real estate owners often failed to provide repairs. Faced with a declining neighborhood infrastructure and influenced by inherited racial prejudice, many whites panicked. They began moving out to the suburbs in large numbers, lowering property values drastically. The despicable blockbusters then bought up entire neighborhoods at market-bottom prices. It wasn't long before the complexion of the Bronx and Brooklyn changed completely. And many of the white flight refugees wound up in Levittown.

Dermot O'Malley had been raised on Flatbush Avenue in Brooklyn, the fourth son of a dockworker. His future wife, Mary Fitzgerald, lived five blocks away, along with her two sisters and two brothers. Both of Tommy's parents were afflicted with the American ethnic scourge: intense insecurity. Tommy's father and mother had grown up during the Great Depression. Financial doom was always hovering just outside their front door. Fear of impending, uncontrolled disaster influenced just about every decision Dermot and Mary O'Malley made. Although it wasn't as if Mary ever had a voice equal to her husband's—she didn't.

Tommy, the family rebel, opted for a secure city job. His sister, Catherine, married young and had four kids by the age of thirty. Michael, his brother, was a divorced fireman who sought solace in a shot glass.

His mother, Mary Elizabeth O'Malley, was, in Tommy's view, a saint. She put up with him, his father, and his brother, all of whom were difficult men. Dermot O'Malley had a volcanic temper and was often frustrated and bitter over life's injustices. Michael O'Malley was shy, introverted, and unhappy without apparent cause. Tommy himself was unpredictable. At times, he could be gregarious, funny, and great company. But, he also had his father's temper and, though he never became a bully, he sometimes took part in unnecessary and destructive physical confrontations. Tommy struggled with conformity, never quite getting it down.

His mother loved her family and friends with a passion most human beings couldn't even contemplate. It was a love devoid of all selfishness. She had few wants of her own, devoted herself to the needs of others, and wanted nothing in return. She not only overlooked all neurosis, but was as kind a woman as could be found this side of Mother Teresa. Her house was usually full of people gathered to experience her support and approval. When his father came home, the visitors tended to vanish.

Mary O'Malley unexpectedly became a widow in 1987, cancer taking her husband quickly. From that time onward, Tommy was his mother's protector. His sister had moved to Virginia and his brother divided his time between the firehouse and barroom, so it was Tommy who was on call. As his mother grew older, the problems mounted. She was still self-sufficient and feisty, but could not handle financial matters, house repairs, or emotional stress on her own. It fell to Tommy to take care of these things. He did so, often grousing about it, but never really minding.

As Tommy exited off the Meadowbrook Parkway and onto Hempstead Turnpike, he winced at the low-budget stores glued together on both sides of the roadway, and he thought back to his childhood. He had been a wild kid, constantly challenging the School Sisters of Notre Dame who attempted to teach him. He was scolded on a daily basis, often being told that he could look forward to taking up residence in Hell. While that threat made many of the other children cower, it didn't bother Tommy at all. He figured that he would eventually arrive there, but so would all his friends, too.

High school was more of the same. Tommy consistently broke the strict school rules of St. Gregory's. His problem was authority. If they told him to do something, automatically, he didn't want to. It was as simple and as stupid as that. But as he grew bigger, Tommy developed into a fierce football player. The sport gave him an outlet for his rebellious energy, and some discipline. He began to see that teamwork could accomplish things. In his junior and senior years, he settled down a bit and performed decently in class.

The turning point in Tommy's life came when he was accepted at Boston University. He would be the first one in his family to go to college. To afford the tuition, he painted houses in the summer. In Boston, he prospered. Though majoring in history, he knew early that law enforcement was the career he wanted. His parents tried to convince him to be a lawyer, but Tommy wanted action. His father's connections in New York's civil service arena made it easy for him to apply to and be accepted by the NYPD without going into the military, which was the preferred route into policing in the seventies.

As Tommy pulled into the driveway of the family home, he saw his mother waving at him through the kitchen window. Built in 1950, the house still had just three tiny bedrooms, one bath, and no expensive conveniences. He laughed to himself recalling the times when five people were sharing the same space. As a child, he did not think of the house as small. It was only when his teenage sister began spending days in the bathroom that the true nature of his living circumstance began to dawn on him.

"Thomas, you look tired," his mother said.

"I *am* tired, Ma. I had to get up early and drive all the way out here." Tommy smiled and hugged his mother. She knew he was kidding.

Age had diminished her looks, but Mary Elizabeth O'Malley still had the vivid, sparkling blue eyes that had made her one of the prettiest girls in Brooklyn. Troublesome arthritis had hunched her posture and begun to gnarl her hands. But she never complained. Her only concession to the terrible disease was to avoid standing for too long.

"So you look good, Ma. There's something different about you."

"I had my hair colored, Thomas." His mother's hair had been dyed a subtle shade of red, hiding most of the gray.

"Better quit that, Ma. You're gettin' to be a real babe." Tommy and his mother laughed together. As usual, she fixed him a large breakfast of French toast, bacon, and fruit. She knew he was a coffee drinker and a large pot was ready as he sat down. Tommy's large frame made the small kitchen table seem even smaller. Mary O'Malley pictured her son sitting at the table as a child, covered with neighborhood dust, and smiled to herself.

Mary knew her son better than anyone on earth and she admired him greatly. He had courage and integrity. He had often argued intensely with his father, but with her, he had always been respectful and loving. She knew he had suffered mightily when his marriage collapsed, but he never reminded him of his problems, and she tried very hard to comfort him. Mary had never been particularly fond of Angela Rufino, thinking her immature and selfish, but no one could have predicted the woman would become a religious fanatic. Mary herself went to Mass three times a week. But few in her circle understood the charismatic Catholics or their almost frightening religious zealotry. Those people, she thought, made the Jehovah's Witnesses look like agnostics.

As Tommy plowed through his meal—he had eaten quickly ever since he was a little boy—his mother sensed his depression. She looked at her son and felt the tenseness he exuded.

"Tommy, something's bothering you, isn't it?"

Wiping his mouth with a yellow paper napkin, Tommy looked at his mother. Although he often kept things from her, he never misled her. He knew she loved to participate in his life, so he decided to fill her in. "I'm working on a complicated case, Ma. One of the suspects lives out here. He's also kind of involved with a friend of mine and I'm a little worried about her."

"*Her?*" Mary O'Malley, like most mothers, was extremely interested in her son's female friends.

"Yeah, reporter by the name of Ashley Van Buren. You might have read some of her articles in the *Globe*."

Mary O'Malley was a radio person. John Gambling on WOR was her favorite. She didn't know of Ashley, but nodded anyway. "Do you think your friend is in any danger?"

"Probably not physically. The guy we're looking for is smart and has a game plan. If it is our guy out here, I don't think he'd draw attention to himself by hurting Ashley. But he might use her for his own purposes."

"What are you going to do?" asked Mary, who was always very interested in her son's career.

Tommy finished his coffee and poured another cup. "I'm not sure. I'm going to see this guy later today. He lives on the North Shore,

Sands Point."

"That's big money over there, Thomas."

"I know, Ma. I'm an investigator, remember? Anyway, let's talk about you. How much did you give the Pope this month?"

Mary O'Malley smiled and looked down at the small kitchen table. As always, she was enjoying her son's visit. The two talked for about an hour, then Tommy paid some of her bills and looked over the mail. At five minutes to one, he settled into his father's old easy chair to watch the Giants play the Cleveland Browns. Usually he would have totally concentrated on the game, but today was different. Today, he was thinking about Ashley Van Buren.

· · ·

Ashley awoke at ten a.m., rolling over to find herself alone in Shannon Michaels' king size bed. She was naked and a little sore from the previous night's exertions. Sitting up, she read the clock and flopped back down. 'How could I have slept so late?' she wondered

Downstairs in the kitchen, Shannon was making a healthy breakfast for two. Sliced fruit, low fat yogurt, English muffins dabbed with honey. Designer coffee was brewing, a Brazilian blend, and Evian water had been poured. He was surprised that Ashley had slept so soundly. He himself could never relax in a strange bed.

Ashley finally kicked the thick comforter off her body, roused herself from bed, and walked into the bathroom adjoining the master bedroom. A huge shower stall stood before her on the right, a floor-to-ceiling mirror on the left. What she saw in the mirror mortified her. Before falling asleep, she had not washed, and mascara had streaked her face. She looked like the bride of Frankenstein.

Ashley quickly turned on the shower water. Four water jets caressed her body. The hot water began to relax her. She might still be a mess when she got out of the shower, but at least she'd be a clean mess.

Shannon heard the shower running, climbed the stairs, and left towels and a robe for Ashley. He had already collected her clothing, which had been strewn all over the living room. He knew this would be an awkward time for Ashley, so he quickly went back downstairs, giving her maximum privacy.

Ashley toweled herself off, found a blow dryer, and worked on her hair while analyzing her emotional state. 'I should not have let last night happen. It was fun, but that's no excuse. He assumed control over the evening and I feel foolish for succumbing.' Ashley knew she was in a vulnerable state, and she was distinctly unsure where things were going. She hated both of those feelings.

As Ashley entered the kitchen wearing one of his thick terrycloth robes, Shannon sensed she was feeling less than exhilarated. He knew he had to think quickly, do just the right thing. He turned to Ashley, smiled, and said just one word: "Muffin?"

Despite her uneasiness with the morning after, Ashley smiled as he held up an English Muffin. She appreciated the light touch. 'No need to discuss anything,' she thought. 'That would come later.'

"It looks a little burnt."

"Oh, I'm sorry, that's *my* muffin. Yours is toasting as we speak, and it will be perfect. I promise. If not, I'll commit ritual suicide." They both laughed and enjoyed the breakfast. Ashley then borrowed an iron and pressed her wrinkled clothing. Ninety minutes later, she was driving back to the city. She felt better, but recognized she still had to come to terms with what had happened.

• • •

Shannon Michaels had agreed to see Detective O'Malley at four that afternoon. Shannon did not like the intrusion on his weekend but was somewhat curious about O'Malley because of Ashley's tie to him. From the tone of his voice on the phone, Shannon ascertained that O'Malley was not a person to take lightly. The interview would be interesting, he thought.

At 2:30 that afternoon, Tommy O'Malley finally reached Ashley Van Buren by phone. Speaking to Ashley from his mother's house, he was intensely curious about her whereabouts that morning, but was careful not to press her too hard.

"So, what have you been up to?" Tommy asked.

"Just the usual. Running around, breaking stories, breaking hearts." Ashley was trying to sound casual but suspected she was not fooling O'Malley. She immediately thought he detected a slight bit of apprehension in her voice. "Where are you?"

"Out at my mother's. I think I told you I'm gonna interview

Michaels today. You haven't talked to him, have you?"

Ashley paused. She knew O'Malley picked up on it, and she wasn't going to lie to him. "I saw him last night. He is definitely expecting you."

Tommy felt a twinge in his stomach. He was jealous. He wanted to ask her a bunch of personal questions. But he knew this would hurt his chances with her. He struggled, but kept it professional. "So, what did he say about the meet?"

Ashley knew the detective was not pleased. All warmth had left his voice. "Not much. Just that he was expecting you. Tommy, this is a guarded man. He doesn't exactly open up about things."

"I wouldn't know."

Ashley felt Tommy's anger over the phone. She liked the detective, but she didn't want to deal with that now. She kept her voice even. "So, will you call me after you talk with him?"

"You're a tough person to reach."

"Oh, did you try before? I didn't get any messages on my machine from you."

"Yeah, I called earlier. Didn't want to bother leavin' a message."

"Well, I must have been in the shower." No way was she going to tell him *whose* shower.

Tommy knew the conversation was getting strained. He decided to switch tactics, saying in a mock gruff voice: "Well, next time you take a shower, Ash, I expect to know about it in advance. Then I can get a warrant and break into your house."

Ashley laughed, relieved. She didn't want to lose her rapport with Tommy O'Malley. "I'll make sure I do that, Detective. Now call me later, okay?"

"Sure, see you."

Mary O'Malley saw her son hang up the phone and knew he was upset, but as always, he didn't display any emotion to her. She gave him a big hug, hard to do because he was so large, and kissed him on the left side of his face. "Things will work out, Thomas. The Lord is watching over you."

"Tell him to send me some evidence, Ma. Fast. I'll see you again soon. Say hello to Cathy and Mike for me. And by the way, Jackson says hello and wants you to know that he's the brains of the partnership."

Mary O'Malley laughed as she watched her son walk down the

narrow driveway to his car. She waved as he backed out into the street and drove off. She was worried about him. There was something about the current situation that she didn't like. Innately, she felt her son was in some danger. As Tommy disappeared around the corner, Mary O'Malley turned toward the cross hanging on the kitchen wall and said a prayer.

CHAPTER TWENTY

LONG ISLAND
NOVEMBER, 1994

He saw them in his rear view mirror: three teenagers in a white, vintage Ford Mustang coming up fast, weaving in and out of traffic. Tommy O'Malley was heading north towards Sands Point, going about sixty in the center lane of the three-lane Northern State Parkway. 'These kids must be doing ninety,' he thought as the Mustang quickly switched lanes and drove up behind Tommy's unmarked police car.

The teenagers were immediately hemmed in—the cars on both sides of Tommy were doing about the same speed. Unable to pass, the young driver began banging his hands on the top of the steering wheel in frustration. Watching in his rearview mirror, Tommy saw that the Mustang was just a few feet away from his rear bumper. He was being tailgated viciously and Tommy hated being tailgated, especially so obnoxiously. He tapped his brakes and the Mustang almost hit him. In the mirror, he could now see rage on the driver's face.

Tommy put on his directional signal and waited patiently for the car on his right to pull up a little. After about fifty yards, it did. Tommy then shifted into the right lane. Immediately, the Mustang bolted forward. Tommy looked over and the kid sitting in the front passenger seat gave him the finger as he whizzed by.

Rolling down his window, Tommy attached the portable red police light to the top of his car and gave chase. He was out of his jurisdiction but it didn't matter. He switched on his radio, called the New York State Police, and told the dispatcher his problem and location. A trooper, he was informed, was up ahead on the highway and would be waiting.

The Mustang continued on for about a mile but pulled over when the State Trooper's police car appeared behind it. Tommy arrived on the scene seconds later, pulled his car onto the shoulder of the highway directly behind the trooper's vehicle, and approached the three teenagers, then sitting in their car laughing. The Trooper was already out of his vehicle and talking to the driver through the rolled-down window.

"Out of the car, boys." The trooper's voice was hard and loud, competing with the heavy bass of rap music pulsating from the Mustang's radio speakers.

The driver, a skinny kid with pimples, emerged first. He wore his baseball hat backwards, an oversized shirt hanging outside his baggy pants. 'What a cliche,' Tommy thought.

Tommy flipped his shield open and shook the trooper's hand. He then filled him in on the Mustang's antics. By now, all three surly looking teenagers were standing together alongside the car. The tallest one, a blond haired boy who had been a passenger in the back seat, interrupted as Tommy and the trooper talked.

"Hey, man. We dint do nothin', man. What's this all about?"

The state trooper looked like a cop recruiting poster: an ex-Marine weightlifter with a flattop haircut and mirrored sunglasses. He was not in a good mood. Besides being bored doing traffic duty on Long Island, he was working on Sunday when he usually watched the pro football games.

"Shut up and stand over there," the trooper said harshly. "Now, will the driver please step forward and produce a license, registration, and insurance card."

The pimply faced kid casually shrugged and said, "Left 'em home."

Tommy shook his head and smiled to himself as he saw the trooper remove his sunglasses, his eyes narrowing. It was all over. He walked around the Mustang and up to the driver. "Nice car. Yours?"

"My dad's," the pimply boy said tersely.

"What does your dad do?" Tommy asked.

"Dentist."

"So he's got plenty of money to get you out of trouble, right?"

All the boys smiled defiantly. "Maybe," the pimply faced kid sneered.

"I'll tell you what, Officer," Tommy said loud enough for everyone to hear. "I would like to press charges against this young man for reckless driving, speeding, and failure to heed a police request to stop."

Then Tommy walked toward the kid who had given him the finger. Suddenly, the teenager looked doubtful, his false bravado fast slipping away. Like the driver of the car, he wore his black Chicago White Sox hat backwards, and was chewing gum. Tommy stopped a few feet away from the kid, looking down into his eyes. "And I will also press charges against this person for harassing an officer of the law. That middle finger got anything else to say, son?"

"Okay, gentlemen," the state trooper said, "hands on top of the car, legs spread apart. You are all under arrest, and your car will be impounded. Please follow my directions at all times."

Tommy walked over to the Mustang and watched as the trooper patted the boys down. He didn't particularly like the situation, remembering his own wild days as a kid. But things were different now. He was beginning to despise a permissive culture that allowed teenagers to disrespect just about everything. In his own younger days, he may have broken some rules, but he took his punishment like a man. These kids, Tommy thought, didn't have a clue about what it took to be a man and probably never would. They were spoiled and damaged by the privileges of wealth.

Tommy knew the three teenagers standing before him would get off lightly. In fact, the case would probably be dropped. But he also knew that lawyers would have to be hired and most likely would soak the parents. Good. These three kids and their parents needed to be taught a lesson. That speeding Mustang could have easily killed somebody.

As the boys were about to be put into the back seat of the trooper's car, Tommy pulled the pimply kid aside. "You know, son, it would be extremely convenient for you if I lost my temper."

The kid looked at Tommy, confused but impenitent. "Yeah, why's that?"

"Because then you'd really *need* a dentist."

• • •

Tommy O'Malley was late for the interview, much to Shannon Michaels' surprise. O'Malley, he had thought, would be anxious to see him, especially after all the phone calls. As for himself, Shannon knew he had little choice but to speak with the detective, however risky it might be. Dodging O'Malley would serve no purpose. No matter what he said or didn't say, Shannon knew he would remain a suspect. There was no point trying to convince the man of his innocence. O'Malley would believe what he wanted to believe.

Unlike Ashley Van Buren, who was hoping that Shannon was innocent, Shannon believed that Tommy O'Malley was looking to nail him as the killer. For Shannon, the only benefit of the upcoming interview was to put O'Malley on notice that any half-assed attempt to pin the crimes on him would result in reprisals against O'Malley himself and the NYPD.

Shannon knew the authorities still had very little evidence in the murder cases. Ashley had told him that the Massachusetts State Police had all but shut down the Martha's Vineyard investigation, and up until the night before, Ash believed that investigators in Malibu had turned up nothing. But that would not stop Tommy O'Malley, Shannon thought. If Ashley's assessment of the detective turned out to be true, O'Malley was under tremendous pressure, and would stay on the Ross case until cracking it.

The late afternoon sun had dipped behind the tall trees surrounding Shannon's house, and the wind was blowing in hard from the water. A cold night lay ahead as Shannon walked around his yard, dead brown leaves swirling about his feet. Shannon Michaels was actually looking forward to his upcoming battle of wits with Detective O'Malley. Shannon's ego craved that kind of stimulating confrontation. He smiled to himself. People used to ask why villains would sit for an interview with a person like Mike Wallace on "60 Minutes." It was an ego thing. They wanted to see if they could hold their own with a tough guy like Mike. They usually couldn't.

But Shannon Michaels, preferring that O'Malley leave him alone after this single interview, knew it was vitally important that he handle himself well when talking to the detective. So, before taking a walk outside to clear his head, he had spent two hours in his library going over strategy. In the interview, he was going to be frank. He did not want to anger O'Malley, but would not be intimidated by him either. He knew his rights and was prepared to invoke them. He would take the direct approach that had worked so well with Ashley. The detective would ask his questions and then, he hoped, vanish quickly and forever.

At twenty minutes after four, Tommy O'Malley pulled into the long circular driveway leading to Shannon Michaels' home. 'Another rich TV guy,' Tommy thought. He wished his mother could have a house like this.

Shannon Michaels greeted Tommy O'Malley at the front door and ushered him directly into the library. Tommy apologized for being late, turned down the offer of refreshments, and did not attempt any small talk. He kept his face expressionless and his tone of voice even. Since he needed Shannon Michaels' consent to even speak with him, Tommy knew he had to stay as low key as possible. He wanted to dominate the interview, get as much information out of Michaels as possible, but not alienate the man. If Michaels asked him to leave, he'd leave. He had no hard evidence against Shannon Michaels and therefore no cause to use his police powers.

During the introductions, the two men, like expectant prizefighters, stood eye to eye, a few feet apart, in the thickly carpeted library Shannon had added to the back of his home. The room was dominated by hundreds of books and built-in oak bookcases that covered three entire walls. On the fourth wall hung dozens of journalistic award plaques Shannon had won during his career.

Shannon was surprised by, and a bit uncomfortable with, O'Malley's height. At 6'3, Shannon was used to looking down on people. But he had to slightly raise his eyes to O'Malley, who was an inch taller.

Shannon motioned for Tommy to sit in a black leather reading chair that was soft and comfortable. Shannon himself sat across the room at a small table. On the table were a Sony micro tape recorder and a note pad.

"I hope you don't mind, Detective, but I'm going to tape this interview for my own protection. This GNN situation has been very difficult for me. I've been getting calls from reporters, and I've been told that I may even be a suspect in the case."

"Who told you that?" Tommy asked, his voice low and emotionless.

"I can't divulge sources, Detective. But I have to ask you straight out: Am I a suspect in the GNN murders?" Shannon, who had turned on the recorder, was now staring hard at Tommy O'Malley.

"Not at this time, Mr. Michaels. I'm just here to ask you a few questions about the case. Background stuff."

"Fine, but there are some ground rules before we begin. I'm sorry to be so blunt, but this is a very serious matter." Shannon picked up a pen, made a check on the top of his note pad, and continued. "If at any time I become a suspect in this case, I will not speak to you. All communications will have to be directed to my attorney. If the New York City

Police Department deems me a suspect, or informs anybody that I am one, I will initiate a civil law suit. Any connection between a murder investigation and myself would severely damage the chances of resuming my career in broadcast journalism. I'm sure you understand that."

What Tommy understood was that the guy was trying to scare him. A major lawsuit against the department pissed everybody off including the mayor. Unless the suspect was clearly guilty, a police officer's career could be badly hurt by a civil lawsuit, warranted or not. The brass downtown did not like to deal with these things. Lawyers could make a cop's life miserable.

"In addition, Detective," Shannon went on, "anything I say to you in this interview, which is taking place on Sunday, December 4, 1994 at approximately 4:30 in the afternoon, is off the record. I do not wish to be quoted either publicly or privately. What I am telling you is for your ears alone. I am simply providing you with background as a professional courtesy. If you violate my trust, I will consider legal action. I also am not prepared to answer any direct questions about the criminal investigation surrounding the Global News Network because I know nothing about it. If you do ask me any questions specifically pertaining to your investigation, I will terminate our conversation. For the record, do you understand my conditions for speaking to you?"

O'Malley was more amused than anything else. That was quite a speech, and the guy had only looked at his notebook twice. He was ice. "Yeah, I understand. But let's get going before that tape runs out." O'Malley smiled and thought, 'No way this guy is going to control the interview.'

His first question was a softball: "Tell me about your career, Mr. Michaels. Give me a verbal résumé."

Shannon Michaels had no problem with that, just as O'Malley had anticipated. Tommy was an excellent interrogator. He carefully practiced the first rule of the interview: get the subject talking about himself. Relax the person. Take the confrontational tension away. Besides, Tommy liked hearing about other people's lives.

It took Shannon about three minutes to run down his career. His speech was precise and relaxed. He knew O'Malley was warming him up. It was exactly what *he* would do in a television interview. Interrogation is an intellectual game won by the player who's mentally faster afoot, and who can rapidly take advantage of an opening or an indicated weakness. Since O'Malley and the authorities had no eyewitnesses to the GNN crimes, and no physical evidence that could lead them to a suspect, their only hope in solving the case, Shannon knew, was a confession by the killer. That's what O'Malley would have to aim for.

"Tell me a bit about your personal background, Mr. Michaels. You mind if I take a few notes as well?"

"Suit yourself, Detective," Shannon answered, though he didn't particularly like the note-taking. "I was born and raised in Denver. My parents were divorced when I was ten. Fortunately, I was an only child so my mother earned enough money to support me. She was a secretary. My father was what the English call a layabout. He wasn't around much, and didn't help my mother financially."

Tommy noticed that Shannon's voice had become almost a monotone. His upbringing seemingly meant little to him.

"In school I was a wise guy, but fairly intelligent," Shannon continued. "I worked delivering newspapers so I could have my own money. That's where I picked up on journalism. After high school, I drove up to Boulder to attend the University of Colorado. Did very well. Then I got a job at a TV station in Grand Junction, Colorado, as I told you. That started me off."

"Are you still close to your mother?" Tommy asked.

"She died eight years ago. Brain tumor."

"I'm sorry." Tommy paused looking for a reaction from Shannon Michaels. None was evident, so he continued his questioning. "Ever been married?"

"Too busy with the career."

"Any relatives?"

"Well, my father's still alive, if you want to call it that. He lives in some low-rent trailer park in Arizona. He got in touch after seeing me a few times on GNN. Hinted around that he needed some money. I send him a yearly Christmas card. That's about it."

"Don't like the guy?"

"Not much."

Tommy wasn't surprised. He figured Shannon Michaels for a loner, an overachiever who depended solely on himself. There was something cold about the man, that was for sure.

"Was your father an abusive man?" Tommy knew the question was tough, but it needed to be asked.

Shannon Michaels looked first at Tommy, then at the tabletop. He was trying to decide whether to answer. Mental images hit him hard. He finally made up his mind.

"My father let the bottle get the best of him. It destroyed him as an effective human being. He was very smart and charming, but he couldn't control himself. He drank. We suffered. End of story."

Tommy didn't push it but got what he was after. After questioning hundreds of killers, he knew that many of them had been abused as children. Their brutal experiences broke down their humanism, made them unfeeling. In many cases, child abuse warped their entire lives. The situation was well-known to criminal lawyers. They often used it as a defense for clients charged with murder. In California, the Menendez brothers were using the abuse defense for all it was worth.

Shannon Michaels sat calmly, waiting for the next question. Tommy continued looking at the man, unable to comprehend how Ashley Van Buren could be involved with him. Yeah, he was handsome. But he was so icy and methodical. Ashley could surely sense that.

Tommy made a steeple with his fingers and asked, "Any interests, hobbies, Mr. Michaels?"

"What do you want? To date me, Detective?" Shannon smiled without any warmth. "History and current events. I like to read and visit interesting places. And I'm fascinated by law enforcement. Did you know, Detective, that according to criminal investigation manuals, only an exceptionally strong personality or a criminal indurated by bitter experience can withstand a prolonged, skillful police interrogation without incriminating himself in some way? That's why the Supreme Court decided in favor of the criminal defendant in *Miranda v. Arizona*. Also, if a person does remain silent while being questioned by the authorities, his chances of being acquitted of any charge are inestimably improved?"

"I think I knew that," Tommy said. "But I'm sure I don't know what 'indurated' means."

"It means hardened, unfeeling."

'Just like you,' Tommy wanted to say. But he didn't.

Instead, he asked another personal question: "Got any religious affiliation, Mr. Michaels?"

Shannon knitted his brow. "Not really. Never felt the need. How about you, Detective? Are you religious?

"Your standard issue Irish Catholic."

"You really believe that stuff?" Shannon asked.

"I do. Especially the part that says, 'Thou shalt not kill.'"

Shannon Michaels frowned again. He was starting to dislike O'Malley intensely. "Let's get down to it, Detective O'Malley. How can I help you?"

"Tell me who's killin' the TV types."

"Someone in TV, I suspect. But, of course, I have no idea who it is."

"Why somebody in the business?" asked Tommy, his body language non-confrontational. He wanted Michaels to start speaking about the case.

"As I'm sure you know by now, all three victims were awful people. They all had enemies within the industry. They ruined many careers."

"Including your own?"

"I have no comment on that question, Detective. It might pertain directly to the case." Shannon smiled. Staying one step ahead of O'Malley was clearly satisfying him .

"People don't usually go around killing their coworkers. Why do you think this case is different?"

Shannon paused, tapped his fingers together, and drew a breath. "I want to make it clear that I am speaking hypothetically now, okay? I am theorizing." O'Malley nodded. Shannon continued. "Working in television can be like a drug. You can get addicted to it, the action, the glamour, the money. When you work in big time TV, people are impressed. Doors open. You have a major piece of the American dream: status. So when that is taken away, the fall is hard. And the business is so small that once you lose an important job, it's difficult to get another one. Many people get washed out, never to return."

Shannon Michaels paused again, looking off to the side of the room. Tommy thought he might be thinking about his own situation. After about thirty seconds, Shannon continued, "Put yourself in the place of someone fired unfairly from a TV position that he or she had worked extremely hard to acquire. The rage that person might feel could be tremendous. And there's absolutely nothing that person can do. If you sue, you'll never work in the industry again. There's an unwritten blacklist for those who sue. The unions are a joke. They can't do a thing because most TV types are under personal service contracts, which give the companies the right to terminate them at will. All management has to do is pay off their contracts, just like professional sports teams do.

"So, logically," Shannon continued, "it makes perfect sense that, again hypothetically, a TV person could snap. If it happens at the Post Office, there's no reason it couldn't happen at the broadcast center."

As he listened to Shannon Michaels speak, Tommy O'Malley knew something was very wrong. His instincts shouted at him. The guy spoke too clinically about murder. He reminded Tommy of a Mafia hitman. Those guys could discuss killing and maiming people with absolutely no emotion whatsoever. What was that great line in *The Godfather*? "Leave the gun, take the cannolis. We'll kill the guy and then eat dinner." Shannon Michaels was like that, Tommy thought. Passionless in discussing heinous crimes.

Even while speaking, Shannon sensed that O'Malley was measuring him, judging him. The detective's face remained impassive, but something about his body language had changed. Shannon felt the man had made a decision.

Tommy tapped his pen against his chin as Shannon finished his analogy about the Post Office. "I've got to ask you this question, Mr. Michaels. Is there anyone you know at GNN or anywhere else who you believe is capable of a killing rage?"

"Just as I do not want to be labeled a suspect, Detective, I would never implicate anyone else, even off the record, unless I had definite proof and, of course, I do not. Again, I know nothing about the case you're investigating. What I will say is this: Almost everybody on earth is capable of killing rage. Certainly you are, Detective. And so am I, for that matter. If circumstances pushed us over the edge, most of us would react violently. Think about someone hurting your wife or mother. What would you do?"

"I like to think I'd control myself."

"So would I, but we don't know, do we?"

"But a normal person doesn't kill over a job," Tommy said. "Whoever is doin' this is psychotic." He looked Shannon Michaels straight in the eye to see if name-calling rattled him. It didn't.

"Maybe. Or maybe the person sees it a different way. Here's an example: A group in Texas is offering a bounty of five thousand dollars to anyone who kills in the legal protection of his family, home or personal property. The group is called Dead Serious, and I believe they are.

Anyway, some might think this group is doing something evil, encouraging violence. But others might say the group is standing up for what's right. Many people are fed up with criminals who go unpunished by a justice system that obviously doesn't work."

"But there's a big difference between threatenin' somebody's family and gettin' fired from a job," Tommy said.

"Is there? For many people, their job is their life. The job gives them the means to provide for their family and loved ones. Taking that away is a very serious matter, yet it is done all the time, often arbitrarily. I don't think it's a stretch to say that someone could feel justified in killing a person who unfairly takes away the most important thing in that person's life."

"Come on," Tommy replied. "If that was acceptable behavior, we'd have anarchy."

"I'm not saying it's acceptable behavior, Detective. I'm saying that in some rare cases, it's understandable. I believe the person or persons you are looking for have been exposed to psychologically brutal behavior in the workplace. I think whoever the killer is looks upon himself, or herself, as an avenger. That's simply my theory. I'm not debating you. You know a lot more about these things than I do."

Tommy O'Malley looked at Shannon Michaels and saw a smug, conceited man who thought he was intellectually superior—not just to Tommy, but to the world. He despised the man's condescending tone. Michaels had the same kind of bloated self-importance that Tommy had seen in Lyle Fleming. 'These TV guys really are pricks,' Tommy thought.

But much more importantly, Tommy sensed a detachment in Shannon Michaels, a coldness, a quiet rage. This man spoke much more passionately about the reasons for killing than he did about the murders themselves. And he knew the people who had been murdered! Tommy, growing uncomfortable, shifted in the leather chair and tried another tactic.

"I think whoever is killin' these people is a coward."

"Really? How so?" Shannon was interested.

"A courageous person takes what life gives him, does his best, and accepts the knocks. He doesn't become some kind of brutal vigilante, hidin' in the shadows, throwin' women off balconies. That's the behavior of a sick coward and no civilized society should tolerate it. Whoever thinks that murder is a solution for bein' wronged is a very sick person."

Shannon Michaels did not react. He knew O'Malley was trying to make him angry. He was too smart to take the bait.

"Interesting point of view, Detective," Shannon said, curious to see if he could get O'Malley to respond emotionally. "I think you know Ashley Van Buren, the reporter. She feels the same way about the case as you do. In fact, just last night in my living room, she practically echoed your words here today."

Tommy O'Malley felt a rush of anger. The man was turning the tables, baiting *him*. He fought not to show any sign of annoyance, but blood ran into his cheeks.

Shannon saw O'Malley flush slightly. 'So this detective has feelings for Ashley,' he thought. 'A weakness. Advantage, Michaels.'

Tommy knew he had lost momentum, but also knew he had locked in on a very interesting suspect—one he would enjoy taking down if the evidence permitted it. Shannon Michaels was a cold-blooded , arrogant bastard. Tommy couldn't believe the man was provoking him with the reference to Ashley.

"So, Detective, is there anything else I can offer? If not, I have a question for you."

"Go ahead," Tommy said stiffly, still smarting over the reference to Ashley.

"From what I've read and from what Ashley has told me, you don't have much hard evidence in the case. Now, I believe it's true that most New York City homicides are solved because of information provided by informants. So how are you going to find this killer if he's acting alone and keeps his mouth shut?"

"We've got some leads, Mr. Michaels. That's all I can tell you right now. But if I were the deranged person who was doin' this, I wouldn't rest too easy." Tommy paused looking hard at Shannon Michaels. "We *will* solve this case."

"Well, I wish you the best of luck, Detective. We need more dedicated men like you."

'Again that condescending tone,' Tommy thought. Shannon pursed his lips and the two men stared silently at each other. Each knew what the situation was. And each knew it had become very personal. Tommy O'Malley wanted to get up and knock Shannon Michaels on his arrogant ass. Shannon Michaels wanted to humiliate this detective, who was so judgmental, so holy in his ignorant righteousness. What right did this common policeman with the New Yawk accent have to insinuate that Shannon had committed a crime? Tension enveloped the room. Neither man would look away from the other. Finally, Tommy felt the standoff had gone on long enough and broke the silence. "Ashley tells me you have a place out in Eastern Long Island. Can you give me the address?"

"Sorry, I can't do that, Detective. Writing is very difficult for me and I must have complete isolation. No phone calls, no visitors, no interruptions. If I lose my concentration, I might not get it back for days. Nobody has my address out there, not even Ashley. I hope you understand."

Tommy knew that was complete bullshit from somebody who could concentrate in a typhoon. His anger briefly stirred by the latest Ashley reference, Tommy concentrated on breathing evenly. "What kinda book you writin'?"

"It's a romance novel, if you can believe it. Kind of like a 'Bridges of Madison County.' Figure I'd try to make some money."

Tommy did not want to leave just yet. He knew that Michaels would probably not consent to see him again. He desperately tried to think of something that would put Michaels off balance. He knew if he mentioned Shannon in the context of the investigation, the dialogue would cease. He knew that threats and intimidation tactics were useless. Michaels would just use those against him. In the end, Tommy disappointed himself. He couldn't come up with anything to rattle the bastard. "Well, I guess that's it for now. I hope we can speak again."

"It would be my pleasure, Detective," said Shannon Michaels. "Meantime, good luck in your investigation. I hope you can put a stop to these terrible crimes."

Shannon Michaels stood up and looked at Tommy O'Malley with a cocky grin. Thinking that the man might actually be mocking him, Tommy once again wanted to pop the guy. But he replaced that violent thought with a different one: 'If this guy is the killer, and I think he is, I will definitely take him down.'

For Michaels, it had been an exhilarating interview. He felt he had bested the detective, even subtly humiliated him. Shannon was tempted to hurl one more remark about Ashley Van Buren at Tommy as he walked toward the door. But he resisted. He'd see this O'Malley again. And next time, it would be on his own terms.

• • •

Tommy O'Malley got little sleep that night. His fury and frustration saw to that. He replayed the interview over and over in his mind. He conjured up scenarios where he nailed Michaels as the killer. But, in reality, Tommy had no hard evidence. And the son of a bitch had succeeded in rattling him with the Ashley remarks. Tommy's muscles tensed.

Minutes turned into hours, and Tommy O'Malley felt emotionally exhausted. 'Why not just take the guy out yourself?' he thought. Justifiable homicide. It was very rare, but Tommy had heard of cases where cops did just that—eliminated a dangerous killer whom they could not obtain evidence against. The fantasy was sweet. As he conjured up various methods whereby Shannon Michaels lost his life, Tommy felt a strange, soothing sensation. His body began to relax, and the frustration melted in his mind. The more violent the fantasy, the more vivid his feelings of contentment and satisfaction. And then, finally, Tommy O'Malley confronted the seductive force that had flooded his mind with pleasure. A potent drug had been planted and harvested within his exhausted mind. The drug was called revenge.

CHAPTER TWENTY-ONE

"Well, I don't think we have to ask how *your* weekend was, do we Ashley?" The voice belonged to Bert Cicero, the *Globe*'s assignment editor, as he briefly interrupted his coffee drinking to offer a smirking greeting to his star columnist.

"What are you talking about now, Bert?" Ashley said, a bit of reserve in her voice. It was eight thirty in the morning and she had just arrived in the newsroom. 'All cryptic comments before Monday at noon should be outlawed,' she thought.

"Check out your office, hon. Somebody suddenly likes you a lot." Cicero grinned his most lascivious grin, replete with yellow teeth. Ashley was convinced no woman on earth could find that grin attractive.

Propped up against her office door were two long white boxes. Red ribbons tied them together. Flowers, probably long stemmed red roses. Everybody knew it from the boxes. In the *New York Globe* newsroom, receiving roses was as rare as showing compassion.

Ashley unlocked the door, put the boxes on her desk and opened the card. "Unforgettable—that's what you are..." was written in neat black ink. It was signed "Love, S." Even though the words sounded plagiarized from a Nat King Cole ballad, Ashley found the sentiment endearing.

The flowers were, of course, beautiful. So was the gesture, Ashley thought. She was surprised. She never expected the man to be thoughtful. Maybe the gamble she had taken with him would turn out to be a winner.

Ashley sat down in front of her computer terminal feeling pleased but also apprehensive. The GNN case was taking up a major amount of her time, and she was not developing as many other column ideas as she should have been. Her column for the next day was a hard-edged look at attorneys who represent killers in murder cases. Specifically, attorneys who charge huge amounts of money to defend obviously guilty people, and then try to get them off on legal technicalities.

Ashley's take was that such lawyers were sleazy and their practice extremely destructive to the criminal justice system. But she was having a hard time getting anyone to say that for attribution. People were afraid. O.J. Simpson's so-called dream team of lawyers was a powerful bunch. Even William Kunstler, as outrageous as any attorney, was feared in law enforcement circles. And Alan Dershowitz. Forget him. Nobody wanted to mess with a Harvard professor. Lawyers could hurt people who criticized them. They could uncover embarrassing things about people. They were to be feared.

Ashley's phone rang and she decided to pick it up rather than go through the voice mail routine. "Ashley Van Buren."

"Hey, it's Tommy. Got a minute?"

"Anything for you, Detective. You know that."

"I wish that were true, Ash." Tommy's voice was business-like. Now that he strongly suspected Shannon Michaels, it upset him even more that Ashley Van Buren was involved with him. "Look, I talked to your boyfriend over the weekend."

"He's not my boyfriend." Ashley sounded defensive.

"He's not anyone's friend, in my opinion. I've got a lot to tell you about him. When can I see you?"

"I'm free tonight."

"Good, I'll swing by your place around eight. We'll get a drink."

"Fine, but don't hang up yet, Detective. I need your expertise on something."

"I'm not going to like this, am I?"

"I'm writing a column on criminal lawyers who defend killers even though they know their clients are guilty. Obviously, it's a hot topic with the Simpson case and the Menendez brothers."

"There are plenty of lawyers who'll do that if the money is right or they get their mugs on TV," Tommy said.

"So what do you think about it?"

"Are you going to quote me, Ash?"

"I'd like to, Tommy, if it's okay with you." Ashley used her sweetest, most endearing voice.

"You know the D.A. will get his colon inflamed if I talk publicly about defense lawyers. That kind of thing can always be used in court to show prejudice, blah, blah, blah."

Ashley sighed. "Tommy, nobody with any credibility will talk on this subject and things need to be said. You know that. Won't you stand up on this one?"

"'Stand up.' Very good, Ash. Police jargon. Okay, I'll give you some copy. But I'm an idiot for doing it." Tommy knew he was caving in for one reason and one reason only: He was completely infatuated with Ashley Van Buren.

"Attorneys who knowingly manipulate the justice system to get criminals off are just as guilty as the criminals themselves," Tommy told Ashley as she typed notes into her computer. In his twenty-one years on the force, he continued, he had seen hundreds of sleazy lawyers beat the system for men and women who had committed thousands of brutal crimes.

Tommy doubted that the lawyers responsible were feeling any pangs of conscience inside their lavish homes in Scarsdale and on Park Avenue. And, yes, everybody was entitled to a defense. But when an attorney is faced with overwhelming evidence that his client has murdered someone, yet still tries to free that person through legal trickery, then that lawyer becomes an accessory to murder. And if the person kills again, the lawyer should also be charged in connection with the subsequent homicide.

Ashley asked Tommy to slow down—his words outran her fingers on the keyboard—and this was just the kind of strong stuff she needed. After a brief pause, Tommy added that, to some attorneys, money and publicity were more important than human life or justice.

As an example, Tommy cited the guy who shot up the Long Island Railroad, killing six people. In the beginning, the shooter was defended by William Kunstler, who actually asserted that the killings were understandable because his client had "black rage." Kunstler said the man was angry because he believed he was being discriminated against, and asked the jury to acquit him of murdering six innocent people he had never seen before. Tommy said the whole thing made him sick.

"What it all comes down to," Tommy said, wrapping things up, "is the lawyer's ability to rationalize. Raising questions of evidence in a murder case is one thing. Deliberately trying to manipulate a flawed system in order to free an obvious killer is quite another thing. Lawyers should be held responsible for the consequences of their actions just like everybody else."

Ashley was clearly pleased with the interview. She gently chided Tommy for being a fascist, telling him that the justice system would totally collapse if lawyers were held liable for their clients' criminal behavior after being acquitted and set free.

If they just shot a few of the worst lawyers outright, Tommy retorted, that might send a message to the others. Tommy signed off, happy to have perked Ashley up. He was looking forward to seeing her that evening.

• • •

"The tee shirts are in!" Tommy looked up as Rosa Gonzalez, the homicide squad's secretary, made the official announcement. He got up from his desk and walked over to a large brown box. In it were three deep stacks of black shirts with large white lettering which read, "This Job Is Murder." Underneath, in smaller letters, were the words "Be Nice to Homicide Cops." Tommy grinned and took three extra-larges for himself, three larges for some friends, and one small for Ashley. 'Trinkets are always effective,' he thought to himself.

Next on Tommy's list of things to do was to call psychologist Anthony Lomanto, an old friend of his, who often testified in criminal cases for the prosecution. Lomanto was a Vietnam vet who had come back in one piece and then signed on with the NYPD. After ten years on the street, he gave it up. His wife was a wreck because of his undercover work, and his two kids wanted to see more of him. Using a family inheritance to live on, he went back to Hofstra University full time, getting a Master's Degree in Psychology.

Tony Lomanto was often used by the NYPD to interview borderline loonies, and to evaluate the criminal tendencies of felons who were evading capture. Lomanto wrote sharp personality profiles, giving detectives helpful psychological sketches of the most dangerous suspects. He also frequently testified for the prosecution in murder cases, debunking defense psychologists who testified for money that So and So's violent behavior wasn't his fault because of "you name the reason."

Tommy liked Tony Lomanto because he was a straight shooter who spoke in language both understandable and useful. Tommy needed to get inside the head of whoever was killing the television people. Since he knew more about Shannon Michaels than David Wayne at this point, he dialed Lomanto up and gave the psychologist every bit of information he had about Michaels, as well as his own impressions of the man. He then faxed Lomanto Shannon's picture and résumé, asking the psychologist for a complete workup. By one in the afternoon, Tony had it done.

"You've got a real problem on your hands here, Thomas," Tony Lomanto began. Tommy already knew that, but he quickly backed off. Knowing that most shrinks loved to steer conversations in their own directions, Tommy chose not to inhibit or rush his friend. He wanted to hear everything the man had to say. The more he talked, the better.

Tommy settled back in his chair, putting his open notebook on his lap. "Tell me about my problem, Tony, and tell me how to catch him."

"It ain't gonna be easy," Tony said, lapsing into his native Brooklyn accent. "Even though he might not be your man, I believe Shannon Michaels is your classic narcissist. That is, he has an excessive love and admiration for himself. True narcissism is a rare personality disorder that's found in only about one percent of the population, although that number rises to about fifty percent in Beverly Hills." Tony laughed at his own joke. Tommy also laughed, but mainly because he appreciated Tony helping him out.

"Anyway, this Michaels looks like a textbook case. Here's a guy whose ability to function in life is based entirely on his accomplishments, or so it seems from the data you've supplied. He's a man who needs attention to function. It's food to him. He also feels that he actually deserves attention from everybody, that he's special, that *his* needs are more important than the needs of other human beings. Know anybody else like that, Tommy?"

"Just my ex-wife." Both men laughed. Tommy was jotting down notes.

"Most of us have elements of narcissism in our makeup, but a full-blown narcissistic personality can turn extremely dangerous if a person's need for attention isn't met. You see, the narcissist is preoccupied with thoughts of his own power, success, beauty, whatever. These things are always on his mind. He has no empathy for others who operate outside his ego. But here's an interesting wrinkle. The narcissist can also be very loyal to those people who give him what he wants. He can be charming, engaging, and persuasive. If someone is giving him attention, or gratifying him, that person may receive a tremendous

183

amount of goodwill. But if the narcissist does not continue receiving what he craves, he'll immediately withdraw that good feeling."

Ashley Van Buren's face quickly jumped into Tommy O'Malley's mind. So that was it. Shannon Michaels was a completely different person around Ashley, probably charming the pants right off her. Tommy frowned at the thought.

"So what you're tellin' me, Tony, is that Shannon Michaels can present different faces to different people?"

"It's more than that. He can actually *be* different people. He can compartmentalize his behavior. For example, if you humiliate a narcissist, he can fly into a rage, even kill you right on the spot if he has low impulse control. You see that with psychos on the street all the time. Idiots killing people because they 'dissed' them. But the narcissist's rage is specifically directed. It isn't all over the place. A few hours after he kills, the narcissist could be calmly making love to a woman who worships him."

"Tell me more about this rage business," Tommy said. "I'm havin' trouble convincing people that a big shot rich guy like Michaels could actually murder someone."

"It's called righteous slaughter."

"What?" Tommy had never heard that term, though he thought he had heard them all. "Righteous slaughter?"

"Yeah. If you completely humiliate a narcissist, you can ignite a bomb. If you take away his ability to get positive attention and then compound the problem by bringing negative attention to him, chances are you've made a mortal enemy of him. The narcissistic personality can easily become enraged and feel that he's morally justified in retaliating against people who hurt him. He sees nothing wrong in demonizing those who bring him pain. And the bigger the humiliation, the more drastic the retaliation. Remember, the narcissist does not feel for other people. 'If they die,' he thinks, 'well, they definitely deserved it.' That's righteous slaughter."

"So how does all this apply to Shannon Michaels?" Tommy asked.

"Well, if I'm readin' the guy's profile right," Tony Lomanto continued, "his career was the source of his feelings of omnipotence and grandiosity. His TV job gave him daily ego gratification and excitement. The narcissist needs excitement. Because Michaels was a success on television, it reinforced his opinion that he was a very special human being.

He got the attention he craved, the admiration of thousands. Being on TV was like a drug to him and when it was taken away from him, he had to find a substitute drug."

Tommy frowned. "Which was?"

"Planning and carrying out the executions of those people who had humiliated him. The substitute for his career in TV is his career as a workplace avenger."

"I don't know whether I can buy that, Tony," Tommy said.

"Look at it this way. The guy gets his feelings of power and excitement by doing the executions. He gets plenty of attention because everybody is writin' about the mystery killer. His ego is gratified because he's gettin' away with these crimes. He's smarter than the cops, stronger than his enemies. And he is satiating his rage. Remember, every time he thinks about the people who wrecked his career, his fury burns. Most of us cool off after a while. The narcissist never cools off."

"So, Michaels, or somebody like him, is having a great time doing this stuff?"

"It's not quite that simple. From what you've told me, Shannon Michaels is a man without a support system. He's single, with few close friends or relatives. Nobody loves him. As a boy, he was probably abused or ignored by his father and did not have a very strong bond with either parent. His mother was out of the house working. So Michaels is the Lone Ranger. He's distant and cold, although, again, he can be charming and warm when he wants to be. But Michaels is not the kind of guy who has a great time doin' anything. Most of his feelings have been destroyed. That's why he might be able to throw a woman off a balcony and propel steel into a man's brain—without even a wince. The guy is numb and probably has been since childhood. He has anhedonia, a reduced ability to experience pleasure. He also can't feel anybody else's pain. The only time he feels anything at all is when his ego is getting massaged, or when somebody is attackin' it."

"What about remorse?" Tommy asked.

"Forget it. The guy has experienced what we call psychic trauma. The worst thing that could happen to him has already happened. His career blew up. I know I'm runnin' long here, Tommy, but do you have time for a war story? It might be helpful."

"Sure, Tony. Take your time."

"Okay, in March of 1968 I was in the Marines, stationed in the

Central Highlands of Vietnam. I was just a grunt, a ground soldier tryin' to stay alive. I was assigned to a Marine Combined Action Platoon that was made up of thirty-five guys and a dog: eleven Marines, twenty-four ARVNs—South Vietnamese—and Buster, the German Shepherd. Anyway, every few days we'd go out lookin' for the enemy. Only we didn't look too hard. Some villages were friendly, so we'd stay close to them. Other villages were nasty, full of Charlie. Those, we'd avoid.

"One of the worst places was a hamlet called My Lai, and we all knew it. It was Viet Cong controlled, a good place to stay far away from, especially at night. Well, you remember what happened at My Lai. American soldiers went in there and butchered almost six hundred Vietnamese, mostly women, children and old men. And those soldiers would have killed even more except an American chopper pilot set down and ordered his crew to train their guns on the guys doin' the killin'. The pilot would have smoked those grunts if they hadn't allowed him to take some of the wounded kids into the chopper and fly them off to the hospital. Now, how intense is that?"

"Geez," was all Tommy could say.

"A few weeks after the massacre, which was kept so quiet that the press didn't find out for months, I'm at this firebase near My Lai. These grunts from the American Division's Charlie Company, the platoon involved at My Lai, were there drinkin' beer. They start talkin' about what they did in the village. I hadn't heard anything about it. So I'm listening to these sons of bitches describin' how they blew apart these unarmed people, babies included.

"Finally, I got really pissed off. I mean I just snapped. I screamed at them: 'What is this shit?' They start screamin' back, cursing me out, saying people from the village were helpin' Charlie. He was killing us, so, in effect, the villagers themselves were killing us. Emotion was flying all over the place. These guys had seen their friends blown apart by booby traps. One guy in their platoon had his balls blown off. I thought they might even smoke *me* before some lieutenant came in and cooled things down.

"Anyway, bottom line, these guys had no remorse whatsoever. They wound up screamin' that the slants at My Lai got what they deserved. I couldn't believe it. Years later, when I went back to school, I learned that they were experiencing 'psychic trauma.' These American soldiers became animals because of what they had seen and experienced. Not an excuse for their behavior, just an explanation."

"So you think Shannon Michaels is traumatized?" The psychologist could hear the skepticism in Tommy's question.

"I think the guy took a major blow to the psyche. That, combined with his personality disorder, could have made him a killer."

Tommy leaned forward, putting his elbows on his desk, cradling the phone in his hands. Rosa the secretary was waving at him. "Can you hold for a minute, Tony? I'll be right back."

"Jackson on line two for you, Tommy. He's calling from California and says it's important."

Tommy punched the phone button. "Livin' it up out there, you swine?"

Jackson Davis snorted. "Doin' your leg work, man. But I got something *very* interesting."

"And I got Tony Lomanto on the other line. Can you call me back in fifteen minutes?"

"You're cuttin' into my beach time, pal."

"You know, Jack, 'Baywatch' could use a brother or two in the cast. You could kick sand in that Hasselhoff's face all day and chase Pamela Lee around the lifeguard stand. Not a bad life." O'Malley laughed. So did Jackson.

"I'll talk to you in thirty minutes." Jackson Davis hung up. Tommy came back on line one.

"Sorry, Tony. You okay?"

"Havin' a blast, Tommy."

"I owe you a steak at Gallagher's. One last question: Say the killer is Michaels. How the hell am I gonna catch him?"

"Let's look at it scientifically," Tony Lomanto began. "I believe Shannon Michaels, if he is the killer, is enjoyin' the game—or at least as much as he can enjoy anything. He's plannin' things very carefully and carryin' the murders out like a professional. But he could very well make a mental mistake. He could get drunk on feelings of invincibility, falsely believin' that his past success makes him invulnerable. That could lead to a bad decision on his part. However, if you do corner this guy, Thomas, be careful. He'll come at you like a starvin' animal."

"I'm not worried about that," said Tommy, sounding a bit too macho for the psychologist.

"Tommy, you might want to rethink that," said Lomanto, using the diplomatic-speak common to therapists. "As I told you, I think Michaels is excited by what he's doing. He likes the mental challenge. He likes beatin' you. That's why he agreed to speak with you when most psychos would have run. But he has a weak point. You can goad him, prey on his vanity. If you can enrage him, he might give you the opening you need. But as you know, that's a dangerous strategy. *You* might survive, but the guy could hurt others around you."

Tommy grunted but didn't say anything. The truth was he would love to go hand to hand with Shannon Michaels.

"Otherwise," Tony Lomanto said, "only a person close to him could provide you with the evidence you need. And there's nobody close to him, right?"

Tommy paused and said, "There may be one person." The sadness in the detective's voice was immediately noted by his friend. "We'll see how it shakes out. I really appreciate this, Tony. You gave me a lot to think about. Let me know if I can ever return the favor."

"I like my steaks rare and expensive."

Tommy laughed. "Just the opposite of *my* personality profile. Common and cheap."

• • •

For David Wayne, it had been a long ride back to New York from Baltimore. After five days of drinking and playing bad blackjack in Atlantic City, he had gone south to visit an old girlfriend in Baltimore. He'd intended to stay just a few days, but things went well—very well. Perhaps because she had left her husband a few months earlier, she nearly killed Wayne in the sack. And could this woman drink! Wayne had known her when she was in the writer's pool at GNN, and they had gone out a few times. Back then, however, the slender woman had been kind of shy. Not any more. Wayne extended his visit by ten days, and, during that time, the topic of Costello and Ross came up quite often. Glasses in their name were frequently raised.

Wayne rode the elevator down from his apartment and strode into his apartment building's lobby. He barely nodded at the doorman, Orlando Soto, so lost was he in thoughts of having a cold beer or two.

Orlando was surprised to see David Wayne. The   powerful-looking man had been away from New York for a long time. "Good afternoon,

Mr. Wayne. How was your trip?"

"Fine, Orlando, just got back in late last night."

"Good to see you again, sir," said Orlando, as David Wayne walked out the revolving door and onto the sidewalk. The doorman then removed a card from his front jacket pocket, picked up the phone, and dialed Tommy O'Malley's private number.

• • •

The article in *Broadcasting and Cable Magazine* described the upcoming convention of the Radio and Television News Directors Association, the RTNDA, in great detail. It would be held in Fort Lauderdale, Florida, at the Marriott Hotel, the week of December twelfth. GNN anchorman Lyle Fleming would be the featured speaker at the gala dinner on Tuesday evening. After reading the short piece, Shannon Michaels picked up the phone and dialed information, asking for the number of the Marriott Hotel.

• • •

As usual, Jackson Davis was prompt. He called Tommy from the Sheraton Hotel in Santa Monica at 11:30 a.m., Pacific time. Jackson had quite a story to tell.

Upon his arrival in Los Angeles, Jackson went directly to the funeral of Martin Moore, a pitiful event attended by just seven other people. Apparently "much loved" was not a phrase that applied to Martin Moore. Nobody at the service shed a tear, not even the man's two daughters, Jackson noted.

At the cemetery, an attractive young black woman caught the detective's eye. He politely introduced himself. The woman's name was Susan Oliver. She had been Moore's secretary for the previous five years.

It didn't take long for Jackson to find out two things: that Susan despised her late boss, and that she liked Detective Davis very much. Later that evening, the two ate dinner at a swank restaurant called The Ivy at the Shore, and sparks flew. Susan Oliver found Jackson Davis handsome and intelligent. Jackson couldn't argue with her.

The next evening, on their second date, Susan Oliver gave up all of Martin Moore's secrets. The man was a true pig, according to Susan. He would do anything for money. He slanted research all the time to please the executives who paid him. Susan typed up all of the research summaries, so she knew many of them were bogus. What Moore found out from the television viewers he polled was not always what he presented as fact. Susan told Jackson that she felt a terrible guilt because she knew some people lost their jobs because of Moore's dishonest research.

Jackson asked Susan if she had ever heard the name of Shannon Michaels. He was surprised by her reaction. Susan's eyes actually teared up. That was the worst thing she had ever been involved with, she said. Moore and a man named Lance Worthington, the news director at Channel Six in New York, really hated this Michaels. They talked about him all the time on the phone. From what Susan could ascertain, Michaels preferred doing hard news, and thus made it difficult for Worthington to champion the tabloid stories he needed to pull in younger viewers. Martin Moore was always calling the anchorman "that bastard Michaels."

In the spring of 1993, Moore undertook an extensive research contract for Newscenter Six, a polling project that would net him close to two hundred thousand dollars. On-air talent at all New York City stations was evaluated, and Shannon Michaels scored excellent numbers, right behind legendary anchormen Bill Beutel and Chuck Scarborough in the name recognition category. The majority of viewers liked Michaels, and felt he added a great deal of credibility to "Newscenter Six."

But that, said Susan Oliver, is not what Martin Moore reported. He cooked the books. By the time Moore was finished tinkering, the research showed that Shannon Michaels was slipping in popularity, especially among viewers eighteen to forty-nine years old—the prime audience for advertisers. Moore then ordered Susan Oliver to enter the phony data into the computer system. She protested, but Moore made it clear that her job was on the line. "What do you care about this guy?" he demanded to know.

When Susan asked her boss for verification information—that is, the names and phone numbers of the people Martin Moore had polled—he told her that Newscenter Six wasn't interested in verification. The company would take the results Moore provided, and ask no questions.

To her shame, Susan Oliver did what Moore ordered. She had a young daughter to support and needed her $35,000-a-year salary. But after she heard that Shannon Michaels had been fired from his job, all she could think about was her role in the man's demise. Moore and Worthington actually laughed about the firing on the phone. She had furtively listened in on one conversation and almost became nauseous. Both men were ruthless animals, she thought. They had no morals whatsoever.

But Susan Oliver had a conscience and did the only thing she could think of: She called Shannon Michaels. Martin Moore kept a list of all "Newscenter Six" employees, including their home addresses and phone numbers. Susan didn't give Shannon her name, but told him what had happened. The man listened in silence, Susan told Jackson. He did not react. After asking a few questions, he politely thanked her and hung up. She expected the shit to hit the fan, to find out that he had filed a lawsuit or something. But nothing happened. The call eased Susan's guilt a little, she said, but she still felt like a criminal.

Tommy O'Malley was silent until Jackson Davis finished the story. All at once, he erupted: "I knew it, goddamnit. I just knew it. That bastard! That cowardly fuck! I'll break his neck, Jack! That lowlife bastard!

"Easy, Tom," said Jackson Davis, who was now holding the phone away from his ear because Tommy was screaming at the other end. "Calm down, man. Now that we know it's probably him, we hold the cards."

"Not really, Jack," said Tommy, the volume of his voice dropping. He was cooling down but still breathing hard. "The guy's eventually gonna go after Worthington, but that could happen any time. We can't watch him forever."

"True, but this guy's not a patient man."

"He's shrewd, Jack. I met with him on Sunday."

"Man, I'm sorry I missed *that*," Jackson Davis said. "I bet you guys are best pals now."

"His best pal inhabits a warm place, if you know what I mean, Jack. Anyway, you're right. We'll get him. Anything left to do out there?"

Jackson Davis paused, "Well, Susan and I still have a few things we haven't tried."

"I mean in the investigation, Jackson. I can't believe you're gettin' laid on the city's nickel," Tommy snarled. He thought he heard Jackson stifle a laugh.

"What I do for the department!" said Jackson in mock exasperation. "But seriously, the cops out here have very little on the Moore case. These are mellow guys; they're not exactly obsessing over it. I need one more day to look around Malibu, see if anyone saw this Michaels or anybody else on the night Moore bought it. I've been showing Michaels' picture around, but nothing yet. You think the guy is definitely our man, huh?"

"No question. I'll fill you in when you get back. By the way, Jack, what's this Susan look like?"

"Five-ten, long legs, nice round butt, 36 B cup and a smile that lights up your life."

"You're a poet, Jack."

"That's odd. She calls me poetry in motion. Any way, got to go. Work to do. I believe it's eighty degrees. What's it like in Harlem?"

"Fuck you, Jack."

• • •

Tommy O'Malley walked into Lt. Brendan McGowan's office and sat down. McGowan had just returned from a long weekend in the Bahamas only to find three messages from the Commissioner. Each asked the same question: When was the Ross case going to be cleared?

On his Caribbean trip, McGowan had gotten some sun, but he still looked tired. 'He probably looked tired the day he was born,' Tommy thought.

"Nice time, Mac?"

"The wife got sun poisoning."

"Geez."

"Had to go to the hospital and everything."

"Wow."

"Two thousand bucks and she gets sun poisoning."

"Shame."

"What we got on Ross?"

"I know who did it."

Brendan McGowan leaned forward, his eyes gleaming with interest. "But there's a problem, right?"

Tommy scratched the top of his head. He needed a haircut. "Yeah,

I can't prove it."

"Who's the perp?" McGowan asked.

"Guy named Shannon Michaels, former Channel Six anchorman."

"Holy shit in a ten pound bag! Michaels? Are you sure? How do you know?"

"I'm ninety percent certain it's him. I had a sit-down at his place. I think he's the guy."

"Can we get him?" McGowan asked.

"I believe we can. But it's not going to be easy. And the bastard's making noises about suing," Tommy answered.

"That's all we need." McGowan shook his head, which was peeling underneath his comb-over. Irishmen rarely tanned. They usually reddened, then shed. "So what do you need to wrap this up?"

"Surveillance on the guy, number one. We might get lucky. I think he's got another target in mind."

"He's out on the Island, right?" Tommy nodded. "That's gonna get real costly," McGowan said.

"I know, but we gotta do it. I also need to pull his phone records for the past year. I doubt we'll find anything, but we should look."

"That's easy enough," McGowan said. "Any probable cause for a search or a tap?"

"None. And we wouldn't find anything anyway. Mac, this guy has motive and he knows we know it. We got the reason behind the hits, but nothin' else. He's a professional assassin. Every hit has been clean. And he's an arrogant fuck. He looked right into my eyes and denied everything. Between the lines, he realizes that I know what went down. But it doesn't matter. He understands the limits of the law, and he knows we don't have shit."

"All right, I'll authorize surveillance for two weeks, but that's all the department will allow in one stretch except for terrorist cases. Can you shake this guy? Force him to make a mistake?" McGowan asked.

"Possible."

"Damn...Shannon Michaels. Be careful, Tommy. If this thing blows up, it's both our asses. If he sues or goes to the press and we don't have him, we're dead meat."

"I know. There's one other thing, Mac. Another guy, David Wayne, used to work with GNN. He's got motive and no clear alibi as far as we know. I'm pretty sure this Michaels bastard is the perp, but we gotta watch Wayne to protect our backs. Can you put a guy on him for a couple of days while I concentrate on Michaels?"

"Fuck. More paperwork. Alright. But I'm also callin' the Commissioner and lettin' him know we're makin' progress. But I'm tellin' him we don't have a name."

"Fine," Tommy O'Malley said, getting up from his chair. "I'll talk to the surveillance guys."

• • •

The phone rang and Shannon Michaels picked right up. He didn't get many calls, so he never screened them with an answering machine. If he didn't want to talk, he'd just say so.

"It's me—Ash. The flowers are beautiful. Thank you."

"You're welcome," Shannon said. "How are you?"

"Stressed over a column. But the flowers are getting me through it. You really didn't have to," Ashley said while looking out her window at the cold East River.

"Can we get together next weekend?" Shannon asked.

"Don't know yet. I'm still sorting some things out."

Shannon didn't like the sound of that. "Talking to Detective O'Malley again, I bet."

"He doesn't have anything to do with it," Ashley said. "It's just that I have conflicting emotions about us."

"Well, let's talk about it. Besides, I want to tell you about my meeting with O'Malley." Shannon knew that would pique Ashley's interest.

"I'll call you tomorrow. Thanks again for the flowers."

Ashley hung up the phone and leaned back in her chair, staring again at the roses sitting in the glass vase on her desk. She really didn't know what to do about Shannon Michaels. The situation was getting out of control. Never in her wildest fantasies could she have conjured up a situation as farfetched as this. If Tommy was right and she was wrong, she might be falling for a cold-blooded killer. What if she had been intimate with a monster? Could she live with that?

But it couldn't be possible. The guy was so normal. And something about Shannon presented an almost overwhelming attraction to her. She had to talk to somebody about this. Just had to. But it was so bizarre, people would think she was crazy. And she couldn't reveal Shannon's name in the context of murder. That would be unthinkable. What if he really was innocent, as she believed? God, what a mess!

After thinking a few moments, Ashley leaned forward, picked up her phone, and dialed a number she knew well. After two rings, her therapist's secretary came on the line.

• • •

The kid was seventeen but looked four years younger. His head was shaved. Hung from his left lobe were two small silver earrings. And, on his left forearm was displayed a garish tattoo of a knife blade with the letters B.B. at the top of the hilt. The B.B. stood for "Bitchin' Boys," the gang to which he belonged.

Detectives Luke Murray and Esteban Morales were interrogating the teenager in the youth room just to the left of Tommy O'Malley's office. The youth room was usually reserved for kids under the age of sixteen, but Murray and Morales were using it because it was smaller than the regular interrogation room, and the detectives wanted this kid, named Justin Holliday, to feel the walls closing in on him.

Two days prior in Central Park, Justin had been "juggin," gang slang for hanging around, waiting for a few of his friends to meet him. Because certain areas of the Park are known as cruising grounds for homosexuals, it wasn't all that unusual for a kid as young-looking as Justin Holliday to be approached by a gay man in his mid twenties and get propositioned.

But Justin became enraged and chased the man off, cursing him with a fusillade of words that were as base as the English language allows. Later that evening, he and three other members of the Bitchin' Boys returned to Central Park to hunt for the man who had accosted Justin. They found him and another man talking and smoking cigarettes at a known gay hangout just north of the West 72nd Street entrance to the Park.

The Bitchin' Boys wasted no time on small talk. They immediately jumped the two men and started beating them. The men ran, but the one who had propositioned Justin slipped and fell. The attackers pounced on him with savage intensity. Despite the victim's screams for mercy, the four gang members kicked him to death in a matter of minutes. The teenagers then took his wallet, left the park, traveled downtown on the subway, and went to a dance club, using their victim's money to pay the admission fee.

The other man escaped the murderous gang by running through the Park and flagging down a police car on Fifth Avenue. By the time the police responded to the scene, the killers were long gone. But the survivor had gotten a very good look at one of them—Justin Holliday. When homicide detectives showed the witness mug shots of known troublemakers, the man fingered the youth immediately. This was why Detectives Murray and Morales were grilling the gang member in the youth room.

But Justin Holliday was playing the hard case. He wouldn't say a thing, wouldn't give up his pals. And he kept asking for a lawyer. The detectives stalled, knowing three things: that once a Public Defender showed up, the case would get much more complicated; that, because this was a bias crime, the news media would be all over it; and that the information could not be released to the media until the cops located the dead man's family—he came from a small town in Michigan. Once that notification took place, though, and it would be soon, all hell would break loose. The homicide detectives were racing against a shrinking deadline to get Justin Holliday to confess, to write down what he did and who did it with him.

"Tommy, I know you're busy, but could I talk with you for a moment?" A tense-looking Luke Murray was actually wringing his hands, apparently in frustration. Murray probably was getting nowhere with the interrogation, Tommy thought, and wanted to beat the hell out of this punk Holliday, but couldn't do it.

"So, Luke, let's just drown him in the sink. We'll tell everybody he wasn't very proficient in the act of drinkin' water."

Murray smiled for the first time in four hours, then filled Tommy in on the problem. Bias crimes were top priority for New York City homicide detectives. If you couldn't solve them quickly, it was held against you. Tommy listened closely and then suggested a strategy. Murray liked it right away and called for Morales to join them. Esteban locked Holliday in the Youth Room and walked over. He, too, looked frustrated and exhausted.

After speaking with the two investigating detectives for a few more minutes, Tommy unlocked the door and strode quickly into the room, startling Justin Holliday, who had never seen him before. Holliday's light blue eyes were blood shot and his face was pale. Tommy sized him up fast. A big kid, about six feet tall. Looked like he lifted weights. Fingernails bitten to the quick and stained by nicotine. It was obvious the kid badly needed a smoke.

"Hey, man, you no lawyer. You another cop. I wanna lawyer."

"We're gettin' you one, Justin," Tommy said in a calm voice. Everybody screamed for a lawyer these days, the direct result of watching the TV shows "NYPD Blue" and "Homicide." Tommy walked behind the seated suspect, paused, and then circled back, taking a chair directly opposite the tough-looking kid. Between them was a metal table. In front of the suspect, untouched, was the pad of paper and pencil Morales had set down. The teenager was rocking back and forth in his small chair. His breath was foul. Tommy could smell it four feet away.

Tommy had seen hundreds of thugs like Justin Holliday—young people who lived lives of depravity, who hurt other people without a thought. Tommy did not care at all how Justin Holliday had arrived at this particular point in his life. His only thought was to get this kid off the streets. He knew that, even with a conviction, Holliday's prison time would be an insult to the family of the murdered man. Twelve years behind bars was about average for a confessed killer in New York City—twelve years for taking a human life.

"I ain't talkin' ta you, man. I got nothin' ta' say."

"Good, Justin. Then you just listen." Tommy's tone was harder. He leaned toward the kid. "I'm now gonna tell you exactly what is gonna happen to you. The other detectives are takin' a break. They wouldn't tell you this, but I think you should know." Tommy paused. He had the kid's attention.

"First thing is we are going to put the word out that you're ratting on your friends. We're gonna tell everybody on the West Side, and then we're pickin' up all the Bitchin' Boys and bringing 'em in. We're gonna say we really appreciate all the cooperation you're givin' us."

Justin Holliday sneered and said, "Nobody'll believe that bullshit."

Tommy smiled and said, "Yeah, they will. Second thing. You're gonna go over to Riker's. We got some guys inside there who owe us. Big, brutal guys who'll hurt you if we tell them to. Know what I mean, Justin?"

The kid's eyes opened wide. He had been to Riker's Island jail before. He knew exactly what Tommy meant.

"It don't matter where they put you over there, or who you complain to. If we want to, we'll put out the word. Most likely, you won't be killed at Riker's. A bunch of cons will probably just beat the shit out of you. Maybe fuck you a few times. And we all know how much you like that gay stuff. But after you're convicted and sent upstate for a good, long time, you could easily be killed. "

"What the fuck you sayin'? You threatenin' me? You can't do that? I wanna talk to a lawyer." Tommy noticed a bit of urgency in Justin's voice.

"If you break our balls over this case, Justin, you'll do very hard time, at Riker's and upstate. That's a fact and there's nothin' you or any lawyer can do about it."

For the first time, Justin Holliday began to look frightened. "You can't threaten me, man."

"You're absolutely right, Justin," Tommy said as he sat back and rubbed a hand through his hair. "I'm just tryin' to help you out, givin' you a heads-up. I really don't want these terrible things to happen to you, but they will unless you pick up that pencil and write down what you did to that man in the park and who helped you do it."

"No fuckin' way," Justin Holliday said, his bravado clearly fading.

"We have a witness, Justin. Puts you right there. The jury'll believe him. You're gone. You help us out, you might be back on the street when you're thirty. You don't—you're in the ground by twenty. I bet big money on that."

Tommy O'Malley gave Justin Holliday his most malevolent look. The kid couldn't meet his eyes. In his own primitive way, he was thinking.

"The guy was just a fag, man. He came onto me. What am I supposed to do? Fucker deserved it."

"Write it down, Justin. If you help us, we'll help you. And we're the only ones who can help you at this point. Do you understand that?" Tommy's tone softened. He knew the kid would break. These gang bangers were hard cases in groups, but get them alone, strip away their power base, and they were scared just like everybody else.

"What can you do for me?" For the first time, Justin looked Tommy in the eye. Game, set, match. Thirty minutes later, the homicide detectives had a statement written and signed by Justin Holliday. Within two hours, his three accomplices had been picked up. Justin's attorney arrived shortly after that—a tired-looking, bearded man who didn't really care what happened to his client just as long as he could finish up in time to get home by eight that evening. Murray and Morales were extremely happy. Tommy gave them his bill: two steak dinners at Gallagher's Restaurant. One would pay his debt to Tony Lomanto. The other would give him a free meal.

• • •

It was twilight as Shannon Michaels drove along Ocean Parkway heading west. To his left were Jones Beach and the Atlantic Ocean, to his right the coastal marsh. Shannon had walked the beach for two hours, thinking about his situation and Ashley Van Buren.

Navigating onto the Wantagh Parkway, Shannon saw the sun dip behind the horizon. A crescent moon was rising. What he didn't see was the dark, blue Chevrolet about a quarter mile behind him. The car had been following him since he had left his home early that afternoon. The two men in the car had radios and nine millimeter pistols. They were New York City police officers.

• • •

"Tell him to come up," Ashley Van Buren told the doorman through her apartment intercom. The invitation was extended to one Thomas O'Malley, NYPD Homicide Detective.

Tommy had seen many apartment buildings like Ashley's. Second Avenue modern. Forty-three floors. In the lobby, tacky fake leather furniture the color of butterscotch that clashed with the black and white tile floor. A few lonely plants huddled in the lobby corners, and a big sign signaled the world that "All visitors must be announced."

The doormen at these places always seemed to be leering, Tommy thought. They kept track of who went to whose apartment and how long they stayed. They were unbelievable gossips who accumulated information on everyone they could.

Ashley's one-bedroom flat was on the fifth floor. Tommy stood in the elevator alone holding a small bouquet of flowers. This wasn't Tommy's style, but he had a major favor to ask Ashley Van Buren. He hoped the flowers would soften her up.

Ashley opened the door and greeted Tommy with a warm kiss on the cheek. He liked it. The only other person on earth who would do that was his mother. Ashley's eyes lit up when Tommy handed her the bouquet. This was her day for flowers, she thought.

Upon entering the apartment, Tommy's ears met a loud, pulsating noise that seemed to resemble music. "What's that you've got on the stereo, Ash?"

"Hootie and the Blowfish."

"Whatie and the Whofish?" Tommy rolled his eyes. "They are really good, Ash." Tommy brought sarcasm to new heights.

"Okay, what would you like to hear, Detective?"

"Let me introduce you to some good music." Tommy walked over to the stereo, shut off the CD player, and tuned the radio to WCBS-FM, the oldies station in town. A staccato rhythm flowed out of the speakers:

Duke, duke, duke
Duke of Earl, duke, duke
Duke of Earl...

"What's that?" said Ashley, seemingly horrified.

"The Duke of Earl. It's a classic. Come on, you've gotta know this song," Tommy said.

"What song? All I hear is someone shouting in pain."

"Come on. This is a gold record."

"Nothing can stop me now, 'cause I'm the Duke of Earl—yay, yay, yay, ah ooooh..."

"Detective, if you don't change the station right this minute, I'm calling the cops." Ashley broke out laughing, and Tommy smiled through his phony scowl. They compromised on some elevator music by Gloria Estefan.

Ashley brought Tommy a beer, and then poured one for herself. She was still off balance about the entire Shannon Michaels situation—didn't know what was real. And her therapist hadn't been much help. She told Ash to "slow down." Such valuable wisdom for just ninety bucks an hour. Ashley tried to analyze what she was going through but only knew that her feelings were changing every hour on the hour.

"Tommy, thanks again for helping me out with the column. You'll see your words in print tomorrow."

"Can't wait," Tommy said, yawning.

"So what's up with the GNN case?" Ashley asked, sitting down on the love seat adjacent to the couch where Tommy was sitting. She thought he looked weary. There were circles under his eyes and his hair was getting long. He had been funny about the music, but she sensed he had something serious on his mind.

"I've got to ask you a favor, Ash..."

She cut him off. "Tommy, just don't tell me not to see Shannon Michaels. I can't have that. I must make my own decisions." Ashley surprised herself with her vehemence. She was very tightly wound.

"I *want* you to see him."

"What?" Ashley was shocked.

"It's the only way I'm gonna catch the son of a bitch."

Tommy looked at Ashley Van Buren, who clearly was waiting for an explanation, and maybe not the one he had been rehearsing in his mind all afternoon. The one that now came pouring out.

"Look, Ash, I spent an hour with this guy. My gut tells me he's the killer. But I can't prove it, and I don't expect you to believe me until I can. I do expect you, though, to wanna know the truth about this Michaels. So I want you to help me."

Ashley didn't say anything. She had absolutely no idea how she could be of help.

"Michaels says he has a house way out on the island. It's his alibi. He's always alone writin' at his retreat. So, we wanna know if there really is a house that he goes to. And if there is, we want you to look around that house and the one in Sands Point, to see if there's anything out of the ordinary lyin' around. Like, say, receipts from Los Angeles, or Martha's Vineyard, or gloves, stuff like that."

"So you want me to spy on him?"

"Yeah, Ash, that's what I'm askin' you to do."

Tommy looked at Ashley, and then looked down at the floor. He didn't like putting the woman on the spot. He realized that, by asking this favor, he was jeopardizing his personal relationship with her. If she refused to help him, things might never be the same between them again. He also knew there could be danger involved. A man like Shannon Michaels would not be pleased if he found someone snooping around his house. Tommy looked up. His blue eyes were sympathetic, his voice very soft.

"Ash, I hate to ask ya. I really do. But it's the only thing I can think of. We have to get a look inside this guy's life. You're the closest person to him. I'm just askin' for the truth. If you don't find anything, so be it. If you do find something, then you'll finally know what I believe is the true story here. David Wayne could be the guy, I guess. He's back in town, I'm told, and we'll talk to him again. But Jackson has come up with some circumstantial stuff that points directly to Michaels. My gut tells me Michaels is the killer. But without your help, we've got nowhere to go right now."

Ashley Van Buren wanted to just shriek at the top of her lungs. All of this was much too complicated and emotionally draining. How could she spy on someone with whom she was intimately involved?

Tommy saw her pain. His instincts were honed to pick up on emotional confusion. He didn't want to think about Ashley's attachment to Shannon Michaels. He had blocked that out. But here it was on silent display. Tommy began feeling his own emotional pain. He wanted Ashley Van Buren for himself, and was hurt that she felt so strongly for someone else.

Ashley looked at Tommy O'Malley and knew what her answer would be. She had to know the truth, and recognized that this might be the only way to get it. She didn't care about the risk. She only cared about getting rid of the confusion that was turning her life into an emotional bungee jump.

"I'll help you, but for one reason only. I want to know the truth. I can't believe this man is a ruthless killer, but I have to know why you think he is."

Tommy was truly surprised. He thought she would turn him down. "Thanks, Ash. Really, thanks. I know this is very hard for you. And I don't want you to put yourself in any danger. Just casually look around. Don't toss the house or anything."

Ashley did not say a word. She looked away from the detective and covered her face with her hands. When she turned back toward him a couple of minutes later, Tommy saw that she was crying.

CHAPTER TWENTY-TWO

In the late summer of 1993, just a few days after the Labor Day weekend, US troops were engaged in combat against Somali gangsters, and a powerful New York state judge, Sol Wachtler, was sentenced to prison for making bizarre threats against his former lover and her teenage daughter. Newscenter Six and its competitors were already pushing hard on the stories.

For the television news industry, autumn is the busiest, most important time of the year. Local TV stations all across America begin to compete in earnest, gearing up for the vitally important November "sweeps" period. Four times a year, in November, February, May, and July, the A.C. Nielsen Company measures the size of the audience watching each individual television station. These ratings, or numbers as they are called, are used to set the prices advertisers pay for commercial time on specific TV shows. The higher the ratings, the more the station can charge. Thus, the "sweeps" periods are vital. And the November "sweeps" are the most important of the four because they're the first ratings measurement of the new TV season, which starts in September and ends in May. November numbers set the tone for the entire season.

Shannon Michaels was extremely competitive, and he understood the ratings system as well as anyone. In fact, he made it his business to monitor the ratings every day. In large cities like New York, the Nielsen Company provides overnight ratings. That way management can see what the audience is watching every day of the year.

As he sat in his spacious office at the far end of the Newscenter Six newsroom, Shannon knew that Channel Eight, "New York's Hometown Station," was gaining audience and creeping up on his own Channel Six, which had been rated number one at the six o'clock news hour for the past three years. Michaels did not like the situation. When he took over as the primary anchorman of Newscenter Six in 1983, ten years before, the station had been a mess.

It took four years of hard work to get the news product to a respectable level. Good reporters were hired and paid well. Tough investigative stories were encouraged, and each reporter was given the mandate to angle as much information as possible through the eyes of the people the story affected most. In other words, the reporters were asked to make their reports as personal as possible. Once the new tone of the newscast was set, a brilliant promotions woman was brought in from NBC to create a compelling advertising campaign touting the aggressiveness and special New York touch of Newscenter Six. The ratings slowly advanced, and the six o'clock broadcast became very competitive.

Shannon Michaels was, in large part, responsible for the turn-around of "Newscenter Six." He worked closely with management, suggesting strategies and personnel. He also wrote most of the news copy in a straightforward, no-nonsense, New York style.

Though born and raised in Colorado, Michaels became an aficionado of all things New York, learning all he could about how the mammoth city and the surrounding suburbs—including half the state of New Jersey—had developed over the years. He turned himself into a New Yorker, to the point where he could even do a perfect Brooklyn accent on demand.

Newscenter Six got a major break in December of 1988 when Channel Eight's legendary anchorman, Preston Millard, was pulled over for driving under the influence. When two New Jersey state troopers searched his car, they found an ounce of cocaine in the glove compartment. The tabloid newspapers went wild. Millard, who had built his image as a solid family man, was humiliated and forced to take a long leave of absence. Channel Eight's news product collapsed.

It took another two years but, by early 1991, Newscenter Six had become the dominant force in television news in New York City, beating, by a fairly wide margin, the four other stations that broadcast an early news program. That first-place ratings finish coincided with yet another major development: the arrival of new News Director Lance Worthington, who couldn't have walked into a more splendid situation—except for one thing. Shannon Michaels had worked with four news directors since coming to Newscenter Six. The high turnover was due to promotions and burnout, not lack of ability. In Shannon's estimation, Worthington was by far the worst qualified.

Shannon Michaels and Lance Worthington clashed almost immediately. Both men possessed huge egos, and both could be ruthless. Worthington was six years younger than Michaels and had made his reputation in Dallas by introducing flashy technical gimmicks. The computerized graphics he championed lit up the TV screen. His whizbang approach gave the newscast a high tech look that younger audiences found especially appealing. Worthington also loved scandal and gore. If the story was sensational, Lance Worthington was all over it. His news programs in Dallas were great ratings successes.

But Shannon Michaels firmly believed that Worthington lacked the basics required of a news manager. He had never covered news in the field. He didn't recognize a good reporter from a hack. And he was obsessed with research, so other people were always telling him what direction the news should take. A true newsperson, Shannon thought, knew that direction instinctively.

Shannon's office door was closed as he perused the latest overnight ratings sheet dated September 9, 1993. Once again he saw what he had been seeing for the past six months: Channel Eight was rising in the ratings, while Newscenter Six was stagnant. It had taken Channel Eight a couple of years to reorganize, but the station now had a new, young anchor team: A former Miss Connecticut and a good looking man from Seattle. Channel Eight had also hired a retired New York Met to do sports, and the guy was amusing and energetic. If the trend continued—and Shannon was a firm believer in momentum—Channel Eight would pass Newscenter Six in the ratings by November. To Shannon, that was intolerable.

He placed the blame squarely on Lance Worthington. The man was not spending enough money to cover breaking news, and had fired some excellent reporters who wouldn't sex up their news stories. Shannon had strongly protested but, increasingly, management was backing Worthington. This, of course, made Shannon furious. He was not about to lose everything he had worked so hard for because of some idiot news director. Even though the GNN disaster had happened more than ten years ago, Shannon knew that his career could not withstand another debacle.

After leaving GNN, Shannon was a damaged commodity in the news business and his agent was forced to call in serious chits to get

Shannon the anchor position at Newscenter Six. In the end, only two reasons explained his getting the job at all: The station was desperate, and he agreed to work cheaply. In the first year of his contract, Shannon earned $150,000, a pittance compared to what other New York anchors were making. Ten years later, his agent negotiated Shannon's salary into the stratosphere: $1.1 million per year, plus a few perks—another major reason Shannon had to protect the station's news franchise.

As Shannon leaned back in his swivel chair, he placed his hands behind his head and stretched his long legs across the side of his large, wooden desk. His feet hung in the air like two fishing poles over the side of a bridge. The major news story on this Friday, the tenth of September, was the mutual recognition agreement reached between Israel and the PLO. Many Americans cared little about this historically pivotal development.

But in New York, because of its large Jewish population, it was a huge story. New York's Jews not only comprise a significant part of the city's television news audience, they follow current events—especially in the Middle East—quite closely. Shannon, after personally covering stories in Israel, had stayed very well-informed on Middle Eastern affairs. Now, Israel and the PLO had mutually recognized one another's existence, and Shannon decided he should travel to Israel and file reports from there throughout the following week.

On the opposite side of the newsroom, Lance Worthington was in his office interviewing a very pretty young girl. When his telephone buzzed, Worthington became visibly annoyed. When his secretary told him Shannon was on the line, he seemed even more irritated.

"See what he wants, Betty." Worthington was never anxious to speak with Shannon Michaels.

"He wants to talk to you about a breaking story."

'Damn,' Lance Worthington thought. He was enjoying talking to this girl, and she was behaving as if she were impressed with him. Worthington was married, but he still carried on a very active social life.

"Tell him I'll see him in ten minutes."

Exactly ten minutes later, Shannon Michaels walked into Lance Worthington's office. As usual, Worthington was on the phone. Motioned to take a seat, Shannon noticed that the news director's sandy blonde hair was thinning a bit, and that he had cut himself shaving recently. Worthington's skin was so light it was almost translucent. He was slim and well dressed, favoring buttondown collars on his starched shirts. Like most of the managers at Newscenter Six, he wore suspenders.

Worthington hung up the phone and looked at Shannon coldly. This was a departure, Shannon thought. Usually the news director displayed no emotion—until you got him riled up, which Shannon often did. Shannon noted the slight scowl from Worthington, but did not react.

"Lance, I think we should go to Israel over the weekend. I can report from Jerusalem all next week on the agreement."

"I don't think so, Shannon."

"Don't you even want to hear my reasoning?"

"Not particularly."

The curt comment cut into Shannon and triggered his temper. When he could, he avoided talking with Lance Worthington because of the negative vibes between them. But he was not about to let this pissant disrespect him.

"Well, you're gonna hear it anyway, Lance." Shannon drew out the man's name to emphasize the sarcasm. "In case you haven't noticed, we are slipping in the ratings. The numbers have been soft since last spring. Meantime, Channel Eight is gaining. I believe we can re-energize the newscast by doing some hard-hitting reporting on the road. Our ratings went through the roof when I covered the collapse of the Berlin Wall, the LA riots, and the San Francisco earthquake. The PLO thing is big in New York with our Jewish audience."

"I know who the audience is, Shannon." Lance Worthington's voice was harsh, condescending. Shannon was surprised. Worthington wasn't usually this aggressive with him. "The network can cover Israel. We don't need to spend all that money sending you over there. I don't believe having you in the Middle East will help our numbers. Besides, I may have something else for you to do."

Shannon looked at the news director and asked, "Such as?"

"We may be getting an exclusive with Joey Buttafuoco's best friend."

Shannon Michaels laughed out loud, deeply offending Lance Worthington. "This is a joke, right Lance?"

"No joke. Everybody is all over this story. You know that."

"Fine, and we've been reporting the whole, disgusting mess for more than a year. Great. We have plenty of reporters who can talk to these revolting people. I'm not going to do it."

"You'll do it if I say so," Lance Worthington said.

Shannon Michaels should have known from those words that danger was present in the room. Instead, he ran right into the trap. "Look, Lance, we've had this discussion before. I'm not going to do the tabloid stuff. The audience respects me as a serious journalist and if I start chasing the sleaze stories, my credibility will be damaged. We've been doing the Amy Fisher story to death on the broadcast. If that's what you want, so be it. But it ain't brain surgery. The younger reporters can handle it. I don't want to be involved."

"Well, then, maybe we'll have to get somebody who *will* be involved."

"Is that a threat, Lance?"

Rubbing the small brown scab under his chin, the one caused by his shaving mishap, Worthington told Michaels in what seemed an overly calm voice, "I think you should have your agent call Mitchell Ryder."

For the first time, the seriousness of the situation struck Shannon. Mitchell Ryder was the General Manager of Channel Six. His nickname was the "Velvet Shiv." One didn't want to meet with Mitchell Ryder unless it was absolutely essential.

Lance Worthington tapped his Waterman pen against his desk. He knew he had stunned Shannon Michaels and was enjoying the anchorman's discomfort. He had waited a long time for this moment and now it was happening. Martin Moore had come through with the research just the way he said he would. Worthington now had a loaded cannon aimed directly at Shannon Michaels. The fuse was about to be lit.

For one of the few times in his life, Shannon Michaels did not know what to say. He knew he was in a precarious position. A sleazy weakling like Worthington would never suggest a meeting with Ryder unless something was going on. But what could it be? Shannon had no idea, but sensed that whatever it was, it was bad.

"What's this all about, Lance?" Shannon's voice was soft. His eyes stared intensely at the news director.

"I can't get into it now. Better let your agent handle it with Mitchell." And Lance Worthington smiled a smile that made his face resemble a skull—a smile that made Shannon Michaels want to strangle Worthington with extreme prejudice.

Shannon Michaels got up from his chair and strode from the room. He never spoke with Lance Worthington again at Channel Six.

• • •

The "Velvet Shiv" lived up to his nickname. In a twenty-minute meeting with Shannon Michaels and his agent, Aaron Aber, Mitchell Ryder said that he regretted doing so, but he was relieving Shannon of his anchor position immediately. Ryder went on to say that while the station appreciated the fact that Shannon had worked hard to improve the fortunes of Newscenter Six, the new research was damning. Shannon's popularity was slipping among younger viewers. Those between eighteen and forty-nine were showing a preference for Channel Eight's news. What could he, Ryder, do? "You can't argue with the research," he said.

There was also a problem with Shannon's attitude toward Lance Worthington, Ryder continued. The news director was the news anchor's boss—something Shannon apparently did not want to acknowledge. Channel Six and Ryder himself had full confidence in Lance Worthington. He had cut costs and introduced innovative technical procedures. "We believe he is the future," Mitchell Ryder said.

Shannon listened to all of this silently, which wasn't his style, but he knew a done deal when he saw one. Aaron Aber drew up a settlement with Channel Six that called for Shannon to be paid his salary for nine months, until his contract was up. Channel Six was legally obligated to honor the contract in that fashion, but the "Velvet Shiv" made a big show publicly of the station's "generosity" towards Shannon. Ryder told all the newspaper reporters exactly how much Shannon was making, off the record of course, and how Channel Six was "taking care of him." In addition, the reporters were fed information that indicated Shannon's viewer appeal was dropping among New Yorkers and that he was "a major pain in the ass" to deal with at the station. "You know those anchor egos," the reporters were told off the record.

The next day, all the New York papers scorched Shannon Michaels, except the *Times*, which ignored the story completely. In general, print journalists resent broadcast journalists, mainly because the TV reporters make so much more money. To their less well-paid brethren, the demise of a major TV anchorman is always hot copy. And in Shannon's case, the headlines were almost gleeful, all of them echoing each other: "Anchor away: Michaels thrown overboard."

When the newspaper reporters called Shannon for a comment, he declined to speak. That angered and frustrated the newspaper people, and further tilted their stories against him. Shannon anticipated the reaction but realized that anything he said would sound bitter, and that wouldn't help much. So he shut up and absorbed the most public humiliation of his life. Shannon thought he was tough enough to endure it, that his life after the brief ordeal would somehow improve. He was wrong.

CHAPTER TWENTY-THREE

Shannon Michaels sat at an outdoor table in one of the most elegant tavernas the Plaka neighborhood had to offer. He was closely watching a strange, demented-looking dog, zigzagging up Mnissikleous Street and heading toward the Acropolis. The dog was a mixed breed—totally white except for the top half of its tail, which was black. The moment the dog's nose touched the stucco wall on one side of the narrow street, he would immediately turn tail and head for the other side. Back and forth he bounded, looking like a pinball with a protruding tongue. Must have drunk a bowl full of ouzo, Shannon thought.

Athens was the second stop on Shannon's desperate trip of escape. Back in New York, he could no longer stand the constant questions about his dismissal from Newscenter Six. He could no longer face people who regarded him as a failure. So, he had flown to London and checked into the Hilton Hotel on Park Lane. Seeking some company, he called an old friend named Liam Mooney.

In 1990, Mooney had helped Shannon with a series of reports on the Irish Republican Army. Although not officially part of the IRA, Mooney did a fair amount of business with the group and had been able to put Shannon in touch with high-ranking members of the outlawed organization. It took Shannon months of negotiation, but he finally convinced the IRA leadership that he would treat them fairly.

The result was Shannon Michaels' Emmy Award-winning series of reports for Newscenter Six on the inner workings of the terrorist group, including how donated American dollars were used for IRA medical treatment and travel expenses. Shannon feared that the IRA would be angry because his reports were precise and balanced. To his surprise, word got back to him through Sinn Fein, the political arm of the IRA, that the commanders thought his reporting was fair and somewhat flattering.

Now, in November 1993, Liam Mooney's wife took Shannon's call from London. Her husband, she said, had traveled to Athens the day before, and would be in the Greek capital for about a week. She then gave Shannon a number where he could be reached. Shannon knew that Athens was a major meeting spot for Middle Eastern arms dealers and Western moneymen who wished to acquire deadly hardware for their clients. Although Liam would never say, Shannon immediately suspected that guns were the reason the Irishman had traveled to Greece.

It took three days of calling, but Shannon finally reached Liam Mooney. The Irishman sounded happy to hear his voice and, on the spot, invited him to meet him right away in Athens. Faced with torrential rain in England, Shannon quickly opted for the balmy climate of Greece. He booked a flight the next day on British Airways.

Liam Mooney was already twenty-five minutes late for their meeting, but for Shannon, it was not a problem. He was sipping a Coke and watching the tourists chug up the steep streets of the Plaka, the ancient neighborhood directly below the Acropolis. After years of neglect, it had been commercialized, and now featured the finest in overpriced Greek souvenirs and cuisine. The sun was out, but a cool breeze warned that winter was quickly descending from Northern Europe. Soon Athens would be cold, but on this day the temperature was pleasant and Shannon was enjoying the warm sun.

Shannon plucked another ripe olive from the ceramic dish in front of him. It was delicious. Greece had the best olives on earth. He stretched out his long legs and sat back on the small wooden chair. The taverna was quaint. Long wooden tables were covered with checkered cloths, a stone floor looked like it dated back to St. Paul, and wooden beams crossed the ceiling. It was a relaxing place and one well suited to the Greek national pastime: sitting around in cafés watching the world go by.

Suddenly, Liam Mooney was standing in the taverna. Shannon never saw him coming. He just appeared. Mooney was a small man in his late fifties, with red cheeks and light blue veins atop his nose. He wore an old navy blue blazer, baggy brown trousers, and scuffed brown shoes. His blue eyes twinkled as he shook Shannon's hand and said in a thick brogue: "Good of ya ta come, lad. Is it a beer you'll be havin'?"

Two Lowenbraus, the most popular beer in Greece, appeared on the table before Shannon could even reply. Amazing, since Greek service was notoriously sluggish. Evidently, Liam Mooney was well known in this taverna.

"Ah, these steep streets can give a man a terrible thirst," Liam said. "I'll lift a glass in honor of Socrates, if ya don' mind."

Shannon laughed. He didn't drink beer, but Liam would literally drink enough for both of them. Liam Mooney was an outrageous rogue—charming, ruthless, generous, spiteful, cultured, and crude, all in the same package. And his guile was legendary. This was a man who managed to live in London for twenty years, remain one of the IRA's most trusted advisors, and yet never get arrested. In fact, some of his best mates were officers in the New Scotland Yard. Liam, Shannon concluded, was indeed one of a kind.

Liam Mooney was also perceptive, and immediately picked up on Shannon's unspoken melancholy, though he was valiantly trying to hide it. After a few minutes of small talk, Liam looked Shannon directly in the eye and said, "So, lad, now that the small talk is done, I'll be wantin' to know what happened to ya. That is, if you've got a mind to tell." Mooney's accent was full of that up-and-down Irish lilt that so charms Americans.

Shannon took the next fifteen minutes to explain his situation in detail. He knew Liam Mooney to be a detail man—one who would be interested in the Machiavellian aspects of his story. Shannon had received the phone call from Susan Oliver, Martin Moore's secretary, three weeks prior, and he was still seething with anger. He hoped Liam could give him some perspective.

Liam absorbed Shannon's story quickly. It was a scenario he was all too familiar with from his own life: betrayal and deceit. Growing up in the Devils Flats Catholic ghetto in Belfast, Mooney had witnessed social injustice on a scale few could comprehend. As Shannon finished his story, Liam ordered another round. He did not immediately react and silence enveloped the table. When the new Lowenbrau bottle appeared, Liam took a long pull and said, "So what are ya gonna do about it, then, lad?"

"What *can* I do about it?" Shannon shot back. "It's over. I'm done."

"Are ya, now? That sounds like surrender to me."

Shannon was perceptive enough to know that Mooney was driving at something, that he was dancing around what was truly on his mind. Shannon thought for a moment, and then asked the question that

Mooney wanted him to ask, "Okay, Liam, what would you do if you were me?"

Liam Mooney took another deep swallow of beer. He scratched his unkempt, stringy brown hair. "Well, I've got a tale for ya, if ya have the time, that is?"

"Sure," Shannon said.

"When I was a lad of eleven, me and some mates in the Flats would run errands for the IRA. Take notes back and forth, get them cigarettes, tell their wives they'd be late. Weren't many phones around in those days. Me mates and I would be paid a few quid a week for our work, and we had a purpose in life. Otherwise, we'd have just hung around, kickin' the football and smashin' each other.

"Our instructions were very definite: Swallow the notes if the Brits pulled us over, which they often did. Everybody was gettin' searched in those days, especially if ya left the Flats and went inta town."

Liam Mooney paused, seemingly deep in thought. Then he continued. "One day, I'll never forget it, there was a soft mist fallin' and I was runnin' over to the Falls Road with a message. And don't I see a Brit patrol comin' round the corner lookin' like the devil's delivery men. Bloody hell, says I, and I swallow the note straight away. But the damn Brits see me chewin' the paper. I take off runnin' but I don't know where I'm goin' cause of the unfamiliar surroundins. So they chase me down an alley and I'm trapped.

"I'm tryin' to be brave, ya know, but I'm scared. Eight a those soldiers surround me, havin' a good old time. Laughin' and pushin' me. Then one asks me what I swallowed. I say nothin.' The Brit slaps me hard across the face. Then he slaps me again. I go down, but they yank me back up. I'm still holdin' my tongue and the truth is, I don't know what the message says, I didn't read it."

Mooney paused again, took a pull, and set the bottle down. Shannon thought he saw moisture in Mooney's eyes. "So now we're in the alley and the fuckers are gettin' impatient, doncha know. One of them slaps me again and I hit the ground. This time they jump me, takin off my bleedin' shoes and socks. I didn't know what they were up too, but I'm bloody scared and I start ta cry. The Brits laugh and one of 'em knocks over a trash can that was in the alley. Out roll a bunch of empty milk bottles. The fuckers take the bottles and smash 'em on the ground. Glass flies all over the place. I still don't know what they're doin.'

"Then two of 'em pick me up and throw me onta the broken glass. Remember, I'm bloody barefoot. And bloody is the word. The glass shards cut into me hands and feet. I'm bleedin' like a pig, cryin' like a hungry baby. The pain was somethin' I'll never forget. They pushed me back down on that glass three times before they quit and walked away. As soon as they were out a sight, I start crawlin' down the alley, tryin' to get to the street. I'm still bleedin' like the crucified Christ. Finally, I pass out."

"Jesus," Shannon said.

"*He* didn't help me," Liam Mooney continued. "Nobody could help me. And nobody could do anythin' about it. No court, no law, nothin.' Well, some old ladies found me layin' there in the alley, took me in, and cleaned me up. I couldn't walk, so some Provos from the Flats came over and picked me up in a car. When I got home, me Mum was furious. Me dod was drunk and didn't care. But it was left ta me. What was I gonna do?"

Liam Mooney stopped speaking and looked at Shannon. He was waiting for the question. The Irish love participation. "So what *did* you do, Liam?"

"Two months later, when I was back on me feet, I went to see the commander of the Provisional IRA, the Provos, in Armagh, outside of Belfast. I explained my situation and told him I wanted ta sign on. The man already knew what had happened and agreed ta give me a mission: to put a canvas bag underneath the bar in a pub where British soldiers drank their pints. The Provos believed a boy of eleven could get in and out of the pub with little problem. And I did it. I didn't look in the bloody bag but I knew what it contained. And I didn't care to hang around afterward when the bomb went off. Six Brits died, and fifteen were sent home less than whole. So, what do ya think of that, lad?"

"Sounds like they deserved it," Shannon said.

"'Tis war," Liam Mooney said. "Same as you got."

"What?"

"Same as you got, lad. These people took your life's work and destroyed it. They hurt you, the same as those soldiers hurt me. And from what I'm hearin', not a damn thing will happen to those sods who ruined ya. And they'll probably do it again ta someone else. Or am I wrong, here?"

"No, you're not wrong," Shannon Michaels said.

"So the question of the ages, lad, is what are ya gonna do about it?"

Shannon Michaels did not answer. In truth, he did not know what to do. He lived in America, not Northern Ireland. He was a professional journalist, not a terrorist. What *could* he do?

Liam Mooney was not about to offer a solution. It was not his way. When asked, he advised, but he did not encourage. He knew he had posed a difficult question to Shannon Michaels, one that the man would eventually have to deal with. But Liam had one more thing to say on the matter.

"If ya decide to act, lad, there's a man to contact for help. His name is Sean and he lives in South Boston. I'll give you his number before ya leave. Mention me name or he'll never talk to ya. If you have questions about retribution, this is the man to see. And remember, lad, this is a tough world. As the ol' sod Mao Zedong was fond a sayin': 'Proper limits have to be exceeded in order to right a wrong, or else the wrong cannot be righted.'

"In other words, you can forgive those who have trespassed against you—as the Church teaches. Or you can take another road, and make damn sure these devils never trespass again. It's up to you, lad. Up to you."

Shannon stared at Liam Mooney. He did not know what to say. He did, however, have an option he had not seriously considered before.

CHAPTER TWENTY-FOUR

MANHATTAN
DECEMBER, 1994

Just as Tommy and Jackson were pulling up in front of Newscenter Six, across town on 78th and First, they heard the call on their car radio. A sidewalk Santa had been shot dead on Broadway and 97th Street. Using his portable phone, Tommy called to say he and Jackson were too busy to take on the investigation. He was told that two other homicide detectives could get quickly to the scene—that he and Jackson could go ahead with their appointment.

The detectives walked into the lobby of Channel Six, which was dominated by huge pictures of the on air talent. Tommy and Jackson paid special attention to the blown-up photo of Diana Troy, the blonde anchorwoman who, it was rumored, was having an affair with the NYPD's Director of Communications, who was a woman. It was great dish, and most cops couldn't get enough of it.

"I think we should put Ms. Troy under surveillance," Jackson said.

"Yeah, you and Bob Guccione," Tommy replied.

"I'm glad you brought that up," Jackson said. "The articles in *Penthouse* are extremely accomplished, I want you you know."

"I concur, Jack. It is a profound, erudite publication. I wonder if Mr. Worthington reads it."

The female security guard stationed at the lobby's entrance overheard the banter and looked strangely at Tommy and Jackson. The two detectives produced their shields and smiled at her. She looked more confused than ever.

"Mr. Worthington is expecting us," Jackson said.

"Go right up, Detectives. Fourth floor."

As Tommy and Jackson entered the empty elevator, Jackson said, "That cute security guard thinks we're perverted."

"Thinks *you're* perverted. She likes *me* a lot," Tommy replied.

"How do you know?" asked Jackson, first frowning, then grinning. This was going to be good.

"It was the way she looked at my shield. I could tell she got hot just by the way I presented it. You, on the other hand, had a limp wrist."

"You're crazy. The ex-wife been calling you late at night again?"

"That lovely woman downstairs thinks I am an extremely attractive man, Jackson, and that is an undeniable fact."

As Jackson Davis rolled his eyes, the elevator door slid open, revealing the vast office space of Newscenter Six. More pictures of the on air talent lined the light blue corridor walls. Tommy and Jackson walked over to a secretary who looked like she knew what she was doing. She did, and they were quickly ushered into the office of News Director Lance Worthington.

Worthington barely got up from his chair to shake hands. He looked bored. "Coffee, gentlemen?"

"No thanks, Mr. Worthington," Tommy said. "We won't take much of your time, but it has come to our attention that you personally may be at risk."

That statement heightened the news director's interest considerably. Worthington had read about Martin Moore's death and figured the detectives were merely questioning TV people like him who had done business with Moore.

"How could I possibly be at risk, Detectives?" asked a rather incredulous Worthington.

Jackson spoke softly. "I just returned from L.A. and your name came up in connection with Martin Moore's murder."

Lance Worthington looked surprised. "Really, how so?"

"We have information indicating that Mr. Moore may have rigged some of his research results," Jackson Davis said. "We believe that his killer may have been hurt by that and decided to take revenge. Do you know anything about bogus research done by Martin Moore, Mr. Worthington?"

Lance Worthington's pale cheeks reddened, and his voice became indignant. "I certainly do not. Martin Moore was the consummate professional. He did a major project for us and the results were very well documented. If someone is telling you different, Detectives, that person is way off base."

Tommy and Jackson knew the news director was lying. They saw it in the way he tensed up when Jackson laid out the bogus research accusation, and they heard it in the overly defensive way he delivered his denial. Moore's secretary, who had told Jackson about the rigged research, was a very reliable, convincing witness who had no reason to lie. Worthington had plenty of reasons.

"What if we told you, Mr. Worthington, that we can prove Martin Moore falsified the research he provided your organization?" Tommy asked.

"I wouldn't believe it."

"Do you have any verification on the research Martin Moore gave you?" Tommy was leaning forward, trying hard to intimidate Lance Worthington, trying to force him to tell the truth.

Worthington's eyes jumped back and forth between Tommy and Jackson. He was thinking furiously, 'Verification. Christ, these guys *have* done some digging.' Tiny beads of sweat formed on his blond hairline. He decided the best defense was a good offense.

"I don't know anything about any rigged research, Detectives, and I resent the implication that I do. All research done for Newscenter Six is confidential, as it would be in any business. I'm sure you understand."

"We might not understand *phony* research, Mr. Worthington," said Jackson, his voice soft but menacing. Though they were trying to catch a killer, not reform the broadcast industry, he was signaling that they would make Lance Worthington and his superiors sweat a great deal more later, if necessary. Abruptly, Jackson changed the subject.

"The main reason we're here is to tell you that if the person who killed Martin Moore did so because of Moore's business ethics, then you should be aware of it. We can't say any more than that, but you should be careful. Security here is okay, but how about at home? Do you have security there?"

Lance Worthington was inwardly relieved that the research questions had stopped. He cleared his throat and fought the rising tension in his stomach. "Well, I live in Alpine, New Jersey and my home is equipped with a silent alarm that is wired right into the local police headquarters. I also have motion sensors on my house, and two small dogs."

"That should do it," Tommy said. "Are you plannin' a trip any time soon?"

"Just going to a convention in Fort Lauderdale next Monday. I'll be there for three days."

"Where are you staying?" Jackson asked.

"The Marriott Marina."

"Well, be alert, Mr. Worthington. The guy who killed Martin Moore is a pro. Highly effective." Tommy reached into his jacket pocket, handing the news director his card. "If you come across anything suspicious, please call me immediately. I'd also alert the Alpine police if I were you. Maybe they could watch your house for the next few weeks."

"Aren't you overreacting, Detectives?"

Tommy looked at Jackson. They both had reached the conclusion that the news director was a weasel and a liar. Why waste any more time on him? "Maybe so, Mr. Worthington. But give us a call if you see anything unusual, okay?" Tommy stood up quickly. Jackson knew Tommy couldn't stand to be around guys like Worthington. The detectives waved, instead of shaking hands, and walked from the room.

Outside, the weather was turning cloudy and cold. Tommy and Jackson walked around the corner and into a deli. There was one on nearly every block in New York City. The detectives ordered two corned beef sandwiches on rye with mustard, and two large coffees.

"That Worthington is quite a guy," Jackson said while waiting for his order.

"Michaels is going after him," Tommy said, his eyes looking around the deli.

"I know," Jackson answered.

Tommy continued to look around the deli, seemingly in thought. He tapped his fingers against the silver counter and turned to Jackson. "We've got to end this, Jack. No more righteous slaughter. This time we've got to get the bastard."

• • •

Murphy Brown was getting old. Not Candace Bergen—she was holding up just fine. But the scripts for her sitcom just didn't have the punch they used to have. At least that was Ashley Van Buren's opinion. Ordinarily, Ashley was not much of a TV watcher. But on this night she was watching the tube with a vengeance, punching the remote control like a maniac. She was trying to divert herself from a phone call she had to make, a phone call to Shannon Michaels.

Finally, she could put it off no longer. She dialed Shannon's number and sat back on her couch. He came on the line after three rings.

"Hi, this is Ashley. How are you?"

"Better, now that I'm talking to you."

"Always the smooth, slick guy, Mr. Michaels."

"Always the cynical, doubting gal, Ms. Van Buren."

Ashley laughed. The man was quick, no question. "So I'd like to see you soon, if you're not too busy, that is."

"Never too busy for you."

"I was thinking maybe I could take a ride out to your writer's retreat. I love the water. I'd really like to see it."

Shannon paused, measuring Ashley's voice. It was casual, but a little rehearsed. Shannon sensed the woman had thought out her request very carefully. Was this an O'Malley thing?

"Ash, you know I like to keep it private. It's the one place in the world where I have complete privacy. Besides, the house has absolutely no amenities. It's very basic."

"Well, I'm basic too."

"No, you're not Ash. You're complicated. Very complicated. Why do you really want to go out there?"

Ashley was ready for the question. "It has to do with trust, Shannon. I just get the feeling sometimes that you're suspicious of me. By showing me something special, you'd be demonstrating that you trust me."

That was a good answer and Shannon knew it. He didn't really like the situation, but felt he could handle it. "Okay, Ash, you're on. I've got a heavy deadline early next week. But I could show you around on Saturday. Then we could go back to Sands Point and have dinner."

"Let's play it by ear. It'll be fun. I'll drive out there on Saturday morning. It's about two hours from the city, right?"

"Maybe a little more. But, fine, I'll see you out there. I'll fax you directions tomorrow. Remember, the place has no phone. So if something comes up, call me at Sands Point. When I'm out in Mattituck, I go into town once a day and use the phone booth to check my messages. Are you sure you want to brave the elements on eastern Long Island?"

"I'm looking forward to it. Good night, Shannon."

"Sleep well, Ash."

As Shannon hung up the phone, he could hear the wind howling, blowing in off the Long Island Sound. The night had turned nasty. Sleet was falling against the windows, and Shannon stared into the fire he had lit about an hour before. Showing Ashley the house in Mattituck would be no problem, he thought, but he was still suspicious of her interest. It had to be O'Malley checking Shannon's alibi. He knew Ashley still had doubts about him, and O'Malley had seized on that. Well, there was nothing he could do about it. If he wanted to continue to see Ashley, which he did, he'd show her the house and ask her to keep its whereabouts confidential.

Shannon then turned his thoughts to Lance Worthington. In town later at a pay phone, he dialed up the Marriott Marina hotel in Lauderdale, told them his name was Worthington, and said he was confirming his reservation. The hotel told him the dates and then, upon his request, assigned him a room number in advance. Shannon now knew where Worthington would be staying during the RTNDA convention. That was useful. The problem was that Worthington would be surrounded by TV people, most of whom would know Shannon Michaels by sight. Worthington would have to be taken by surprise—in private and swiftly—and his getaway would have to be especially well-planned. For the first time, thought Shannon, he might have to use a weapon to carry out his mission.

Weapons were strongly discouraged by Sean, the mysterious Irishman about whom Liam Mooney had spoken in Athens. Shannon, after leaving Liam in the Greek capital, had gone on to Delhi, Bangkok, and Hong Kong. But he kept replaying in his mind the question Mooney had posed during their first conversation: Should he take vengeance against those who had hurt him? The answer he kept reaching was yes.

Upon returning to New York, Shannon called Sean's number, reaching him at a bar in South Boston. The bartender took Shannon's name and number, and told him that Sean would be in touch. Three days later, Sean called collect from a pay phone.

He had a thick brogue, even stronger than Liam's. His voice sounded friendly, but wary. If Shannon would like some advice, he would be glad to provide it, he said, but only over the phone. And, in return, Shannon would have to make a sizable donation to the Northern Ireland Relief Association.

Shannon asked Sean what his area of expertise was. The Irishman laughed sardonically and said he was a consultant on "sanctions."

Shannon knew that was a euphemism for assassinations. In the course of three phone conversations with Sean, the man laid out the general rules of the modern assassin. He did this indirectly, using the term "business plan" as a metaphor. He told Shannon, for example, to always pay cash for any "services and supplies"—credit cards, even phony ones, he pointed out, could be traced.

Sean also told him he was a firm believer in never using a home phone for business, never carrying your real identification, and always taking your target by surprise. As for training, Sean suggested that Shannon learn the basics of karate, as well as running or swimming a good distance at least four times a week. In the ruthless "world of business," Sean liked to say, "you can never have too much endurance."

Sean also told Shannon that he could provide him with a false passport, for a fee of course, and that a phony driver's license was easy to secure through *Merc* magazine. He suggested to Shannon that on his missions, he should disguise himself in a very simple way—changing his eye color with contact lenses, and wearing facial hair and a hat whenever possible. Sean's last piece of advice had to do with attitude and decision-making: If he wasn't positive that his target deserved to "retire," then Shannon should pass on the mission. Doubt always leads to mistakes, he emphasized.

And he wrapped up with a few real-life stories that pointed up the wisdom of never actually carrying a deadly weapon on one's person—there are hundreds of ways to injure someone without using an illegal weapon, Sean advised.

Shannon digested the information, but waited six months before finally deciding on a course of action. During that time, he took a karate course and got himself into excellent shape. To quell his inner rage, he also tried everything from Transcendental Meditation to Yoga. Nothing worked.

It was nearly midnight before Shannon snuffed out the fire and headed upstairs to bed. But he couldn't sleep. Lance Worthington, the last one left and, perhaps the worst of them all, had to be dealt with. Imposing sanctions on him required an unusual amount of planning. Every time Shannon pictured Worthington's smug face during their last conversation, his jaw clenched. "I hope you're enjoying yourself tonight, Lance," Shannon whispered to no one but himself. "You don't have too many nights left."

CHAPTER TWENTY-FIVE

Ashley Van Buren was lost. Having driven the Long Island Expressway its full length, she exited at Riverhead, just as Shannon had instructed. But now as she passed empty vineyards and potato fields, she was beginning to lose her bearings. And there was absolutely no one around to help her.

Ashley had never visited the North Fork of eastern Long Island before. She had often taken the bus, the Hampton Jitney, to the South Fork during the summer to join the thousands of Manhattanites who made the Hamptons their summer headquarters. It was a scene that made Ashley somewhat uncomfortable.

The ocean beaches from Westhampton to Montauk were exquisite, but the constant posturing was exhausting. Social status was ostentatiously on display in the Hamptons, and the pressure to appear successful and powerful was intense. Just to get a table in a restaurant on summer weekends was a major challenge to one's place in the social pecking order. Even where one was seated in the restaurant was extremely important. It could make or break an entire evening.

Young professionals swarmed to the Hamptons, renting space in houses, called shares, at exorbitant prices. A small three-bedroom house would often be home to ten people over a weekend. It was all too much for Ashley, who preferred to vacation in the relative quiet of Cape Cod.

But in December, Eastern Long Island had returned to its natural, desolate state, and Ashley badly needed directions. As she drove along Route 25, she wondered where all the yearlong residents were. Finally, an oasis appeared in the form of a combination gas station and food mart. She gassed up and asked the overweight attendant to pinpoint her exact location. Luckily, she was not far from Shannon's house.

Driving quickly past the Old Steeple Community Church, Ashley turned northward at the tiny village of Mattituck. She crossed the railroad tracks and took the next right, heading east toward Orient Point.

All around her was beauty—low rolling hills and quaint farmhouses. It was a regular "Field of Dreams," she thought.

Shannon's house was located atop a steep cliff, directly overlooking the Long Island Sound. Ashley turned off a small farm road and onto the property. Out of view, about a hundred yards away, a blue sedan was parked. Inside, sitting low in the front seat, were two tough-looking New York City policemen.

Ashley drove down a long, dirt driveway flanked on both sides by high hedges. At the end of the driveway was a clearing big enough to park a half dozen cars. A small A-frame house painted white with black shutters sat peacefully in front of her. Shannon had said it didn't look like much, and he was right.

But behind the house was something quite fantastic, as Ashley discovered when she took a quick peek outside. The glass-enclosed living room overlooked a small back yard, and then it was a seascape view all the way to Connecticut, which was visible in the distance. A long wooden stairway descended to the beach, which stretched for miles in both directions. The small house itself was surrounded on both sides by pine forest. It was extremely private. Ashley loved it immediately.

Despite his initial suspicion, Shannon Michaels was happy to see Ashley Van Buren. He greeted her with a deep kiss and, because it was cold, quickly ushered her into the house and sat her down. Shannon had some New England clam chowder simmering, and served it up along with two tuna sandwiches and coffee. Ashley was disarmed immediately.

"This is great, Shannon, the perfect place to write a book."

"It is that. Not a distraction for ten miles."

"How did you find this place?" Ashley asked.

"It was easy. After Labor Day, all the summer rentals end. If you drive out here, you can find plenty of places. This one is owned by a schoolteacher in Queens. It's been in his family for decades. He uses it in the summer, and was thrilled to get a long winter rental."

Ashley stared out the huge window that covered the entire back of the house. In the corner, she noticed a mounted telescope. The house was everything Shannon Michaels had said it was, she thought. Tommy O'Malley would not be pleased to hear that, but it was the truth. And the truth was what Ashley Van Buren was after.

• • •

The New York Knicks were losing and Pat Riley looked mad. His face looked mad, that is. The rest of him always looked the same: well groomed, in an oily way, and well pressed. Tommy thought the guy was a great coach, but somehow didn't trust him.

Tommy was lying on his couch watching the game and feeling sorry for himself. It had been a terrible week. Nothing was breaking on the GNN case, and he had been scolded by the NYPD's assistant director of communications—he wasn't important enough to hear directly from the Director. No, the assistant director had called him and said, in a snotty tone, that the commissioner would appreciate it if O'Malley would alert the police press officers before he talked with any newspaper people.

This, of course, was in response to Ashley Van Buren's column on defense lawyers. The press flack told Tommy that the consensus downtown was that his remarks were "simplistic." The between-the-lines translation, Tommy knew, was that he was not smart enough to articulate a reasoned position on the lawyer issue.

Tommy didn't argue with the press flack because he knew that anything he said could and would be held against him. After the flack finished his condescending remarks, Tommy uttered just one word: "Fine." He did alert his boss, Lt. McGowan, to the call, and McGowan told him not to sweat it. Tommy wasn't sweating. He was pissed off. The department, he believed, was filled with more self-important jerks than ever before.

Tommy watched as Knick John Starks missed a three-pointer, but his mind continued to wander. The surveillance on Shannon Michaels had only turned up the location of his rented house in Mattituck. But just the fact that there actually was a house angered Tommy. Now Michaels had an alibi. It was flimsy, but it existed. The phone records of Shannon Michaels also turned up nothing incriminating. None of his calls went anywhere near Martha's Vineyard or California.

And then there was Ashley. Tommy hated the fact that she was out there with Shannon Michaels. He hated the fact that, unless Shannon really screwed up, Ashley was Tommy's only hope. And a screw-up was doubtful. The man was meticulous—the guy had received expert training, Tommy believed. These killings were professional hits, not the work of some out-for-revenge amateur.

Tommy's dark thoughts about Shannon Michaels were interrupted by the phone. Anything was better than thinking about this frustrating case, so he picked up immediately.

"Tommy, this is Angela," his ex-wife began.

'Jesus Christ,' Tommy thought as he looked toward his ceiling, 'why are you persecuting me?'

"How's it goin,' Ange?" he said instead.

"Fine, Tommy, very well." Tommy thought her voice sounded unusually calm. The fact that she was doing "fine" was a radical departure from her norm. "And you?"

"Happy as the proverbial clam, Ange. What can I do for you? I know I'm all paid up because my checking account is empty."

"I'm just calling to tell you something, Tommy." Angela paused. And paused again. Tommy knew she was purposely keeping silent.

Finally, he said, "Yes, Angela?"

"I'm getting married."

Tommy sat upright. What a lightning bolt! He recovered quickly enough from the shock to calmly ask: "Who's the lucky guy?"

"You don't sound surprised, Tommy. Have you been spying on me?"

Tommy was back on familiar ground. "Yeah, Ange, I'm lookin' in your window every night. You know how much time I have on my hands."

Angela Rufino O'Malley ignored the sarcastic remark. "I'm marrying Sal Lamonica. He's a deacon in the church. We're in love, Tommy, but we need your help."

"What?" Tommy said, surprised again. "Why would you need my help?

"We need an annulment from the church, so you have to fill out some forms and come to an interview with the priest."

"I *have* to?"

"Please, Tommy. Sal won't get married without the annulment. He says Jesus won't recognize the marriage."

"Well, maybe if I talked to Jesus..."

"Don't be sacrilegious, Tommy. Talking like that is a serious sin."

Tommy O'Malley couldn't believe it. All he wanted was to go back to watching the Knicks game. Now he was in trouble with Jesus!

"Send the forms over, Ange. I'll fill them out. I'll tell them that I have a pact with Satan. They'll let you off the hook."

"You must take this seriously, Tommy. The priest says that, when we took our vows, we were too immature to understand the true nature of a Catholic marriage. So we might be able to get an annulment."

"Well, he's half right anyway. Look, Angela, I'll help you out with this, but I'm not payin' for it. Sal Whatever will have to do that. These annulments are expensive, aren't they?"

"But Sal doesn't have any money. He's devoting his life to Christ."

Tommy bit his lip. Typical Angela, trying to put the arm on him for the annulment fee. He could have said at least ten nasty things. But he didn't. "Ange, I'll help out, but Sal is payin'. Period."

Angela Rufino O'Malley didn't like that one bit. "I'll talk to him about it," she said.

"Oh and Ange? Give him a big hug for me." Tommy knew it was a cheap shot, but he couldn't resist.

"Goodbye, Tommy." The click on the other end of the line was emphatic. Tommy tried unsuccessfully to refocus on the game. It didn't bother him that his ex-wife had found someone. He actually wanted her to remarry. Financially, it was beneficial to him. But he was constantly amazed and disappointed at the self-absorption all around him. Angela Rufino had been his wife, had said she loved him. Now, she just wanted to use him. Angela couldn't care less about Tommy or his life. He couldn't believe the woman's nerve, asking him to pay for her annulment.

But if he confronted Angela, he knew she could easily justify the request—at least to herself. Her thinking was, and always had been, 'If it's good for Angela Rufino, then it's good in perpetuity and nothing else matters.' As John Starks missed another three-pointer, Tommy stared at the TV and thought that Angela Rufino truly represented the crass selfishness that had infected America. That he had ever been married to such a woman added black layers to his already smothering depression.

• • •

"So, O'Malley thinks I'm a vicious serial killer," Shannon said, watching closely for Ashley's reaction. There was none, and she continued chewing her sandwich. "Just because I didn't like those two GNN people, he is convinced I'm a murderer. And he doesn't have a

229

shred of evidence against me. It's so ludicrous."

Ashley dabbed her lips with the paper napkin Shannon had provided. She didn't know what to say. She sucked in her left cheek and raised her eyebrows in a quizzical way. "I just think he's frustrated and looking at a number of suspects," she said.

"And I think he's jealous because you're spending time with me."

Again, Ashley felt uncomfortable. "Why do you think that?" she asked, knowing full well why Shannon thought that.

"During our conversation at my house, I mentioned your name to him. The guy got all flustered. You should have seen him. I think he likes you, Ash."

"What's not to like?" said Ashley, smiling. But Shannon, feeling uneasy, decided to press her.

"Why do you think O'Malley is coming down on me?"

Ashley decided to answer the question honestly. She didn't like playing games. "His information is that the three people who were killed all hurt you, hurt your career. Come on, Shannon, if you were in his position, you'd think the same thing."

"And how 'bout you, Ash? What do you think?"

"I believe you when you say you didn't do it. But I know that Detective O'Malley has to follow every lead he has."

Shannon stared at his companion. She had tied her blonde hair back and was wearing a red turtleneck sweater and black jeans. And she looked great. Her green eyes stared at him questioningly, as if waiting for some revelation. Shannon decided to change the mood.

"Well, I don't blame the detective for being infatuated with you—I know *I* am."

Ashley saw the man's sly smile. She knew he was teasing. He wasn't the type to confess undying love. "Well, I guess that comment is dessert," Ashley said. "But a little overly sweet, if you ask me."

Shannon laughed. The woman had spunk. He truly hoped she wasn't working with O'Malley.

Ashley took a sip of coffee while looking at the man across the table from her. As always, he was not completely relaxed. And she was curious about something. "Do you miss working in TV, Shannon?"

The question took him aback. But his answer came quickly. "I miss doing something that I was good at, but I don't miss the pressure and I don't miss a lot of the people. I worked very hard to develop myself as a journalist and as a performer, and it seems a shame to waste those skills." Shannon got up and walked to the old, overstuffed couch. He eased himself down on to the sofa, resting his right arm across the back of it.

"That's what most newspaper people don't understand. When you do TV news, you have to be able to handle the pressure to perform. You can't just write a good story. You have to look into that camera and convince people that you know what you're talking about. You can't be threatening, or nervous, or silly, or inarticulate. You can't fumble your words or lose your train of thought. You have to come across as a nice, smart, honest, objective newsperson who is also perfectly groomed. And we both know that's the way most newspeople are in real life, right?"

Ashley laughed and said: "Yeah, and I'm Oprah Winfrey."

"Now there's a perfect example, Oprah Winfrey. This woman is an enormous talent. She started out doing the weather on local TV. But she made it big because she convinced people, through the television camera, that she was just like them. She was performing, but it looked so natural. Now, because she's a huge celebrity, the audience expects Oprah to know everything, to be able to solve all their problems. They look to her as a role model and advisor. She's no longer just like them. She's much more. Can you imagine the pressure on her to perform every day under those circumstances? It must be excruciating."

"But she makes forty million dollars a year!" Ashley said.

"It doesn't matter, and anyway, she deserves the money. She makes the people who sell her show three times that. But money doesn't alleviate pressure. It just makes it worse. If you're paid the big bucks, then you have to carry the ratings. So not only do you have the pressure to perform flawlessly, but you also have to worry about how many people are watching. That kind of pressure makes people crazy."

"But you loved it," Ashley said, playing with the handle of her coffee mug. "You liked the challenge."

"That's true. I liked the competition. I liked to win. But the success and money came at a big cost."

"Really, what do you mean?" Ashley asked.

"Your feelings become hardened. You fight so many battles with people who try to hurt the broadcast. Sometimes they're just ignorant, but sometimes they're lazy or disinterested. And once in a while it's blatant sabotage because they dislike you. No matter why, there's conflict nearly every day. You get hurt, and then you lash out at others. It's like getting calluses on your heart."

'Not a bad line,' Ashley thought, filing it away.

Shannon was staring out the window. The sky was gray, the pine trees swaying under a light breeze. Shannon turned his eyes back to Ashley. "You know, the anchorpeople are the quarterbacks. And although they're not allowed to call the plays, they are held responsible for the final score. Plus, the bosses can fuck things up royally and the anchors don't have the authority to stop it. That's why most anchor people don't even bother to fight anymore. They just shut up and hold on for as long as they can."

"But you didn't do that."

"No, and look where it got me. The bastards took me down hard. But I took a lot of money out of there, so I guess I shouldn't be feeling too sorry for myself."

"But you are," Ashley said.

"Yeah, I guess I am. Many TV people are good at that because they're always thinking about themselves. It's a self-obsessed business. 'How are things going to impact on *me*? Is this person my friend or my enemy? I'll get him before he gets me.' That kind of thing. It's a brutal way to live."

"But you'd go back." Ashley's green eyes swept over Shannon. She could see he was struggling to contain his emotions.

"Yeah, I probably would. I'm so jaded I'd go back into the jungle. That's pretty pathetic, isn't it?"

Ashley remained silent. It was obvious how much Shannon's career meant to him. But it was a destructive force, Ashley was convinced. "Why do you think the TV business attracts so many bad people?"

"The same reason politics does. Power. There's tremendous power in television news. If you're calling the shots, you can help someone tremendously, or you can crush that person. With a well-positioned negative word, you can ruin a career or endeavor forever, virtually unchecked. You can make the most powerful people on earth tremble. By deciding what stories the public will see and hear, you can influence history. People who are greedy for power realize that television is the most influential tool ever invented. For some, it's a place to be reached, no matter the cost. You can make more money on Wall Street, but nowhere else can you accumulate personal power as fast as you can in television."

"And power corrupts," Ashley said.

"It's not that simple. Many people working in TV were corrupt before they even got there. Somebody once said: 'The TV industry is the health club for megalomaniacs.' Well, all the ego exercise equipment is in place."

"And you worked out pretty hard there, didn't you, Shannon?"

Shannon didn't mind the question. He wore his ego without shame. He got up off the couch, and walked over to the telescope by the window. "Yeah, I guess I did."

Putting his eye to the telescope finder, Shannon aimed to the northeast, scanning the Long Island Sound. Despite the cloudiness, there was good visibility, and he shifted the telescope to the left. The Sound there was choppy and empty of boats. But then he caught a glimpse of something that briefly startled him. He moved the scope back, spotting a small motor launch. Then he zeroed in and got an additional shock. A man in the boat was standing, his binoculars trained on Shannon's house.

"What the hell is he doing?" Shannon said, just loud enough for Ashley to hear. "What's going on?"

Ashley was startled by the change in Shannon's demeanor. He was clearly agitated. "What's wrong?" she asked.

"Damned if I know." Shannon manipulated the lens to get a better look at the boat, seeing two guys wearing navy blue high-neck sweaters and matching woolen caps. The guy with the high-powered glasses had lowered them and was talking with the other man. Shannon thought he might have caught them looking at him.

"I've gotta check this out," Shannon said, grabbing his jacket and walking quickly out the back door. Ashley walked over to the telescope to see for herself. The boat was about fifty yards off shore, and the men in it looked like they were preparing to leave. Ashley suspected the men in the boat were cops.

With Shannon down the stairs to the beach and out of sight, Ashley saw an opportunity. Up against a window in the living room was a huge desk, with a small personal computer on top. She went over and opened up the desk drawers, but saw nothing out of the ordinary: just writing paper, pens, paper clips, staples, and envelopes.

Ashley looked up and saw the small boat moving eastward at a rapid clip. Suspecting that Shannon would soon be coming back, she quickly went to check out his bedroom. On the nightstand next to his small bed was a leather-bound organizer. Without hesitation, she walked over and opened it. A number of papers spilled out onto the floor. 'Shit.' Ashley knelt down and gathered them up. If Shannon caught her snooping around, she didn't know what he would do. The man was tightly wound.

Suddenly, she heard a scratching sound at the window. Ashley's heart leapt and she jerked her head up, staring at the window pane. A pine branch swayed back and forth. Ashley could feel her heart thumping as she took a deep breath and listened closely for any sound coming from the backyard. Nothing.

She continued to flip through the loose papers. There were scribbled notes and what looked like telephone numbers, but no names. One of the phone numbers was circled. Ashley stared hard at it and wondered if she should she copy it down. No, there wasn't enough time. She repeated the digits in her mind, hoping to memorize them. Closing the organizer, she placed it back on the nightstand and quickly stood up.

"What are you doing, Ash?" said a voice cold and low. Shannon Michaels stood in the bedroom's doorway.

"Kind of a small bed, don't you think?" Ashley said, trying to force a twinkle into her eye. It didn't work. "I figured I'd tour the rest of this mansion while you were out. What gives out there, anyway?"

Shannon didn't answer. At first, he just stood there, his eyes narrowing. Then he took a step toward her and stopped. She was deeply afraid. Slowly he turned around, trying to calm himself. He knew the two men in the boat were spying on him. He strongly suspected that Ashley had told the police where his house was. And now he had found her in his bedroom, skulking around. All his warm feelings for her were quickly evaporating.

"Ashley, did you tell Detective O'Malley where I'm staying out here?" Shannon's voice was hard but calm.

"No, I did not."

"Well, I think the two guys in the boat were O'Malley's men. They were definitely spying on me. He probably had you followed."

"I don't think he'd do that," Ashley said.

Shannon didn't reply. He walked back into the living room, his mind racing. He was being watched. And there was a chance that Ashley was in on it. He felt his anger rising. "Ash," he said, "let's take a walk outside."

• • •

The Church of St. Monica on East 79th street was built in Italian style in the late nineteenth century, and its interior was massive: stone floors and walls, high arches, a hand-painted ceiling, and dark oak pews. In truth, Tommy O'Malley preferred this kind of church to many of the more modern Catholic churches, which were often glass and teakwood affairs. St. Monica's was cool and dark inside—the stained glass windows kept light to a minimum. Hundreds of flickering candles flanked the altar, providing the traditional, medieval-like atmosphere Tommy associated with Catholicism.

The five o'clock mass on Saturday afternoon was sparsely attended. Tommy himself didn't usually attend. Though he tried to go to mass every Sunday, he sometimes missed. On this day, though, he felt he needed to pray.

The elderly priest began the ceremony in a barely audible tone, but Tommy's mind was elsewhere. He was worried about Ashley Van Buren. His surveillance team had informed him about Ashley's arrival at Shannon Michaels' house. The cops went on to say that two Suffolk County policemen were helping out by watching Michaels from a small boat on the Sound. Tommy had cursed, knowing that a careful man like Shannon Michaels might very well notice that kind of surveillance, and suspect that Ashley had brought it with her.

The Epistle of St. Paul dealt with rejecting false gods, but Tommy barely heard it. Instead, he silently asked for the ability to stop Shannon Michaels, and to keep Ashley Van Buren from being harmed in any way. Tommy rarely prayed for himself. But he firmly believed that by trying to stop a killer, he was doing God's work. Tommy finished his intense personal meditation and looked around. The congregation was standing for the Gospel of St. Mark. He had been concentrating so hard on his thoughts that he had missed the Gospel signal and was still seated. The elderly lady situated further down his pew looked at him disdainfully.

Tommy stood up and listened as the priest read the Scripture. All his life he had believed that an active God oversaw what happened in the world. His mother had instilled in him a deep feeling of faith, but it was sorely tested by the evil he saw nearly every day. He had remained steadfast. He had vowed to die a believer, no matter what happened.

The mass continued for a long time, too long in Tommy's opinion. The elderly priest's sermon was about some obscure point of theology and Tommy could barely sit still. His apprehensions made it just about impossible for him to concentrate on anything but the murder case.

Walking back to his apartment after mass, Tommy slowly acknowledged that Christmas was coming. The decorations along Third Avenue lit up the night. Tommy, of course, had not even thought about Christmas yet. But seeing the seasonal displays, he knew exactly what he wanted his Christmas present to be: Shannon Michaels in handcuffs.

• • •

With the setting of the December sun, the beach was turning colder, and Shannon Michaels' disposition didn't warm things up at all. Ashley Van Buren knew the spy boat had upset him. What she didn't know was what would come next. And that made her fearful. After walking a few hundred yards in silence, Shannon finally said, "You know, this is really unfair. I'm a suspect in a murder case and I haven't done a damn thing. Even you aren't sure about me. How would you feel if you were in my position?"

"I wouldn't feel good about it, Shannon. I'm certain of that."

"And there's absolutely nothing I can do, is there?"

"Not that I can think of," Ashley said, relieved he was talking to her in a natural way.

The couple continued to walk in silence. Small stones crunched under Ashley's boots. Old hollowed-out shells of horseshoe crabs dotted the sand. After about fifteen minutes of walking, Shannon stopped and looked out to sea. "I guess I'll just have to live with the situation, and the tragedy is that while they are wasting time and manpower following me, there's a killer on the loose. I wonder how the police will react when they finally catch him?"

"When that happens, you'll have quite a story to tell. I'll do a column on it if you want." Ashley was trying to be helpful. She still had seen no indication that Shannon Michaels was a killer. And the fact that he was so upset at being a suspect made her feel somewhat sorry for him.

It was dark when the couple returned to the house. Shannon had been silent for most of the walk back, seemingly lost in thought. As the two strolled into the living room, Shannon said, "I'm sorry I'm not very good company today. This whole thing has really thrown me. I'm not used to being hunted."

"That's okay, Shannon. I understand completely. If it were happening to me, I'd be a wreck. Anyway, tomorrow is a work day so I've got to leave, but I hope we can see each other again soon."

"Sure. Maybe next weekend."

"And if you just need to talk or anything, give me a call, okay?"

Shannon didn't answer but stood in front of the doorway, blocking her exit. Outwardly calm, she began to feel uneasy again. Shannon just kept staring at her.

Finally, he smiled uneasily and Ashley followed suit. 'It was going to be okay,' she thought. She didn't want to give up on Shannon Michaels yet, but she also sensed something changing. Deep inside, her inner voice was talking. And, for the first time, Ashley Van Buren was ready to listen.

• • •

"Tommy, this is Ash."

As he picked up the phone, Tommy O'Malley was in the middle of eating his dinner—half a barbecued chicken and green salad. "Ash, where are you? Are you all right?"

"I'm at a rest stop on the Expressway and I'm fine, Tommy. Why wouldn't I be?"

"You know why."

"I don't know any such thing, and I'm afraid I have bad news for you. I didn't find anything incriminating at Shannon's place. And now I have to ask you something." Ashley paused. Her voice was businesslike.

"Go ahead," Tommy said.

"Did you have me followed to Shannon's house?"

"No, we've had surveillance on the guy for three days. It had nothing to do with you."

"Well, he spotted your surveillance people. And he's really angry. And, you know what, Tommy? I kind of don't blame him."

"Come on, Ash. How are we gonna catch this guy if we don't watch him?"

"What if he didn't do it, Tommy?"

"And what if he did, Ash? Are we supposed to just sit around and not try to find out? If he's innocent, so be it. He was inconvenienced for a few days. No big deal." Tommy's voice was a bit loud, so he lowered it. "You didn't find anything in his house, huh?"

"Nothing strange at all. I did memorize a phone number he had circled, but it turned out to be nothing."

"Tell me about nothing, Ash."

"It's just the number of some hotel in Fort Lauderdale. I know because I called it."

Tommy stood up and a rush of adrenaline hit him, but he kept calm. Lance Worthington was going to Fort Lauderdale on Monday. "What hotel, Ash?"

"The Marriott Marina."

"Ashley," Tommy said very slowly. "What was nothing to you could be a major development for me. A guy we think Michaels may be after is going to a convention in Lauderdale. And that convention is being held—"

Ashley, giving no thought to the potential danger to herself, quickly interrupted. "When do we leave, Detective O'Malley?"

• • •

At four in the morning, Shannon Michaels walked out the back door of his cliffside house and descended the stairway steps leading to the beach. A full moon hovered near the horizon, giving off just a trace of light. Stopping at the tenth step, Shannon slowly dropped to his knees. Using a small spade, he dug into the side of the cliff, which was a few inches underneath the protruding stairway.

After penetrating a few inches, the spade hit metal. Shannon removed the small, oblong-shaped container. It held his bogus driver's license, his brown contact lenses, a pair of surgeon's gloves, a new false mustache, and a new Phoenix Suns cap. Placing all but the gloves into a paper bag, he put the empty container back into the dirt and covered it up.

Shannon walked back up to the house and stuffed the paper bag into a large canvas traveling bag nearly full with packed clothing and essentials. He then left the house again, walking silently down the long driveway. Dressed completely in black, including a woolen cap, Shannon approached the narrow lane that provided access to his house, then stopped. He strongly suspected that someone would be watching his driveway entrance. He was right.

Approximately one hundred yards east of him, he spotted something odd—a car parked on the street. Mattituck residents kept their vehicles on their own property, not on the street. Shannon couldn't see into the darkened car, but believed one or two men were in it.

Shannon walked back to the house and readied his plan. He quietly put the canvas travel bag in the trunk of his car, donned the gloves, and tore up an old black tee shirt. Taking the rags with him, he cut across the pine forest flanking his house. It was very dark, but Shannon's night vision kicked in and he made his way cautiously through the trees. He knew he would have to move quicker coming back, so he was careful to note the terrain.

Shannon emerged from the trees and onto his nearest neighbor's front lawn. Walking silently toward the street, he realized he was now behind the parked car. He proceeded quickly out into the lane. He was moving with purpose now, keeping very low.

Inside the unmarked 1994 Toyota Camry, Patrolman Anthony Calabrese was nearly asleep. This was the worst detail he had had in months. Boring as hell. And cold. The policeman turned the ignition on every ten minutes just to warm things up inside, but he was still uncomfortable. He looked at his watch. Two more hours before his partner, who was sleeping in a nearby motel, would relieve him.

A crawling Shannon Michaels was less then twenty feet from the car when a noise startled him. The engine shut down. Shannon hit the pavement and lay prone, waiting for someone to emerge. A rather small man did, quietly opening and closing the driver's-side front door. The man stretched his arms and walked a few feet away from the car. His back to Shannon, he straightened up and began to urinate.

Shannon's heart was beating quickly. He hugged the cold pavement. If the man turned around, he would see Shannon's white face. Shannon mentally prepared himself for a confrontation.

Anthony Calabrese got his relief, and then began to feel cold. 'No sense staying out here,' he thought. The policeman opened the car door and slipped in behind the wheel.

As soon as the car door closed, Shannon resumed his crawl and within seconds was directly in back of the Toyota. He brought himself up to a kneeling position, removing the rags from his jacket pocket. Using short, precise movements, Shannon stuffed the rags silently into the Toyota's tailpipe, making sure to thrust them in as deeply as possible. The entire exercise took about fifteen seconds; crawling away from the car took about ten times as long.

Picking his way through the pines, Shannon moved rapidly. He was out of breath by the time he reached his own car. Turning the motor over, he figured there was a good chance the man sitting in the other car would hear it. But, with luck, it wouldn't matter.

Patrolman Calabrese did indeed hear a car engine fire up. In the still of an Eastern Long Island night, any sound carries a long way and Calabrese had wisely kept the driver's side window open a crack. He was instantly on alert. It was the first sound he had heard in five hours. Slowly, he turned his ignition key. The engine turned over but sputtered. 'Too much off and on,' Calabrese thought.

Shannon Michaels rocketed out of his driveway and made a sharp right turn. The policeman waited a few moments to turn on his lights. He did not want the suspect to know he was being followed. When Calabrese finally did press down on the accelerator, there was barely a response. The car lurched forward, then rolled ahead slowly. When Calabrese floored it, the engine coughed and jerked forward again. The policeman hit the floor brake. It didn't work. 'What the hell?' he thought.

Smiling to himself, Shannon figured it would take the cop at least a few minutes to find the rags. He knew that by stopping up the car's tailpipe, the cop's Toyota would lose engine vacuum. The power booster would fail and the entire system would shut down. If the cop was a car enthusiast, he would find the problem quickly. If not, he'd have to call a tow truck. Either way, Shannon was long gone and clear.

Shannon also anticipated that the policeman would radio for help and that other patrol cars might be alerted to look for him on the Long Island Expressway. So he kept to the local roads. He had plenty of time to get to the airport.

•••

Ashley Van Buren was spent. Her emotionally wrenching experience at Shannon's house had left her depressed and anxious. As she lay on her bed and stared at the ceiling, the only thoughts that gave her comfort were those of Tommy O'Malley. She respected the fact that Tommy had kept her apprised of the investigation. She knew that she had unwittingly provided a key piece of information, and that other cops would have played it cozy, neglecting to tell her that point A led to point B. Tommy was a man of his word—and Ashley knew so few of them.

Reaching slowly for the phone, Ashley dialed up the assignment desk at the *Globe*. She informed the weekend editor, Ed Kowalski, that the GNN case was heating up and that she might have to get on a plane fast. Kowalski began to stammer, his nerves showing, and said he'd call Bert Cicero at home and ask him to okay the trip. Then he'd get back to her. 'Typical,' Ashley thought. 'Everybody covering their own ass.'

Tommy O'Malley was also on the phone. As soon as he had tied together the information about Worthington, Michaels, and the Marriott Marina in Lauderdale, he called Jackson Davis. Both men now believed that there was a good chance Shannon Michaels would go after Lance Worthington at the Radio and Television News Directors Convention. The event ran Monday through Wednesday of the following week. Michaels, they guessed, would probably head south on Sunday, giving him time to prepare.

Tommy ordered that all New York flights to Fort Lauderdale from Sunday morning onward be monitored by undercovers. That meant the departure gates would be surreptitiously staked out. Tommy was certain that the police surveillance team assigned to Michaels in Suffolk County would track the man to whatever airport he chose to use, but he always tried to have a backup strategy. Because the detectives had already checked the credit card records of both Shannon Michaels and David Wayne, they knew that if either was the killer, he would be smart enough to use only cash while traveling.

Tommy also figured that their man would not travel under his own name, but had the airline reservation systems checked anyway. As expected, the exercise turned up nothing in Shannon Michaels' or

David Wayne's name. To help with airport surveillance, Tommy had their GNN publicity pictures faxed to the Port Authority police at both JFK and LaGuardia. Copies were quickly made and passed along to the NYPD surveillance teams.

Jackson Davis then called a friend of his, Fort Lauderdale Homicide Detective Julio Lopez. Tommy and Jackson knew they would need surveillance in Florida, and Lopez was the man who could make it happen. That Lopez had played football at Penn State with one of Jackson's brothers was a stroke of extremely good luck.

The disastrous bad luck was the Mattituck stakeout. Patrolman Calabrese radioed in for help and a mechanic discovered his car problem in minutes. When Tommy got the call shortly after five on Sunday morning, he went ballistic. Rags in the tail pipe. A kid's trick that Eddie Murphy had used in one of his *Beverly Hills Cop* movies. Tommy couldn't believe it. Now they had no idea where Shannon Michaels was. Tommy was so angry he smashed a coffee mug against his kitchen wall. He knew he was far too emotionally vested in the case, much too wired. But he also knew there was absolutely nothing he could do about it.

There was, however, something Tommy could do to locate his suspect. He quickly dialed the commander at the Port Authority police office, telling him he needed to be alerted immediately if anyone paid cash for a ticket to Fort Lauderdale. He asked the commander to request that all airline ticket reps immediately report any cash transaction to Florida. Tommy thanked God he had put his backup plan into effect. Though they had lost Michaels, Tommy was confident they'd pick him up again if he tried to fly to Florida.

• • •

At six o'clock Sunday morning, Shannon Michaels turned his black Buick Park Avenue into the parking lot of the Harvest Diner on Northern Boulevard in Bayside, Queens. He had spent the last couple of hours driving around and formulating strategy. Shannon had one more mission to complete, and Florida was the perfect place for it. O'Malley and his minions were on his tail, but they had no idea where he was, or where he might be going. So, Shannon figured he would confront Lance Worthington in his hotel room, dispatch him quickly, then fly back to New York before anyone ever discovered the news director missing. It was the same strategy he had used with Ron Costello on Martha's Vineyard.

After ordering orange juice and a bagel, Shannon imagined how frustrated Tommy O'Malley would be on discovering that yet another TV type had been killed. Shannon smiled at the thought. O'Malley wouldn't be able to handle it. The embarrassment would be too much. Perhaps the big detective would then overreact and make a mistake.

Shannon's new plan was simple. He would park, disguise himself in his car, and then proceed to the airline ticket counter at LaGuardia. Using an alias, he would pay cash for a ticket on the eight a.m. Delta flight. He'd be in Lauderdale in three hours, plenty of time to check out Worthington's hotel. The convention schedule had been printed in *Broadcasting and Cable Magazine*, so Shannon knew that nothing formal was set for between four and six in the afternoon. Shannon would make his move before the gala dinner on Tuesday evening, when Lance Worthington would probably be in his room getting ready for the festivities.

Shannon left the Harvest Diner and decided to drive around the borough of Queens. He wanted to get to LaGuardia as close to departure time as possible, so he could board the aircraft and fly off without much waiting.

The streets were nearly deserted. Sunday mornings in winter were the quietest time of the year in New York. The drive gave Shannon extra time to think and, as he drove into the open-air parking lot in front of the Delta terminal, he wondered about Ashley Van Buren. Sad to say, his instincts told him that she was now Tommy O'Malley's ally. 'Well,' he thought, 'it has been fun.'

The flight was wide open and, after receiving $750 in cash from Shannon, the sleepy-looking airline agent punched out the one-way ticket. Seat 10A for "Sean Hardnett." Shannon then walked down the long corridor and through security. He bought the *Sunday New York Times* and meandered slowly toward his departure gate.

A few hundred yards behind him, two NYPD detectives were already talking to the Delta ticket agent. He had called the airport police office immediately after finishing a cash transaction with a "Mr. Hardnett." They got a description of Hardnett and immediately called Tommy O'Malley at home.

Shannon had a bad feeling. Perhaps he was getting paranoid. His inner voice told him not to take the flight, but there was no reason not to. He got up and walked over to the next waiting area, where he sat down and observed the terminal. Nothing seemed out of the ordinary. After a few moments, he got up and boarded the plane. 'Nothing to worry about,' he said to himself. 'No one on earth besides me knows my intentions. No one could possibly know I'm going to Lauderdale.'

• • •

Tommy O'Malley did not believe in coincidence. A 6'3, well built man paying cash for a one-way ticket to Lauderdale fit Michaels' description pretty closely. The ticket agent said "Mr. Hardnett" had brown eyes and a mustache, but Tommy did not doubt for a minute that this man was Shannon Michaels in disguise. He told the two detectives on the case to stay away from the suspect, that nothing would be accomplished if the man aborted the trip. Tommy then hung up and immediately called Jackson Davis, who had fallen back to sleep.

"He's on his way down, Jack. Let's mobilize quickly. Get the Lauderdale guys on him and meet me at the airport. There's another flight going down there at eleven."

Tommy quickly dialed another number. An answering machine picked up. "This is Ashley. Please leave all the information you want, and I will get back to you." Beep.

"Ash? Tommy. It's showtime. Shannon Michaels left for Florida early this morning. Jackson and I are taking the eleven on Delta. I kept my promise. See you when I see you."

Five minutes later, Ashley Van Buren stepped out of the shower. She had heard the phone ring but her hair was full of shampoo, so she let the machine pick up. Dripping wet, she walked over to the phone and pressed the message button. One minute later she was booking her flight on Delta.

CHAPTER TWENTY-SIX

Fort Lauderdale had changed greatly over the past twenty years. No longer was it the small town that Connie Francis had immortalized in the movie "Where The Boys Are." The wild college kids were just a memory, neither economically needed nor welcomed in the upscale beachside environs. Lauderdale was now a small city with big city problems. White flight from Dade County, where Cuban immigrants had taken over, had fueled a real estate boom in Broward Country, where Fort Lauderdale was located.

But the imported prosperity did not trickle down to the poor living in Southwestern Broward, on the edge of the Everglades. Like many American towns, Lauderdale had become a city of stark contrast between the haves and have-nots. Beautiful waterfront estates on the east side of town. Sweltering two-bedroom shacks further west. But the wild card in Lauderdale was the transient factor—unattached people who floated down to South Florida during the winter looking for work or thrills or both. Lauderdale was one of the few places left in America where strangers sometimes outnumbered the locals.

Shannon Michaels knew Lauderdale well. He had actually lived in the northern part of the city, off Commercial Boulevard, for a short time in the early eighties, when he was covering Latin America for GNN. He thought of the town as wide open, as an easy place to do just about any kind of business.

The Fort Lauderdale Airport, medium sized and clean, was a much better facility than Miami's chaotic, antiquated airport thirty miles south. At nearly eleven in the morning, Shannon walked off the plane in Fort Lauderdale's airport. Carrying his canvas traveling bag, he tried to appear casual and relaxed, but something continued to nag at him. It was a feeling he couldn't identify, but one he didn't like.

Shannon could see that the airport terminal was beginning to crowd up. Early December was the beginning of "the season" in South

Florida, the time when the snowbirds up north flew down to get warm. From the gate, Shannon walked quickly toward the main terminal, his eyes hidden behind dark glasses, his false mustache rubbing against his upper lip. He discreetly scanned the area as he walked. He did not see anything to put him on alert.

The young Hispanic woman thirty feet behind Shannon was wearing a light blue janitorial uniform and carrying a broom. From the description provided by the NYPD, she immediately recognized the tall man wearing the black baseball cap, and stayed with him as he headed toward the exit. The moment Shannon walked through the electronic doors leading outside, she stopped and removed a small radio from the back pocket of her blue pants. "He's getting into a cab," she said.

The taxi was spotless, and the driver was an American. Shannon was shocked. Most South Florida cabs were in deplorable shape and driven by recent immigrants. "Yankee Clipper," Shannon instructed the elderly cabby, who nodded. Shannon thought he might be a retiree supplementing his income.

The yellow taxi pulled into the traffic flow, which was regulated by a brown-clad Broward County deputy sheriff. The cab driver was cautious, but not timid. His cab quickly broke out of the bottleneck and headed down a road that led to the airport exit, palm trees visible on all sides.

Four cars behind the taxi, a white Ford Taurus with two men in the front seat was keeping pace. 'This is going to be easy,' its driver thought.

The taxi driver was nearly clear of the multilevel parking lot in front of the airport terminal when Shannon's voice startled him: "I'm extremely sorry, sir, but it appears that I've left something very important on the plane. Could you take this exit right here and go back?"

"The return to airport" sign was just ahead. The cabby had no trouble merging into the left lane and making the U-turn. Shannon peered out the back window. He would definitely notice any car following him back into the terminal. He saw a white Taurus hesitate, but then head toward the airport exit.

The Fort Lauderdale cop in the passenger seat of the Taurus spoke into the radio: "Suspect is going back in. Probably wants to see who's following him. We'll pull over on Route One and wait for instructions."

A voice from inside the terminal answered, "Roger that. We'll pick him up here if he gets out of the cab. There's only one way out of the airport, so stay put."

Shannon Michaels apologized again and gave the cab driver twenty dollars for missing a fare. He then hopped out of the taxi and walked back into the terminal. Methodically, he searched the area with his eyes. Nobody was paying any attention to him. 'Good.'

A circular cluster of phones, five in all, stood to his left just a few feet away. Shannon sauntered over and punched in a number that would connect him to South Boston. He paid for the three-minute call with quarters. A man with a thick Boston accent answered: "Sweeney's."

"I need to talk to Sean this evening, sir. Might that be possible?" Shannon kept his voice low and authoritative.

"Could be. Who should I say is callin' ?"

"Shannon, like the river. A friend of Liam Mooney."

"So, where can he reach you?"

"He can't. I'll have to call him. Perhaps I could ring you later and you can tell me when he's available."

"I'll do my best. Call around six."

"I will, thanks. Bye."

Shannon picked up his bag and walked out into the warm sun. Florida's climate, inferno-like during the summer, is benign most of the winter months. Shannon looked to his left and saw two cabs remaining in the taxi line. The first one drove over.

"Route One and State Road 84 please." This time the cab was well-worn, and the driver Bahamian.

As the taxi pulled away, a young woman in a maid's blue uniform interrupted her floor sweeping long enough to speak into her radio: "He's in a red checker, heading your way." The cops in the Taurus nodded, and put their white vehicle in motion.

• • •

Tommy O'Malley and Jackson Davis, using police department funds, had purchased coach tickets, but were assigned first class seats. When space permitted, most airlines were good about upgrading New York City's finest. The detectives had been sitting in the departure lounge for a few minutes when a very attractive blonde walked up to the counter. Jackson poked Tommy, then reading *The Daily News* sports page.

"*She*...has arrived," said Jackson, deliberately overemphasizing the she.

"I wonder how she knew what was going on."

Tommy looked up sheepishly. "I told her. She did me a major favor."

Jackson looked amused. "I bet."

"Fuck you," Tommy said.

Ashley walked over, a wide smile on her face. "Detectives, how nice to see you both this morning." She wore a black leather jacket and tight blue jeans. To Tommy, she looked a bit tired.

"You know Jackson Davis, don't you?" Tommy was trying to sound gruff. He didn't quite pull it off.

"Yes, I think we met when I visited your lavish headquarters."

Jackson smiled. "Going for some sun, Ms. Van Buren?"

"Sure. And I believe I'm sitting across from you gentlemen in first. My, the city certainly is generous these days. Does Rudy know about this?"

"Nothing's coming out of the mayor's pocket," Tommy mumbled. "We were upgraded."

"As well you should be." Ashley's green eyes were shining. She was enjoying Tommy's obvious discomfort.

Ashley was just about to utter another smartass remark when the boarding announcement was made. Tommy and Jackson rose from their seats, and the three approached the ticket-tearing flight attendant. Wordlessly, Tommy took Ashley's carry-on bag from her hand and carried it aboard himself.

• • •

The taxi dropped Shannon Michaels in front of the Sinbad Motel, one of seven seedy motels lining a three-block strip along Route One, a few blocks south of the 17th Street Causeway in Ft. Lauderdale. The Sinbad was perfect for Shannon. The management there would take his cash while checking him in under any name he desired. The rate was $32.50 per night—and "Mr. Hardnett" would be staying for just one night.

The Ford Taurus drove on past the Sinbad and turned right at the next corner. Another unmarked car was radioed and, within minutes, pulled into a hardware store parking lot across the street from the motel. Until the New York boys showed up, the two homicide detectives in the brown Ford station wagon would watch Shannon Michaels.

Shannon unlocked Room 17, which was on the ground floor facing a small, littered parking lot. The room was dank and hot. The window air conditioner, he discovered, had been turned off, and Shannon immediately rectified that. The machine groaned as he flipped the switch to high. Two small twin beds stood side by side, each with matching stained bedspreads. The TV was bolted onto the dresser. Obviously, there was no honor system at the Sinbad. A small closet flanked the small bathroom, and one lone wire hanger hung off the wooden rail like a listless bat. His room was one step above a jail cell.

Shannon walked into the bathroom and drew back the shower curtain, startling a large Palmetto bug—a giant roach that is as much a part of Florida as Disney World. The bug waved its antennae, then sauntered toward the shower drain. It acted very put out.

At the very back of the motel room was one small window. It was high up on the wall and Shannon opened it with great effort. The rusty attachment bar finally gave way and Shannon felt a rush of humid air enter the room. He quickly closed the window, which was obviously there for ventilation purposes only. It was much too high to see through, and much too small to crawl through.

The room television received only three channels, but one of them was broadcasting the Miami Dolphins-Cleveland Browns football game. Shannon had a number of hours to kill, so he sat back on the sagging bed and watched Dan Marino go to work. He admired the skill of Marino and a few other NFL quarterbacks. They were like surgeons. Precision under pressure. The game, however, was a lackluster affair, and by halftime, Shannon Michaels had fallen asleep.

• • •

As Jackson Davis, Tommy O'Malley, and Ashley Van Buren walked off the plane, Julio Lopez, the Fort Lauderdale homicide detective, was there to greet them. Resplendent in plum-colored sports jacket, tan slacks, and brown Gucci loafers, Lopez showed off a smile of perfectly straight white teeth.

"Good to see you, man," Lopez said, hugging Jackson. Introductions were made and Julio actually kissed Ashley's hand. Tommy thought it was a bit much, but what the hell, Julio was really helping them out.

Fighting political battles that would have defeated most men, Julio Lopez had risen through the ranks of the Fort Lauderdale police department at a time when Latino officers were widely considered inferior by the white men who ran it. Sometimes the glamour of Florida obscured the fact that it was part of the Deep South. But Julio was a man with a plan, and his strategy included overlooking petty crap like prejudice. After graduating with a degree in English from Penn State, he resolved to live in a warm-weather city and carve out a successful professional life for himself. He chose Fort Lauderdale and law enforcement.

During the eighties, Lauderdale, and all of South Florida, were awash in narcotics. Julio made his name then as an undercover drug cop. Using fluent Spanish and finely honed street smarts, Officer Lopez made bust after bust. After three years, he was promoted to Detective, an astoundingly quick rise. He continued working narcotics until he was fingered by a corrupt cop who was his friend—or so he'd thought.

Acting on the corrupt cop's information, three members of the Los Diablos drug gang kidnapped Detective Lopez, drove him to the Everglades, and were preparing to hack him into pieces with machetes. Fortunately for Julio, two gang members began arguing and one shot the other dead. Panic ensued, giving Julio enough time to free his tied hands and slip out of the car. He then ran like hell into the Glades and hid out until the other two gang members gave up looking for him. After that experience, Detective Lopez transferred to Homicide.

During a conference call from New York, Tommy and Jackson had briefed Julio on the Shannon Michaels case. Lopez was brought up to speed on the situation—except for the appearance of the beguiling Ashley Van Buren. When Tommy told him that she was a newspaper reporter, Julio's expression demanded an explanation. "It's a long and boring story," Tommy said.

Accepting Tommy's dodge, the Lauderdale detective took the three New Yorkers to the Pier 66 Hotel, across the Intracoastal Waterway from the Marriott Marina. During the drive from the airport, Julio explained that although Michaels had tried to slip surveillance, they still had him under eyes at a sleazy motel. He could spare one two-man team for a few days and he himself would be available to help out if necessary.

While Ashley listened silently beside Tommy in the back seat of Julio's Lincoln Town Car, Jackson and Lopez caught up with each other's lives in the front. This was one hell of a story and Ashley was taking it all in. She was also feeling very guilty for doubting Tommy O'Malley. How could she have been so wrong about Shannon Michaels? All the pieces fit. He was going after the man who had arranged his humiliating dismissal: Lance Worthington. Yet, Ashley, believing all of Shannon's denials, had trusted him. Now, she felt foolish and used. She knew she would have to apologize profusely to Tommy O'Malley as soon as they could have a private word together.

Following hotel check-in, Tommy, Jackson, and Julio went out to the outdoor bar to map strategy—Ashley went to her room after Tommy promised to call her once a plan of operation had been agreed on. Julio gave the New Yorkers two small portable phones so communications could be constant. Julio himself was in radio contact with his surveillance team, which continued to watch Shannon Michaels from a station wagon across the street from his motel.

All three detectives agreed that Shannon Michaels had to be taken down *only after* attempting some kind of illegal act. To stop him prematurely would create a legal mess. They could probably arrest him for suspicion of murder, and might even be able to make a case. But it would be a weak one. Michaels had money and could hire the best attorneys available. In order to ensure a conviction, the cops knew they had to catch Shannon Michaels just prior to an act of violence. Because Michaels, or whoever the GNN killer was, operated without the use of a deadly weapon, the timing of the arrest would be all the more crucial.

This meant two things. Ethically, Lance Worthington would have to be alerted that Michaels could be targeting him at the convention. But doing so might jeopardize the stakeout—any unusual activity could, in turn, spook Michaels. Under the detectives' plan, Julio Lopez would call Worthington and tell him that his life could be in danger, that two police officers would be stationed in the room next to his, and that he would be watched closely but surreptitiously while out in public. If Worthington requested visible protection, it would have to be provided.

Julio Lopez then sprang a surprise on Tommy O'Malley and Jackson Davis. Smiling broadly, Julio asked the detectives to follow him into the

hotel parking lot where, parked side by side, two identical highly polished Mercedes-Benz sedans gleamed in the sunlight. "Thought you
guys would like to do the town in style," Julio said. "These are courtesy
of a local car dealer who also moved cocaine. We busted him and seized
his whole inventory. Now we got cars you wouldn't believe."

Tommy and Jackson looked at the black and gold cars and smiled.
If you have to sit around staking out somebody in a car, a big Mercedes
is the place to be. The three men then walked back into the lobby of the
Pier 66. The hotel, a Lauderdale landmark, is a high-rise, cylinder-
shaped structure affording wonderful water views. The detectives talked
for a while in the lobby lounge and decided that they would divide the
stakeout on Michaels into six four-hour shifts. That way the cops could
stay fresh in case quick action had to be taken. Jackson would take shift
number one, beginning at seven that evening.

As Julio Lopez got up to leave, the three detectives agreed that they
would talk by phone every couple of hours. Julio promised to keep his
team on the suspect until Jackson arrived. As Lopez drove away, Jackson
turned to Tommy and said, "That guy is tremendous. Can you believe
the wheels?"

"We owe him, big. That's for sure," Tommy said. "I've got to check
in with Ashley, Jack. Where you gonna be?"

"At the pool, getting ready for my role in 'Baywatch,' of course."

Tommy laughed. "I can't wait to hear about you and Pamela."

• • •

That afternoon, Ashley Van Buren met Tommy O'Malley in the
revolving bar atop the hotel. She was wearing white shorts, a blue *New
York Globe* tee shirt, and sandals. Tommy was already seated at a
window table when Ashley walked over and plopped herself down in
an overstuffed chair.

"Whatcha doin' big boy?"

Tommy turned away from his view of the Atlantic. 'It was nothing
compared to the view of Ashley,' he thought. "Doesn't take you long to
get tropical, does it?" he said.

"Just call me Annette Funicello."

"Wasn't she before your time?" Tommy asked.

"Ever heard of cable, Detective?" Ashley answered.

"You're such a little wiseass, Van Buren. You know that?"

"I know that. It's a large part of my charm. So, what's the plan now that we're having fun in Florida?"

"Well, we're gonna stake him out. He took some precautions at the airport but I don't think he knows we're onto him. We've gotta catch him doin' a crime, or else all we have is circumstantial. Four-hundred-dollar-an-hour lawyers raisin' reasonable doubt can beat that any day."

"When do you think he'll make his move?" Ashley asked.

"Tuesday," Tommy answered. "He'll probably nose around tomorrow. See what he's up against at the hotel. See where Worthington goes and who goes with him. He's a deliberate guy, this Michaels. He'll plan this out very carefully."

"What about Worthington?" Ashley asked. "Does he know what's going on?"

"Jack and I already talked with him in New York. Julio's gonna call him tomorrow. Worthington's an arrogant bastard, but we'll tell him what's up. Course, we can't tell him that we suspect Michaels, because that would wind up in the scandal sheets in a heartbeat and we'd be liable for civil action if we can't catch the guy. We're walkin' a thin wire here."

"Will Worthington help you?"

"Probably not. Guy's a pain in the ass. Knows it all. Thinks we're overreacting. Guys like that always think nothing bad can happen to them. We know what he did to Michaels, and it was pretty damn ruthless. That's what makes this such a tough case. The people Michaels has killed were all morally bankrupt. The dregs of the earth. But no matter how bad the victims were, nobody's entitled to kill them. Nobody has the right to this kind of revenge. If we allowed it, we'd all be doomed."

Tommy was speaking so rapidly he didn't notice Ashley's reaction. When he finally paused, a tear was running down her smooth cheek. Tommy was caught completely by surprise.

"What's wrong?"

"I can't believe I didn't see Shannon Michaels for what he is. It's just so humiliating. I... I..." Ashley buried her face in her hands and began to sob quietly.

Tommy O'Malley leaned forward in his chair, reached across with both hands, and gently rubbed Ashley's shoulders. He felt very sorry for her. He remained silent until she finally looked up at him, her face red, her eyes moist. "Ash, it could have happened to anyone. The guy is really smooth. Don't beat yourself up about it. You followed your heart and that's all you can ever do."

Then Tommy O'Malley moved close to Ashley Van Buren and kissed her.

• • •

At 5:30 in the afternoon, just two weeks before the official first day of winter, it was already dark in South Florida. Shannon Michaels flipped off the TV and left his hotel room, walking briskly south on Route One toward a Waffle House restaurant. Shannon had no idea that, from their parked car across the street, two policemen were alertly watching his every move.

Shannon entered the small restaurant, got some change, and was directed to the wall phone outside the men's room around the corner. It took him just a few seconds to dial up Sweeney's Irish Pub on Broadway in South Boston.

The unmarked station wagon had started up when Shannon entered the Waffle House and stopped directly opposite the restaurant. The two homicide detectives peered into the place through the glass window. They did not see Shannon Michaels.

"Holy shit, he's not in there," said the older of the two cops.

"I'll check it out," the younger man said, quickly getting out of the car and walking across the street.

The bartender who answered Shannon's call gave him a number with instructions to call it in thirty minutes. There was a good chance, the bartender said, that Sean would pick up. If he didn't, Shannon was told, he should call the bartender back tomorrow.

Shannon thanked the man and hung up the phone. 'Fine, I'll grab some food and call from here,' he thought. Rounding the corner, Shannon saw a young, casually dressed man standing in front of the cash register looking intently around the restaurant. When the man saw Shannon, a tiny hint of recognition registered in his face. It was a twitch, nothing more. But Shannon caught it.

The man nonchalantly ordered a coffee to go and left the restaurant, walking north. As Shannon sat in a corner booth perusing the menu, he knew two things: The man who had just departed was following him, and he was a cop. Shannon figured the guy had temporarily lost sight of him when he went to make his call. Now Shannon was confused. 'How could they have known?' he wondered. 'How the hell could they have known?'

The fried chicken was undercooked and the potatoes were greasy, but Shannon would not have eaten much no matter what had been put in front of him. He was anxious and his mind raced with theories. How had Tommy O'Malley figured out he was going to Lauderdale? An educated guess was all Shannon could come up with. O'Malley had probably tied him into Lance Worthington, and once he found out that Worthington would be attending the convention, and that Shannon had skipped the surveillance, he figured Shannon would head to Lauderdale. 'Good detective work,' Shannon thought. That thought angered him.

For about ten minutes, he sat in the booth staring out the window. Then he paid the check and returned to the phone booth around the corner. He had Sean on the line within seconds.

"You'll be needin' somethin' then," the Irishman said before Shannon could say anything.

"A new license. Name, state, doesn't matter. Height 6'3, eyes brown. And I need it by tomorrow."

"Aye. It'll cost ya, lad. Five hundred."

"Done."

"So where are ya, then?"

"Fort Lauderdale."

"You're in luck, man. We have a branch office just to the north. Lauderdale-by-the-Sea. Call the Dingle Pub. Ask for Max. I'll ring him now, let him know what a good lad ya are. And bring a nice color picture of yerself."

"Yeah, a picture. Listen, Sean. Can you get me a false set of whiskers? Salt and pepper, closely trimmed, top notch. I'll get the beard from your guys and then have the picture taken. Great. Thanks. If I can ever repay you..."

"Don't worry lad," the Irishman said. "You'll be the first ta know." The line went dead. Shannon smiled.

• • •

At precisely seven that Sunday evening, Jackson Davis turned his Mercedes into the hardware store parking lot, waved at the cops he was relieving, and took up his post. Over the phone, the older cop told Jackson that Shannon was in his motel room, that there was no back door, and that all was quiet.

Shannon was watching "60 Minutes" and thinking. His plan depended on some luck, but was fairly straightforward. But should he go through with it now that O'Malley was on to him? It was a tough call. His adrenaline was surging, but, for the first time, serious doubts entered his mind.

• • •

Tommy O'Malley sat at the table and counted the forks. There were five of them. Why? 'With her Boston brahmin background, Ashley Van Buren would certainly know the answer to that one,' Tommy thought.

"Now, Ash, about these forks?"

Ashley laughed. She knew Tommy was mocking the restaurant, Le Soufflé, situated on the Intracoastal Waterway. "It's on the *Globe*, Detective. So make sure you make good use of every one of those forks."

An absolutely stunning yacht passed by the restaurant—"The Monique," with Delaware tags. 'The ship must be more than a hundred and fifty feet long,' Tommy thought. 'And it has its own little helicopter on deck. Isn't that cute?'

"You know, Ash, that could all be yours if you hung out down here," Tommy said. "Marry some export guy or something, and you could be floating around on that. Of course, we'd have to dump Monique. Change the name to 'The Ashley.'"

Ashley emitted a little laugh. She was beginning to relax, but still felt embarrassed over misjudging Shannon Michaels. She had always felt comfortable with Tommy O'Malley, but now her feelings toward him were changing. She wasn't exactly sure how and, in her current emotional state, she didn't think she was capable of thinking clearly. But she knew that something was happening inside her. She met Tommy's eyes for a few quick seconds and then dropped her gaze.

"You know, Detective, you can be a very intimidating man."

"But charmingly intimidating, or so I've been told."

"Oh, yeah? By whom?" Ashley was smiling.

"By the buffs."

"Buffs? Who are *they*?" Ashley looked quizzical.

"They are the ladies who pursue cops, who are attracted to intimidating guys like me. They're groupies, only we call them buffs." Tommy was smiling wickedly. Ashley thought he looked like an overgrown teenager.

"I see," Ashley said. "Do you know many of these buffs?"

"Hundreds."

"You must have an extraordinary amount of energy, Detective."

"Oh, I do. And if I wasn't so shy, I could really put it to good use." Tommy grinned. Ashley just shook her head.

"I wish I were a lesbian," she said.

• • •

While Tommy and Ashley dined, Shannon Michaels fitfully reached the most important decision of his life. For a full two hours, he lay on the motel room bed debating whether or not to abort his mission. The cops knew his target. That much was obvious. But no one in Florida had seen his face undisguised. No one could place him at the scene of a crime. If he could get Worthington and return to New York before the body was discovered, he would be untouchable.

But Shannon also knew the police would be closely watching Lance Worthington. The man might even be provided with a bodyguard. So he decided that if he had no clean shot at the news director, he would not take a chance. He'd get the hell out. Shannon's rational side kept repeating, 'Forget this one, you'll get another chance down the road.'

It was the thought of Tommy O'Malley, however, that caused rationality to lose out. Shannon Michaels believed that if he outwitted O'Malley and killed Lance Worthington, he could ruin the detective's career and eliminate his last big TV nemesis. The story of O'Malley's slipups would get out—Shannon would see to that through anonymous calls to journalists. 'This *is* the ultimate chess game,' Shannon thought. 'I've already taken O'Malley's queen—Ashley Van Buren. Now it's time to checkmate the detective right off the board.' Shannon Michaels' heart began to beat quickly. He was getting pumped up. He could do this. He could take Worthington and O'Malley down together.

His decision made, Shannon walked into the bathroom and

checked his disguise in the scratched up mirror. Then he stood on a chair and pried open the small back window, jamming his canvas carrying bag into the open space. It was a tight fit but, using all his strength, Shannon eventually pushed the bag through and let it drop to the alleyway behind his room.

Picking up the cheap plastic ice container sitting next to the paper drinking cups in his room, Shannon walked to the front door. 'This is it,' he thought. Controlling his breathing to assure that it was measured and normal, Shannon opened the door and began a slow stroll toward the ice and soda machines located in the breezeway separating the motel office from the main building's guest rooms.

Watching from across the street, Jackson Davis immediately spotted Shannon Michaels. Even though Shannon wore a hat and phony mustache, his height and bearing caught Jackson's eye. He watched carefully as Michaels walked down the narrow corridor in front of the motel. Despite the dim lighting, Jackson could see Shannon holding something and heading for the illuminated soft drink machine. "Probably getting a drink and some ice," Jackson thought, leaning forward toward the steering wheel.

Shannon stopped at the soda machine, reached into his pocket and pulled out some change. Jackson saw the motion and relaxed. Then, suddenly, the change dropped from Shannon's hand onto the concrete floor. Jackson watched carefully as Shannon bent down to pick the money up. It was darker in the breezeway and Jackson momentarily lost sight of Shannon as the tall man rooted around, seemingly looking for the dropped coins.

As soon as Shannon lowered himself from view, he began running in a crouch. Bent at the waist and staying low to the ground, he was out of the breezeway and into the back alley within seconds. He scooped up his bag, which was lying right where he had dropped it, and sprinted the length of the motel. But to his horror, there was no exit. The fence that separated the Sinbad from the houses built directly behind it was at least twelve feet tall. There was no way Shannon could get over it.

When Shannon Michaels failed to emerge from the breezeway, Jackson Davis knew he had been duped, and he was out of the Mercedes in less than ten seconds. He ran quickly across the street. He recognized instantly that he was in trouble.

Shannon was frantic. He knew he had only seconds to get away.

At the far end of the fence, he saw a metal dumpster nestled in the corner. He ran as fast as he could, leaped onto the green cover, threw his bag over the fence and pulled himself over the top of the wooden barrier. He landed hard in somebody's backyard. Immediately, a dog began to bark.

Jackson Davis heard the dog as he rounded the corner into the motel alleyway. Shannon Michaels was gone and Jackson quickly saw how he had made his escape. The odds of running Michaels down now were slim, Jackson thought. Cursing to himself, he decided to return to the car and radio in. He hoped a quick police response could contain Michaels within a small radius. In South Florida, unlike New York, taxi-cabs do not cruise the streets, and Jackson figured Michaels could not get very far on foot.

Shannon Michaels was sweating heavily. The humid night air was sucking the wind out of his lungs like an ocean whirlpool. His chest heaved as he climbed still another fence and finally found himself on a small street in the middle of a lower middle class neighborhood. Wiping the sweat from his eyes, Shannon walked quickly south, looking back over his shoulder for any sign of a tracker. His destination was just blocks away. Once there, he thought, he would look for an escape opportunity. If he didn't find one, it was no big deal. He hadn't broken any laws in Florida.

"Tommy, I lost him." Jackson Davis did not add another word. He knew it was damage control time.

O'Malley, instantly frowning, said into the cellular phone, "Is he still in the area?"

"Yeah, he slipped over the fence behind the motel just a couple of minutes ago. He knows we're on to him. He's still nearby."

"Okay, I'll call Julio and we'll flood the area. Don't worry about it, Jack. This stuff happens."

"Not to me it doesn't. I'll find this guy. I'll tell you later how he made the slip. It was super slick."

"Okay, Jack." With Ashley Van Buren looking on, their dinner nearly complete, Tommy hung up the phone and savagely punched the digits on his phone to reach Julio Lopez.

"Julio. Tommy. He slipped Jack. Yeah, it's a bitch, but we think he's still in the area. Can you call out the militia? Good. We've gotta get him sighted again. I'm goin' over to the motel, find out what happened. Good. I'll see you there in fifteen minutes."

...

Five blocks away from the Sinbad Motel was a country music dance club called Midnight Cowboy. Shannon had been to this Lauderdale institution before. And he knew the place was usually full on Sunday nights, which were always set aside as "Ladies' Night." Ladies drank for free, and, for obvious reasons, that attracted men.

It took Shannon less than three minutes to reach the saloon. He stood in the shadows of the packed parking lot for a few moments, cooling down. He did not want to raise any attention, but he needed to get out of the area fast. He figured the police would be pouring in momentarily.

Two young men in khaki shorts were sprinting around the Midnight Cowboy parking lot. Cars were backed up outside the club entrance and these valets couldn't keep up. Shannon watched the scene for just a few seconds. It was obviously chaotic. The parking guys were doing their best, but they were heavily outnumbered by trendy new cars.

As Shannon moved toward the valet shack, he spotted a white Ford Explorer. The valet had just hopped out of it and run back to the shack, hanging the vehicle's keys on a hook with the number 405. Shannon moved quickly but smoothly, walking up and removing the keys to the Explorer in one deft motion. Keeping his eyes on the frantic kid who had parked the Explorer, he waited until the valet was occupied with another car. Within thirty seconds, Shannon had the Explorer on the road heading north.

The vehicle wouldn't be missed, he thought, until its owner came out of the club, and that would probably be much later.

...

Jackson Davis was embarrassed as he explained to Tommy O'Malley and Julio Lopez how Shannon Michaels had eluded him. Tommy felt sorry for his partner. He knew that what had happened to Jackson could have happened to any cop. Shannon Michaels was sly, smart, and quick. What bothered Tommy was how Michaels figured out he was under surveillance.

Meantime, the Lauderdale police remained on full alert. Shannon's description had been broadcast city wide, and units cruised the area where he had last been seen. In addition, plainclothes cops on foot canvassed the area around the Sinbad Motel. The hunt was low key, without sirens or flashing lights, but intense. The cops were told not to confront the fugitive, but not to let him out of their sight either. It was clear to all involved that some major heat was on this tall guy with the mustache.

• • •

As it turned out, the mustache was gone. And so was the baseball cap. Shannon had thrown them into a dumpster. All that remained from his original disguise were the brown contact lenses. Shannon pulled the Explorer onto I-95 heading north. He didn't leave the interstate until the Pompano Beach exit, far away from any police check of Lauderdale motels. He spotted a flea bag motel just off the highway and checked in, carefully keeping his head down and avoiding eye contact with the Cuban clerk.

After receiving his key, he got back into the Explorer and headed toward the ocean. It took him almost twenty minutes to reach the upscale Coral Reef Hotel and Spa. He parked the Explorer in the huge lot and hailed a taxi to take him back towards I-95. The cab dropped him six blocks from his new motel.

• • •

Ashley Van Buren was waiting for Tommy O'Malley's call. She lay on top of her bed wearing only a tee shirt and panties, watching the late edition of Eyewitness News on South Florida's "One and Only TV Ten." The Dolphin victory over the Browns took up half the newscast. Various Miami players were interviewed. All of them said virtually the same thing: "We were fortunate, you know, to win. Just very fortunate, you know?"

Ashley yawned and thought back to the day's events. Her confidence remained severely shaken. Bad judgment is bad judgment, and that's what she had demonstrated in dealing with the devious Shannon Michaels. She should have been much more cautious. That she had given her body to a killer made her shudder every time she thought about it.

The phone rang. It was Tommy O'Malley. "Bad news. We lost the guy. It's over for tonight. Tomorrow we'll stake out the convention hotel."

"Maybe he'll go back to New York now," Ashley said.

"Possible, but I don't think so. I get the feeling that our boy Shannon is addicted to the game, and that he'd like to embarrass us."

"You mean he'd like to embarrass *you.*"

Tommy sighed. "Yeah, I guess that's right. This is a personal thing, isn't it?"

"Tommy, I can't imagine it being any more personal. Just be careful. I think he's dangerous. I don't think Shannon Michaels is going to allow anyone to arrest him for murder."

"Quite a change of heart, Ash."

"Yes, I'm very aware of that," said Ashley, sounding very sad. Tommy didn't push it.

"Anyway, I'll call you in the morning and you can ride with me," Tommy said. "He knows both of us so we'll have to stay in the background. But we'll have people all over the hotel. If he tries for Worthington, we'll get him."

"I appreciate you letting me come along, Tommy." Ashley's voice was low. Tommy thought she sounded like a little girl.

"Hey, you gave us the big break."

"Yeah, but I didn't even know what I was doing."

"Ash."

"Yes?"

"Don't tell anybody that, okay? I'm sayin' you got this guy down cold and that's why you're here."

Ashley laughed softly. "Okay, I am a super-sleuth. See you tomorrow." And she hung up.

CHAPTER TWENTY-SEVEN

FORT LAUDERDALE
DECEMBER, 1994

The next day, the temperature outside the Marriott Marina Hotel hit a scorching eighty degrees early—at 11:48 a.m. Inside, as 1994's Radio and Television News Directors Convention got underway, six policemen, including Jackson Davis, were working undercover. The four men and two women had assumed a variety of hotel jobs—from parking valet to bellman. Jackson played bartender in the lobby lounge, where he could observe everyone who entered or left the hotel.

Lauderdale's Marriott Marina was located on the 17th Street Causeway, directly on the Intracoastal Waterway. In the back of the main building was a large pool where many of the guests congregated. The hotel itself was nice but not luxurious. It stood fifteen floors high and featured the usual two restaurants and a nightclub. By noon the whole place was swarming with news executives, many of whom were severely hungover from the night before.

Tommy O'Malley and Ashley Van Buren were parked in the lot directly in front of the hotel. Tommy had positioned his Mercedes so that it was well back from the main entrance, but facing the hotel's facade. From his vantage point, he could see all movement in front of the hotel.

Tommy had the windows rolled down and the car radio on low. His police radio lay on the floor and a portable phone was clipped to his belt. Ashley sat next to him reading Fort Lauderdale's *Sun-Sentinel*. She had five other newspapers with her as well. Both Tommy and Ashley knew it could very well be a long, hot day.

• • •

After eating a light breakfast at a little pancake house a few blocks from his motel, Shannon Michaels called a cab and was dropped on the ocean side road, A-1-A, in the small town of Lauderdale-by-the-Sea, just north of Fort Lauderdale. He continued on foot, walking a half-mile along A-1-A to the Dingle Pub. There, two tough-looking men were waiting for him with a brown paper bag containing the false beard Shannon had requested. The men eagerly accepted the five one-hundred-dollar bills Shannon produced for the driver's license, and another crisp fifty for the whiskers. The men did not bother with any small talk, simply telling Shannon to come back when he had the photo for the license. "By the way," one of the men said, "your new name'll be George McCoy."

Shannon's next move was to begin extensive intelligence gathering. Weeks before, he had laid the groundwork for Lance Worthington's demise by calling the Marriott Marina, pretending to be Worthington, and requesting a room with a northern view—one that faced the Intra-coastal Waterway. Over the phone, he had been assigned Room 615. With any luck, Lance Worthington would accept that room without question.

Knowing Worthington's room number and location initially gave Shannon a slight advantage over the police. But now that they were looking for him, he knew that Tommy O'Malley and his gang would double their close watch of Worthington. All of this meant that Shannon could not go to the hotel until he was ready to act. Even in disguise, he could not risk it. So he designed his plan for simplicity and speed. If things went smoothly, he could dispatch Worthington in seconds and be out of the hotel and on his way in less than five minutes.

It was now early afternoon in south Florida. Shannon, dressed in white shorts and a blue Toronto Blue Jays tee shirt, and wearing his new beard and old sunglasses, strolled down the main boulevard that separates the wide sandy beach of Fort Lauderdale from the seaside shops and apartments.

After getting his photograph taken, Shannon returned to the Dingle Pub, waited an hour, and was finally handed his new license. He then walked south for two miles and now was in the heart of Lauderdale. Traffic was heavy as driving tourists slowed, gawking at the ocean and chic stores and hotels. Shannon, tired and wet from all his walking, turned left down a side street and into the office of Dune Rent-a-Car.

Ten minutes later, Shannon was driving an almost new 1995 Cadillac El Dorado. Eight cylinder engine, plenty of power. Shannon gave the car rental manager ten one-hundred dollar bills—a week's rental and deposit—paid in cash because, as Mr. McCoy put it, "I don't believe in credit cards."

Driving the Caddy south on A-1-A, Shannon came to the end of the Lauderdale beach strip and began traveling west as the road veered in that direction. He passed over the large drawbridge spanning the Intracoastal waterway and lightly hit the brakes as he passed the Marriott on his right. There was just one road leading in and out of the hotel. If anything were to go wrong with his plan, where he parked his car would be vitally important. Attached to the west end of the hotel was a two-story concrete parking lot. The second tier was exposed to the sun and elements, and was reserved for drivers who parked themselves. The ground level, for cars using the valet service, was covered. Neither seemed right for his future purposes.

But just west of the Marriott Marina was a small, rectangular single-story office building. A short row of hedges separated the building's tiny parking area from the huge hotel parking lot. When the time came to confront Worthington, he would park his car in front of the office building, slice easily through the hedges, and walk from there onto the hotel property.

Shannon continued driving west until he reached Route One. There he turned left and headed for the airport. Minutes later he was driving around the airport on Perimeter Road, a small, lightly traveled service road located directly underneath the brand new highway extension, 595. His purpose was to closely check the various gates along the road that kept pedestrians from entering the airport grounds. He had plenty of time to do so.

As he cruised the north side of the Fort Lauderdale Airport, Shannon noticed a sign that read, "Restricted Area—No Trespassing." He turned the Cadillac left and slowly proceeded down a narrow road to a locked metal gate. To the right was a small building housing an export company based in the Turks and Caicos Islands, or so the sign said. To the left was a Federal Express office. Shannon parked his car in front of the gate, which stood between him and the airport runways. The fence housing the gate was twelve feet high and topped with razor wire. The lock on the gate was old and rusted. Very rusted.

Shannon looked out over the compact airport. It had three active runways, and air traffic was relatively light. Security was nowhere to be seen.

Fort Lauderdale International Airport had an interesting history, and Shannon Michaels knew it well. The first story he had ever filed for GNN was about this very airport. During World War II, the Lauderdale airport had been a small but important naval air station. American torpedo bomber crews trained there. The most famous graduate of the Lauderdale naval flight school was George Bush. On December 5, 1945, five U.S. Navy Avenger planes took off from Lauderdale on a routine training mission. They never returned.

That was the beginning of the infamous "Bermuda Triangle" legend. The planes were dubbed "The Lost Patrol," and the mystery was never really solved to anyone's satisfaction. Shannon's report focused on the Bermuda Triangle theory well before it had been exploited to the hilt by the rest of the media.

As Shannon stared at the airport control tower on the south side of the field, he reminded himself that, for his last mission, he might need an especially well-honed escape plan. This time, he had lost the element of surprise. If he had to escape pursuers, Shannon thought, the airport was where he would go. If he was being chased in the dark, the inside of the airfield offered his best chance of vanishing. It was an obstacle course, full of junked planes and debris, and was illuminated only by small lights flanking the runways.

Shannon studied the terrain carefully, noting the small paved roads, the ditches, the standing hazards. If he could get inside the airport grounds ahead of the posse, and drive quickly across the field, he had a good chance of disappearing. He seriously doubted that the chase would ever happen, but he decided to prepare himself, in a disciplined way, for every eventuality.

Sweating now, Shannon got back into his car and drove to the other side of the airport. There he found another gate, with the number 152 written on it. Again the lock was rusted. In fact, this gate looked as if it hadn't been used in decades. Three burnt out planes stood yards away on the inside of the airport property. Probably used for fire training. 'Perfect,' Shannon thought.

Continuing his private tour, Shannon drove west to a fork in the road. He bore left, crossing a small overpass that took him above the primary highway in Florida: I-95. On the other side of the overpass, approximately a two hundred yard run from Gate 152, was a restaurant called "Something Fishy." Shannon stopped the car and got out. The sun was blazing hot. He looked around. Not a soul in sight. Apparently Something Fishy was open only for dinner, although there were a half dozen cars in its parking lot.

Shannon thought hard. Now that he had carefully examined the airport and its environs, he believed he could pull off the sanction of Lance Worthington without complication but, if all hell did break loose, he needed every advantage he could get.

Shannon again felt moisture on his forehead and an itching on his chin. He hated the damn beard. Swearing to himself, he got back into the air-conditioned Cadillac and drove east. He had some shopping to do.

• • •

The buzz on his belt told Tommy O'Malley that he was wanted on his portable phone. It was Julio Lopez calling from Lauderdale police headquarters. At three in the afternoon, Tommy was actually pleased to be talking on the phone, something he ordinarily despised. Sitting in the car for hours at a time was getting to him, although Ashley Van Buren was dealing with it better. She was asleep.

"That Worthington is really a prick. You know that, Tommy?"

"No doubt, Julio. What happened?"

"Well, I finally reached the bastard. Of course, he didn't return my calls. Said he was busy in meetings all day. So I told him we had a tip that he might be in some danger and the guy went off on you and Jackson. Said you're overreacting, blah, blah, blah. I couldn't get a word in. Finally, I told him to give it a rest. I then asked him to unlock the door between his room and the one next to it because two of my guys were in there. He said he'd think about it. Can you believe this clown?

"Anyway, I told him that we'd like to stay out of sight because we don't want to spook the guy we're chasing, but that if he wanted protection, we'd assign someone to stay with him. I think I heard the jerkoff yawn at that point. He said he didn't need a bodyguard. So I gave the guy my number and told him to call me if he saw anything unusual. I also suggested that he not let anyone into his room and, if somebody broke in, to scream like hell. My guys would be alert around the clock. And get this Tommy. The guy didn't even say thanks."

"Gotta love the media, Julio."

"Fuck 'em. How you holding up?"

"Bored to shreds," Tommy said. Ashley awakened long enough to smile.

"Well, it's just one more day," Julio said. "Are you gonna stay there all night?"

"Gonna knock off at nine. My hunch is he'll make his move tomorrow. He's probably putting his plan together right now. But if we see him, we'll be way ahead. No word on him around town?"

"Nothing, Tom. The guy's gone to ground. But we're all over the hotel. If he shows up, we'll get him. I'll bet Jackson's having a fine time mixing drinks."

Tommy laughed. "I don't think Jack knows a Singapore Sling from a Mountain Dew. But seriously, Julio, we can't thank you enough. We owe you."

"No problem," Julio said. "And one more thing, Tommy. We ran a check of all hotels and rental car agencies from Miami to Pompano, but nobody fitting Michaels' description showed up."

"I'm not surprised. The guy's a walkin' Jack Higgins novel. He's in some kinda bullshit disguise," Tommy said. "Tomorrow, Julio. And thanks again."

Ashley glanced at Tommy. He looked wilted and exhausted, even with the air conditioning running in the car. "Tommy, I think I'm going to walk back to the hotel and take a shower."

"Can I come?"

Ashley gave him a seductive look that seared his nerve endings. "Quite the professional attitude, Detective," she said.

"Sleuths do not live by clues alone," Tommy replied.

"Call me if anything happens, Columbo," said Ashley. "I'll see you later."

• • •

Lance Worthington was a man with an undisturbed conscience, a man who considered introspection to be an unnecessary distraction. As he readied himself to participate in the afternoon seminar, "How to Handle Broadcast Talent," he was feeling very pleased with himself. He had come a long way in ten years.

After graduating from Northwestern University, he had entered the world of local television news and risen quickly. Now he was a news boss in New York, the largest market in America. And in a few hours, he would be telling other news executives from around the country that a "tough love" approach was the only way to handle anchormen and women. If they didn't do it your way, he would say, then show them the door. The TV audience is distracted and forgetful. Viewers shift loyalties quickly. Newsreaders are overpaid and overrated. Most of them can be easily replaced.

That was Lance Worthington's guiding rule: Everyone was expendable except him. And he had been ruthless in enforcing his law, leaving a trail of wrecked careers in each of the four markets where he had been boss. But look where the hard line had gotten him, he thought. He was earning a quarter of a million dollars a year, and he wielded incredible power. His wife and two kids were well taken care of, and he was the envy of his friends. He had proven that in a tough business, he had the stuff to prosper.

For him, all that stood in the way of a perfect day was the warning he had received from the police. It nagged at him. Martin Moore had been deliberately murdered. That much was obvious. And the cops knew exactly how Moore had operated. Worthington sensed danger, but not the physical kind. He was more worried about exposure in the research scam than he was about some "mad killer." Somehow he just couldn't imagine himself a target. But he would be careful nonetheless.

Worthington knotted his silk tie and poured himself a Scotch from the hotel room mini-bar. He needed a lift. After all, he would be addressing some powerful people in thirty minutes. He wanted to be light on his feet, and Scotch melted his inhibitions.

But what Lance Worthington was really looking forward to was the next night's gala convention dinner, the one featuring Lyle Fleming as the keynote speaker. Worthington knew the dais would be loaded with network executives, and he wanted to meet as many as possible. Network news was the next stop on his journey to the top. At least that's how he had planned things. Worthington hoped to make a solid impression on the network types with his no-nonsense management style.

The news director drained his drink and walked into the bathroom. He took a last look at himself in the mirror. His blonde hair was slicked back, and his dark blue suit was freshly pressed. He had the air of success about him. He could feel it. He would take no prisoners at the seminar. He was ready and able to tell the industry exactly how to deal with difficult anchor talent.

• • •

It took Shannon Michaels less than an hour to buy the items he needed to complete his mission. A strip of shops along Route One in Dania, a small town just south of Lauderdale, provided him with a walking cane, a hacksaw, a box cutter, and a blue polyester sports jacket size 44 long.

He then drove south into Hollywood, Florida to another rent-a-car agency called "Rent-a-Heap." There he paid five hundred dollars in cash, including deposit, to use a 1992 Ford Taurus for three days. The tan car sputtered a little, but handled fine as he drove directly to the parking lot of the "Something Fishy" restaurant about five miles away. Shannon parked and walked to a phone booth just outside the restaurant's front door. He called "Babe's Taxi" and a bright yellow cab arrived ten minutes later. The ride back to his parked Cadillac in Hollywood took fifteen minutes.

Shannon, needing darkness to implement his scheme, still had a few hours to kill. He decided to have dinner and try to unwind. He drove west on Griffin Road until he found a small Italian restaurant.

• • •

After sitting around in the hot car all day doing nothing, Tommy O'Malley was exhausted. He sprawled out on his hotel bed, thinking black thoughts about what he would do to Shannon Michaels if he caught him in any illegal activity whatsoever. The room was cool, but the air did not take the edge off Tommy's angry frame of mind. He wasn't in the mood to chat, but he had promised to call Ashley Van Buren.

"What's up?" Tommy asked after dialing up her room.

"The paper's pissed off," Ashley said in a disgusted tone.

"Well, I can't understand why. They should be grateful that you're down in Florida in December hunting up crime stories."

"You would have made a great assignment editor, Tommy. You

missed your calling," Ashley said.

"So why are they mad?" Tommy asked.

"Because I can't write anything. I keep telling them that I'm on a huge story but I can't give them the juicy details. I can't even mention Shannon's name. If I do, it will be all over the city, and that would be big trouble, right?"

"Big trouble? That would be the end of the world, Ash. If we don't nail the guy and his name gets linked with the investigation, my next job will be in Mayberry."

Ashley sighed into the phone. "I know. I keep telling my editors to be patient. And they keep screaming at me."

"I bet you're not used to that."

"Screw you, Tommy. You're about as sympathetic as Jack the Ripper. Why are you calling, anyway?"

"Because I like you," Tommy said.

Ashley smiled to herself but maintained her hurt tone of voice. "Well, you've got a very strange way of showing it."

"Yeah, I've heard that before. Bottom line, Ash, there's nothin' new. Everybody's tired. Everybody's tense. Tomorrow it all goes down."

"It better or I'm in deep trouble," Ashley said.

"It will. I have a feeling, Ash. Tomorrow is it."

"So what time do we begin sitting in the car?"

"Six a.m. When the sun comes up, we should all be in place."

"Just call me Katie Couric," Ashley said. "And Tommy, try not to be so cranky in the morning, okay?"

"Anything you say, Katie."

• • •

Shannon Michaels put the blade of the sharpened hacksaw on the rusted steel. A half dozen strokes were all it took. The lock was hanging by the proverbial thread. It was midnight, and a light breeze blew in off Runway 27 Right. Shannon examined the steel gate that blocked entry to the Lauderdale Airport. It would hold until something hit it.

A few minutes later, Shannon repeated the same exercise on the opposite side of the airport. Now he had two gates that could be smashed through with ease. The first part of his plan was done.

Shannon returned to the Cadillac, turned on WIOD, the talk

station, and began driving back to his motel, oblivious to the radio voices. Tomorrow would be the most challenging day of his life, he thought. Tomorrow he would finish what he had started.

CHAPTER TWENTY-EIGHT

A physically ill Lance Worthington let out a deep groan as the early morning sun poured into his hotel room and awakened him from a dead sleep. He had gotten so drunk the night before that he had forgotten to pull the curtains—so drunk that he had collapsed on the bed and fallen asleep fully clothed.

As Worthington's eyes slowly opened, his head throbbed. How many shooters had he consumed after his hard-assed presentation at the seminar? He had lost count. And now his body was punishing him. His mouth silently begged for liquid. His throat was parched—a classic case of hot pipes. Worthington tried to sit up. The movement made him nauseous and dizzy. But he had to get water.

As he stumbled into the bathroom, he cursed. It was already eleven in the morning, and he had missed the first seminar of the day. 'Fuck it,' he thought. The most important thing was to get himself together in time for the dinner that evening. He looked at his pale face in the mirror and made a decision: He would spend the rest of the day recovering from his overindulgence, and really concentrate on impressing the network executives that night.

Thirteen miles away, Shannon Michaels felt strong and alert. He was sitting on his hotel room bed going over his plan for the fifth time. There could be no mistakes, he thought. O'Malley and his crew would be waiting to pounce. Both he and they knew the window of opportunity was small. Lance Worthington would be leaving Lauderdale on Wednesday.

Shannon decided to strike around 6:30, a half hour before the special cocktail hour for news executives began in the hotel ballroom. He assumed that Lance Worthington would be primed to circulate among his peers, well prepared for the political gamesmanship that always takes place at RTNDA ceremonial dinners.

For Tommy O'Malley and Ashley Van Buren, it was another day of fitful waiting. The only plus was the overcast weather. A nice breeze was blowing in from the Atlantic, and the inside of the Mercedes was not nearly as hot as it had been the previous day. But the waiting was excruciatingly dull. While Ashley was somewhat relaxed, reading the local papers through her sunglasses, Tommy squirmed. He hated every minute of this sitting around. He was not built for inactivity.

Even the conversation between Tommy and Ashley was strained. After all, how much can you say to the same person hour after hour after hour without becoming extremely annoying? More than once, Tommy suggested that Ashley return to the hotel and hang out there. He would call her if anything developed.

But Ashley knew that in order to get the strongest story possible, she had to see the entire scenario unfold. If Shannon Michaels finally appeared, she knew that things would happen very quickly. There would be no time for her to return from the hotel. She would have to tough it out in the car. Besides, she kind of enjoyed watching Tommy's sedentary agony.

The day passed slowly for Shannon Michaels, Lance Worthington, Tommy O'Malley, and Ashley Van Buren. Each spent most of the time lost in private thoughts. At five in the afternoon, Shannon put down the novel he couldn't concentrate on and began arranging his supplies. And with that, Shannon put the end game in motion.

Reaching into his canvas carrying bag, Shannon pulled out a pair of surgeon's gloves and stuffed them into the back pocket of his tan slacks. The box cutter purchased the day before went into his front pocket. He then put on his new blue, polyester jacket over a plain white sports shirt. A porkpie hat went atop his head. With his salt and pepper beard, he looked like a man in his fifties. Finally, he put on dark glasses, picked up his cane, and walked out the door.

After ten minutes of driving, Shannon Michaels pulled the Cadillac into an Exxon station with a public phone. He quickly dialed the Marriott Marina and asked for Room 615.

"Yes," a weary sounding voice said into the phone.

"Mr. Worthington, Graham Barker here, the assistant manager." Shannon's accent was imitation British. "I'm just calling to make sure everything is going well with your stay."

"Well, to tell you the truth, Mr. Barker, the hotel is quite noisy. I've been trying to get some rest and it's been very difficult."

'Typical Worthington,' Shannon thought. 'Always trying to pull little power plays.' "I am *extremely* sorry about that, sir. Would you like me to send security up to quiet things down?"

"No, don't bother," Worthington said. "But I *am* getting a bit low on Scotch. The mini-bar needs to be restocked."

"I'll take care of that straight away, sir. And if you need anything else, please do not hesitate to call."

"Fine." As was his custom, Worthington didn't say thank you.

Shannon hung up the phone and walked back to the car. It was a three-mile drive to Worthington's hotel and he took it slowly, again going over the plan in his mind. As he turned into the small parking lot next to the Marriott, the one he had selected during his reconnaissance, Shannon visualized Lance Worthington lying dead on his hotel room floor. His plan was perfect. It would work.

Tommy O'Malley was fighting to stay calm. It was now dark outside and he was again worn out from another day of doing absolutely nothing. But his anxiety was mounting. 'Where is the bastard?' he wondered, 'It's getting late. Maybe the degenerate has gone home after all. Shit. If I go back to the office with nothing, it's my ass.'

The car radio briefly interrupted Tommy's thoughts. On the all-news station from Miami, the big story was the murder of another Haitian radio talk show host. Ashley listened intently, but Tommy had heard it over and over during the day. He continued to watch the hotel entrance, which was now very busy. Guests were checking in and the valet parking attendants were running their butts off.

Tommy and Ashley could see every person who walked into the front entrance of the hotel, including a bearded man bent over and limping badly. Using his cane to steady himself, the man proceeded very slowly through the center revolving door—the side doors were reserved for use by bellmen. 'A shame,' Ashley thought. 'The man didn't seem to be all that old.'

• • •

Jackson Davis was exhausted. He had poured more drinks in the previous two days than in his entire life. And he had already been on his feet six hours straight that day. But there were compensations. During his two twelve-hour work shifts, he had received two hundred

dollars in tips and three women and one man had blatantly propositioned him—this despite the fact he wasn't being particularly friendly.
Jackson's attention was focused on each person who walked into the
hotel lobby, not on his drinking customers.

Jackson Davis had never seen so much polyester in his life. It
seemed to be standard issue for South Florida visitors. So when a
limping man in a light blue double knit sports jacket slowly shuffled by,
it hardly registered with Jack. He noted the man and his dopey little
hat, but his eyes did not stay on him for long. The man hobbled slowly
around the corner of the lobby and disappeared into the elevator.

The knock on the door startled Lance Worthington. "Mini-bar," a
voice called out. Worthington thought it was about time. He got up off
the bed, pulled on a terrycloth bathrobe, and opened the door. If he had
bothered to look through the security peephole, he would have seen a
man standing with his back to him. But Worthington didn't look, and
immediately turned *his* back to the man who entered his room.

"I need all the Scotch you can spare," Worthington said in a rather
harsh voice.

Worthington had barely gotten the last word out of his mouth
when he suddenly felt a synthetic fabric cover his mouth. A split second
later, he felt a sharp pain on the left side of his neck. Fortunately for
him, his nerve endings then went dead, and he couldn't feel the razor-
sharp box-cutter blade slice through his throat. Shannon Michaels,
having covered Worthington's mouth with his left hand, used his right
hand to brutally slash the man's jugular vein. Blood filled Worthington's throat and rushed up through his nasal passages. Because he could
make no sound now, Shannon removed his gloved hand from the
man's mouth and stepped in front of him.

"It's a cutthroat business you're in, Worthington," Shannon said
softly. "Say hello to Martin Moore for me."

Exactly two seconds before he lost consciousness, Lance Worthington's brain sent a signal of recognition. Shannon Michaels saw it in the
dying man's eyes. His mission was complete.

Lance Worthington now lay silently on the floor, where his blood
trickled onto and stained the brown carpet. Shannon Michaels turned
away, walking into the bathroom and rinsing off the box cutter and
gloves. He folded the gloves carefully and placed them in his front
pockets along with the cutter. Then he removed a wash cloth from the

bathroom and used it to cover his hand as he opened the hotel room door and placed the "Do Not Disturb" sign on the outer handle. It was the same move he had made in the Ron Costello assassination. He then picked up his cap, which he had placed on the floor outside the door in case Worthington looked through the peephole. Mini-bar attendants did not usually wear porkpie hats while on duty. His cane was lying next to the cap.

There were a couple of people at the far end of the hallway, but they took no notice of the limping man with the cane. Shannon knew he had to get rid of the wash cloth, but couldn't risk dumping it in the hotel garbage. He folded it and put it in his back pocket.

In the room next door to Worthington, unbeknownst to Shannon Michaels, two Lauderdale detectives were stretched out on their double beds reading. They heard nothing but the continuing sound of the television newscast that Lance Worthington was presumably watching.

It crossed Shannon's mind to take the stairs back down to the lobby, but he rejected the idea. He wanted to blend in with the crowd and a hotel stairway was a lonely place. The elevator stopped twice on the way down, and Shannon followed three people into the lobby—two rather overweight women squeezed into tight shorts, and one bellman. The bellman, who was actually an undercover cop, was distracted by the sight of the corpulent women, and did not notice the bent-over man in the polyester jacket as he limped slowly through the lobby. Shannon remained bent over, and avoided eye contact with everyone. Jackson Davis spotted him again but again thought nothing of it. 'Just another guest,' he thought.

When Shannon reached the revolving door that led out of the lobby and into the open air, he straightened up just slightly. He limped into the triangular space slowly, staying in character. He didn't see the two young children a few yards in back of him running frantically toward the doorway.

Suddenly, they crashed into the glass behind Shannon, pushing the whirling door into the back of his legs. He stumbled and the door's circular motion propelled him hard into the small outside courtyard. Trying to stay upright, Shannon missed two beats on his limp. Watching from the Mercedes, Ashley Van Buren saw the missteps.

"Tommy, look! That man there! He was limping badly a few minutes ago when he went inside the hotel. But he just about leapt out of the revolving door."

Tommy O'Malley was out of the car in two seconds. Shannon Michaels, who had quickly resumed limping, noticed movement in the parking lot. He turned his head and immediately saw a big man racing toward him. Instinctively, he knew it was O'Malley. And O'Malley left little doubt. "Hey, hold it right there," he shouted in his authoritative cop's voice. Shannon Michaels, briefly unglued, took off.

Ashley Van Buren was also running, but she was heading for the lobby. She wanted to alert Jackson Davis and the rest of the police. She didn't want Tommy O'Malley to confront a possible killer alone.

Shannon Michaels, now sprinting for his life, believed he could outrun O'Malley, but feared that the cop would shoot at him. He was just crazy enough to do something like that, he said to himself. He again heard O'Malley's loud voice screaming at him to stop. He never looked back.

Shannon zigzagged, running between the rows of cars in the covered valet parking lot. He did not want to give O'Malley a clean shot. His eyes were on the short row of hedges about fifty yards away. He would be there in seconds, and then into his Cadillac. In case a quick exit was needed, he had purposely left the car doors unlocked. As he ran, he reached into his front pants pocket for the keys. He found them, but as he removed his hand, the surgeon's gloves, which were in the same pocket, fell out. 'Shit. Physical evidence,' he thought. But he couldn't stop to pick up the gloves. Stopping would mean certain capture.

Tommy O'Malley, losing ground, realized he could not catch the fleeing man. But his rage drove him onward. He strongly suspected he was chasing Shannon Michaels but could not make a positive identification. He figured the man had a car waiting. O'Malley had to see the car.

Jackson, Ashley, and four Lauderdale undercovers ran out of the lobby in time to see Tommy a couple of hundred yards away and running hard. Jackson then made a decision. "Let's get the cars," he yelled. "Tommy won't catch him on foot. We'll drive over and pick him up."

Shannon, having reached the Cadillac, was pulling out of the small parking lot when Tommy came crashing through the hedges. Shannon looked back, gave a slight wave, and then floored the vehicle. It bolted onto Marriott Drive, tires squealing. Tommy leveled his pistol and fired at the car's right front tire. He missed.

Jackson Davis, with Ashley Van Buren in the back seat, screeched to a halt on the Drive and Tommy ran toward the Mercedes. Directly behind the car, two unmarked police vehicles came to a stop. Everyone had seen the Cadillac take off. Radio calls were already being made to Lauderdale police cruisers citywide.

Speeding along the small hotel road—the one that runs parallel to the 17th Street Causeway—Shannon tried to clear his head. He was in deep trouble, and his only chance of getting away was the airport. He had to get there and hope his escape plan was good enough to throw off his pursuers. "Goddamnit!" he cursed, "Again that fucking O'Malley."

Tommy dove into the front passenger seat of the Mercedes and, before he'd closed the door, Jack had put the car in motion. The fleeing car was in sight, about a quarter of a mile ahead. Tommy was perspiring heavily and hyperventilating, but his senses were acute, and he forced himself to be calm. "I think it's him. That bastard, Michaels. Just keep him in sight, Jack," Tommy said. "Just keep him in sight."

Ashley Van Buren wisely said nothing. She was stunned by how quickly things were unfolding. She nervously checked her seat belt. This was going to be a hell of a ride—maybe even a dangerous one.

The traffic signal ahead was red, but Shannon Michaels was not stopping for anything or anyone. He pumped the gas and the Cadillac shot through the light and across the causeway. An oncoming car braked hard but not in time, hitting the side of the Cadillac's back fender. Shannon didn't give it a glance.

A sports car appeared directly in front of him. Shannon swerved to the right but hit the sports car almost directly in the gas tank. After the collision, he braked, reversed the car, and floored it—out of reflex as much as anything else. The tires screeched, and the Caddy lurched away from the crunched sports car. Shannon then hit the brakes hard and jammed the gear into drive, speeding down Eisenhower Boulevard past Joe's Bel Air Diner.

Jackson Davis, despite police sirens wailing behind him, still had to slow his Mercedes down to get across the causeway. By now, police cars were racing toward South Fort Lauderdale from all directions, but no one knew exactly where the fugitive was heading. And, as yet, no one knew exactly what the fugitive had done.

Tommy's portable phone rang. It was Julio Lopez, his voice tense. Lance Worthington had been found lying on the floor of his hotel room. His throat had been cut.

"He got Worthington," Tommy said to Jackson and Ashley. "Cut his throat right under our eyes. I can't believe it. That fuckin' Michaels. Don't lose him, Jack."

Jackson Davis was annoyed by Tommy's order. It should have gone unsaid. But Jackson understood. He knew that Tommy wasn't thinking about words. He was obsessed with capturing the man in the Cadillac.

Shannon Michaels willed himself to think clearly. He was outrunning the pack, but knew there would be more cops up ahead. As he sped down Spangler Boulevard toward Route One, he decided he would not surrender. He could never spend a day in prison. He would rather be dead.

Shannon's Cadillac was doing ninety as he approached a major intersection. Directly ahead was State Road 84, which would lead him to the Lauderdale Airport. But he had to cross over Route One to get to the State Road and that was a problem. At least ten cars were stopped at the intersection light, and Shannon was bearing down on them.

When he saw the Cadillac's brake lights suddenly illuminate, Jackson stared in disbelief: the Caddy had swerved onto the sidewalk at a tremendous rate of speed, plowing through garbage cans and over front lawns. On the corner of the intersection was a self-service gas station. The Cadillac turned into it and roared through the narrow space between gas pumps, sideswiping at least two cars. Cursing, Jackson was forced to stop behind the cars lined up at the intersection waiting for the light to change. He could not jump the curb for fear of hitting civilians.

Shannon glanced in his rear view mirror and saw that the police caravan had momentarily stopped. He sped out of the gas station and turned the Cadillac south onto Route One, going the wrong way on the divided highway. The cars coming at him desperately swerved away trying to avoid a head-on collision.

Shannon sped into the intersection that had stopped his pursuers and turned right. The Cadillac bolted quickly into a stream of oncoming traffic going north on Route One. Once again a car clipped the Cadillac's bumper, this time knocking it completely off. Shannon's response was to floor the gas pedal. He rocketed onto State Road 84, heading west.

As cars, hearing the sirens, pulled over in front of him, Jackson got moving again. But he had fallen back. Tommy was cursing wildly and slamming his huge fists into the dashboard. Ashley was mute. Jackson had lost sight of the Cadillac and knew they would now have to count on the local police to close in on all sides. 'This is not some goddamned movie,' Jackson told himself. 'I can't endanger innocent lives to catch a murder suspect.'

Shannon Michaels had no such compunctions. His life was on the line and he knew it. He sped wildly, going west on State Road 84, passing over a set of railroad tracks, and turning left on Southwest Fourth Avenue heading south toward the airport. Two police cruisers coming from the opposite direction spotted him and took up chase. He had a couple of hundred yards on them.

Jackson saw the police lights turn left and again gunned the Mercedes. He now had it up over one hundred miles per hour. Though he was closing fast on Michaels, he was worried. The police cars had turned into a residential neighborhood.

It took Shannon Michaels just seconds to reach Perimeter Road, where again he briefly reviewed his plan. He would smash through the gate he had prepared the night before and drive onto the airport runways. Once there, he would kill his lights and proceed quickly across the field in darkness. Upon reaching the south side of the airport, he would crash through the other gate he had tampered with.

After driving another hundred yards or so, he would abandon the Caddy, sprint across the highway bridge, and proceed to the Ford Taurus he had left in the parking lot of "Something Fishy." With luck, the police would lose him momentarily inside the airport and have no idea he had a second car waiting. And, once free of his pursuers, he would drive north to Georgia using local roads. There he would assess his situation. Shannon knew that he could never go home again. But at least he would be free, he had some money in bank accounts outside the country, and Liam Mooney had promised to help. Perhaps he could live quietly in Ireland.

Shannon again glanced in the rearview mirror, noticing that the police cars were gaining on him. 'Jesus, they're really moving,' he thought. He saw his turn coming up. Without braking, he jerked the car to the left, taking the corner on two wheels. He once again floored the gas pedal and blasted through the weakened airport gate. It shattered in two directions. Step one of the plan had worked perfectly.

"I can't believe it. He's going into the airport," Tommy O'Malley said. "Why the hell is he doing that?"

Jackson Davis did not reply. He was rapidly closing the distance behind him and the two police cars closest to the fleeing Cadillac. But in his mind, Jackson was beginning to see what was developing. The airport is a big space. A big, *dark* space.

The runway on the north side of the Fort Lauderdale Airport is nine thousand feet long and handles the biggest planes that land there. Seven minutes before Shannon Michaels sped across it, a Delta Airlines 727 coming in from Atlanta had used the runway for a perfect landing. But when Shannon reached the concrete strip, it was empty.

The police cars chasing the Cadillac did not pause at the broken airport gate. They drove right through it. But now the police had to slow down. They were on unfamiliar ground and visibility was limited. The only lights were on the ground, lining the three runways. As Jackson Davis drove through the gate a few seconds later, he noticed that the cruisers were bunching up. "Look at that, Tommy," Jackson said. "That's just what the bastard wants: us to be tentative."

"Get him, Jack. Don't slow up." Tommy was concerned about Ashley, who was uncharacteristically quiet in the back seat. But he knew they had to take the risk. They had to speed through the darkness hoping they would not drive off the north-south tarmac. Jackson, by gunning the Mercedes again, overtook the police cars. Tommy strained to see in front of him, barely making out the outline of a dark speeding car a couple hundred yards ahead.

It was Shannon who saw the light in the sky first. It was coming in fast from the west. He had no way of knowing it, but a Lear Jet, model 35A, was cleared to land on the General Aviation runway that loomed a half mile in front of him. On the Lear were three businessmen from Baton Rouge, Louisiana, one pilot and one co-pilot. The Lear, traveling one hundred and fifty miles per hour, would be down on the ground in forty-five seconds.

At first, Shannon shuddered when he saw the plane coming in, but then he saw an advantage. The cops would now have to stop cold in order to let the plane pass safely in front of them. If he could beat that Lear across the runway, he could escape. The police would never catch up to him or find him. He would win.

"Jack, look at that." Tommy O'Malley's voice was tense. "It's a plane. It's gonna land right in front of us. Shit."

Jackson Davis hit the brake, slowing the Mercedes, and looked up to his right. "No way the Caddy beats that across," he said.

Ashley Van Buren was also measuring the plane. "You don't think he'll race it across, do you Tommy?"

A worried Tommy O'Malley did not answer. If the Cadillac got across the runway before the plane, it could vanish into the darkness. Tommy's phone rang. Julio again. "Do you see that fuckin' plane?"

"We see it!" Tommy shouted.

"I've got units closing on the other side of the airport. And choppers on the way, but they're still not in place."

"So if he beats the plane, he could disappear?" Tommy's voice was rising.

"We'll get him, Tommy," Julio replied. "We know the car."

"Jesus," said Tommy, hanging up. "The bastard's got a shot, Jack. We got to get him. Floor it."

Jackson Davis looked at Tommy O'Malley. "We got Ashley in the car. We can't risk it."

"GO JACK," Tommy screamed. "GO!"

Jackson's right foot drove the gas petal to the floor. The eight-cylinder engine shuddered and the Mercedes instantly bolted forward. Ashley was pinned to the back seat, her right hand tightly gripping the doorjamb.

"The pilot might abort the landing, Jack. We've got to stay on Michaels," Tommy screamed.

Up ahead, Shannon Michaels was trying not to look at the approaching plane. He was concentrating on driving as fast as he possibly could. The Cadillac's speedometer read one hundred and twenty miles per hour.

The Lear was going one twenty-five when its wheels touched the runway. The landing was a piece of cake, the pilot thought. Another great pay day. Off to his left, the copilot noticed police lights flashing. He had seen them on approach, but they had been distant, and air traffic control had not warned him about anything. Now the lights looked much closer. He wondered what was going on.

Unable to gauge just how fast the approaching plane was going,

Shannon saw it touch down and heard the jet's engines begin to roar down the runway. But he couldn't stop. If the cops saw his brake lights, they'd know his position. He gritted his teeth and pumped the gas pedal hard. The Cadillac was almost out of control. If he hit anything, the Caddy would surely flip over.

It was the copilot who saw the dark blur first. "What the hell is that?" he yelled, startling the pilot. Both men's eyes locked in on a dark object approaching the runway from the north at a high rate of speed. In a few seconds, the car would be directly in front of them.

"Holy shit, it's a car on the side tarmac," the copilot screamed. "And there's another one behind it, coming up fast. Can you pull up?"

"No," was all the pilot could say as he struggled to slow down and control the plane on the runway.

Jackson Davis made his decision instantaneously. Realizing that his Mercedes would not beat the jet across the runway, he yelled almost violently, "Hold tight!" Jackson braked, jerking the steering wheel to the right—his power side. The left side of the Mercedes lifted precariously off the ground. Jackson, his face a mass of perspiration, fought for control and prayed the car wouldn't overturn.

As the car tottered, seemingly in midair, Ashley screamed. Then it landed on its wheels with a thud, spinning a full three hundred and sixty degrees. Tommy peered out the front window, clearly seeing the jet and Shannon's speeding car approach each other in a race of death.

Shannon Michaels heard the plane's deafening noise grow even louder, its two powerful engines being pulled back. But he continued straight ahead, pushing the car to the limit. Suddenly, the Cadillac hit a bump on the tarmac. It shot into the air. Shannon fought to keep his composure and control. The car hit the pavement and bounced. When it came down, it bounced again, losing speed. Shannon glanced to his right. The jet's front light blinded him. In a flash, he was past it. He had made it. He had beaten the odds.

But Shannon's thoughts of victory suddenly vanished when he heard a loud thump followed by a crunching sound. All at once he felt a spinning sensation that disoriented him. He had indeed beaten the Lear Jet across the runway but, at the last possible moment, the speeding plane's right wing had clipped the Cadillac slightly above the right rear tire. The car flipped over immediately and spun around like a huge, metallic top.

Upon impact with the car, the Lear Jet veered sharply to the right. Its landing gear collapsed and the body of the plane met the concrete runway at a speed in excess of one hundred miles an hour. The intense friction ignited a shower of sparks that flew into the three thousand pounds of reserve fuel that had begun pouring out of the fuselage.

All this happened within ten seconds. Nobody inside the plane had a chance. The Lear Jet exploded while the passengers and pilots were still strapped into their seats. All aboard were killed instantly.

As the Lear Jet was skidding, Shannon Michaels was trapped inside the overturned Cadillac. He sat upside down, bleeding from the head but still thinking clearly. Either he would crawl out of the car, or he would die. When he heard the terrible screeching of the plane's steel body meeting concrete, he realized he had only seconds to make his escape.

Shannon managed to unbuckle his seat belt, but the inflated air bag had him pinned against the driver's seat upside down. He reached into his pocket for the box cutter. The sharp razor would be able to puncture the bag. As the pulled the cutter out, Shannon Michaels heard a tremendous roar and felt intense heat—the backdraft from the explosion. The Lear jet had begun disintegrating and the shooting flames were engulfing the Cadillac. Shannon felt something hot oozing onto his body from above him. Parts of the car were actually melting and the floor, which was now the ceiling, was a mass of scorched dripping iron.

A pain unlike any he had ever experienced seared through him. Every pore in his body seemed to be on fire. The box cutter fell from his burning hand as Shannon screamed in agony. Instinctively, he rotated his head, desperately searching for an escape route. His pain intensified. Suddenly, the heat was causing his brown contact lenses to disintegrate into his eyes. He blinked frantically, but saw nothing. With his last bit of desperate energy, he twisted his body trying to free himself. A slab of sizzling white hot metal fell directly on his head. Death for Shannon Michaels came one second later.

As Tommy O'Malley and Jackson Davis stood watching the conflagration just one hundred yards away, Ashley began to sob uncontrollably. The two men cast their eyes downward but said nothing. What was there to say? The airport fire engines wailed in the distance, and flames lit up the night. Watching the explosion and fire had almost a hypnotic effect on those present. Police radios crackled, but the cops themselves remained silent.

Finally, after the firefighters and rescue teams had arrived and the flames began to subside, Tommy put his arm around Ashley Van Buren and hugged her tightly. She looked up at him with tear-filled eyes. Tommy stroked her face while remembering that Tony Lomanto, his psychologist friend, had come eerily close to predicting the outcome of the case: "If you can enrage him," Tony had said, "he could give you the opening you need...but that's a dangerous strategy. *You* might survive, but the guy could hurt others around you."

It had happened that way. And as Tommy thought back upon what had transpired that evening—about the human carnage that Shannon Michaels had caused—he felt no satisfaction in knowing that Michaels had received his due, that he could kill no more.

In his heart, Tommy knew he had done his best. But he also knew that it had not been enough.

EPILOGUE

It was the clearest sea Ashley Van Buren had ever gazed upon. Sitting in a plastic sand chair, her feet submerged in the azure waters of Caneel Bay, she looked out through her sunglasses at a real-life postcard picture. For the first time in six months, she was relaxed, totally relaxed.

Life had changed dramatically for Ashley Van Buren. Her page one stories on the Shannon Michaels murder case not only stunned the city of New York, but were syndicated nationwide. Almost immediately, book agents were after her, closely followed by movie people. Following weeks of being wooed, she signed contracts which guaranteed her close to half a million dollars, and she didn't even have to write the book. A professional collaborator, a "ghost" in writing parlance, would be brought in to help her bang out the text. Ashley could even continue working at the *Globe* while the book-writing was underway.

Hollywood was a similar story. Ashley was flown to Los Angeles and courted by some of the most powerful film makers on earth. She stayed in a lavish suite at the Belair Hotel and schmoozed with Michael Douglas, Martin Sheen, and Oliver Stone, among others. It was a fantasy run that would lead to still another book—one that she herself would write. She had kept meticulous notes on her Hollywood seduction.

Ashley had offered to share her tremendous good fortune with Tommy O'Malley and Jackson Davis, but the two detectives were adamant about not cashing in. Every time she told them of another incredible offer, they mocked her—even threatened to tell the *National Enquirer* nasty things about her if she didn't quit bugging them about signing contracts. The attitude angered her.

In the end, Ashley did manage to get Tommy and Jackson nice consulting fees on the movie project, but they weren't even grateful. They made her pay for every dinner at which the project was discussed, and they ordered the biggest steaks allowed by law.

After four days in the Caribbean sun, Ashley's skin was medium brown. Her orange-leaf-pattern bikini set off her sunglow nicely. She took a sip of Evian and sighed contentedly. 'If only life could be like this all the time,' she thought.

The sun was descending—it was after four—and Ashley decided to pack it in. She dragged her chair back from the shoreline, and proceeded to her oceanfront bungalow. Stripping off her bathing suit, she walked into the huge shower. She pulled the lime green curtain across the entrance, and set the water for a tepid seventy-five degrees. The spray felt great against her skin as she ducked her head underneath the nozzle. Closing her eyes, she concentrated on the tingling sensation of water flowing against her body.

Suddenly, another sensation intruded. Ashley felt two large hands wrap themselves around her breasts and hot breath on the back of her neck. She opened her eyes wide and giggled. "I thought you drowned out there, Snorkel Man."

Tommy O'Malley was naked and at attention. "Drowning is not an option," he said, "unless, of course, you beg me to perform unnatural acts right here in this shower."

Ashley laughed and kissed Tommy O'Malley hard on the mouth. Her painful, dangerous ordeal had turned into one of the most joyous times of her life. True, she still had her bad days emotionally. In fact, the horrendous scene of the fire on the airport runway would never leave her—and was occasionally triggered by the mere sight of an airplane in flight. But her time with Tommy O'Malley since the Lauderdale tragedy had given her a sense of peace she had never experienced before.

Out of confusion and chaos, Ashley Van Buren had found clarity and happiness. And, as she wrapped her slender arms around Tommy's thick neck, she hoped those new feelings would deepen and last forever.

Acknowledgements

For me, writing a first novel was a harrowing experience. The following people provided me with invaluable information and/or encouragement that kept me going, even though, at times, the project looked hopeless. Those listed are not in any kind of logical order.

Maureen O'Reilly, Detective John Schlagler, Detective Daniel Rodriguez, Detective Gaeton Fonzi, Jane Dystel, Gloria Jean Sessler, Mary Ann Yastremski, Dr. Kathy Levinson, Jim Reynolds, Makeda Wubneh, Deidre O'Brien, Erica Orloff, Jay Garon, Liz Smith, Bill Bratton, Col. David Hackworth, Arthur Hailey, Vincent Bugliosi, Catherine Crier, Janet Pawson, Art Kaminsky, Byna Zimmerman, Lou and Mary Jo Spoto, Keith Paglen, and especially Bruce Bortz—the most perspicacious editor and publisher around.